Caroline is originally from Yorkshire and spent a year living in Paris before reading PPE at Oxford University. She trained as an actress then fell into a career in finance, going on to write various commercial fiction novels under various pseudonyms. She's also written comedy for the BBC and Comedy Central.

Caroline now lives in London with her husband and two young children. When not writing, she's mostly reading, travelling and aspiring to have a life as interesting as the women she writes about.

instagram.com/caroline.lamond
x.com/carolinelamond

CW01425832

Also by Caroline Lamond

Well Behaved Women

THE SOCIALITES

CAROLINE LAMOND

ONE MORE CHAPTER

One More Chapter
a division of HarperCollins*Publishers*
1 London Bridge Street
London SE1 9GF
www.harpercollins.co.uk
HarperCollins*Publishers*
Macken House, 39/40 Mayor Street Upper,
Dublin 1, D01 C9W8, Ireland
This paperback edition 2024

1

First published in ebook by HarperCollins*Publishers* 2024
Copyright © Caroline Lamond 2024
Caroline Lamond asserts the moral right to
be identified as the author of this work

A catalogue record of this book
is available from the British Library

ISBN: 978-0-00-852768-6

This novel is entirely a work of fiction. The names, characters and incidents portrayed in it are the work of the author's imagination. Any resemblance to actual persons, living or dead, events or localities is fictionalised.

Printed and bound in the UK using 100% Renewable Electricity
by CPI Group (UK) Ltd

To Ces, Vix & Abs, who I've known for about as long as I've been writing this book

PART I
The Schoolgirl

Chapter One

Roehampton, England

September 1922

The glove was white cotton, unblemished as a conscience after confession. The hand it encased belonged to Maureen's nanny, Nurse Ranger, who held onto her charge so tightly that it was painful. Bone crushing into tender flesh. The cruelty was intentional; this wasn't a gesture of reassurance or comfort, but one of control and spite.

The pair stood in a residential street in the London suburb of Roehampton, the autumnal breeze stirring up dust and detritus that swirled around their ankles. Maureen swallowed, staring up at the sprawling mansion in front of her, its arched Gothic doors criss-crossed with steel bars and studded with metal bolts. Doors to keep the rest of the world out.

Or the inhabitants in?

Nurse Ranger rang the bell and they waited in silence. No one answered, and Maureen entertained a fleeting hope that her nanny might permit them to turn around and go home, as though taking the boat across the Irish Sea had been a mere caprice, not an unchangeable reality that was to shape the rest of her life.

Maureen's mother hadn't been able to accompany her to England. Mary was, once again, absent from the family home; ill, and convalescing, Maureen and her younger siblings had been told. Nor would her beloved father's poor health allow him to make the long journey in comfort, so Nurse Ranger had been tasked with bringing eleven-year-old Maureen to her new school. A different country. A fresh start.

Out of the frying pan and into the fire.

Maureen's upbringing had been far from idyllic. The O'Sullivan family had moved regularly, according to her mother's whims, but had now settled outside Dublin in a grey stone castellated mansion overlooking the Irish Sea. Nurse Ranger was just one in a long succession of nannies to have passed through the household; some stole, some drank, some clashed with Mary O'Sullivan, but all were heartless and cruel once the grown-ups were out of sight, impressing upon Maureen that she was ugly, wicked, unlovable and unloved, the words repeated so often that Maureen took them for truth.

She had dreamed about leaving home; had, in fact, run away a number of times as a child, returning to anger and punishment. But at least she'd been with her father and her siblings (for Maureen was the eldest of five; others had been born and failed to survive infancy, which in part explained the great sadness that lived within her mother), and the landscape of Killiney was familiar to her: the rugged coastline and the sweeping bay and the north Wicklow hills beyond. The building in front of her now was austere and forbidding, and Maureen felt a surge of anger that she'd been sent here, away from everything she knew, as though she were being punished—

Her thoughts were interrupted as the heavy doors groaned open, rattling and clanging like a spectre in a Victorian melodrama, to reveal a young nun who gestured that they should enter. Maureen stiffened, reminded of the nuns at her convent school in Dublin whom she'd hated with a passion, vowing to break every rule that they set.

This woman radiated disapproval, though her features remained impassive, as she led them along a corridor that smelt of beeswax and incense. Maureen glanced up at Nurse Ranger, tight-lipped and sour-faced, her habitual expression. She was wearing a brown cloak with a brown cloche hat, dullness blending into the monochrome walls of the convent like camouflage. Maureen was a veritable butterfly in her blue silk dress and red velvet coat, a colourful interloper who didn't belong.

Behind a wooden door lay a cavernous hall. Gloomy light fell in shafts through the narrow windows, dust motes hanging in the air. Despite the room's size it felt claustrophobic, dominated by a particularly gruesome statue of the crucifixion mounted high on the wall. The thorns drove cruelly into Christ's temples, blood dripping from his feet where the nails had been hammered through. Maureen winced and averted her eyes.

A door banged, and her head snapped back up. Framed in the archway at the far end of the room was a tall, striking figure with keen eyes and an imperious bearing. The Reverend Mother Ashton Case crossed the room towards them. The walk was long, and Maureen had time to feel fear as she approached.

'Thank you, Sister. Now, please go and find a girl to show Maureen to her dormitory. We will be in my office.'

The nun who had accompanied them bowed her head before swiftly, silently, crossing the hall and slipping out through the far door, as the Reverend Mother Ashton Case observed Maureen with an unflinching stare.

'Welcome, Maureen,' she said, though her tone betrayed no sign of the sentiment. Then she turned and walked back across the hall, as Maureen and Nurse Ranger followed, out of the far door, along another corridor and into an office that was sparse and spare. It contained a plain wooden table, upon which a copy of the Holy Bible sat prominently, a painting of the Sacred Heart adorning the otherwise bare walls.

The Reverend Mother Ashton Case took a large book from the shelf behind her, bound in blue leather and trimmed in gold. She took a seat and indicated that Nurse Ranger and Maureen should do the same, before taking a fountain pen from her desk drawer and making an entry in scratchy writing. The book was upside down to Maureen, but she could make out the words:

O'Sullivan Maureen Paula Sept 1922

Mother Ashton Case added Maureen's parents' names, her address, and her date of birth before turning the book round and pushing it across the desk towards Maureen, tapping on the paper with her finger: 'There. Your signature.'

Maureen hesitated. The pen felt heavy and unwieldy in her small hands; she was terrified that she would blot the ink and spoil the page. Willing her hands not to shake, she wrote her initials and surname.

'Now it's official,' said the Reverend Mother Ashton Case gravely. 'You're a Roehampton girl. You must set an example to others and follow in the way of Our Lord. Can you do that, Maureen Paula O'Sullivan?'

Maureen felt as though something heavy was pressing down on her chest. She wanted to speak but her mouth was dry. 'I…' she began, but was saved from replying by a tentative knock at the door.

'Enter,' said the Reverend Mother Ashton Case in clipped tones.

Unable to help herself, Maureen twisted round in her seat, intrigued, as the door slowly opened. The girl who entered was the prettiest Maureen had ever seen, with thick, dark hair in a neat ponytail and incredible blue-green eyes. She wore the standard uniform of a navy-coloured dress with a white Peter Pan collar and her build was slight – she was perhaps a year or two younger than Maureen – her features arranged in a way that could only be described as beautiful. When she smiled the effect was heightened, her rosebud lips curving upwards, a glimpse of mischief discernible beneath the surface. Maureen instantly took a liking to her.

'Vivian, this is Maureen O'Sullivan. A new girl,' said the Reverend Mother. 'Take her to get her uniform then show her to her sleeping quarters. She is to be in Nazareth dormitory.'

'Yes, Mother,' Vivian replied. Her voice was high and musical, well-spoken with no discernible accent.

'Pray to Our Lord to comfort you, Maureen, and remember that there is no need to feel homesick – home for a Catholic is wherever God can be found,' added the Reverend Mother. 'Now say goodbye.'

'Goodbye.' Maureen turned to Nurse Ranger, unable to keep the triumph from her voice. Whatever lay on the other side of this door had to be better than the life she'd come from.

Vivian held out her hand and Maureen took it.

'Let's go and get your uniform. Your dress is awfully pretty, but you'll have to leave that, I'm afraid. Then it will be almost time for supper – I think it's boiled ham tonight...' Vivian chattered on, as she led Maureen out of the room and into the school. Maureen listened happily and didn't look back.

'What's it like here?' she asked quietly, suddenly vulnerable after the elation of leaving Nurse Ranger.

'You'll get used to it,' Vivian assured her. 'The girls are delightful, and sometimes we have the most tremendous fun. But it can be rather hard at first, until you get used to it.'

Maureen's face fell as she stared at the long, unwelcoming corridor ahead, with its dark wood panelling and slit-like windows, a chill wind whistling along its length.

'Oh, please don't worry,' Vivian insisted. 'You've got me now, and I can tell that we're going to be great friends.'

She gave Maureen's hand a reassuring squeeze, and flashed that dazzling smile. Gratefully, Maureen smiled back.

Maureen's silk dress had been taken away to who knew where and replaced with a drab serge garment, as required by the Convent of the Sacred Heart. The rough material scratched her skin and the collar was the wrong size, meaning it didn't quite meet in the middle.

After introducing Maureen to everyone, Vivian had gone back to her own dorm, leaving Maureen feeling uncharacteristically shy. She'd missed the start of term, and the others had had time to rekindle friendships or form new ones, but they'd been cautiously cordial and Maureen was hopeful.

Now she was standing, motionless and silent, alongside the eleven other girls from her dormitory in a sparse stone room containing two rows of metal bathtubs. Through the mullioned windows, Maureen glimpsed the twilight sky; autumn had arrived with a vengeance, and the gas lamps on the wall provided little heat or illumination.

An elderly nun entered the room. Her name was Mother Lennox, and she had a sour, whiskery face and downward-sloping mouth.

'Where is your bath shift?' she demanded. Her voice was low, crackling like old newspaper left in an attic.

'I'm sorry?' Maureen's face creased in confusion.

'She's new,' put in one of the others.

'Evidently.' Mother Lennox's tone was withering. 'What is your name, child?'

'Maureen O'Sullivan,' she stated boldly.

Mother Lennox pursed her lips and turned to another pupil. 'Agnes, go and find Maureen O'Sullivan a bath shift and towel. Do you have a nightgown?'

'Yes, Mother. In my trunk.'

Mother Lennox's pale, rheumy eyes were cold as they assessed Maureen. 'It may not be suitable. Agnes, find a nightgown as well.'

'Yes, Mother.' Agnes scurried from the room. The girl at the end of the row – a rather plain, moon-faced child, with a freckled face and untidy plaits – began to giggle nervously, a series of unbecoming snorts erupting as she clamped a hand over her mouth to stifle the sound.

'Silence,' snapped Mother Lennox. 'I suggest you all use this time to contemplate the sins you have committed and ask for forgiveness. I do not believe there is one girl standing before me who has not sinned today, whether in some obvious manner, or whether secretly, in the depths of her heart. God sees it all,' she hissed, white spittle foaming at the corners of her mouth.

Maureen frowned as she tried to recall what dreadful crimes she had committed that day, wondering whether Mother Lennox could read her mind and recollect the misdeeds that Maureen could not. It seemed eminently possible. She cast her eyes down to the floor, hoping to avoid the nun's penetrating gaze. The others had done the same, one girl dropping to her knees with her hands clasped together, eyes closed as she mumbled indistinctly.

Agnes returned carrying a thin, white cotton nightgown, and what looked like a sack, crudely fashioned from cheap cloth. She handed both to Maureen with an apologetic smile.

'Now, girls,' said Mother Lennox. 'Into your bath shifts.'

The spectacle that followed was unlike anything Maureen had ever witnessed. She could only stare uncomprehendingly as the others placed the cloth sacks over their heads, pulling them down over their bodies, then squirming and wriggling, discarded garments appearing on the floor at their feet. Some had the technique down to a fine art and the whole process went off smoothly; others, like Agnes, appeared to be wrestling an imaginary foe, panting and struggling inside the restrictive sack.

Maureen watched in bewilderment, unaware that Mother Lennox was now standing beside her.

'Nakedness is a sin, Maureen,' she murmured, leaning in so close that Maureen unwittingly inhaled the cloying warmth of her breath. 'Did your mother not teach you that?'

Maureen nodded hesitantly. In fact, her mother was not even Roman Catholic; her father, Charles, was in thrall to the Vatican, whilst Mary had tried several faiths – Anglican, Methodist, Spiritualism – before settling on Christian Science. But Maureen doubted Mother Lennox was looking for an explanation.

'Even to catch sight of our own unclothed body is wicked as it may lead to… impure thoughts…' the elderly nun continued.

Eleven-year-old Maureen wondered what on earth she could mean. She'd seen her sisters and brother naked at home, and wondered what was so terrible about it all. Overwhelmed with curiosity, Maureen suddenly longed to examine herself, wondering what made her body so shameful. Perhaps her family weren't like others? Perhaps she didn't have this mysterious, depraved appendage that everyone else must surely possess? Maureen glanced around surreptitiously, catching a flash of ankle here, a glimpse of shoulder there, but saw nothing that helped her understand what Mother Lennox was referring to.

'The bath shift protects you from this immorality,' the nun carried on. 'It enables you to bathe in absolute privacy, without exposure, so that only God knows what lies beneath. Now, hurry up, child.'

The other girls were now changed and standing beside the bathtubs, the oversized cotton sacks hanging forlornly from their bodies. Quickly, Maureen pulled her own shift over her head, cheeks burning as her fingers fumbled with the unfamiliar buttons and hooks of her new uniform. Finally, the task was accomplished. Maureen waited expectantly, wondering what was to happen next in this bizarre ritual.

At a signal from Mother Lennox, the students climbed into the tubs, which had been filled barely an inch or two deep. Maureen did the same and immediately cried out, yelping like an animal in pain. The water was freezing, soaking through the fabric to penetrate the hidden reaches beneath.

'Now, now, Maureen,' Mother Lennox chastised. 'I see you are used to being spoiled at home. That will all change here. Your discomfort is nothing to the pain of Christ when He fasted in the desert. It is nothing compared to His agony when He was nailed to the cross. He died for your sins, and you must suffer in return.'

Maureen shivered violently, her teeth chattering as her body shook uncontrollably. Around her, the others hastily washed themselves and Maureen tried to do likewise, hands plunged into icy water and sluiced over frozen skin. She recalled with horror a memory, long buried: a cold bath, a cruel nanny, being held under the water until she turned blue. Maureen gasped, sucking in the freezing air, her eyes wide with shock and horror.

In the dormitory later that night, the ordeal over but not forgotten, Maureen lay in the darkness beneath a coarse woollen blanket, on top of sheets so rigid and glacial that they must surely have been starched with blocks of ice. Her breathing was light as she listened to the unfamiliar sounds, unaccustomed to sharing a room with eleven other people and their nocturnal coughs and sighs and snores.

She didn't feel homesick; she didn't want to go home. But neither did she want to be here, at the mercy of the nuns and their casual cruelty.

Maureen rolled onto her side and brought her knees up to her chest, wrapping her arms around herself, searching for warmth and comfort in a place where there was little to be found.

Chapter Two

September 1923

I t was almost a year later when Vivian flew through the once intimidating doors of the convent into the main hall, already teeming with giddy girls overjoyed at meeting their friends again after the long summer holidays. The first time she'd set eyes on the Convent of the Sacred Heart, she'd been six years old, and the youngest child ever to be accepted at the school. England had seemed so wildly different to her upbringing in India that she had felt she would never get used to it, the austere buildings and slate-coloured skies an incomprehensible contrast with the vibrant, colourful country of her birth.

The Great Room, which had once appeared so sombre and forbidding, was transformed by bright clothes and babbling voices, as her fellow pupils shared stories of travel and adventure, of boredom and siblings. Right now, the students revelled in this glorious no-man's-land of time, intending to eke all the pleasure they could from these last few minutes of liberty before fashionable clothes were exchanged for uniform, glossy ringlets replaced by functional plaits, joy giving way to gloom.

'Maureen!'

'Darling!'

Vivian caught sight of her friend and hurtled towards her, slipping impatiently through the tightly knit groups. She caught Maureen's fingers and the two clasped hands, faces lighting up in pleasure.

'I love your hair, it's divine!' Maureen gushed.

'Do you like it? Truly?' During the vacation, Vivian had had her long curls cut into a 'shingle', a daringly short bob that perfectly framed her exquisite face.

'I adore it. I shall write to my parents the second I get back to my dorm and ask if I can have the same.'

'Twins!' Vivian exclaimed, and the pair beamed at one another.

'Dearest Viv, I missed you so much. Did you have the most delightful hol?'

Vivian had spent the summer with her grandparents in Bridlington and, whilst she loved them dearly, they were no substitute for her parents. It was a year since she'd last seen her mother – two, for her father, who was now a wealthy and successful broker in Calcutta – and although Vivian looked at their photograph every night, praying fervently that God might keep them safe, her memories were beginning to lose their clarity. She was alarmed to find that she could no longer remember the exact timbre of her father's voice, nor recall with certainty the precise shade of her mother's eyes. But Vivian had been conditioned to always appear gay and cheerful in company; anything else would be most impolite. If the occasional dark shadow flitted across her mind, pangs of melancholy or homesickness assailing her in the night, she pushed them away and buried them deep.

'It was splendid,' she declared. 'And you? It must have been super to be back at home.'

Maureen hesitated, her expression faltering. Before she could reply, she was interrupted by the Reverend Mother Ashton Case, who appeared in the doorway and clapped her hands twice.

'Please make your way to your dormitories as quickly and

quietly as possible. I see you have been permitted to run wild over the holidays. This behaviour will not be tolerated.'

Carried along with the crowd, Vivian and Maureen drifted towards the door that marked the exit from the real world and the entry into the boarding school proper. The pupils dragged their feet, knowing only too well that it would be a whole three months until they made the return journey. It would be Christmas before they saw a face that wasn't one of their teachers or a fellow student – unless they were exceptionally lucky and needed to be hospitalised. A broken leg sustained during a game of hockey, or a vicious bout of whooping cough that was beyond the skills of Matron, might mean that a girl was fortunate enough to temporarily escape the confines of the Sacred Heart.

'Do you know, it was quite the silliest thing,' Maureen began, as they meandered. 'I spent all last year quite desperate to leave this place, and as soon as I got home I was quite desperate to be back here again. Isn't that ridiculous? In fact, the only thing that made everything bearable was knowing that you were going to be here too.'

'How silly,' Vivian giggled.

The two of them made a striking pair, near-identical with their delicate looks and shining chestnut hair. Before the summer vacation, a poll had been conducted amongst the pupils, to vote for the prettiest girl in the school. Vivian had come first, and an astonished Maureen second. Later that day, Vivian had found Maureen crying alone in her dormitory; she'd confided to Vivian that she'd never even considered herself to be pretty, that the words used by her mother and her nanny were: horrid, repugnant, ugly.

'I do believe you've grown even prettier whilst you've been away,' Maureen said, as she studied Vivian admiringly. Even at nine years of age the way Vivian held herself was somehow different from the others, with a graceful quality to her movements, her long neck giving her an elegance like a prima ballerina.

'Oh, now you *are* being silly!'

'Did you miss me? Even the tiniest bit?'

'Of course I did,' Vivian replied truthfully.

They arrived at her dormitory, the scent of fresh lemon and beeswax mingling with the acrid tang of vinegar that had been used to polish the windows. Vivian looked around with something approaching fondness – familiarity at the very least – at the large room with its rows of beds, each with their own small wardrobe and a hard wooden chair. Students were permitted to affix family photographs or religious imagery to the wall, and a delightful rumour had spread that one of the senior girls had tacked up a picture of Douglas Fairbanks in *The Mask of Zorro* beside an image of the Blessed Virgin. When questioned, the girl had claimed it was a photograph of her father – an unconvincing assertion, given the character's distinctive moustache and black eye mask – and the offending item had purportedly been ripped from the wall and torn to pieces by Mother Ashton Case.

'Vivling! Maureen!' squealed Patsy Quinn, as she appeared in the doorway and rushed over to embrace her friends. She was soon followed by more of Vivian's dorm mates, spilling into the room with exclamations of delight. There was Anne Fitzgerald, who was Irish like Maureen, pale little Dorothy Ward, and Catalina Vasquez Orellana, the dark-haired, olive-skinned *señorita* from Granada, who was viewed with suspicion by the nuns lest she be a Moorish spy.

Vivian's trunk had already been brought up and she began to unpack as the girls chattered away, words tumbling over one another in their haste to tell their tales. She worked quickly and methodically as she listened, dresses unwrapped from their tissue-paper lining and hung neatly on the rail, whilst hats and gloves, nightdresses and handkerchiefs were slotted onto shelves. Her parents, keen to make up for their absence, had sent a crate of goods to Yorkshire, and Vivian had returned laden with silks and scarves, jewellery, books, a paint set and a new pair of ballet shoes. The others watched in fascination as she pulled out one delectable item after another. A bottle of cologne emerged and was immediately passed around the group, the young ladies taking turns to remove the stopper from the glass bottle and inhale the musky scent that hinted at the mysteries of adulthood, with its promises of elegant parties and handsome boys.

Next came the foodstuffs: exotic dried fruit (pineapple, mango, papaya); a jar of black plum preserve; a loaf of coconut cake. A dark green box tied with a wide cream ribbon concealed miniature desserts flavoured with pistachio and cardamom, which Vivian immediately opened and offered round.

'Viv, they're divine,' groaned Charlotte Astor, as she forgot a lifetime's training and spoke with her mouth full.

'May I take two?' asked Martha Brown, her voice thick with longing. The nuns chastised her continually ('Gluttony is a sin, Martha,' Mother Lennox would remark nastily), yet Martha remained impervious to their thinly veiled insults.

'Of course,' Vivian smiled.

Following careful deliberation, Martha selected the two largest pieces and the box moved on, as Vivian unrolled a length of silk to reveal a fine gold chain.

Patsy let out a gasp, as though someone had pinched her. 'Viv, that's beautiful.'

'Do you really think so?'

Patsy nodded vigorously. 'I think it's the prettiest thing I've ever seen. You're so lucky.'

'Take it,' Vivian insisted, holding the necklace out towards Patsy.

'Oh, I couldn't possibly,' she breathed, but her face betrayed her desire.

'Of course you can. Do take it, truly. You love it far more than I do already.'

'Well, if you're sure...;' Patsy's voice was hesitant, but her hands were already reaching out for the chain, the others watching enviously as she ran her fingers along the delicate links, clasping it round her neck where it came to rest along her collarbone.

'Lovely,' Vivian declared, delighted to see Patsy so happy. Naturally generous and kind, one of Vivian's greatest joys came from being able to please others. She knew she had settled well at the school, soon becoming one of the most popular girls in her class. The warmth she felt now, seeing the others sprawled on her bed as they joked and giggled and exclaimed over her gifts, was in stark contrast to the first night she had spent under Roehampton's slate roofs. Now the routine was as familiar as the Nicene Creed, the traditions as innate as the Lord's Prayer, the rituals so deeply rooted that they would never be erased.

The heat of the day had given way to a warm, still evening, but the water for the nightly baths remained arctic as ever. Maureen wrestled with the cumbersome bath shift – elbows restricted, hips chafing – lost in her thoughts.

She'd inevitably grown used to the Convent of the Sacred Heart over the past year, but she would never be the blindly obedient, docile pupil the nuns required. Maureen was intelligent but found her classes uninteresting, her rebellious side always ready to defy any instruction she considered foolish or illogical.

She shivered as the cold water found its way beneath the bath shift, her dorm mates occupying the impersonal metal tubs either side of her. The routine never changed, nothing surprising or unexpected to alleviate the tedium, but at least the familiarity left one's mind at liberty to wander, free to dream of far-off lands and storybook romance and—

There was a tap on the door and Maureen looked up, startled. She wondered if she'd misheard. Then the knock came again, sending murmurs rippling through the room. This was unprecedented! Even Mother Lennox was caught off guard, hesitating momentarily before crossing the worn flagstones and opening the door, shoulders set rigid with suspicion.

'If you please, Mother Lennox…' It was a pupil from the lower school and she looked utterly terrified.

'Speak up, child, I can't hear you.'

The girl swallowed and began again, her face white. 'If you please, Mother Lennox, the Reverend Mother Ashton Case has requested that you come to her office. She said it was urgent.'

Maureen's heart began to race as she listened to the exchange. Without a doubt, this was the most exciting thing ever to have happened at bath time. What on earth could be so urgent? And what would Mother Lennox do?

The nun was clearly asking herself the same question; the girls remained mute, but the feverish energy pulsing through the room did not need words to make itself known. Mother Lennox was conscious that the situation could quickly run out of control, the devil sneaking in through the cracks around the window, sliding in on his belly whilst her back was turned and offering larks and high jinks to the susceptible pupils.

'You will finish bathing immediately, then get dressed and return to your dormitory. I expect this to be done in absolute silence. If there is any bad behaviour, rest assured that I shall hear about it, and the perpetrators will be punished.'

Was it Maureen's imagination, or did Mother Lennox glance in her direction as she delivered the warning? But then the holy sister turned and left and the girls were all alone.

There was a pregnant pause, a single moment ripe with possibility. The others obeyed instructions and began drying and dressing, but Maureen didn't move. The invisible thrum in the air was relentless, so loud it drowned out reason. Something had to happen. Something *needed* to happen.

And Maureen had *the idea*.

The idea popped into her brain and lodged itself there. It whispered mercilessly, made itself impossible to resist, until

Maureen had no choice but to act on it, merely the vessel as *the idea* unleashed itself.

'Bother this!'

The others turned to look; Maureen's eyes were aflame, spots of colour high on her cheeks. She began pulling at the bath shift, showing ankles then calves then bony knees followed by white thighs as the bath shift grew higher and the revelations continued.

'Maureen!' exclaimed Josephine Williams.

'I'm going to bathe properly!' she declared, dragging the despised garment over her head and gleefully throwing it to the ground, naked and unashamed.

The move caused a sensation. Her fellow pupils could not have been more astonished had the Blessed Virgin appeared in their midst right there and then. The hum in the room reached fever pitch, an unspoken frenzy of shock and awe and admiration and curiosity, for who could resist a glimpse of the slim, pale body so brazenly on display?

Maureen let out a peal of laughter, shrieking in delight as she splashed icy water liberally over her bare skin. This was liberation! Glorious freedom!

She threw back her head and laughed once again, wondering how anything that felt so good and so natural could possibly be wrong? She was a beautiful bird that had flown free of its cage, lifted on warm winds, joyously heedless of the inevitable consequences.

Chapter Three

May 1924

The Sisters of the Convent of the Sacred Heart adhered firmly to the maxim that *the devil makes work for idle hands*. To keep the devil at bay, the pupils were submerged in a demanding timetable of English, Latin, arithmetic, history and French, alongside a heavy dose of religious instruction. The aim was not to produce scholars, but to turn out personable young ladies able to converse easily in society and land a suitable husband. There were also optional classes in music, dance and drama, led by the younger Sisters, and disapproved of by the Reverend Mother Ashton Case who considered them dangerously self-indulgent.

The long school days began at 6.30 a.m. with a thrice-tolling bell.

'Precious blood of Our Lord Jesus Christ,' Mother Lennox would intone, her expression grave.

'Wash away our sins,' came the pupils' reply, as bleary faces were doused in cold water and hastily patted dry with rough towels.

This morning, as had become their custom, Maureen accompanied Vivian as the throng of girls made their way, two by

two, down the main staircase and into the Great Chapel for early mass. Their uniforms were matching, their T-bar shoes identical in dull black leather (patent was outlawed at the Sacred Heart, lest someone should catch a reflected glimpse of the wearer's undergarments).

At eight o'clock it was time for breakfast, with everyone taking their place at one of the four long wooden tables in the dining room. The meal was basic fare of bread and butter washed down with tea, but today no one was concerned with filling their bellies. As soon as the duty nun had given them permission to leave, the girls raced as fast as they dared to the main noticeboard to read the smudged paper that had been pinned to the centre.

'I got it!' Vivian exclaimed joyfully, as she spun round and gripped hands with Maureen. 'I'm playing Miranda!'

'Oh congratulations! Well, of course you are, how could anyone ever doubt it?' Maureen pushed her way to the front, running her finger down the cast list for the end-of-year production of *The Tempest*. 'Caliban,' she announced triumphantly.

'Is that… good?' Vivian knew that playing a character described as '*a freckl'd whelp, hag-born*' would not be to everyone's taste.

'Absolutely! I'm just thrilled they've given me a real role, instead of making me paint the scenery or sew buttons on costumes. Besides, it might be jolly good fun to play a monster. Look—'

She twisted her face into a grotesque mask, and Vivian squealed in delight.

'It's how I used to scare my brother,' Maureen confessed, mugging even harder as Vivian giggled and the others joined in, the atmosphere growing febrile in the narrow corridor.

'Girls!' Mother Lennox was suddenly upon them, her stealth being yet another weapon in the vast arsenal she used to terrify the pupils. 'This is very unseemly behaviour for Roehampton ladies.' Her narrow eyes darted over each of them, noting who was present, lingering for an extra beat on Maureen before sliding on. 'Very unseemly indeed. You're acting like a pack of wild animals. Perhaps I should speak to Mother Ashton Case about the suitability of putting on this play.'

The words had their desired effect. The girls immediately fell silent, only a single horrified yelp escaping from Dorothy Ward before Patsy Quinn clamped a hand over her mouth. There were few highlights in the monotonous Sacred Heart calendar, and the end-of-year production was a beloved institution amongst the students.

'Maureen O'Sullivan!' Mother Lennox pounced. 'I might have known you'd be at the centre of this. Such a wicked, disobedient child.'

Maureen stared back, eyes blazing at the injustice of being singled out. She knew the futility of trying to defend herself and remained mute, determined not to apologise or hang her head in an admission of guilt.

Ever since that night almost a year ago, when Maureen had bathed naked and suffered the wrath of the nuns, her cards had been marked. Someone had given her away – she'd bet it was that little sneak Josephine Williams – and Mother Lennox had taken great delight in administering three sharp strikes of a wooden ruler across the soft palms of Maureen's outstretched hands. But instead of it breaking her spirit, Maureen had pitted herself against the established order and emerged more defiant and determined than ever.

Unexpectedly, Mother Lennox's thin lips curved into a smile, crepe lines puckering around her mouth. 'I suppose that's all one can expect –' here she raised her voice, ensuring her words were audible along the length of the corridor '– from a girl with a cripple for a father and a lunatic for a mother.'

Unrestrained gasps rippled outwards like the aftershock of an explosion. Maureen blinked once, twice, momentarily dazed as she waited for the full impact to be felt. Family secrets exposed, laid bare to mockery and judgement. Her gaze misted as she clenched and unclenched her fists, nails digging sweetly into flesh.

'How your fellow pupils must *pity* you. I do hope they find room for you in their prayers.' Mother Lennox turned heavily on her heel and departed.

Talk of *The Tempest* swept through the school like a raging fire, all other topics of conversation extinguished as chatter turned to whether Anne Fitzgerald would remember her lines; if Monica Callaghan (twelve years old and thin as a rake) was sufficiently suited to playing Prospero; and would Vivian really, truly be given a full-length dress of white silk, studded with jewels, for her portrayal of Miranda?

That afternoon, the cast had been freed from the confines of the classroom, flooding into the main hall where a rehearsal was to take place on a makeshift stage erected by the caretaker. Mother Regan entered the hall behind the girls, her face alight with anticipation. She taught Religious Studies, and she was both young and kind – two traits unusual amongst the Roehampton staff – with a soft, round face and small eyes hidden behind thick glasses. Gamely, she tried to fashion the excitable girls into some kind of order.

'Act one, scene one,' she announced grandly, the cue for those involved in the opening to rush onto the stage where they fell about dramatically, representing as best they could the storm-ravaged characters of Alonso, Gonzalo, Ferdinand and the Boatswain. (Sebastian and Antonio had been excluded from this scene due to their use of profanities; the Mariners likewise for lewd behaviour.) Mother Maguire, the Latin teacher, had viciously pruned the text, reducing the Shakespearean masterpiece to little more than a summary of its original self. She had scant respect for literature, but a veneration of the Almighty which drove her to purge the play of any blasphemy, violence or sexual references until, like a tree cut down in its prime, only the truncated stump remained with little of the original beauty discernible.

'Excellent. Lovely work,' Mother Regan praised, as the girls finished the scene and staggered off into the wings, transformed from Dukes and Kings back into skinny-limbed infants. 'Now, act one, scene two.'

Vivian, who had been watching the others in rapt silence, eagerly stepped up to the stage, joined by Monica Callaghan as Prospero. She looked out at the dozen pupils sitting neatly on the benches below (backs straight, knees together), and allowed herself to imagine that they were merely a tiny portion of a much larger audience. In her mind, the assembly hall at Roehampton was in fact a grand theatre with red velvet seats and gold rococo decoration, packed to the rafters as patrons clamoured to watch Vivian Hartley's portrayal of Miranda.

'If by your art, my dearest father, you have put the wild waters in this roar, allay them…'

Her eyes were wide with anguish as she spoke of the plight of the sailors. She listened in astonishment as Monica's hesitant Prospero recounted the (heavily abbreviated) tale of how they had come to be on the island, before finally, gracefully, closing her eyes and gently falling asleep. As Vivian's head came to rest on a makeshift rock, the watching girls burst into spontaneous applause, with Mother Regan on her feet for a standing ovation.

'Superb! Just wonderful! And now, enter Ariel.'

Anne Fitzgerald, playing Ariel, had been so wrapped up in watching the performance that she had quite forgotten her scene was next. On hearing Mother Regan's directions, she leapt from her seat and hurried up the short flight of steps at the side of the stage, tripping over the final one in her haste. Her entrance was earthbound and sprawling, her first words spoken in panting gasps as she limped around in a most un-sprite-like manner, regularly demanding 'Line!' from Dorothy Ward who was on book.

Then came the confrontation between Prospero and Caliban. Maureen took her place, screwing up her eyes and mouth to depict the beastly Caliban.

'Do straighten out your face, Maureen,' Mother Regan called. 'I can't understand a word.'

'Caliban is a monster.' Maureen was indignant. 'It's part of my characterisation.'

'Could Caliban be a little less monstrous, so that everyone can hear what you're saying?'

The words were meant kindly, but the girls snickered and Maureen's cheeks flamed hot with humiliation and anger. She remained silent as Monica recited a long speech of Prospero's, the angel and demon on opposing shoulders battling for control as the red mist descended and the devil claimed the victory.

'Excuse me, Mother Regan, but I think this speech has some lines missing.'

Monica Callaghan faltered. Mother Regan frowned. Even Vivian broke out of character and stared at her in confusion.

'I thought Monica spoke her lines correctly – is that right, Dorothy?'

'No, that's not what I meant,' Maureen cut in quickly before Dorothy could reply. She was standing on the edge of a precipice, ready to jump and knowing that the outcome could not be good. Seized by an overwhelming desire to show off, cause trouble, get attention… Maureen couldn't have explained the reason, she only knew that the fury deep in her belly could not be controlled, her voice clear and unwavering as she addressed Mother Regan:

'I believe the script itself has some omissions. I read my father's copy of *The Tempest* in the last vacation, and Prospero has a line when addressing Caliban about *"violating the honour of my daughter"*. Then Caliban replies that he would have *"peopled the island with Calibans"*. Do you know anything about those lines, Mother Regan?' Maureen asked. 'What do they mean and why are they missing?'

The hall had fallen silent. Not all of the girls understood what Maureen had said, but they could hardly fail to comprehend the effect her words had on their teacher. Mother Regan turned scarlet, blinking once, twice, her mouth opening wordlessly. She'd always tried to be fair and kind to the pupils, but now they would discover that even she had her limits.

'Maureen O'Sullivan, how dare you—'

'Is everything all right in here, Mother Regan?'

Every head swivelled to see Mother Lennox standing in the doorway, a petrifying vision in her billowing black habit. She was barely five feet tall, but her presence seemed to fill the whole room. 'I was passing by when I thought I heard... an incident. May I be of any assistance?'

The smallest flicker of annoyance crossed Mother Regan's face, though she quickly regained her composure. Only the taut white line around her lips gave away how furious she was with her colleague for interfering, and how incensed with Maureen for putting her in such a position. She would have to punish the girl now – there was no way to avoid it.

'No, thank you, Mother Lennox. That won't be necessary. I was about to send Maureen to Mother Ashton Case.'

'Maureen O'Sullivan?' Mother Lennox's eyes darted to where Maureen stood centre stage, alone and vulnerable. 'What are you still standing there for, child? Do as Mother Regan tells you,' Mother Lennox snapped, successfully terrifying Maureen and undermining Mother Regan all at the same time.

Mortified, Maureen slipped down from the stage, head bowed as she half-ran across the hall and slunk through the door, away from the staring eyes that followed every step. For once, she didn't relish the attention of her peers.

'Thank you, Mother Lennox,' Mother Regan said with dignity.

The elderly nun nodded with grim satisfaction then turned to follow Maureen, feet shuffling ominously along the cold stone floor, crucifix swinging heavily against her bosom.

'Have you heard the news?' Catalina Vasquez Orellana was giddy with anticipation as she rushed into Vivian's dormitory. Vivian was sitting at her desk, distractedly writing a letter to her parents. 'Maureen has been banned from the play!'

'No! It can't be true.'

'It's all over the school,' Catalina announced triumphantly, in her thick Spanish accent. 'Josephine saw her leave the office of Mother Ashton Case and she was crying.'

'Where is she now?'

Catalina shrugged. 'Perhaps outside? I must go and tell Francesca.' She ran off gleefully, eager to spread the gossip far and wide.

Vivian found Maureen sitting under a sprawling oak beside the lake. Her eyes were red, and she swiped at them angrily with a soggy handkerchief.

'Is it true? Have they forbidden you from being in the play?'

Maureen nodded. 'Yes,' she managed, through hiccoughing tears.

A new fear gripped Vivian. 'You haven't been expelled, have you?'

'No, nothing like that.' Despite her hatred of Roehampton, expulsion was something that Maureen feared: the letter home, the humiliating exit, the wrath of her father. 'Mother Ashton Case said I should pray extra hard for the Lord to deliver me from Satan. That I was too easily suset... sucsept... oh bother, I can't remember the word, but she said I was too easily tempted and I must try to be more calm and serene. But Viv, I don't know if I can!'

She looked so distraught that Vivian burst out laughing. 'You wouldn't be the same if you were quiet and well behaved. Honestly, you'd be the most awfully dull person.'

Unexpectedly, Maureen began to giggle. 'I suppose I would. Oh, Viv, thank heavens I've got you to make me laugh at myself. You love me whatever I do, don't you?'

'Of course. You know I adore you, and it's beastly unfair that you're not allowed to be in the play. I don't know if *I* want to be in it now. It won't be half as jolly without you.'

'Oh, but you must! Don't say that, Vivling. You're so terribly good as Miranda, I'd feel wretched if you didn't take part because of me. Promise me you'll do it.'

'All right then, I promise,' Vivian smiled. 'Now come on, darling, I really think we should go back.'

'Do I look as though I've been crying?'

Maureen's eyes were red and swollen, her cheeks blotchy.

'I'm afraid so, but everyone will understand. I think Catalina has already told the whole school anyway.'

'Oh, bother Catalina!' Maureen exclaimed, as she jumped to her feet and dusted down her dress. 'Who cares about her? As long as I've got you it doesn't matter what anybody says.'

Backstage, Vivian waited.

All her senses were heightened, her eyes glittering brightly, her shallow chest rapidly rising and falling as she tried to calm her racing mind. Her friends jostled and giggled, each dealing with the tension in their own way: Monica Callaghan had turned pale and seemed ready to vomit; Anne Fitzgerald was prone to outbursts of high-pitched laughter and had stuffed her fist into her mouth to muffle the sound; Josephine Williams had turned to a source of comfort none of the others had considered and was offering up a prayer to the Almighty.

The seamen staggered offstage, flushed and giddy, with exclamations of triumph or disappointment depending on how they rated their performance. Taking her cue, Vivian stepped out in front of the glaring lights.

There was no need to fumble for the lines – they came automatically to her lips as though the words were her own and she was speaking them for the first time. She was unaware of the nuns lining the front of the hall, a black, forbidding wall of pursed lips and suspicious expressions. She didn't see Maureen, allowed to watch the play from a standing position at the very back of the hall, her face full of pride as she watched her friend. Nor was she aware of Sonia Brownell, one of the younger pupils, staring up at her in awe. Their parents had known one another out in India, but Sonia had not yet plucked up the courage to approach the pretty, popular, older girl to let her know of their shared connection.

For that brief time, real life retreated, Vivian Hartley ceased to exist, and in her place Miranda lived and breathed, her story more real than anything Vivian had experienced in her cloistered convent school life. The restrictions of the stage brought a paradoxical freedom; she could fly whilst grounded, inhabit other worlds without even leaving the room.

And then it was over.

In the wings it was dark and Vivian felt momentarily afraid, longing to rush back out to the safety of the lights. Mother Regan placed a hand on her shoulder and whispered, 'Well done', guiding her back to the makeshift dressing room as the idea swirling in Vivian's mind slowly crystallised into certainty: when she was older, she didn't want to be a nun, like the Reverend Mother Ashton Case, or merely someone's wife, like her own mother. She didn't even want to be a pilot, or an explorer, which were Maureen's regularly-voiced ambitions.

Vivian wanted to be an actress. A *great* actress.

Chapter Four

June 1925

'La… laboro, labo… um, laboras…'

The classroom was hot and stuffy, the stagnant air an oppressive blanket that smothered the restless girls. They longed to loll in their chairs, to let their rigid spines relax and their tightly-held knees fall apart, but they did not dare.

'… Laborat…'

Josephine Williams was on her feet, visibly wilting in the heat, as she scrunched up her face and tried to remember the Latin verb tables.

'Labor… Labor… *ent*?'

'*Mus*,' shot back Mother Maguire. 'La-bor-a-*mus*,' she repeated angrily, stressing every syllable.

'Laboramus,' Josephine parroted in fright. 'Laboratis, laborant.'

The others listened in tense silence as, one by one, they were called upon to recite the hated conjugations. The time dragged interminably and, although no clocks were permitted in the classrooms, the listless students discerned from the rumbling in their bellies that it was almost lunchtime. The heat was soporific.

Unbidden, Maureen yawned widely, barely remembering to put a hand in front of her mouth as she slumped in her seat.

'At Roehampton, young ladies do not slouch,' snapped Mother Maguire. 'They sit up elegantly. Whereas you, Maureen O'Sullivan, resemble a sack of Irish potatoes. Now, *aedificare*.'

Slowly, her limbs heavy and her brain sluggish, Maureen stood. She opened her mouth to speak but was interrupted by the tolling of the Angelus bell. It rang three times, and the girls looked expectantly towards Mother Maguire.

'Very well, class dismissed. You will be first next time, Maureen.'

'Yes, Mother Maguire,' she replied sweetly, hardly able to believe her luck and crossing her fingers that the nun would forget her promise by Friday's lesson.

Outside the classroom, Maureen caught up with Vivian.

'No, not that way.' Maureen stopped her, tugging on her arm. 'I've got something to show you. It's a secret though, you mustn't tell. Come on!'

Vivian followed, intrigued, the older girl leading the younger along a corridor that led towards the back of the building.

'Where are we going?'

Although not officially out of bounds, they would likely get into trouble if they were found there without a good reason.

'You'll see,' Maureen grinned.

The corridor swung left and the pair hesitated, hearing the noise coming from the school kitchens. There were women shouting and the crash of metal on metal, accompanied by an unappetising smell of boiled vegetables and overcooked meat.

'Go!' Maureen hissed suddenly, taking off at speed. Vivian ran after her, racing towards a door at the far end of the passage. Maureen flung herself against it and it swung open, the girls bursting through into the humid air.

'This way,' Maureen panted, as the yard opened up and Vivian saw half a dozen of her classmates huddled together, their attention focused on something she couldn't quite make out. From behind they appeared skittish and flighty, all standing at strange angles with heads cocked to one side, hips jutting provocatively, one leg extended to show off a shapely ankle.

'Girls!' Maureen snapped, in an uncanny imitation of Mother Lennox. The group jumped in fright, wheeling round to discover it was only Maureen and Vivian, whereupon they collapsed into guilty giggles, high-pitched and hysterical.

'What's going on?' Vivian wondered.

Patsy Quinn put a finger to her lips and beckoned her forward. The others reluctantly moved aside to let the newcomers in and Vivian discerned the cause of their excitement: two delivery men were crossing the yard, carrying wooden crates from their horse-drawn cart to the Roehampton kitchens.

Men!

Maureen looked across at Vivian, eager to see her reaction. She cast her eyes down shyly, before casting them back up again in curiosity, her cheeks pink with a hue that was surely caused by more than the fierce summer sun. Maureen smiled knowingly.

The male of the species was a virtually unknown quantity at the Convent of the Sacred Heart, the nuns largely succeeding in preventing any contact between the young women in their charge and the opposite sex. Father Cole visited the school every morning to celebrate mass, but the elderly, white-haired, corpulent priest was certainly no object of adolescent infatuation. The violin teacher was a man named Mr Britten, his gender being the primary reason why that instrument was so popular among the girls. This very ordinary, rather shy man proved a source of fascination for the testosterone-starved pupils, who would flip their hair and bat their eyelids when speaking to him, the perfect target on which to practise their rudimentary flirting skills.

Now the gaggle watched, enthralled, as the two men strode back and forth across the yard, muscles straining and stretching, foreheads shiny with sweat as they transported the heavy boxes. To Vivian, it seemed a particularly masculine sort of pursuit, thrilling her in a way she could not quite explain.

The older man appeared to be in charge, calling directions and striding confidently ahead. The second, younger man generated far more interest. Indeed, one could hardly call him a man, for he seemed barely older than the girls themselves. His hair was a fine blond, a colour and texture rarely seen past babyhood, and he was long and gangly and held himself awkwardly, as though he'd recently undergone a growth spurt and hadn't fully realised the extent of his new frame. He was all too aware that he was being watched and it made him unbearably self-conscious as he bowed his head, stealing a glance at the girls, who promptly burst into giggles, which in turn caused him to stumble over his own feet.

'All right, son, keep your eyes on your work,' the older man instructed, his south London accent out of place amongst the well-spoken voices of the Sacred Heart.

The boy went to pick up a box, but he fumbled clumsily and it slipped from his hands, crashing to the floor. He instinctively looked over to see if the girls were watching him; his eyes locked with Vivian's marvellous blue-green ones, and he froze in humiliation.

'He keeps looking at you,' Maureen hissed.

'Don't be silly.' Vivian waved away her words, although the notion was exhilarating.

'I'm going to speak to him,' Maureen declared, boldly calling out, 'How old are you?'

The boy's mouth flapped open and closed, his Adam's apple bobbing silently. 'Four'een.' His voice broke mid-word, sending the girls into another spasm of uncontrollable laughter. He caught Vivian's eye and flushed deeply, beside himself with embarrassment.

'Ooh, he really likes you, Viv!' chimed in Charlotte Astor, and the others quickly took up the refrain.

'He *loooves* you.'

'He wants to marry you...'

It was nothing more than childhood teasing, with no malice directed at Vivian, but she felt deeply sorry for the boy. His misery was compounded as his father cuffed him violently round the ear, reprimanding him, 'You're not supposed to speak to the young misses.'

The boy recoiled from the blow, glancing across to see if the group had witnessed the scene.

'He looks at you again!' squealed Catalina. 'He truly loves you. You will kiss him and have babies together.'

There was a shocked silence, and Patsy gasped, for the mention of babies did not conjure up an image of the infant Jesus lying in his crib, but rather the furtive, sinful act of procreation. The girls knew that intercourse and babies were somehow related, but the hows and the whys and the what-went-wheres remained shrouded in mystery, the focus of much speculation and debate. Despite the best efforts of the nuns, the pupils were naturally curious. Their hormones were raging, and the unsubstantiated rumours of what sex might involve were both wildly thrilling and utterly terrifying. After lights out in the dormitories, whispered gossip was passed from bed to bed in the safety of the darkness.

'I've heard it's so painful it makes you bleed,' Anne Fitzgerald asserted one night. The source of the information was an older sister who, at fifteen, was barely more knowledgeable than Anne herself, but she delighted in scaring her younger sibling.

'But if it's so horrible, why does everyone make such a fuss about it?' Vivian had wondered.

'Because what Anne says isn't true at all,' retorted Charlotte. 'It's supposed to be the best thing ever, and that's why the Bible is full of people doing it with their brother's wives and so on – because when you're grown up everyone wants to do it with each other all the time. That's why the nuns are so worried about it, because they think if we do it we'll stop thinking about God and start thinking about *it* instead. That's why *they're* not allowed to do it, you see,' she finished, with a dismissive sniff.

'You're allowed to do it when you're married though,' Dorothy Ward clarified. 'It's just before that makes it wrong.'

'Well, I'm going to do it as soon as I can,' insisted Charlotte, the darkness making her bold.

'Me too,' added Patsy.

'I don't want to do it, ever,' said Anne. 'It sounds horrible.'

'Not even when you're married?'

'Well, perhaps once or twice, so we can have two babies. A boy and a girl. But that's all.'

'Oh yes, I *would* like babies,' Patsy chimed in. 'What about you, Vivian?'

'Of course,' Vivian nodded. 'I shall find a handsome husband, and we'll have a delightful little family.'

'And me,' added Maureen loyally. After all, wasn't that what every woman did? What alternative was there?

'I've heard there are things you can do to *stop* you having babies,' Charlotte announced in hushed tones to a chorus of shocked gasps.

'Like what?'

'I don't know exactly.' Charlotte sounded cross that she'd been questioned. 'Maybe it's something the man does. But it means you can still do *it* and not have a baby.'

'So what's the point of doing it if you don't have a baby?'

The room fell silent, then the speculation continued. Those who had brothers pronounced themselves experts on the male anatomy, based on a fleeting glimpse at bath time, and they willingly recalled what they had seen for the benefit of those who were blessed only with sisters. Learning to kiss using one's hand, or a pillow, or even a fellow student, was common practice, in order to be well prepared for meeting one's future husband. There was even a rumour that two students in the upper school had enjoyed practising kissing on one another so much that they had no desire ever to kiss a man.

Back in the yard, Vivian giggled as she admitted, 'Yesterday, in confession, I made up all the filthiest things I could think of. I was in there for almost twenty minutes and I could see Father Cole through the grill growing redder and redder. At the end he gave me twenty Hail Marys, ten Glory Bes, and told me to come back immediately if I had any more impure thoughts.'

The others howled with laughter, marvelling at Vivian's daring.

Suddenly, Patsy flinched, her eyes darting left to right as she listened intently.

'What is it?'

'I think I heard something—'

'Quick! Run!'

The girls pelted across the yard, feet pounding, skirts flapping, all thoughts of boys and babies and sexual relations flying from their heads.

Chapter Five

October 1926

A new craze had swept the corridors of the Sacred Heart, a fresh obsession taking hold of the impressionable girls. Where once they tramped around the school in straggling clusters, they now seemed to glide in orderly formation, faces composed into wistful expressions. Rarely were they found without a prayer book in hand, a rosary draped around their neck, or some trinket from Rome or Lourdes about their person.

The catalyst for this sudden fervour was a young French nun, Marie Françoise-Thérèse Martin, a humble village girl who had devoted her life to God and died of tuberculosis at the age of twenty-four. In 1925, she had become Sainte Thérèse de Lisieux, with Pope Benedict XV waiving the standard fifty-year interval between death and beatification. The girls of Roehampton were wild with excitement. The nuns did their best to redirect any disturbing adolescent urges onto papal-endorsed idols, and Thérèse was the perfect candidate.

Part of her appeal was that she'd died only thirty years before – a welcome change from the ancient do-gooders of long ago – and the girls were fascinated by the notion of someone with such purity so close to their own age. Goodness was such a terribly difficult thing to achieve. Had the young Thérèse never been tempted to play naughty tricks on her sisters? Had she never had the urge to kiss a boy?

Thérèse's story was all the more seductive because it seemed so *easy*. Known as 'The Little Flower of Jesus' (a title all the girls swooned over and immediately aspired to achieve for themselves), she was famed for her philosophy of 'little deeds', believing it was not necessary to perform great acts during one's quest for holiness and that little gestures would suffice. The Roehampton students took this to heart, pledging to make a difference in whatever small way they could: posies of flowers were left on pillows, glasses of water placed on desks. Perhaps not quite in the spirit Thérèse had intended, the students found themselves caught in a holy one-upmanship of generosity – fetching gloves, sharpening pencils, donating hairslides – as they held firmly to the conviction that eternal salvation could be achieved merely by tidying another girl's desk.

Thérèse's spell was all-encompassing. Even Vivian lost her head to the silliness and flirted with the notion of taking holy orders, imagining the stone walls of the convent to hold the same drama as the bare boards of the stage, the stark black habit as enticing as any West End costume.

Only one girl remained immune to the allure of Thérèse: Maureen. At fifteen years old, she was increasingly rebellious, paying little attention to her studies and revelling in her fearless reputation: the girl who could always make everyone laugh in class; who would never refuse a dare, no matter how outrageous. She'd been known to throw peanuts at the nuns during mass, accumulating a record haul of seventeen in the folds of Mother O'Brien's veil. On one occasion, she shimmied up the tree outside the Reverend Mother Brace-Hall's office to triumphantly hang a pair of knickers from the highest branch. (The Reverend Mother Ashton-Case had died the previous year; in the spirit of Thérèse, many of the pupils were calling for her immediate canonisation.)

Maureen had realised that she had little respect for the nuns. She felt certain that if there *was* a God – something she was by no means sure of – then He could not condone their cruelty, their hypocrisy. She knew, innately, that it wasn't right to treat a child in the way she'd been treated. And so her resentment grew and her fear subsided.

It was a blustery, overcast autumn day when Maureen decided to act upon the plan she'd been hatching. She exited Mother Maguire's class hugging her books to her chest and found Vivian waiting for her in the busy corridor. Regardless of the weather, the girls were expected to take a stroll outside during break time; the fresh air was good for the soul and the complexion.

'You go ahead. I'll catch up.' Maureen intended to keep her tone light, but the harder she tried, the more unnatural she sounded. Her cheeks were flushed, her eyes bright and feverish.

Vivian frowned. 'What are you up to?'

'Nothing.' The denial was swift and unconvincing. 'Honestly, you go. I'll meet you by the tennis courts in ten minutes.'

'Oh, Maureen, you're not about to do something silly, are you?'

'No!' Maureen was disconcerted by how easily her friend could read her. 'Well, perhaps. But the less you know about it, the better. I'll see you outside.'

Maureen grinned as she slipped into the crowd of girls. Vivian hesitated, wondering if she should follow.

'Pardon me, but are you Vivian Hartley?'

The voice was little more than a whisper. Vivian glanced down to see a pupil from the lower school gazing up at her with wide, blue eyes. She had a round, pretty face, flanked by thick blonde hair, and she looked terrified.

'Yes, I am,' Vivian replied distractedly. Already Maureen was out of sight, swallowed up by the blur of uniforms. She was bound to be up to mischief, Vivian thought worriedly, berating herself for her indecision.

'I just… I wanted to say hello. I think you might know my family.'

'Might I? What's your name, darling?'

'Sonia. Sonia Brownell. My sister, Bay, says that you were friends in India, and my par– well, my mother, knew your parents.'

'Really?' Vivian was torn between the courtesy expected of her, and her desire to stop Maureen before she did something reckless. 'I'm sorry, I'm not sure I remember. I was awfully young. Are your parents well?' She was scanning the crowds as she spoke and failed to notice the way Sonia's cheeks grew red, her face crumpling with the onset of tears.

'They… I…'

When Vivian looked back, Sonia had fled.

———————————

At the other side of the school, Maureen hovered nervously outside the Great Chapel. Her heart was pounding so loudly she felt sure it could be heard by every nun in the building.

I could always say I've come to pray. The thought made her smile as she contemplated Mother Lennox's disbelief at that statement. But then the thought of Mother Lennox sobered her again, the smirk disappearing as she remembered what a risk she was taking.

A final glance to check that the corridor was clear, then Maureen pushed open the heavy door and slipped inside.

It took a moment for her eyes to adjust to the darkness of the chapel. The flickering of the candles cast distorted shadows, spectres in the gloom, and Maureen stood very still, ready to run at a moment's notice. It was eerily quiet. Even her breathing seemed to disturb the silence. Her eyes swept quickly over the pews, behind the pillars, around the altar and along the dusty tapestries on the wall. She appeared to be alone, yet she proceeded with caution; it was all too easy for a lurking nun to be concealed by the blackness.

Maureen skirted the aisle, her footsteps soft on the flagstones, her adrenaline racing. As she reached the font she noticed her hands were shaking. She didn't have much time, she realised, fumbling in her pocket for the small bottle she had brought. Without hesitating – without thinking – Maureen did what she had come to do and whirled around, scuttling back to the door. It took all her willpower not to run as fast as she could, bolting for the exit.

Ten steps… eight… six…

She reached for the handle but it slipped through her grasp, the door yanked open from the other side. Then came a moment of sheer terror as a woman charged through and the two of them collided, Maureen unexpectedly engulfed by the warmth of another human being; the yielding softness of stomach and breasts; the fresh, clean scent of soap and rosewater. It was all over in a second, less time than it would take to say Amen, but Maureen thought she might faint with fright.

'Oh! Pardon me!' she blurted out. She glanced up, terrified to discover who this other person might be, but the examination provided no answers: not a fellow pupil, not a nun, but a woman. A stranger. One with dark blonde hair in fashionable curls, a retroussé nose and porcelain skin. A wide-brimmed hat concealed the upper half of her face; her eyes weren't visible, but Maureen felt certain that she'd been scrutinised and committed to memory, to be presently identified and duly punished.

Panic overcoming her, she put her head down and ran, racing down the corridor as though the devil himself was after her.

———

'And what did she look like?'

Vivian was walking in the school grounds, arm in arm with Patsy and Dorothy.

'I've never seen anyone like her before. Especially not here,' Vivian explained, gesturing up at the forbidding convent building.

'Her clothes were exquisite, and she moved so gracefully. She looked so sophisticated, she might almost have been French!'

After Sonia had vanished, Vivian offered up a swift, silent prayer to God that He might keep Maureen out of trouble and hurried towards the tennis courts, knowing that she herself would be reprimanded if found inside during recess. On her way, she passed a young woman, dressed in a chic grey woollen suit. The woman's presence – unusual in itself – was made all the more notable by the fact that she was strikingly beautiful. Despite being barely older than some of the upper school students, she clearly belonged to another world, one outside the restrictive walls of the convent.

'How mysterious,' said Patsy, breaking off to wave as she spotted Maureen sprinting across the lawns to join them. Her face was flushed, and Vivian eyed her suspiciously. 'Vivian's just seen the most beautiful woman,' Patsy told her excitedly.

'Oh, I saw her too!' The comment slipped out before Maureen could stop herself. She faltered, looking down at the ground and willing someone to change the subject.

'Really?' Patsy looked surprised. 'Where?'

'Um… In the corridor. I don't remember exactly.'

'I think she's one of the Old Children,' Dorothy chimed in, referring to the name given to Roehampton's alumni. 'I heard there was someone coming. I think she's been called. She's going to take orders.'

'How shocking!' Patsy exclaimed. 'Such a waste. *And* she has to cut her hair short.'

'Golly,' muttered Maureen, unable to think of anything more perceptive to say.

'I'm sure she could marry any man that she wanted, and it seems such a terrible pity that she never will.' Patsy sighed wistfully. 'Who would you like to marry, Viv?'

'Someone handsome and exciting,' Vivian smiled, her eyes lighting up. 'He would ride a horse and look ever so well on it, and he would have a commanding voice that people listened to.'

'An actor, perhaps?' Patsy teased, as Vivian blushed.

'We were talking about what we want to be when we grow up. Vivling wants to be a great actress of the stage,' Dorothy announced, putting on a dramatic voice that made the others giggle. 'What about you, Maureen? Would you ever take holy orders?'

'Dear me, no! I should think Mother Lennox would expressly forbid it in any case.'

'Well, what *do* you want to be?'

'I should like to be a pilot, and fly all the way to Africa or China or America. And I want to travel the world, and explore the jungle. And become an archaeologist in Egypt.'

'That *does* sound utterly thrilling. But I think—'

Dorothy broke off as she spotted Catalina running across the field towards them, her dark hair streaming out behind her, her skirt flying up in the breeze.

'Have you heard the news?' she panted.

Four heads shook simultaneously, as a cold fear clutched Maureen's heart.

'Mother Brace-Hall is *so* angry. Someone has put ink into the holy water of the chapel. Antonia Rogers arrived today because she is to take orders next week and she tried to cross herself with the water but now her face is blue. It is running over her head. She is trying to wash but Francesca saw her and said she looked terrible. Perhaps she will not take her vows now. Perhaps it is a sign.'

It was at that moment that Vivian caught sight of Maureen's ink-stained hands. Maureen realised at exactly the same time, slipping her hands discreetly inside her gloves.

'Is Mother Brace-Hall terribly cross?' Maureen asked nervously. She exchanged a glance with Vivian, who looked as worried as she did.

'Oh yes,' Catalina confirmed joyously. 'She was absolutely furious and said that when she finds out who did it, they will be expelled *immediately*.'

Chapter Six

SONIA

Roehampton
19th September 1930

Dearest Mother,

I am missing you all terribly but do not worry about me for I am well. Now I am twelve I feel very grown up and quite able to look after myself. I am working hard already, and hope to gain some prizes this year. Mother Graham says my recitations are among the best she has ever heard. I showed her some of the poetry I wrote in the holidays and she said it showed great promise.

It is odd to be at school without Bay, but I am glad you have her at home with you. Maxine and Tilly are here with me and we sit together in all of our classes, except religious instruction because Mother O'Brien insists on splitting us up.

Last night at supper we had beef and it was delicious.

I will work very hard and make you proud, and I will try extra hard not to get into trouble so you have no cause to worry.

Kiss my darling brother for me, I do miss him!

Love,

Sonia

Roehampton
24th September 1930

Dear Bay,

Here I am back at the Sacred Heart, and without you! It seems very strange indeed, and I have yet to stop looking for you in the corridors.

Very little has changed here – Mother O'Brien is still horrible, and Mother Regan still looks as if she will burst into tears in every lesson. A summer by the seaside in Kent has done nothing for her nerves. I am very much enjoying Mother Graham's English class – we are reading Notre-Dame de Paris by Victor Hugo, which I adore. And she liked my poetry! But she advised me not to show it to the other teachers as they might not approve.

Maxine and Tilly send their love. Maxine is so very grown up as she spent the holidays on the south coast of France. She speaks in French, and raves about the French food and fine weather, and really, she is in danger of becoming quite insufferable. How I wish we could have gone away in the holidays but I know it was not possible. I should love to travel and explore. When I am grown up I shall travel the whole of Europe!

How are Mother and Michael? I think of them every day and love them dearly. I hope Michael is behaving, but I know he is a good boy, and you must both take extra care of Mother for me.

How is Father?

I had better leave you now as I must read a whole chapter on mortal sin before bed!

Your loving sister,
Sonia

Liverpool

29th September 1930

Darling Sonia,

What a delight to receive your letter! Indeed you do sound extremely grown up and your handwriting is quite improved from the letters you sent last year. I hardly recognise my baby girl, she is growing up so fast and is far away from me.

But I do not mean to sound melancholy. Bay and I speak of you often – she is a great help to me in the house, particularly as we have had to let Alice go. As you may have been aware during the summer vacation, our financial situation is a little difficult at the moment and it makes no sense to keep a maid when Bay is now at home. Do not tell this to any of your friends at school, for I fear that they would tease you.

Father has been taken on by a small insurance firm, and I hope that he will soon be settled there and our situation will return to normal. I was very sad to let Alice go but… forgive me, I can think of nothing to complete my sentence. How silly!

I am sitting here in the peace and quiet of the parlour, thinking of you. Michael is upstairs in his room and I know he misses you greatly. Such closeness between a brother and sister gladdens my heart.

I keep you in my prayers every night and love you very much.
Mother

Roehampton
8th October 1930

To my darling Michael,

How are you? How I long to hear your news! I feel sure that everything you are doing is far more exciting than life here. I have been telling my friends all about my handsome brother, and they long to meet you.

I am reading 'Notre-Dame de Paris' and when you are older I shall buy you a copy, for I feel sure you would adore it. It is set in an old cathedral in Paris and is about the love between a hideously disfigured man with a hunch and a beautiful gypsy girl. But there is more than just love – there is murder, and the creepy cathedral and gargoyles made of stone.

I will see you at Christmas but the time here goes so slowly. All of the lessons (apart from English) are dull and the food is horrible.

Your ever-loving sister,

Sonia

Liverpool
12th October 1930

Dear Sonia,

Firstly I must apologise for taking so long to reply. I promise I am not neglecting you! I have been kept very busy, and this is the first spare moment I have had since you left.

As you may already know, Alice is no longer with us and this has meant that much of the extra responsibility has fallen on me. I never knew there was so much to attend to in one small house! Always there is washing to be done, floors to be scrubbed, bedding to be changed… Reverend Mother Brace-Hall would be quite ashamed of my hands for they are red and raw, particularly in this bout of cold weather we have been having. I beg of you not to tell your friends about the situation in which we find ourselves – not because of any vanity on my part, but I do fear what would happen if word were to get around the school. Girls of your age (and some of the nuns too) can be spiteful, and I would not wish that upon you.

But enough about me: I am pleased that you do well in your lessons. Keep it up, it may be more important than you realise.

Michael studies hard and reads voraciously. He reminds me so much of you, and I am very hopeful for his future. Perhaps he may win a scholarship to a good school, as I fear we may not be able to afford the fees.

Father has taken a job in a local insurance firm. Mother is pleased (and I am pleased for it keeps him out of the house), but I am concerned that it may not last for long. Do not tell Mother that I have told you, but he is drinking heavily again. He is managing to keep it from his new employers at present but surely it cannot be long until he is discovered and then I don't know what we shall do. Mother bears it with fortitude. She has such strength and kindness: a true angel.

Goodness, this letter is such a length already! I must turn off the lamp now to save the gas but I send my love to Maxine, Tilly and of course, yourself.

Bay

P.S. Do not worry about Mother, I take good care of her.

Roehampton
22nd October 1930

Dear Bay,

It is such a delight to receive your letters for this place is tedious, tedious, TEDIOUS! Really, if the family need my school fees I would be quite willing to give this place up and come home to scrub floors with you! Dearest Bay, I do not mean to make sport of our situation, but honestly, there are days I feel I would happily swap my situation with you.

I am glad that Father is working, if only so that he is away from you and Mother for most of the day. For the same reason I hope that he is successful in his job.

Oh, I heard the most marvellous rumour – do you remember Maureen O'Sullivan? The beautiful Irish girl, two or three years older than you? You told me she was expelled for putting ink in the holy water. Apparently she was discovered by a film director from America, and now she's in the movies in Hollywood! Can you imagine it? It sounds like a fairytale. I wish something like that would happen to me, it sounds so terribly, terribly glamorous and exciting, but I can't act for toffee. Perhaps someone will publish my poems and that will make me rich and famous. Anything to get away from here.

Bay darling, I mustn't complain as I know you're having the most horrible time at home. It's awful to think of you cleaning and scrubbing, but I haven't told a soul here. Maxine says her family are going on a tour of Italy at Easter, and Tilly is to get a new pony for Christmas, so I doubt either of them would understand our predicament.

Lots and lots and lots of love to you all. I hope Michael is behaving without me to boss him around! Do write to me as soon as you have a spare moment, for I long to hear your news.

Your affectionate sister,
Sonia

Roehampton
4th November 1930

Dear Michael,

Do write to me, just a quick note so I know that you haven't forgotten me. Bay says you have been reading – what books have you read? I do think that people who can write are the cleverest people in the whole world, don't you agree? What a marvellous life that must be, to write and create and go on wonderful adventures, all inside your head.

You are so lucky not to have been sent away to school. The nuns are terrifically mean and they only like the boring swots like Alexandra Pattinson who prays every spare second and is class monitor.

Do write back soon,
Love Sonia x

Liverpool
6th November 1930

My darling Sonia,

I do hope you are well and are working hard at your studies. It is wonderful to hear your news, and I am so glad you are happy and have made such good friendships.

I long to have you back at Christmas, but you must prepare yourself for some changes on your return. I need you to be strong and brave and grown up, for life here is a great deal harder than when you left us, and there may be other changes to come. But I do not mean to alarm you. We are all well and making the best of things. Bay is such a help to me, and Michael offers much support. He is growing up so quickly and is becoming a delightful, thoughtful young man.

Make sure you say your prayers every night, trust in the nuns and do what they tell you for they are good people who will help you to become closer to Our Lord.

I send all my love and a big kiss,
Mother

———

Liverpool
20th November 1930

Sonia,

So much has happened that I have only just found time to write to you.

Mr Dixon (I will call him that because he has never been my father and he does not deserve that title. I am sorry to say such a thing about Michael's father, but how glad I am that our darling brother does not take after him) has behaved so despicably that I hardly know where to begin. A few days ago, he stole money from Mother's tin that she had put away for our Christmas presents, and bought himself a bottle of whisky. When Mother found out she called him a devil and poured the whisky all over the back yard. Mr Dixon began to shout all kinds of abuse and Michael ran upstairs, but I remained with Mother. He tried to strike her, but she pushed him and because he was intoxicated he fell. Mother locked the door to keep him outside and told him to stay away from her. She took the suitcase from upstairs (the good leather one) and packed all his clothes and shoes. She seemed quite calm, quite methodical. All this time Mr Dixon was in the yard, shouting and carrying on. I have no idea what the neighbours thought but they undoubtedly heard. Then Mother dropped the case from the landing window and told him not to come back. He hasn't. It was Friday and I dearly wish she had taken his pay packet from him before she threw him out!

Mother and I are both looking for work. I have taken in some sewing for Mrs Harvey at number 37, but that pays very little. I know she cannot really afford it and gave me the work out of charity, but for now I will not question it. Mother is to enquire about a bookkeeping job in a clerk's office tomorrow. We have also written to Uncle Henry to see if he can help us in the meantime, for I do not know how we will pay your school fees next term, and it will be impossible to send Michael to any reputable institution.

I know you are too young to remember our real father, but he was such a good and kind and generous man. I have never told you this before, but I miss him every single day.

Do not reveal to Mother how much I have told you. Do not worry: but you must understand our situation.

Perhaps the most serious part is that I have persuaded Mother to get a divorce, a course of action she would not countenance at first. To you and I it may not seem quite so serious, but Mother is beside herself. I cannot imagine what the nuns would say if they found out, especially that wicked old cat Mother O'Brien. In spite of everything, we still have a reputation to uphold.

I will write again as soon as there is more news, but I beg you once again not to worry unnecessarily. I will look after Mother and Michael, and of course you, my darling sister.

Bay

Bay,

I am in such a state I hardly know what to write. I wish you would come and take me away from here because I truly hate it and have never been so miserable in my whole life. If I came back I could be such a help to you and mother, for even though my sewing is appalling I'm sure I could improve very quickly. Everyone here is hateful, especially the nuns. I am certain that they read our letters, for they are never sealed when we receive them and now they seem to know everything about me. Mother Maguire told me I was a disgrace, and in class yesterday Mother O'Brien said that if I wasn't careful I would end up like my mother! She said it in front of everyone, and they all heard and keep asking me what has happened.

Tilly's parents sent her an enormous doll as an early Christmas present and she won't let me play with it. It's huge – bigger than some of the first years – and it's so pretty but she's so selfish.

I got into terrible trouble today. It was during a hockey match, and the weather was so cold and everyone was so mean that I said I wished I'd been birth controlled so as not to exist. Mother Kelly looked more shocked than I've ever seen anyone look in my life. She made me strip down to my vest and knickers and stand at the side of the pitch for the rest of the match. It was freezing cold and everyone laughed and I wanted to cry but wouldn't give them the satisfaction. I hate Mother Kelly so much. That might be an un-Christian thing to say but I don't think she is a good Christian. She said she was going to tell Mother Brace-Hall, but I don't care. I hope they expel me.

I'm so glad I don't have to see Mr Dixon ever, ever again. I wish he wasn't Michael's father. I wish our real father could come back. Perhaps he is not really dead, but is hiding somewhere, and now Mr Dixon has gone he will come back and make everything all right again.

I am not ashamed of Mother getting a divorce – not that I would ever be ashamed of Mother for anything – but doesn't it seem like a thrilling thing to do? She's just like one of those pioneering women Mother O'Brien always tells us off for talking about, like that lady who threw herself in front of the horse. I want to be just like her. I shall never marry anyway. Boys are far too much trouble – apart from darling Michael of course, but I wouldn't want to marry my brother! But I don't want to be a nun either because they are horrible and I don't care if they are reading this. <u>HORRIBLE!</u>

I cannot, CANNOT wait for the Christmas holidays. I long to see you and I don't want to return in the New Year. Tell Uncle Henry not to worry about my school fees – he can save them for Michael.

Yours in despair,

Sonia

Roehampton

2nd December 1930

Dearest Mother,

Thank you for your letter and your kind words of advice. I am trying very hard to be good, but it is very difficult. I wish all the nuns were as nice as you think they are, but they are not.

I long for Christmas, and I wish I was at home so I could give you a big hug and tell you how much I love you.

Here it is very cold and not very festive. We made chains out of strips of coloured paper but when we tried to hang them in our dorm they were removed. Tilly's parents have sent her a doll for Christmas, but I don't want anything like that. I honestly don't need anything for Christmas so it doesn't matter if you don't buy me anything.

Kiss Bay and Michael for me, and I will see you very, very soon.

Love Sonia

P.S. I am working on a special Christmas surprise for you.

Liverpool
4th December 1930

Dear Sonia,

I have been putting off writing you this letter for a long time, but I feel it is only right that I tell you what has happened here so it will not be so much of a shock for you on your return. I understand that Bay has written to you a little of the situation, but I wanted to explain things myself, and to forbid you from making the same mistakes that I have.

With great regret, and with a heavy heart, I have taken the decision to ask Father for a divorce. It is not a decision I have made lightly, and I pray to God that He will grant me the strength to get through this difficult time. I beg His forgiveness daily, for I can barely reconcile it with my own beliefs. This is not a path I would choose if there were any other way, and it is not a path I wish for any of my children to take. Just this once, do not learn from my example, Sonia.

Work hard on your character. Strive every day to be a good person, humble, generous. I fear for what others may say if they hear of our situation but you must be brave, Sonia. I pray you will not have cause to feel sorrow over my shortcomings, but if you do, remember that Our Lord is the only one who can guide us through this. Open your heart to His love and in His mercy He will guide you from the path of sin.

I think of you every minute, my beautiful daughter, and count the days until we are reunited at Christmas-time.

All my love,
Mother

———

London
10th December 1930

Dearest Sonia,

I have so much to tell you! Our situation has changed so greatly since my last letter, and so quickly!

Mother has found work managing a hotel near King's Cross: so we are now in London, mere miles from you, my darling sister. The hotel is small, and our living quarters are cramped, with just one bedroom and a parlour to share between us. But I do not wish to complain. Mother is so very clever to have found a job and be independent. She is truly an inspiration.

I help her with her duties as much as I can, cleaning and answering the telephone and serving breakfast. Sometimes it's rather fun talking to all the different people who are staying here. Yesterday I spoke with a man who told me he was an explorer, newly returned from China. He said that the people there all have yellow skin and eat dogs!! Now that I've written it down I realise how silly that looks, so perhaps he was playing a trick on me.

This part of London is very dirty and busy, but we have heard about a wonderful zoo close by. Michael is beside himself, and quite desperate to see the camels and the zebras, but we have not yet had the time to take him.

It will certainly be a very different Christmas for us this year, as Mother must work for the entire festive season, and I daresay I shall be serving Christmas dinner to our guests.

The good news is that I am to come and collect you at the end of term! Though I shall feel very strange returning to the Sacred Heart, it will all be worth it to see your beautiful, smiling face. We will have the whole train journey to catch up on one another's news, and there is so much to talk about. I can hardly wait to see you! By the time you receive this letter it will be less than a week away.

Whatever the New Year brings, we must feel thankful that Mr Dixon is no longer in our lives, and make sure to support Mother in whatever way we can.

Your ever-loving sister,
Bay

Roehampton
14th December 1930

My dear Bay,

I am overjoyed to hear of the change in our situation, it is so exciting! The hotel sounds marvellous and I long to meet all the peculiar characters you describe. Mother is both a trouper and an inspiration.

I cannot CANNOT wait to see you very soon, and I can barely contain myself from bursting with excitement that you will be coming to pick me up. I have lots of silly stories to share but will save them until I see you in but a few days' time.

All my love and kisses,
Sonia

PART II
The Ingenue

Chapter Seven

MAUREEN

Dublin, Ireland

September 1929

'You'd think they'd be grateful!'

Maureen burst through the double doors that separated the chaotic kitchen from the large, communal dining room where dozens of Dublin's poor were seated at long rows of tables, consuming their meagre meal. Her face was flushed, her dark hair escaping from beneath the white cap she wore, part of the uniform that marked her out as a volunteer.

'But no, all they do is tell me I'm serving the pudding wrong. You'd think they'd be counting their blessings just to get a piece of pudding!'

'Are you having a toughie today?' asked Dolly O'Shaughnessy, a petite girl with dark blonde hair.

Maureen raised her eyebrows so far that they almost disappeared into her hairline. 'The things they say to me, I couldn't repeat. My mammy would wash my mouth out with soap and water, a good Catholic girl like me,' she joked, hamming it up. 'Mr Connor made a lunge for my bottom and muttered something filthy, so I hit him with the soup ladle. And poor old Mrs Byrne smells as though she hasn't had a wash in months – I held my breath when she passed for fear of being sick into the bread basket.'

Dolly giggled, shaking her head at Maureen's theatrics. The two young women had worked their first ever shift together at the charity-run kitchens just off Temple Street and had soon become fast friends. Both eighteen years old, with a desire to give something back in exchange for their privileged lives, they worked three shifts a week at the soup kitchen in this insalubrious part of the city, north of the River Liffey. The poor would shuffle in from the nearby slums to be given a hot meal, served up by pretty young socialites with a conscience.

The concept of *noblesse oblige* greatly appealed to Maureen, but the reality was far less gratifying – 'bloody awful' was how she regularly described it.

'It's a long way from Versailles,' Dolly commented wryly, raising her voice to be heard over the clattering of saucepans.

'Ah, Versailles!' Maureen pretended to swoon against the ovens, as she recalled her finishing school. 'I had the most marvellous time. We'd sneak out of the grounds at night to meet the French boys, and they'd whisk us up to Paris on the back of their motorcycles. We'd spend the evening dancing and laughing, then home by midnight and our chaperones would never even notice we'd gone. Can you imagine?'

'You're a wild one, Maureen O'Sullivan,' Dolly asserted, secretly thinking how thrilling it sounded. Dolly had never even ridden on a motorbike, let alone been to Paris on one.

'Oh, not anymore. Nothing fun ever happens to me now that I'm back under my parents' watchful eye. You know, when I was at school, the nuns were always warning us about everything – *"be careful of this, don't try that, your soul will be in mortal peril if you do the other"* – and I always imagined that the real world must be a terrible place, full of danger and temptation. But honestly, the most frightening thing I've encountered is James Murphy trying to kiss you after he's walked you home.'

Dolly chuckled. 'That can be pretty frightening in itself. Especially if he hasn't shaved. Or if he's been on the whiskey.'

Maureen smiled distractedly. 'I feel as though... As though I need something more. A sense of purpose. Do you know what I mean? Perhaps it sounds silly to you, but I can't help but think there's a bigger life out there. Sure, all the parties and balls are fun, but they can get a bit tedious after a time.'

Dolly's forehead wrinkled uncomprehendingly. They were two of the most popular girls in Dublin, and the invites never stopped rolling in – to the races, to the Embassy, to balls at Trinity College. What was there to complain about?

'When I was a girl,' Maureen continued, attempting to make Dolly understand, 'I dreamed of doing something pioneering, like flying an aeroplane or excavating tombs in Egypt. And now look at me. Back home in Ireland, serving soup to a bunch of ungrateful—' Maureen hastily bit down on her lip to stop herself saying something inappropriate.

'Not quite the romantic vision you hope for, is it?' Dolly agreed. 'You think, "*This is my vocation. I will serve the poor, and be patient and loving and kind.*" And then you get here and they stink to high heaven and say horrible things and it's all you can do not to walk out every day.'

'Exactly,' Maureen nodded, remembering the Little Deeds of St Thérèse de Lisieux and how the girls of the Sacred Heart had longed to emulate her.

'*And* I can never get the cooking smell out of my clothes,' Dolly went on. 'I must walk down the street reeking of cheap meat.'

Maureen paused, uncertain that Dolly fully understood her anxieties. Since leaving Roehampton, Maureen had been corresponding with Vivian, who had embarked on a Grand Tour of Europe and was having a marvellous time by all accounts. Maureen felt Vivian might appreciate her need for adventure in a way that Dolly didn't.

'There's just not the sense of fulfilment I thought there'd be,' Maureen attempted to explain. 'It might be good for my soul, but it's doing nothing for my sanity.'

'Well, I've got just the thing to cheer you up.' Dolly's blue eyes sparkled mischievously. 'Tickets to the Horse Show!'

Maureen let out a groan. The Horse Show was one of the biggest events on Dublin's social calendar, attended by the great and the good, the beautiful and the well-connected, and tonight was the closing party at the Hotel Metropole.

'But I'm *so tired*, Dolly. And I don't know if Mother will let me go. I've been out every night this week.'

'Of course she will – she won't care,' Dolly chirped tactlessly. 'Your father's away, isn't he? Well, there you are then. Your life's not going to change if you sit at home, is it?'

'No, but—'

'Patrick Murray's going to be there,' Dolly interrupted.

'Is he?'

Patrick Murray was a medical student at Trinity College, with chiselled features and piercing blue eyes.

'Yes, he is, and he asked me 'specially if you were going.'

'Did he?'

'I swear on my life. Oh, do come, Maureen! It'll be the most tremendous fun, and I hear they have a marvellous band,' Dolly added, knowing that her friend could never resist a dance.

Maureen hesitated, closing her eyes as she smoothed her fingers across her forehead, their tips kneading out the tension lines on her alabaster skin.

'All right then, I'll go,' she capitulated, as Dolly squealed and the two girls clasped hands, tearing round the kitchen in a clumsy Charleston before the chef asked what on earth they thought they were doing and they collapsed against the countertops, laughing so hard that they could barely catch their breath.

———

The evening was magical, the air abuzz with sparkling conversation and perfumed with the scent of lilies, roses, freesias and hydrangeas. Tables covered in fine white linen had been laid out around a circular dance floor, and the band played tirelessly, up-tempo jazz numbers in keeping with the young crowd.

The cream of Dublin society rubbed shoulders with leading equestrian figures from across the world, the room filled with a heady mix of bankers, lawyers, military men, and a youthful, work-shy, good-time set who were omnipresent at Dublin's most exclusive events. There was a sense of being amongst the movers and shakers, that *here* was where things happened: deals brokered; acquaintances renewed; romances begun.

Maureen herself looked radiant, even though she wasn't wearing a scrap of makeup. She didn't need to – her lips were a luscious pink, her skin glowing. She'd brushed her hair until it gleamed, and dabbed scent on her neck and wrists, a sophisticated, sensual fragrance that she'd bought in Paris. In contrast to the formal ballgowns some of the old guard were wearing, Maureen sported an audaciously short flapper dress, a stunning creation in cream silk with a dropped waist and gold beading. She had danced all night, whirling from one suitor to the next, all thoughts of tiredness forgotten and the deprivations of the soup kitchen left far behind. And now she had landed in the muscular arms of Patrick Murray. He was a superb dancer – almost as good as Maureen herself – and they made a striking couple as he led her round the floor with the lightest of touches.

'You must be terribly clever. It's such a wonderful thing to be a doctor,' Maureen flattered him, as she gazed up at him admiringly.

'Well, I'm not there yet, there's still a few more years of hard work to go. But I always make time for occasions like this. One must enjoy oneself too.' Patrick smiled, showing clean white teeth.

'What an excellent philosophy.'

'And what about you? Were you a good student?'

'I was terrible,' Maureen confessed. 'I was expelled from my convent school for putting ink in the holy water.'

Patrick threw back his head and laughed. 'No! That's not true.'

'Every word. And after that no respectable school in England would have me. I had to move to France to finish my education.'

'Now I know you're pulling my leg. A pretty little thing like you could never have such a fearsome reputation.'

'You'd be surprised,' Maureen grinned, as she threw herself into the lindy hop, kicking her feet joyously before bursting into applause as the song finished. 'Oh, that was so much fun, I can hardly catch my breath,' she cried, collapsing into a chair next to Dolly, who was resplendent in a pale pink lace dress with a string of pearls reaching past her waist.

'Can I get anyone a drink?' Patrick asked solicitously. 'Maureen? Dolly?'

Dolly declined, indicating her almost-full glass, but Maureen nodded. 'Surprise me,' she giggled, as Patrick made his way over to the bar.

'He can't take his eyes off you,' Dolly squealed. 'You look wonderful together.'

'Really?' Despite Maureen's initial reservations, she was having the most tremendous fun.

'Absolutely. He's one smitten kitten. Evie Clarke thinks he's sweet on her, but he's barely been near her all evening. And in that vile dress I'm not surprised. Oh, did I tell you…'

As Dolly chattered on, discussing the men she had danced with, the ones she intended to dance with, and the ones she wouldn't dance with if you paid her, Maureen's attention was caught by a large group seated directly across the room. They were all exceedingly well dressed in the latest fashions, and not one of them was familiar from the society circuit.

The man leading the conversation had dark, wavy hair and a striking, serious face. His features were animated as he described something to the man on his left, and Maureen could sense his passion as he spoke, waving his arms and slamming his fist on the table to emphasise a point.

On his other side sat one of the most glamorous creatures Maureen had ever seen. Her hair was dyed platinum blonde – unheard of for a respectable Irish woman – and she wore cherry-red lipstick and a languid expression. Her dress must have cost a small fortune, Maureen speculated. Even at this distance, it was evident that the peacock-blue silk was exquisite, beautifully cut and hand-decorated with hundreds of tiny seed pearls.

'Dolly,' Maureen interrupted, cutting off an interminably long anecdote about Dolly's mother's terrier. 'Do you know who those people are?' Discreetly, she inclined her head as Dolly followed her gaze.

'Haven't you heard? They're from America.'

'Well, that explains the hair!' The comment slipped out before Maureen could stop herself, but Dolly laughed wickedly.

'It certainly does. She's an actress, I believe. Roma or Rena something.'

'Goodness.' Maureen was intrigued. An actress from America!

'Yes, they're all in films. She's married to the director – that one, with the dark hair,' Dolly continued, pointing rather obviously at the man Maureen had noticed just moments ago. 'I heard he's won an Academy Award, and they're shooting a picture over here.'

'Is that so?' Maureen fell into a thoughtful silence, which went unnoticed by Dolly as she happily resumed the tale about the dog. Patrick returned with a Gin and It, which Maureen sipped distractedly before placing it down on the table.

'Patrick,' she smiled flirtatiously. 'This is one of my favourite songs. Do you feel like a dance?'

'I don't know where you get your energy from,' Patrick laughed, but he took her by the hand and obligingly led her onto the dance floor. The music was slower, a more sedate foxtrot, and it wasn't long before the two of them had circled the floor and were gliding past the Americans' table. Maureen's heart began to beat a little faster, and she made sure to keep her head up, a radiant smile fixed on her face as though she was having the time of her life.

'What are you laughing about?' asked a bemused Patrick. 'I'm not even saying anything.'

'Well, perhaps you should be,' Maureen returned smartly.

The band segued seamlessly into a popular swing, and Maureen found herself happily (and not entirely accidentally) beside the table of film people. Eager to remain there, she engaged Patrick in small talk and feigned indifference to the famous director seated nearby.

She didn't have long to wait. When the dark-haired man rose from his seat to approach her, Maureen pretended to look surprised.

'Do you mind if I join you?' he asked gruffly. The look he gave Patrick implied he did not expect his request to be declined, and Patrick readily assented.

'What's your name, honey?' the man turned to Maureen, his accent both incongruous and thrillingly glamorous.

'Maureen O'Sullivan,' she replied instantly.

'Nice to meet you, Maureen.' He didn't call her Miss O'Sullivan, as she might have expected, and Maureen wondered what to make of it. She put his lack of formal manners down to his nationality. 'My name's Frank. Frank Borzage. I'm a film director. Tell me, have you ever done any acting?'

'A little,' she said truthfully, unwilling to recall the disastrous role of Caliban.

'And what do you do now? Do you work?' His questions were short and to the point, and there was something about his brusque manner that unnerved Maureen. It wasn't that he was rude, exactly – more that he was unexpectedly direct, a busy man eager to cut to the chase.

'I work with the poor.'

'Nice, nice. Do you like it?'

'I hate it.' Maureen's luminous green eyes flashed defiantly, the candlelight playing across her features.

Frank eyed her carefully for a moment, admiring her spirit and assessing her potential. She was undoubtedly attractive, with an innocence and naivety that American audiences would adore, and his instincts rarely let him down. 'Say, how'd you like to move to California, kid?'

'California?' Maureen repeated dumbly. Standing mute beside her, from where he'd been watching the entire exchange, Patrick's mouth fell open in shock.

'Yeah. Los Angeles, to be exact,' Frank confirmed, a smile spreading across his face. 'Hollywood.'

Chapter Eight

New York Harbour, USA

October 1929

'Do you see her, Ma? Can you see it?'

Maureen and her mother were standing on the upper deck of an enormous ocean liner, wrapped up tightly against the stiff Atlantic breeze. On the horizon, the Statue of Liberty hove into view, growing larger by the second as the RMS *Baltic* ploughed through the ocean towards its destination. Lady Liberty was an iconic sight and a wide-eyed Maureen pointed excitedly, the euphoria contagious as her fellow passengers did the same.

The majority of those on board were just like Maureen – sailing to a new life in a brave new world, not knowing what lay ahead – although she had reason to believe that her prospects were brighter than most. Many had gambled everything they had on a one-way ticket with no guarantee of work or lodgings when they reached the United States; Maureen had signed a six-month deal with Fox, so her immediate future was secure, but she was all too aware that when the contract expired she could be on a return ship, heading back to Ireland and the life she'd hoped to leave behind.

Beside her, Mary O'Sullivan raised a hand to her eyes, squinting as the late autumn sun reflected off the water. When she spoke, she sounded awestruck: 'There's a sight I never thought I'd see. She's a grand lady, that's for sure.'

The skyscrapers of New York loomed in the distance, rising above the construction taking place in the race to build bigger, bolder, higher. Maureen considered herself to be a sophisticated young woman of the world, but she'd seen nothing like this in Europe. It was hard to believe that in this fantastical city, ordinary people were going about their daily business, carrying out the mundanities of eating and sleeping, working and procreating.

Leaning over the rail beside her, Tommy Clifford's eyes were bulging. Just eleven years old, he'd also been 'discovered' by Frank Borzage, and signed up to appear in the same film as Maureen, *Song o' My Heart*. Unlike his co-star, Tommy had never before left his native Ireland, and the city couldn't have been more of a contrast from the green valleys and granite mountains of County Wicklow where he'd grown up.

'New York – is that all there is to it?' he said with an affected swagger, and Maureen laughed, seeing the way he was drinking it all in, overwhelmed by the incredible sight laid out in front of him. She knew exactly how he felt – excited, hopeful, completely out of his depth.

The ship blew its horn to announce their arrival and Maureen felt an unexpected surge of adrenaline. She was really here and she was really doing this. America! Land of the free and home of the brave – wasn't that what they said?

Her life over the past couple of weeks had been a veritable whirlwind. On the morning following the Horse Show, Maureen had met with Frank at his office for a screen test, and it had gone well enough for him to make her an offer on the spot. She'd taken the contract home to show it to her father, newly returned from London, and begged for his permission to travel to the United States and appear in a film. Despite his obvious reservations, and his distrust of what he termed 'motion picture people', Charles O'Sullivan had always harboured a soft spot for his first-born child and could see how badly Maureen wanted this opportunity. He eventually agreed, on the proviso that her mother accompany her, to act as chaperone.

Maureen would have accepted any stipulations that her father had laid down, and before the ink was dry on the contract she had embarked on a flurry of shopping and packing, saying goodbye to her brother and sisters and her friends. She hadn't been back to the soup kitchen since the night she'd met Frank, but Dolly had been over to the house every day after her shift with endless questions and non-stop chatter, watching enviously as Maureen threw her best clothes into a large leather trunk.

'Come along now, we'd better go get ready.' Mary touched her daughter lightly on the arm, breaking into her thoughts. 'Mr Borzage left very specific instructions.'

Frank had travelled to America ahead of them but his office had taken care of all the arrangements, and their five-day ocean crossing had been completed in style. Despite their luxurious living quarters Mary had not enjoyed the journey, having been seasick a number of times, and she was keen to be on terra firma. They would spend five days sightseeing in New York before departing once again, this time by train, taking the Santa Fe line across the Midwest and arriving three days later in Los Angeles, California.

'You go, I'll follow. Just five more minutes,' Maureen pleaded, hardly able to tear her gaze away from the land which held so much promise.

Mary watched her daughter for a moment, her eyes narrowing. 'Now don't you be letting your head swell, young lady. Your father and I would never have agreed to this if we imagined you'd become a… a conceited show-off. It's not too late to tell Mr Goldstein and Mr Borzage that we've changed our minds, and ask them to put us straight on the next ship back to Ireland.'

The Socialites

It is *too late*, Maureen thought defiantly. She knew that her mother would find it far too humiliating to go back on her word like that. Despite everything she'd said, Mary was just as dazzled by the 'film people' as Maureen was. Besides, there was a signed contract in place, and extracting Maureen from that would require lawyers and payments and all manner of things her mother would never involve herself with in a million years.

But Maureen merely smiled and said nothing. Perhaps she was finally growing up, she reflected, this new opportunity heralding the start of a calmer, less impulsive Maureen. And perhaps this time alone with her mother would finally start to heal the divide that had grown between them over the years.

As a child, Maureen had bitterly resented her mother for her continual absences – both literal and emotional. Mary had spent long periods of time away from the family home in Killiney, and when she *had* been physically present she'd been cold and capricious, critical of her eldest child and at times downright cruel. At Roehampton, Mary's condition had proved a source of embarrassment, the nuns making vicious remarks that Maureen didn't always understand but which aggravated her feelings of shame and anger.

It was only as she entered adolescence that Maureen had begun to understand, and to forgive. She recognised that the terrible injuries her father had sustained in the war had taken their toll on her mother's mental health, triggering a dependence on alcohol and a series of nervous breakdowns that required convalescence and specialist care. Time and maturity had begun to heal the wounds, and Maureen would even go so far as to say that she'd enjoyed Mary's company on this trip.

'You needn't worry, Ma,' Maureen smiled sweetly, the Atlantic wind tugging her hair free from its scarf, letting it billow freely around her face. 'Hollywood won't change me.'

'Five more minutes,' Mary agreed sternly, as she turned and walked back to their cabin, leaving her daughter alone with a head full of daydreams.

Staring out at the skyline, Maureen experienced an unmistakeable rush of excitement as she thought about everything that had happened so far. The escape from her stifling, unfulfilling existence seemed almost unbelievable; the idea of returning unthinkable. However handsome and charming a man like Patrick Murray might be, Maureen knew that she had no wish to settle down and become the respectable wife of a Dublin doctor.

The great steamship sailed onwards, skirting Liberty Island with its famous statue, the light reflecting from her copper robes, her flaming torch thrust high into the sky. Laughing out loud with pure joy, Maureen leaned over the railing and stretched out her hand towards Lady Liberty. This leap of faith was undoubtedly daunting, the prospect of what lay ahead formidable, but Maureen knew that if she could overcome her fears then the rewards would be life-changing.

———

Maureen barely recognised the girl that stared back at her, reflected in the enormous mirror surrounded by bare lightbulbs. She looked like herself, only better – prettier and fresher, her skin more luminous, her lips fuller, her eyes wider and more arresting. She was playing an Irish country girl, so the overall look was subtle, but Maureen felt transformed.

'The lights of the set will wash you out,' explained Ruby, the make-up girl, as she applied rouge to the apples of Maureen's cheeks whilst Mary looked on in disapproval.

Her hair was styled in Marcel waves and pinned, her costume a simple fawn-coloured dress with a wide collar and bow. If only her schoolfriends could see her now, they'd never believe it. As soon as she had a spare minute, she would write to Vivian and tell her everything that had happened. Although – Maureen caught herself – she wouldn't want to sound too triumphant, for she remembered how Vivian had once harboured acting ambitions of her own.

Maureen's stomach was somersaulting like an Olympic gymnast as she was led from the costume trailer onto the set for her very first scene, Mary walking stoutly beside her. The warmth of the Californian sun hit her as soon as they stepped outside. Despite it being November, the day felt hotter than an Irish summer.

The buildings on the Fox lot were the size of aircraft hangars, and separated by narrow walkways. As Maureen passed between them she caught a glimpse of the mountains in the distance, sage and ochre, patches of vegetation amidst the scorched scrubland with a backdrop of clear blue sky. The view couldn't have been more different from the lush green hills of County Wicklow, where the rolling grey clouds swept low overhead, but there was something alluring in this new landscape.

'Ma, I've been thinking. I'd like to go to the ocean when I have a day off,' Maureen confessed. She'd been speaking to some of the cast and crew during rehearsals, and the prospect of wide sandy beaches and warm sparkling sea was too tempting to ignore.

'Let's get your first day over with,' Mary said tartly, 'before we start thinking about a day off.'

Maureen fell quiet, thinking that she should have known better than to confide in her mother. Though still only eighteen, she was growing in independence with every challenge she faced. Arriving at a new place, cultivating friendships and navigating a new environment were nothing new to her; Roehampton had been her training ground, and finishing school had given her the opportunity to perfect those skills. Hollywood was more intimidating than either of those, the stakes far higher, but Maureen still felt confident that she could steer her course with aplomb.

And she wanted to stay here, she was sure of it. She'd had only the merest glimpse of the motion picture industry, but already she wanted more.

The first night they'd arrived, fresh off the train as the sun was setting, Maureen and her mother had taken a taxicab from the station to the house the studio had provided for them. Their route had taken them along Sunset Boulevard, and Maureen had been wide-eyed as she took in the stores and restaurants, the profusion of neon and the hordes of people out enjoying themselves despite the late hour. They turned from Sunset onto Hollywood, passing Grauman's Chinese Theatre, the famous picture house which was showing the latest releases. Crowds were clustered outside, measuring their steps against the concrete footprints of their idols, and Maureen drank in the enormous posters featuring Mary Pickford, Gloria Swanson and Buster Keaton, wrapped in a daydream that one day it would be *her* face up there, *her* movie that the masses were flocking to see.

'Hey, Maureen! Are you coming for drinks tonight? Everyone's heading to Cocoanut Grove when we finish.'

It was one of the supporting artists she recognised from rehearsal – Ralph, she thought his name was. She grinned enthusiastically, and was about to reply when her mother cut in.

'No,' Mary replied tersely. 'She's not.'

Maureen caught his eye, signalling an apology. 'Yes,' she mouthed. 'I will.'

Ralph gave her a laughing thumbs-up and Maureen felt a joyful flip in her stomach, enjoying the heady sensation of being young and attractive and about to film her first movie. Her mother was a heavy sleeper; still adjusting to the time difference, she'd be out like a light by nine o'clock. It would be just like finishing school, Maureen thought wickedly. She could sneak out of the house and flag down a taxicab. Cocoanut Grove couldn't be too hard to find…

'Oh my,' breathed Mary as she stepped onto the soundstage.

Maureen, following behind her, was no less impressed, her mouth falling open involuntarily. It was as though Ireland had been replicated in miniature inside an aircraft hangar. A painted backdrop of rolling hills and lush greenery, with a winding river and blustery sky, dominated one wall. In the foreground, a traditional stone cottage had been constructed, with a pretty garden and even half a dozen real sheep gambolling on the freshly laid grass. Maureen had seen it in rehearsals but the atmosphere was completely different now that filming was about to begin.

Today the building was a hive of activity with sparkies, chippies, extras, all dashing to and fro. Huge cine-cameras were mounted on tripods and cranes, with cables snaking across the floor and lights strung overhead, as serious-looking men in suits frowned and barked commands. Maureen felt a surge of adrenaline and nerves that threatened to overwhelm her, as goosebumps prickled on her arms. She'd practised until she was word perfect, but she was terrified of getting something wrong – forgetting a line, missing a mark or some other mistake that would cost time and money. She was eager to impress everyone. She hadn't even begun and already she wanted to do this all over again.

Mary was led to the side and offered a chair from where she could observe the action. Maureen stepped onto the set, waving a greeting to little Tommy Clifford, who looked as though he were in his Sunday best, wearing a suit and tie with a jaunty flat cap. Then the star of the picture, John McCormack, made his grand entrance, a make-up artist fussing to powder his shiny forehead, as he strode across to his opening position.

The assistant director called for silence on set and the clapper boy marked the take as Frank Borzage – the director who'd plucked Maureen, fairy-godmother-like, from the obscurity of a Dublin party to the glamour of Hollywood – stepped forward, his gaze sweeping over the set and the performers.

Maureen took a deep breath. The next few moments could change her life.

'Aaaand… Action.'

Chapter Nine

Los Angeles, USA

June 1931

The cherry-red Corvette screeched to a halt as Maureen pulled onto the Fox Studios lot in West Hollywood. She drew admiring glances as she stepped out in a chic new suit in cornflower blue, with cream court shoes and an extravagant hat that she had bought that very morning. She was down to her last $250, but she'd been feeling impulsive as she drove past the boutique on Rodeo Drive and the hat had looked so darling in the shop window that she simply had to have it.

Maureen had recently finished shooting *Skyline*, her sixth motion picture for Fox, where she played a young Irish girl in love with a troubled Irish boy. Her first film, *Song o' My Heart*, hadn't performed well at the box office, but Maureen had proved popular and Fox were keen to work with her. The reviews she'd been garnering over the past few months were increasingly positive: '*Proud and lovely*', said the *Los Angeles Record*. '*The acting technique of Miss O'Sullivan improves with each picture*', proclaimed the *Hollywood Daily Citizen*. Even the notoriously vicious critic Louella

Parsons could find nothing bad to say, telling her readers, '*You will love Maureen.*'

Two weeks ago, after *Skyline* had wrapped, Maureen had returned to Ireland. It was her first trip home since she'd left for America almost two years before, and on her arrival she'd been treated like a superstar, thrilled to discover that she had a legion of fans in her motherland.

The Maureen who returned to Saintbury, the family home overlooking the sea, was certainly different to the one who'd left, she reflected – confident, worldly, sexually experienced. It was as though she'd outgrown Dublin, and she felt pulled between two worlds, one foot in both. It made her realise more than ever that L.A. was where she wanted to stay, that she *had* to make a success of her career. She didn't want the lives of her siblings or friends, working as a typist, or a shopgirl at Arnotts, or husband-hunting at every high-profile social event like Dolly.

Relations with her mother were still strained, but Maureen had been overjoyed to see her beloved father again, spending many happy hours curled up on the old wingback leather chair in his study whilst they discussed her new career. Despite Charles's initial misgivings, he was now immensely proud of his eldest child, and supported her wholeheartedly.

'You've got to let them know what you're worth,' he told her animatedly, his paralysed arm lying prone in his lap. 'That studio's making a small fortune out of you, and they're paying you a pittance. You need to stand up to them. Show them who's in charge.' As a military man, it was a subject close to his heart.

'But Pa, the studios don't work like that,' Maureen protested. 'There are hundreds – thousands – of young girls just like me who'd gladly take my place in a heartbeat.'

Charles shook his head. 'No. They're not all like you. Fox took you halfway across the world for a reason, and you've got to make sure they give you your due.'

Buoyed by her father's advice, Maureen sped down to Fox Studios the day after she returned to America, bowling across the lot and into the offices. She was nervous but determined not to show it, outwardly full of bravado as she prepared to ask the head of the studio for a pay rise.

It felt like the plot of one of her movies, Maureen realised with a smile – the plucky young heroine, the underdog, David taking on Goliath. She would be charming, she told herself, full of chutzpah, and in a happy Hollywood ending Walter S. Parker would roll over like a puppy and concede to her every demand.

'Good morning,' she called out brightly to everyone she saw. Her familiar voice was warm and lilting, bubbling with expectation, and her heels sank into the plush carpet as she made her way along the warren of corridors. Her greetings were returned politely but she wasn't a fool and could imagine how the pool of secretaries regarded her: a minor success with ideas above her station; just nineteen years old and girls like her were ten a penny, they'd think dismissively. Well, Maureen wasn't like the others and she wasn't to be underestimated, she thought fiercely, her father's encouragement ringing in her ears.

'Take a seat, Miss O'Sullivan,' she was told, as she arrived outside the office of Walter S. Parker.

Maureen sat down on a plush green chair, picking up a paper from the low table beside her and glancing idly through the headlines. Depression, starvation, unemployment. The stock market had crashed the week after she arrived in America, and in the two years since its effects had deepened. There were photographs of families queuing for bread; jobless men, quiet and dignified, holding placards announcing their desire to work.

How terrible, Maureen thought distantly, but these lives felt so far removed from her own existence they might as well be on the moon. The place she inhabited was full of life and colour, dreams and vibrancy; it was nothing like the world she saw in the newspaper, desperation etched in dull shades of grey.

Maureen was aware that the studio itself had had problems. Financially crippled by the Wall Street crash, it had gone into receivership, its founder, William Fox, dramatically flung into jail.

A new president had yet to be appointed, and in the interim Fox was being run by a temporary and fluctuating motley crew of acting heads like Walter S. Parker.

But this was Hollywood! Maureen cheered herself with the thought. In these dark, uncertain times, the public longed for something to cheer them up – their weekly escape into a life of fantasy and excitement. Surely the motion picture industry was invincible!

Like her father said, they were making a fortune, so why shouldn't Maureen stand up for herself? They thought that just because she was young, a woman, a foreigner, she wouldn't dare to demand her due. They supposed they could fob her off with a few hundred dollars a picture, and bog-standard roles in B-list movies. Well, she'd show them, Maureen thought, her eyes blazing with righteous indignation.

By the time she was shown into Walter's office, Maureen felt like a boxer going into the ring.

'Mr Parker will see you now,' his secretary announced.

'Thank you,' Maureen said, her voice gracious but her gaze steely.

The room was luxurious, with a kidney-shaped desk made of gleaming walnut, and thick cream carpeting. The man in front of Maureen was of considerable girth, in an expensive-looking mocha-coloured suit. He wore a red silk tie, and his dark hair was parted in the middle and slicked down with oil. A partially smoked cigar rested in an ashtray beside him.

The image only strengthened Maureen's resolve. Of course Fox could afford to give her a salary increase, just look at this place!

'Miss O'Sullivan.' Walter S. Parker didn't shake her hand, but indicated the small, rather hard chair opposite him. 'I'm glad you've come to see me,' he continued. 'There's something I need to speak to you about.'

Maureen was surprised but decided to take it as a positive. 'Oh yes?'

'But first, why don't you tell me why you've come to see *me*.'

'Well,' Maureen paused and gathered her confidence. 'I feel I deserve a pay rise,' she announced brightly, coming straight to the point.

Walter S. Parker's reaction was not what she had expected. His jaw dropped visibly, heavy jowls quivering in amazement. The silence continued so long it began to feel uncomfortable.

Walter recovered and appeared to smile. 'You do?'

Maureen nodded.

'And why do you think this? I'd be interested to hear your reasons.'

Maureen cleared her throat. 'Well, I've been working for you continuously ever since I arrived from Ireland and I've appeared in six pictures now. *A Connecticut Yankee* in particular did very well. *The Princess and the Plumber*… well, that was just a blip. But I'm committed, talented and I really feel as though I'm going places…' She trailed off, unsettled by the effect her well-rehearsed speech was having on its recipient.

Walter's jaw had steadily dropped once again, so low that Maureen feared it might dislocate. Then he threw back his head and guffawed, his cheeks growing red as his belly rolled and shook. Finally, he recovered himself, wiping his clammy forehead with the silk handkerchief from his jacket pocket.

'Miss O'Sullivan, you're undoubtedly a very lovely young lady, but let me explain something to you. You don't mean a thing to this studio. Nothing,' he repeated for clarity as he saw the confusion cloud Maureen's eyes. 'You're not an actress on the rise, you're a failure. D'you know how the *New York Times* described you in *The Princess and the Plumber*? "Poison".'

Maureen inhaled sharply.

'How'm I supposed to work with that?' he asked bluntly, spreading his hands wide across the desk.

'But surely—'

'There are no buts,' Walter cut her off. 'No ifs, no buts, no second chances.'

'Then… what are you saying?'

'Miss O'Sullivan, I'm afraid this is the end of the road. Your contract has been terminated. You're fired,' he added, to ensure the message was not misunderstood.

Maureen felt her eyes start to fog, her head swimming. Already Walter was distracted, his sausage-like fingers picking over a contract as though he'd forgotten she was even there. Maureen suppressed a wave of panic as her future flashed before her: ignored, forgotten, disposable. At nineteen years old, her Hollywood career seemed already washed up, but she didn't want this adventure to end.

She swallowed hard, determined to keep her dignity. Steadily she rose to her feet, smoothing down her skirt and resettling her hat. *That damned hat.* Perhaps she could take it back and get a refund – she would need the money.

'Good day to you, Mr Parker,' she said smoothly, her Roehampton stiff-upper-lip training finally finding a use.

Walter S. Parker barely looked up as she left his office.

Maureen entered the studio on Wilshire Boulevard, gratified to see that everything looked clean and professional, just as it should be. Ed Tucker was one of the best – the reason Maureen had withdrawn her last remaining dollars from her bank account to spend on a photographic session with him. It was undoubtedly a risk, but better than going back to Ireland, cowed and defeated.

After her meeting with Walter, she'd slunk home to lick her wounds and cry her heart out. She thought of calling Vivian, but was too embarrassed to admit what had happened – not to mention the fact that she could barely afford the international call. She felt sure, though, that Vivian would tell her not to give up so easily. Wasn't rejection all part and parcel of show business? The sooner she developed a thick skin, like rhino hide, the better.

'Miss O'Sullivan? Very pleased to meet you.' Ed Tucker emerged from a back room and extended his hand. Maureen smiled and shook it firmly. 'And may I say how much I enjoyed your performance in *A Connecticut Yankee*.'

'Thank you,' Maureen returned, her tone friendly but guarded. She was quickly coming to realise that, in this town at least, people only told you what they thought you wanted to hear.

'So, what kind of look are we going for today?'

Maureen saw his eyes glaze over as he asked the question, thinking he already knew the answer. You couldn't swing a cat without hitting a starlet in Hollywood, and Ed had shot them all: Janet Gaynor, Loretta Young, Fay Wray, each one clad in a pretty dress with just a whisper of make-up, no deviation from the virginal, girl-next-door persona.

'Something young and fresh?' he suggested, trying to keep the note of boredom from his voice. 'A wholesome, feminine image?'

'If you don't mind, Mr Tucker, I'd like to try something a little different. Exotic, perhaps. More like Myrna Loy or Claudette Colbert.'

Maureen was gratified to see Ed stop what he was doing, hearing something in her voice – something firm, yet dignified. He straightened up and looked at her, a long, appraising stare that she returned defiantly. *So this one had some spunk after all!*

While Ed readied himself, adjusting the lights and changing the lens on his camera, Maureen set herself up in the small dressing room, painting on daring red lips and kohl pencil lines around her eyes. She'd never even worn make-up before she came to America, and now look at her! Her mother would never approve, and that strengthened her belief that she was doing the right thing. She ruffled her hair, making it a little wilder, a little wavier than in previous headshots – as though she'd just rolled out of bed, she thought, suppressing a giggle.

Then came the clothes. Out went the pastels and the delicate florals. Instead, the colours were bolder, the fabrics more sensuous – a high-collared jacket in black velvet, adorned with a jewelled brooch; a cashmere jumper that slid off the shoulder; a strapless ball gown accessorised with long black evening gloves.

When Maureen emerged from the dressing room wearing a low-cut cream silk dress that clung to her slender figure, Ed, perched high on a stepladder adjusting a light, wobbled dangerously and almost lost his balance.

'You Irish girls scrub up pretty good,' he managed, steadying himself against the light frame.

Maureen bobbed him a curtsy. 'Why, thank you, Mr Tucker,' she giggled, doing her best impersonation of a Southern belle.

From behind the camera, Ed watched his subject with growing admiration. The girl was a natural! One moment she was a tempestuous gypsy girl, the next a Spanish Infanta. *And didn't that camera just drink her right up, like she was a shot of bourbon after a hard, working day.* The eyes – often so dull and lifeless in many of the actresses Ed had shot – were alive and ablaze, a suggestion of recklessness in the set of her mouth.

Dozens of eager young things had passed through Ed's studio over the years, all dazzled by dreams of stardom, most chewed up and spat out by the system, disillusioned and deposited back in their small-town lives. But as Ed Tucker watched Maureen shine and captivate in front of his lens, he was willing to bet his last dime that she'd end up a star.

Chapter Ten

VIVIEN

Devon, England

February 1932

The day was cold, and Vivian was wrapped tightly in a long cashmere coat with a black felt hat as she walked through Holcombe village, arm in arm with her friend Hilary Martin. The pale afternoon sun reflecting off the stone houses did little to warm the two girls as the biting February wind blew in off the Channel, and they clung to each other as they fought their way along the seafront. Vivian could taste the salt on her lips, stirring memories of places she had visited with her parents: Dinard on the Normandy coast; San Remo on the Italian Riviera; the French seaside town of Biarritz.

'And is it true what they say about Italian men?' Hilary pressed, eager for any snippets of information about a life more thrilling than her own. Vivian's parents had leased a house in the nearby village of Teignmouth, and Hilary's father, Geoffrey, was an old acquaintance of Ernest Hartley's. Their daughters had hit it off immediately, and Hilary was wild with excitement at the arrival of this glamorous visitor.

'Darling, they're just as handsome as everyone says they are. Dark and swarthy, with tanned skin and eyes like melting chocolate. The convent at San Remo was such a bore – the Mother Superior was as venomous as a snake – but the boys weren't scared of her and came right up to the back gate to talk to us. My Italian improved enormously, but I'm afraid I only learned the bad words.'

'Why didn't you stay there?'

'Well, someone wrote to Mother, and she wasn't awfully happy at the way I was behaving. She came to Italy to drag me away, and then we moved to the west coast of Ireland, which was deathly dull after San Remo, but I still managed to find some fun.'

'And is that where you fell in love with the waiter?' Hilary's head was reeling.

'Oh no, that was Munich. And I wasn't really in love with him, I just had a little pash and Mummy got awfully annoyed.' Vivian paused, gazing out over the choppy green sea as the waves crashed and foamed in great white crests. A few fishing vessels braved the swells, pursued by seagulls that wheeled and dived behind the boats, their mournful cries carried back to the two girls on the shore.

At eighteen years of age, Vivian had grown into an exquisitely beautiful young woman. Since leaving Roehampton five years ago she'd been travelling around Europe, attending various convent schools and enjoying a traditional Grand Tour with her parents. In every country, men flocked to her: in France, they stared overtly; in Italy, they whistled; in Austria, they invited her for coffee, all captivated by her arresting looks and dancing blue-green eyes. Making men fall in love with her felt like a game at which she had swiftly become an expert.

Vivian knew that Gertrude had become increasingly concerned by her capricious behaviour and this, coupled with Ernest losing a considerable sum of money in the stock market crash, meant her mother had made the decision that the family should return to England. There, Vivian would attend the right social events and meet the right people, with the ultimate aim of finding a husband – something Vivian was determined to do on her own terms, and not with one of the chinless wonders her mother paraded before her.

'Where else did you go?' Hilary asked, not wanting the stories to end.

'Well, of course Paris was divine, and I adored Salzburg – the scenery was beautiful. And in Zurich three men proposed to me.'

'*Three!*' Hilary squealed.

'And I accepted one of them.'

Hilary's mouth fell open.

'But Mummy found out and stopped it. I insisted the engagement go ahead, but she refused to give her permission.'

'I… I've never been proposed to,' Hilary managed to stammer.

'Oh, I wouldn't worry, darling. Mother says there's oodles of time. But I think it would be delightful to be married, don't you?'

Hilary nodded enthusiastically.

'If I end up as a spinster then Mummy will only have herself to blame,' Vivian giggled.

'Oh, I can't ever imagine you being a spinster,' Hilary insisted, glancing across at Vivian with an expression approaching reverence.

'You're so sweet, and I've had such a lovely time today,' Vivian sighed, as they headed back towards the village. 'You must come over for supper one evening.'

'Really?' Hilary's eyes shone with excitement.

'Of course, it'd be such fun.'

The two girls turned off the coastal path and were walking along the road that led towards St George's Church when a sudden gust of wind threatened to blow Vivian's hat away. Instinctively, she grasped it, resettling it squarely on her head and smoothing down her hair. As she looked up, she became aware of a man approaching on horseback. He moved at a leisurely pace, clearly in no rush as the horse ambled past the church towards them.

As the man drew closer, Vivian discerned his features more clearly. His hair was blond with a slight wave, his eyes blue, and he looked older than her. His build was pleasing – strong, yet slim – and he wore tan breeches with a thick tweed jacket. His forehead was creased, his expression pensive, as though ruminating on some weighty issue.

So much consideration was he giving to the mystery matter that he barely noticed the women until he was almost upon them. Recovering himself, he saluted them, but it was an informal acknowledgement, not the sharp, regimented gesture of a soldier. The man nodded at Hilary, glanced for a moment at Vivian, then nudged his bay mare in the flanks and moved on.

'Who's that?' Vivian asked, as she watched him ride away. He reminded her of Leslie Howard, one of her favourite film stars.

'His name's Herbert Leigh Holman,' Hilary told her. 'But everyone calls him Leigh.'

'He looks like the perfect Englishman,' Vivian breathed.

'He's a barrister in London, but he grew up here and his parents still live in Holcombe so he comes back often.'

'I'm going to marry him,' Vivian declared.

Hilary laughed, assuming that Vivian was joking. 'He's all but engaged to my sister,' she explained. 'Mother says he's certain to propose to Dulcie before the end of the month.'

Vivian stared after him, digesting the information. 'He hasn't met me yet.'

'Sorry?' The wind whipped along the street and whistled past Hilary, the words lost on the breeze.

Vivian smiled charmingly, the edges of her mouth tilting upwards in that endearing fashion. 'Nothing. It was nothing, darling.'

It was the evening of the Devon Hunt Ball and Leigh Holman was nervous. His palms were damp and he thrust them anxiously into his pockets, feeling the cool metal of the ring that he'd concealed there. His fingers traced the smooth gold band, his thumb caressing the raised surface of the single diamond. The ring had belonged to his grandmother. Leigh worried it might be slightly too small for Dulcie, but if that was the case they could get it altered, he supposed.

Discreetly, he checked his appearance in one of the long gilt-edged mirrors that lined the walls of the hotel ballroom, pleased to see that he looked smart in the white tie that his mother's housekeeper had carefully pressed. Yet his face was pale, and his clear blue eyes were anxious.

It was ironic, Leigh thought, the way he felt completely at ease in a court of law but thoroughly discomfited when it came to matters of the heart. He was naturally reserved – perhaps even a little old-fashioned – and not a romantic, but at the age of thirty-one, he was coming under increasing pressure to settle down. His mother, and his colleagues in chambers, intimated that it would be the proper thing to do. And Dulcie was from a good family, friends of his parents…

Leigh turned the arguments over in his mind again, as he'd been doing for weeks. Dulcie was a sweet, exuberant girl, and although he worried she might find him somewhat stuffy, he believed he had plenty to offer. He had a good, stable career, was well connected, and had his own flat in London – one which could be exchanged for a larger property when a spouse and family came along.

Leigh caught sight of Dulcie as soon as she entered the room. She was with her mother and her three sisters, all of them gossiping intently, all of them decked out in a bewildering array of luridly coloured satins.

She hadn't seen him yet, and he ducked into the crowd, playing for time.

Don't be such a coward, Leigh berated himself, extracting his handkerchief and wiping away the sweat beads that peppered his hairline.

He watched the party circle the room until they found an empty seat for Mrs Martin next to her good friend Mrs Morgan. Clare Martin, the youngest sister, was immediately asked to dance by a gentleman that Leigh didn't recognise, whilst Hilary looked around expectantly, as though searching for someone. Dulcie stood slightly apart from the group. Dressed in a garish fuchsia gown, which did nothing for her broad shoulders, she was fiddling irritably with the clasp on her purse.

Leigh cleared his throat. This was his opportunity. His mouth felt as dry as the Sahara and he glanced around, wondering if he could procure a brandy.

'Leigh!'

'John!'

'Wonderful to see you, are you well?' Sir John Fieldman was the local magistrate and had known Leigh since he was a boy. His face was florid, his tie undone and thrown loosely around his neck.

'Yes, very well, thank you. And yourself?'

'Oh, excellent. Excellent. Now, Leigh –' Sir John leaned closer to make himself heard above the din, flecks of spittle flying from his lips as he spoke '– may I introduce Miss Vivian Hartley?'

Leigh blinked, as the most dazzling creature he had ever seen appeared in front of him. She wore a beautiful gown in a deep sea-green, and she was tiny, the fine boning of her dress emphasising her delicate waist. She had the most mesmerising eyes, and Leigh found himself quite unable to speak.

'How do you do?' Vivian came to his rescue, extending her hand politely. 'We've almost met before,' she told him. 'Last Wednesday. You were riding by the church in Holcombe, and I was out walking with Hilary Martin.'

At the mention of the Martin sisters, Leigh winced almost imperceptibly, but Vivian carried on smoothly, 'You certainly looked dashing astride that horse.'

'Thank you,' Leigh inclined his head self-consciously. 'Yes, I remember you too.' And he did – the strikingly beautiful girl with Hilary had certainly caught his attention.

'I'll leave you young people to it,' Sir John boomed, striding away as the band finished their song and struck up a waltz.

Vivian placed a hand on Leigh's arm, looking up at him from under long dark lashes. 'Well, aren't you going to ask me to dance?'

'Oh, of course.' Leigh recovered himself and led her onto the floor.

He was not the most natural of dancers, but moved with a grace and confidence that covered any flaws. Vivian was adept at polite conversation, and Leigh soon felt at ease as he guided her around the floor. Her skin was cool, and the hem of her dress brushed against his trousers.

'I must say, I find Holcombe quite the most charming little village. It's so peaceful to be back in England,' Vivian told him, shaking her head slightly so that her dark hair spilled out over her shoulders.

'Have you been travelling?'

'Like Napoleon himself! Paris, Biarritz, Salzburg, Zurich… It's been quite exhausting.'

'Goodness, what an accomplished young woman you are.'

'Oh yes,' Vivian agreed, although she was clearly making fun of herself. 'I was born in India, you see, so perhaps travelling is in my blood. Although I'm quite ready to settle down now,' she added hastily, as Leigh caught her meaning and smiled.

'I was born and bred in Devon,' he told her. 'My family have lived here for generations, and my parents have a house in Holcombe. It's a good place to escape from all the hustle and bustle of London.'

'Oh, what do you do in London?' Vivian wondered, although she remembered full well what Hilary had told her. She remembered *everything* that Hilary had told her about Herbert Leigh Holman.

'I'm a barrister, at Temple Gardens.'

'Goodness, how impressive!'

'Oh, it's not really,' Leigh insisted. 'I expect it seems terribly boring to you. In fact, I have to be back there tomorrow.'

'So soon?'

'I'm afraid so. I'm booked on the afternoon train to Paddington.'

Vivian frowned, clearly disappointed, but brightened as she confided, 'I'll be in London soon myself. I'm going to be an actress.'

'Are you indeed?' Leigh looked amused.

'Yes, I am.' Vivian's reply was swift and firm, and Leigh felt obliged to apologise for not taking her seriously.

In the silence that followed, he cleared his throat. 'I feel like such a fool for asking, but I wondered whether… Well, what I mean to say is… Do you think we might possibly be able to meet…?'

Vivian hesitated. 'Well, I'm going to be very busy…' she began regretfully.

'Oh, of course, of course,' Leigh agreed immediately, wondering what on earth had possessed him to even ask the question. Now he felt ridiculous, wanting to excuse himself as quickly as possible.

'… But I'm sure I'll have a spare second to meet you, Mr Holman,' Vivian finished, smiling up at him. Her marvellous eyes sparkled mischievously, and Leigh found himself wrong-footed yet enormously relieved.

The waltz came to a halt as the band switched to a more up-tempo number. Leigh opened his mouth to speak then felt a touch at his elbow.

'Leigh?' Dulcie was glaring at him, her hands on her hips. 'It's terrifically warm in here, isn't it? Mother suggested we might want to take a walk outside.'

'I… er…' Unconsciously, Leigh pushed the ring further into the depths of his pocket. Attempting to change the subject, he asked awkwardly, 'Dulcie, have you met Miss Vivian Hartley?'

'Yes,' Dulcie replied coldly. 'She's a friend of my sister's.'

'Ah, yes, of course.'

The discomfort was palpable, the moment broken by Dulcie asking more insistently, 'Leigh?' She jerked her head impatiently in the direction of the door.

Vivian smiled bewitchingly, the dimples appearing in her cheeks. Ignoring Dulcie, she looked straight at Leigh. 'It was wonderful to meet you, Mr Holman. Have a delightful evening.'

In a flash of emerald and sea-green, she was gone.

Chapter Eleven

London, England

December 1932

The church of St James in Marylebone was Roman Catholic in persuasion, Gothic and majestic in design. The blackened stone turrets and distinctive arched buttresses loomed large over the residential buildings which had sprung up all around it, the ancient rose window keeping quiet watch over one of the smartest parts of the city.

Outside, the last few guests trickled into the church, their vibrant clothes and hats brightening the dull December day. Patsy Quinn and Jane Glass remained on the pavement, chattering excitedly as they huddled together to combat the chill, their peach satin dresses offering little protection from the elements.

Minutes later, a chauffeur-driven Rolls-Royce Phantom drew up and the bridesmaids gave a little cheer as Ernest Hartley stepped out, looking dapper and distinguished in his morning suit, and strode round to open the car door for his daughter. Smiling shyly, Vivian emerged wearing a simple white satin gown and crocheted Juliet cap, and carrying an enormous bouquet of roses and lily of the valley which quite overwhelmed her. She'd spent the previous week in bed, laid low by a vicious bout of the flu, and she was pale and slender and more ethereal than ever.

'Oh darling, you look beautiful. You truly do,' Patsy breathed, leaning in to kiss her.

'You're so lucky,' sighed Jane. 'I can't believe you're getting married. The first out of all of us.'

Patsy confided, 'Leigh looks awfully handsome. He's exactly the kind of man I'd want for a husband.'

The two of them fluttered around, fixing a stray wisp of hair, smoothing fabric so that it fell perfectly. Vivian remained poised as they fussed and exclaimed, a queen amongst courtiers.

She knew, then, that she had made the right decision. Her friends' envious glances and congratulatory comments confirmed that Vivian had achieved what was expected of her: a good marriage; a handsome husband; an assured, comfortable future. She had spent years feeling as though she were waiting for her life to begin – rushing towards adulthood, away from her parents and her stifling schooldays – and now, thanks to Leigh, it had.

Ernest stepped forward, holding out his arm for Vivian to take. 'Are you ready, darling?'

Vivian exhaled slowly, turning to meet her father's enquiring eyes. Her gaze was steady as she inclined her head, the gesture almost regal.

'Are you sure?' Ernest pressed, his voice low. 'You know I think that Leigh's a splendid chap, but your mother has her reservations and—'

Vivian cut him off. Her face was radiant, her reply brooked no argument.

'Daddy, I've never been more certain of anything in my life.'

Following the ceremony, a reception was held at The Savoy hotel on the Strand, in an elegant private salon overlooking the

Thames. Vivian had changed into her going-away outfit – a chic blue woollen suit trimmed with silver fox fur – and was surrounded by a group of her girlfriends, whilst Leigh chatted to his colleagues from chambers. The room was filled with well-heeled, well-to-do people, socialites and a smattering of aristocrats, along with family members and a number of Vivian's schoolfriends from Roehampton. Maureen had sent her apologies; she was unable to attend due to filming commitments in Los Angeles.

'How wonderful to be Mrs Leigh Holman!' Patsy exclaimed, embracing Vivian.

'Do you feel different, now that you're married?'

'How will you be spending your first Christmas together?'

'Where are you going on honeymoon?'

The questions came thick and fast and Vivian answered them graciously.

'We're travelling to Germany and Austria, for three weeks in the new year. Leigh's arranged everything. It'll be so pretty, with the snow on the Alps and the darling little villages.'

'The fresh mountain air,' chimed in Dorothy Ward.

'And the romantic old *Schlösser*,' Jane added, as Vivian laughed.

'So what will you do with your time, now that you're married?' asked Charlotte Astor. 'Won't you be frightfully bored?'

'Of course she won't,' Patsy rebutted. 'She'll have her wifely duties to attend to.' As soon as the words were out of her mouth, Patsy realised what she was implying. Her cheeks coloured as the others burst into giggles. 'I just meant… running the house and so on…' she tailed off, clearly embarrassed by the innuendo.

'I'm to be presented at court next summer,' Vivian explained, sparing Patsy's blushes. 'Leigh's cousin has agreed to sponsor me, which is terrifically sweet of her. There she is – you see the tall, slim woman in lavender, talking to my mother?'

'Presented at court?' Dorothy breathed, reaching for a salmon vol-au-vent. 'That's almost as exciting as getting married! Maybe even more so. Anyone can get married – not everyone gets to be a deb.'

'What are you going to wear?'

'I've got everything planned already,' Vivian confided, her eyes sparkling. The thought of going to the palace – all that pomp and ceremony, being part of history – was thrilling. 'I want to wear a huge taffeta gown with puffed sleeves and a long train, and ostrich feathers in my hair.'

'I'm sure the King will be enchanted!'

'And Queen Mary will find you charming.'

'But won't you miss your acting classes, now that you're married? I know how you enjoy them, and I was quite certain you'd be whisked off to Hollywood, like Maureen.'

'Or become a huge star in the West End.'

For a moment, Vivian faltered. It was true that she adored her classes at the Royal Academy of Dramatic Arts, where she was studying voice and movement, Shakespeare and Restoration comedies. Despite her engagement, she had never truly given up her dream of becoming a great actress, and Maureen's success had shown her that it *was* possible. But for now she smiled and said, 'Yes, I think I shall miss them. But Leigh says they were a silly diversion to keep me occupied until the wedding, and I suppose he's right. I'll be far too busy running the house and being a good wife to have time for anything as frivolous as that.'

She caught her husband's eye across the crowd and smiled. He really did look proud as punch, and Vivian felt a huge surge of affection, her spirits lifting as she raised a hand to wave at him.

'Do let me see your ring again, Viv,' begged Charlotte, seeing it sparkle as it caught the light.

Obligingly, Vivian held out her left hand, displaying the dazzling diamond band as the girls cooed effusively.

'It's so pretty!'

'Just divine.'

'Here – try it if you like.' Vivian quickly slipped it off, feeling self-conscious as everyone looked at her hands. She'd always been concerned that they were too large for her delicate frame, preferring to conceal them in gloves to deflect attention whenever possible.

'It fits! Ooh, look at me, I'm Mrs Holman.' Charlotte pouted, holding her hand against her face and striking a pose. The girls collapsed into another round of giggles, not noticing as Vivian's mother wove her way through the guests towards them, resplendent in a calf-length *eau de nil* dress accessorised with a mink stole and an elaborate hat.

Gertrude smiled as she saw how happy her daughter was, clearly in high spirits as she enjoyed a joke with her friends. One of them was waving her arm around elaborately, a jewelled band on her finger glinting beneath the chandeliers…

'Vivian!' Gertrude snapped, her tone startling them. Charlotte hastily removed the ring and handed it back, sensing that she'd done something wrong.

'Vivian, don't do that again. It's terribly unlucky. You must never, ever take off your wedding ring.'

The girls were suitably chastened, shamefaced at their complicity. Charlotte was mortified – Gertrude was a fearsome woman – but Vivian merely rolled her eyes.

'Oh, Mummy, that's such awfully old-fashioned tosh. Silly, superstitious nonsense.' Defiantly, she pushed the ring back onto her finger and held it up for Gertrude to see. 'There, look. All fixed now.'

Gertrude shook her head in exasperation. Vivian knew that her mother had reservations about her marriage. Although Gertrude both liked and admired Leigh – he was undoubtedly a gentleman, steady and dependable – she wasn't sure he was the best match for Vivian, and was concerned that the thirteen-year age difference might prove problematic. She'd even suggested that Vivian should speak to a priest, implying that an outside influence could more successfully impress upon her that a Catholic marriage was for life. Vivian, however, had balked at the idea and pooh-poohed her mother's concerns, insisting that she was in love with Leigh and that was an end to the matter.

'Leigh's organised for the car to arrive in thirty minutes, so say your goodbyes and don't keep him waiting,' Gertrude said sternly.

'No, Mummy, I won't,' Vivian replied sweetly, as she finished her glass of champagne and reached for another.

The mirror in the entrance hall was frightfully plain and dull, Vivian noted with displeasure, as she checked her reflection. She'd been meaning to replace it ever since she moved in three months ago, but somehow hadn't quite got around to it yet. Well, she would insist to Leigh that they drive out to the Cotswolds this weekend; there were a number of delightful little antique shops that she loved to visit, and she felt sure that they could find something there. Something striking yet timeless that would brighten up the whole corridor.

In fact, the entire apartment could do with redecorating, Vivian thought, looking round at the ugly wooden panelling and the dowdy furniture. Immediately after the wedding, she and Leigh had begun living together in his former bachelor flat in St John's Wood and, whilst Vivian had done her best to add a tasteful, feminine touch, it was still far from the stylish marital home she had imagined.

She picked up her handbag, checking that she had everything she needed, then jumped as she heard the rattle of a key in the front door.

'Leigh, darling! You're home early.' Vivian stood on her tiptoes to kiss him, wincing as she heard the overly bright, unnatural note in her voice.

'I'd finished my client meetings for the day so thought I'd bring my files home and work in the study. I shan't disturb you, my darling.'

'Oh, don't worry about that.' Vivian smiled nervously.

Leigh set down his briefcase and looked at her more closely, taking in the fur coat, the leather gloves. 'Are you going out?'

Vivian hesitated for a fraction of a second. 'Yes, I'm … going to see Madame Gachet. You know how I always enjoyed my French classes, and it seemed a shame not to keep them up.'

'Oh, absolutely,' Leigh agreed. 'You have a real talent for languages.'

'I shan't be home late,' Vivian rushed on, as she hastily settled her hat on her head. 'I'll be back well before supper. I've asked Mrs Bradley to prepare veal cutlets in mushroom sauce, how does that sound?'

'It sounds delicious.'

'Wonderful.' There was an awkward pause. 'Well, I'd better go. I don't want to keep Madame Gachet waiting.'

'Have a wonderful afternoon, darling.'

'You too, my love.'

Vivian hurried out of the door into the afternoon drizzle, her heart hammering as she hailed a taxicab and guiltily gave the driver the destination. She wondered if Leigh could tell she was lying. Perhaps she wasn't quite as good an actress as she'd thought.

The cab pulled away, the London streets a rainy blur as they skirted the edge of Regent's Park en route to Fitzrovia, past the fine terraced houses and the leafless trees that were tentatively beginning to bud in a springtime renewal.

Vivian didn't like lying to her husband, but it was better for both of them this way. What he didn't know couldn't hurt him and, if anything, it strengthened their marriage, providing the excitement she was craving, giving her an outlet, a release. Undoubtedly, she loved Leigh. Of course she did, he was her husband. But, at nineteen years of age, Vivian felt that she was awfully young to be cooped up in the house all day, with little stimulation or purpose. Leigh employed both a cook and a housekeeper, so the household chores were more than adequately taken care of, and, in truth, she was finding life rather dull. By nature, she preferred to keep busy, and her years at Roehampton had led her to associate idleness with dissatisfaction and guilt.

Vivian had imagined that being the wife of a barrister would be far more fulfilling. Prior to the wedding she'd glamorised her future role, a romanticised vision of hosting cocktail evenings and dinner parties, accompanying Leigh to social events as the model wife and ideal companion. The reality was that Leigh was devoted to his job, spending long days in court and late nights in chambers.

When they'd been courting, life had been a whirlwind of outings to the opera and the theatre, concerts and restaurants and day trips to Henley or Brighton, long weekends with friends in the countryside. The honeymoon had been equally delightful, discovering quaint little shops and cafés together, but all of that seemed to come to an abrupt end on their return, and Vivian was wild with envy when she met up with her old schoolfriends and heard about the parties and nightclubs they'd attended, the gallery openings and the ski holidays to Courchevel. Some were even working as models, or as extras in films. Not to mention Maureen's success in Hollywood, her career documented in fashion magazines and the newspapers Leigh read each morning over his boiled egg with toast.

The taxi pulled up outside the address on Gower Street and Vivian alighted, glancing left and right discreetly to ensure that none of her husband's acquaintances happened to be in the area. Satisfied that no one had seen her, Vivian slipped quickly through the main door of the building, beneath the sign that read: Royal Academy of Dramatic Arts.

Despite what she'd told Leigh, Vivian wasn't taking French lessons, nor was she meeting Madame Gachet. She was taking acting lessons, resuming the classes she'd so loved before they'd said their vows.

Vivian still had ambitions; they hadn't withered when she said her vows, and she was no longer content to merely be someone's wife. It wasn't Leigh's fault, but Vivian wanted more from life. She'd imagined that marriage would be her escape, away from school and her parents and towards a path that she could carve for herself, but she'd been horrified to discover that she felt more trapped than ever in a terribly conventional relationship. Vivian expected that she'd be able to charm Leigh, as she always had, into seeing her point of view, but he'd made it clear he didn't approve of her aspirations.

Leigh considered performing an unrefined pastime, unbecoming to a married young woman of good social standing. Vivian's focus should be on running the household, and it was entirely unnecessary for her to work when he could provide amply for them both. But for Vivian, the lure of the stage was too great, her passion refusing to simply dampen and die.

It wouldn't be for long anyway. She would have to give up her classes at the end of this term, Vivian thought to herself, as she called hello to the receptionist and made her way up the main staircase, one hand cradled protectively over her stomach. She hadn't told Leigh yet, but Vivian was almost positive that she was pregnant.

Chapter Twelve

Copenhagen, Denmark

August 1934

'Are you glad I brought you here, darling?'

'Oh, Leigh, it's wonderful. So pretty with the coloured buildings and the boats. And look at all the people riding bicycles!'

'I'm so pleased you're enjoying it. You haven't seemed… quite yourself recently.'

'Darling, you are funny,' Vivian smiled, as she hooked her arm through Leigh's and gazed up at him. They were strolling through the streets of Copenhagen, walking along Strøget on the way back to their cruise ship. 'And where's the next stop on our grand tour?'

'Helsinki tomorrow, and then on to Leningrad.'

'I'm longing to see the Winter Palace.'

'Mmm,' Leigh agreed distantly, his mind wandering as they passed the distinctive shopfronts offering furniture and fashionable clothing, fine porcelain and traditional pastries. This trip away had been arranged rather hastily – an out-of-character move for Leigh, who wasn't prone to spontaneity – but Vivian's recent behaviour had alarmed him. Her need for company and diversion was greater than ever; she was forever dragging him to some West End nightclub, or throwing dinner parties at their home that continued into the small hours, fuelled by gin and parlour games and growing ever more raucous long after Leigh had retired.

He'd hoped that motherhood would settle Vivian but, if anything, it seemed to have had the opposite effect. She showed little interest in their daughter, beyond her maternal obligations, and there was a distinct restlessness about her, a skittishness that left her eyes glittering feverishly, her gestures infused with a nervous energy.

'Darling, look,' Vivian cried, tugging at his arm and pulling him through the crowd towards a fountain, where a small group had gathered to watch a street performer. He was dressed as Pierrot, with his characteristic painted face and voluminous white smock. His mouth drooped with sadness, a lone tear on his face, as he pulled out a red rose and offered it shyly to a little girl standing nearby. Vivian burst into applause, her face radiant in the bright Scandinavian sunshine. There was something almost childlike in her delight, Leigh realised, as he watched his wife watching the performance, thoroughly absorbed in the action. Which reminded him—

'I do hope Suzanne's all right.'

'Is that what you're fretting about? I'm sure she'll be perfectly fine. You've employed a small army to look after her.'

'Yes, but a child needs her mother.'

'She doesn't need me, Leigh. She's nine months old—'

'Ten—'

'—And anyway, she's far more attached to Nanny than she is to me.'

Leigh sighed. He'd already learned that there was no reasoning with Vivian when she was in this mood. 'I think I'll send a telegram, make sure all's well at home.'

'As you wish. Oh, do you think we have time to see the Little Mermaid? I'd so love to see her.'

Leigh smiled indulgently, taking her hand. 'I'm sure we will, darling. Let's go down to the harbour and find out.'

———

When they returned to the ship, a telegram was waiting for Vivian.

'Perhaps it's Suzanne.' Leigh's face was taut with anxiety. 'Perhaps something's happened.'

Vivian tore it open, her eyes skimming over the paper as she took in the words. She was breathless as she exclaimed, 'They want me for a film!'

'Pardon?'

'A film!' Vivian was ecstatic. Finally, things were starting to happen! She couldn't remember when she'd last felt so excited. 'Oh Leigh, how thrilling. It says I have to report to the production office on Monday.'

'But we're in Riga on Monday.'

'If I leave immediately, I could make it.' Vivian flew across the room, dragging her trunk from where it was stored in the wardrobe. 'When's the next ship to England? I'll call the porter, he'll know. I have to get off before we set sail again.'

'Vivian, stop this at once. You're being ridiculous.'

'This is the opportunity I've been waiting for.' Vivian snatched up the telegram once again, re-reading it to ensure its message hadn't changed. 'It's called *Things Are Looking Up* and it stars Cicely Courtneidge and I'm to play a schoolgirl.'

'A schoolgirl? Heavens above!'

'Don't be such an old fuddy-duddy,' Vivian chastised, pulling armfuls of clothing from their hangers and depositing them into the open suitcase. She wouldn't allow Leigh to ruin her moment. Surely he realised how momentous this was for her?

Instead, Leigh watched in disbelief. 'Vivian. Vivian!' he repeated, his voice growing louder. A vein was raised on his temple, his body rigid. 'You *cannot* do this. I forbid you from leaving.'

Vivian let out a peal of high-pitched laughter. 'You *forbid* me? Now who's the one being ridiculous?'

'Darling, please don't go. I booked this trip so that we could spend some time together and it's barely even started. What about the Winter Palace?'

'Oh, bother the Winter Palace. They're going to pay me thirty shillings a day!'

'We don't *need* thirty shillings.'

'Perhaps not, but I *need* to do this. Don't you understand? I'm wasting my life stuck in that house all day with Cook and Nanny and the baby. It's just dull, dull, DULL!' Vivian slammed the trunk shut, her breath coming fast.

Leigh looked taken aback by Vivian's vehemence. The words were unspoken, but there was an implicit criticism of *him*: of his reserved manner, his lack of dynamism. For a moment, the pair eyeballed one another, each waiting to see who would make the next move.

'How did they know you were available for a film?' Leigh's voice was calm, conversational.

'I'm sorry?'

'This production company – how did they know your name, how to contact you, that you were even interested in being in their silly film?'

Vivian hesitated. 'I had some photos taken.'

Leigh raised his eyebrows, shock registering on his face.

'I went to a photographer and sent the pictures round to various casting agencies. Everyone's doing it,' Vivian protested. 'Beryl's been in half a dozen films, and Hazel posed for Cecil Beaton,' she added, naming two of her friends who were, like her, aspiring actresses. 'Not to mention Maureen being the toast of Hollywood since that Tarzan film.'

'Yes, but those girls don't have husbands or children. They don't have a house to run or responsibilities.'

'Sometimes I wish I didn't either.' The words were out and she couldn't take them back. Leigh looked crushed, and Vivian realised she'd gone too far. Guilt threatened to overwhelm her, but she stood firm. This was a confession that had long been in the making.

In the early days of her marriage, Vivian had thought that becoming a mother might fill the void inside of her, but she soon realised she'd been mistaken. She hadn't enjoyed being pregnant, her diminutive frame expanding to elephantine proportions, host to an alien creature living and growing inside of her.

The birth itself had been as horrific as she expected, and the postpartum rush of hormones unsettled her mind for weeks afterwards, the mental toll no less taxing than the physical one.

One moment she would break down and weep, the next rise up on a tide of euphoria, feeling as though she could build an empire. Then Nanny took over and everything settled down. Suzanne was an adorable, mewling creature who'd inherited her father's looks and his easy temperament, and she looked as pretty as a picture in the outfits Vivian picked out from Harrods.

But she found the daily drudgery of motherhood unbearable, the smells and secretions nauseating. Instinctively, she avoided it as much as she could, telling herself she was temperamentally unsuited, but secretly wondering whether there was something wrong with her. As the first of her circle to get married and have a child, she had no one she could comfortably speak to about it. She loved Suzanne – that wasn't in question – but she had no desire to spend hours shaking a rattle or playing peekaboo or whatever else one did to entertain an infant all day long.

Her ambition burned more brightly than ever, a glimpse of glamour amidst the humdrum of her daily routine. She needed stimulation and activity and, though she was loath to admit it to herself, her small life as Leigh's wife and Suzanne's mother was simply not enough.

'I'm sorry, Leigh.' Vivian was chastened, but didn't waver. 'I really am. But I have to do this.'

Without even waiting for the porter, Vivian dragged her suitcase out of the cabin and shut the door behind her.

The band was playing, the beautiful people were dancing, and the Colony Club in Mayfair felt like the centre of the world. The great and the good, the aspirational and the influential, drank and dined beneath the sparkle of the chandeliers, the champagne flowing freely into coupes ostensibly shaped like the breasts of a French queen. Peggy Ashcroft and Ralph Richardson played host to a noisy troupe of thespians, their table crowded and convivial, whilst Ivor Novello lingered by the grand piano, surrounded by a coterie of admirers. The night was full of promise; even the waiters were devilishly handsome.

Vivian sipped her martini and revelled in the glamour. Dressed in a silky silver evening gown by Balmain, backless and form-fitting, she was every inch the bright young thing, the rising star poised for greatness. She'd recently spent three weeks filming *Things Are Looking Up* and she sensed that she'd made an impact. Despite being merely an extra, the camera repeatedly singled her out for close-ups, and she'd impressed the director so much that he'd given her a line – *'If you're not made headmistress, I shan't come back next term.'* Vivian had thoroughly enjoyed the whole experience.

Her success had made her more determined than ever to continue with her acting, regardless of her husband's opinion. True to her word, Vivian had cut short their holiday and travelled back to England, whilst Leigh had continued the cruise by himself and had a miserable time, missing his wife terribly. They'd spent more than a week apart, and Leigh had returned full of apologies for his heavy-handed reaction, whilst Vivian herself had been eager to forget the argument and put aside any bad feeling. The matter of her potential acting career, however, remained far from settled.

Tonight, she was positively radiant, as she danced and drank and flirted. She felt like a different person when this side of her was allowed to take hold, as though there were two personalities locked inside her – one bold and sparkling and captivating, the other side darker, capable of selfishness and cruelty. She supposed all of these different facets were what made her whole, and would bring depth and authenticity to her acting.

'Enjoying yourself?' Beryl Samson appeared beside her. Blonde and vivacious, Beryl had had small roles in several films, and was proving to be a good friend to Vivian as they accompanied one another to parties and plays around town.

'Absolutely. Thanks so much for inviting me. I'm having a fabulous time.'

Beryl grinned. 'I thought you might. Come over here, there's some people I want to introduce you to.'

Intrigued, Vivian followed Beryl through the throng, where they joined a small group by the bar. Amongst them was a man in his late thirties, with dark hair and a heavy face. He was tall and broad-shouldered, smoke curling from the cigarette between his fingers.

'John, this is Vivian, the friend I was telling you about,' Beryl introduced them. 'Vivian, this is John Gliddon. He's just opened a theatrical agency.'

'Is that so?' Vivian gave him her most dazzling smile, knowing full well its effect. 'And how is business, Mr Gliddon?'

'Call me John,' he replied affably. 'I was bemoaning the lack of beautiful young English actresses to Miss Samson, but she was determined to prove me wrong.'

'What did I tell you?' Beryl laughed. 'You just have to know where to look. I'll leave you two to chat.' She winked at Vivian and walked away.

'So, I hear you're an aspiring actress,' John said, seeming

genuinely interested. 'Beryl speaks very highly of you. She thinks I should snap you up.'

'I rather think you should,' Vivian shot back, guessing – correctly – that John Gliddon might admire a spirited woman.

'Do you have any acting experience?'

'I completed two terms at RADA, and I've recently filmed a small speaking role in a Cicely Courtneidge picture. So not very much at all so far, but perhaps with your help that might change.' Vivian inclined her head deferentially, and John found himself thinking how utterly engaging she was.

'You should be playing leads, not minor parts,' he told her straight, mentally scanning his lists of producers and directors, new plays or upcoming films she might be suitable for.

'I couldn't agree more.'

'Well, we certainly seem to be on the same page.' John stubbed out his cigarette and reached into his jacket pocket. 'Listen, here's my card. Why don't you come to my office tomorrow morning and we can talk further.'

Vivian took the card from him, tucking it neatly into her purse. 'Perfect. I'm looking forward to it, Mr Gl—' She stopped and corrected herself. 'John.'

———

The following day, Vivian arrived at 106 Regent Street fifteen minutes early. She looked immaculate, in a chic black Mainbocher skirt-suit edged with white piping, her dark, wavy hair pinned back from her face to emphasise her extraordinary features. After her conversation with John Gliddon the previous evening, she'd made her excuses to Beryl and left early, making sure to drink a large glass of water before bed to mitigate the effects of the martinis. Vivian was determined that everything would go perfectly at this meeting.

She couldn't shake the feeling that momentum was building in her career; that *this* was what she was born to do, and everything else was secondary. At Roehampton, the girls had been trained to be first-rate wives and mothers, to further the reaches of the Empire that Vivian had been born into. But the world was changing, and Vivian, like Maureen, recognised that an unconventional life could be a far more fulfilling one. It was the uncertainty itself that made it exciting.

As Vivian stepped out of the taxi, she was so preoccupied with thoughts of her imminent meeting that she almost didn't notice the young woman in a calf-length checked skirt and long-sleeved cream blouse who stepped across her path.

'Vivian?' she said uncertainly.

Vivian did a double-take; it took a moment for her to recognise, and then place, the young woman, who looked around sixteen.

'Sonia,' the woman filled in helpfully. 'Sonia Brownell. We were at Roehampton together.'

'Oh yes, of course,' Vivian beamed, delighted to see her old acquaintance. Sonia was almost five years younger than Vivian, but the small, communal nature of the Sacred Heart meant that they had known one another, united by sports matches and end-of-year productions. 'How are you? Have you escaped yet?'

'A few weeks ago,' Sonia grinned. 'It's heavenly. I'm planning to go to Switzerland soon.'

'How wonderful! Finishing school?'

'Something like that...' Sonia seemed evasive, and Vivian didn't want to pry.

'Well, it's been delightful to see you, but I must go, darling. I have an appointment with a theatrical agent.' In Vivian's excitement, she couldn't resist confiding.

Awe and incredulity were writ large on Sonia's face. 'That's super! How thrilling. Well, best of luck, though I'm sure you don't need it. I remember how marvellous you were at school.'

'Thank you,' Vivian smiled, buoyed by the timely compliment.

She kissed Sonia on both cheeks and the two women said their goodbyes.

Vivian inhaled then let out a long, slow breath, her heart racing as she made her way inside the distinctive building with the ornate, stone façade, taking the stairs to John Gliddon's offices on the first floor.

John had been an actor and director himself and Vivian knew that he had the contacts to help further her career. His move to agenting was relatively recent and, despite its prestigious location, his office was rather bare. It consisted of two small adjoining rooms – the outer one for his secretary, the inner for John himself. Vivian noticed a drooping aspidistra sitting sadly beside a filing cabinet, framed pictures leaning against a wall where no one had yet found the time or inclination to hang them.

John greeted her warmly, looking somewhat worse for wear. He clearly hadn't felt the same need to get home early last night and arrive with a fresh head today. But his three-piece suit was smart and well-tailored, and he was clean-shaven and smelt of expensive cologne.

'Right, let's get down to business.' John leant back in his chair, crossing his legs as he looked at Vivian with interest. 'If I'm to represent you, I need to know that you're serious about this. I need clients who'll turn up on time, work hard and be professional – it's my reputation on the line too.'

'Oh, absolutely,' Vivian assured him. Punctuality, politeness and hard work had been drummed into her since she was a child.

'Are you married?' He glanced at Vivian's hands, which were encased in white gloves as usual.

'Yes, I am.'

'And is your husband supportive of your acting ambitions?'

'He…' Vivian hesitated, choosing her words carefully. 'He's a barrister. He'd rather that I stayed at home, to be frank with you. But he absolutely understands that this is what I want to do, and that I won't be dissuaded.'

John nodded. 'Would you be willing to use a stage name?'

'I… Yes, of course. If it's necessary.' The thought had never occurred to Vivian. 'How about Suzanne Stanley?' she suggested, saying the first thing that came to her.

John shook his head. 'No, that's not right at all. Too cold. Too hard. How about… April Morn?'

Vivian burst out laughing, stopping abruptly as she saw the look on John's face. 'My apologies, I didn't think you were serious.'

'You don't like it?'

'I think it's ghastly,' Vivian said honestly. 'What about Mary Hartley? That's my middle name and my maiden name.'

John pulled a face. 'Dull. Forgettable. And the Cockneys will call you Mary 'Artley.'

Vivian smiled. She liked John's candour, his natural charisma. He was charming without being obsequious. 'What's so very wrong with Vivian, anyway? It's served me extremely well for twenty years.'

'Well, it's neither one thing nor the other, you see. People won't be able to tell if you're a man or a woman. How about you change the spelling? It's far more feminine with an "e".'

'All right,' Vivian agreed easily. 'But what about my surname?'

They lapsed into thought, the seconds audibly ticking by on the clock on the wall behind John's desk. An idea was forming in his mind; it could be brilliant, or it could be a disaster.

'Your husband…' he began. 'You said he wasn't very supportive?'

'Well, I didn't mean… That is, he wants me to be happy and—'

'I'm not asking about that.' John waved his hand, cutting her off. 'What's his name?'

Vivian frowned. 'Herbert. But everyone calls him by his middle name – Leigh.'

John sat back in his chair looking pleased with himself, the proverbial cat who'd got the cream. 'How about Vivien Leigh?' he suggested. 'Your husband can't possibly object to that.'

Vivian's face lit up, and she laughed delightedly. 'How terribly clever of you! Yes, I rather like that.' She held out her hand across the desk and John leaned forward to shake it. 'Hello, I'm Vivien Leigh,' she told him, trying it out for the first time. 'And I rather think I'd like you to be my agent.'

Chapter Thirteen

SONIA

Neuchâtel, Switzerland

May 1936

'This is heavenly.'

Sonia lay back and sighed, throwing a hand across her face to shield her eyes from the sun. She was sprawled on a chequered woollen picnic blanket, in a pretty valley carpeted with soft grass and wildflowers. Snow-topped mountains loomed large in the distance, the craggy peaks of La Berra and Gruyère straddling the void between earth and sky, whilst ahead of her stretched the wide, flat calm of Lake Neuchâtel.

'Sonia! Sonia, *regardez-moi*!'

Sonia rolled over, propping herself up on her elbows. She burst into laughter as she saw her friends Madeleine and Paul, up to their ankles in water, paddling at the edge of the lake. Madeleine raised a hand to wave and almost lost her balance on the slippery rocks, grabbing Paul's arm to steady herself.

'What a delicious idea.' Sonia popped a handful of blueberries in her mouth and gazed across at Jean-Pierre, who was lounging on the rug beside her. He was eighteen, a year older than her, with sandy-coloured hair in a slick side-parting, and long, gangly legs in khaki shorts. 'We should all go swimming to cool off.'

Jean-Pierre smiled regretfully. 'I can't. I don't know how to swim.'

'You don't know how to swim? And you live by this beautiful lake?' Sonia's tone was teasing, her French impeccable. 'If I'd grown up here, I'd have gone swimming every day.'

'Why swim when you have a boat?' Jean-Pierre shrugged, and Sonia laughed flirtatiously, her blonde curls bouncing as she tossed her head. Jean-Pierre stood up, stretching his limbs without taking his eyes off her. 'Would you like to go for a walk?'

'*Oui, bien sûr.*' Sonia accepted the hand Jean-Pierre was offering as he pulled her to her feet and the pair strolled away from the lake, following the path towards a small patch of woodland. The noise from their friends soon grew distant, the copse cool and quiet and seemingly deserted. Jean-Pierre didn't let go of her hand.

'So how do you like Neuchâtel?'

'I adore it. I feel so free here,' Sonia said truthfully. 'It's wonderful to have finally left school and be away from my mother.' She had finished her studies the previous summer, delighted to have fled the Roehampton regime. Any further education was, unfortunately, out of the question; although Sonia was undoubtedly intelligent, her mother, Beatrice, was simply unable to afford any reputable university or finishing school. Instead, Sonia had been sent to stay with their friends, the du Pasquier family, in Switzerland. Their daughter, Madeleine, was seventeen like Sonia, and the two girls had been attending classes together at the local college.

Though Sonia had no real idea yet of what she wanted to do with her life, she was enjoying her freedom and her studies, and was charmed by the beauty and elegance of Switzerland and its people. She didn't worry about what tomorrow might bring, luxuriating in the present.

'The scenery is beautiful, *non*?' Jean-Pierre pressed, waving his hand in a vague gesture intended to incorporate the whole of the Swiss countryside.

'Oh, very beautiful.'

'Just like you.' They stopped walking, and Jean-Pierre seemed nervous suddenly. 'Sonia, I… I would very much like to kiss you.'

'Go on then,' she retorted smartly, though her heart was thumping in her chest. 'What's stopping you?'

He reached out to stroke her hair, bending down in the same clumsy movement, and their lips crashed together. His eyes were closed, his movements awkward and uncertain.

'Wait,' Sonia said softly, pulling away from him. A flicker of anxiety crossed his brow. 'Like this,' she explained, kissing him slowly, gently, letting him take the lead as his confidence grew.

Jean-Pierre wasn't the first boy Sonia had kissed. She'd made the most of her freedom since leaving Roehampton, and had discovered that not only did she like kissing, but she was very good at it. Every boy she embraced felt like flicking a finger to the nuns.

They stumbled backwards against the gnarled trunk of a pine tree, the rough bark pressing through the light material of Sonia's dress. Jean-Pierre's body was heavy against hers; though he was slim, he was almost a foot taller than she was, folding himself awkwardly to reach her. One hand slid speculatively to her breast, palming the soft flesh as his breathing began to quicken.

'Sonia!'

They both heard Madeleine's shout, instinctively pulling apart.

'Jean-Pierre! Where are you? We need to leave.'

Sonia smiled at him, a secret smile, full of promise. Jean-Pierre's eyes were dark, his cheeks flushed.

'We'd better go,' Sonia murmured, raising her voice to call out, 'Yes, we're here. We're coming.'

Her eyes gleaming wickedly, she set off at a run. Jean-Pierre gave chase, and with his long strides soon overtook her. Sonia grabbed at his shirt, pulling him back, and he scooped her up into his arms as she giggled uncontrollably.

Madeleine was packing away the picnic paraphernalia as the pair returned, giddy and breathless.

'What's the hurry?'

Madeleine nodded towards the lake where fierce black clouds were gathering on the horizon. Paul was attempting to hoist the boat sail and Jean-Pierre ran to help him, scrambling to secure the jib.

'Get in,' Paul shouted, as Madeleine picked up the picnic basket and Sonia grabbed the rug, her hair whipping around her face as a squally breeze took hold. She realised that she and Jean-Pierre had been too preoccupied to notice how the sky had darkened, shrouding the sun and sending the temperature tumbling.

'*Attention!*' Madeleine shrieked, as she scrambled on board and Paul pushed off from the shallows, sending the boat rocking violently. The boom swung wildly and Sonia cried out as she ducked to avoid it, losing her footing and almost upsetting the small craft as Jean-Pierre grabbed for the ropes, hands flailing to reach them as they were lashed by the wind.

'I'm cold,' Madeleine said, shivering and clamping her arms tightly across her chest. All four were dressed for the sunshine, with short sleeves and bare legs, but fat spots of rain had begun to fall, soaking their clothes and chilling their skin. Sonia snatched up the blanket and slid along the seat towards her friend, intending to huddle together for warmth, but the boat tilted dangerously and Sonia screamed.

'We should go back,' Madeleine wailed. The waves were growing larger every minute, mercilessly battering the tiny vessel.

'Don't be stupid!' Paul's eyes were wide, his fear making him angry. 'We need to get home.'

Madeleine burst into tears, her teeth chattering as she pulled the blanket around her shoulders. The wind had quickly pushed them out into the lake, the shoreline no longer within easy striking distance. They were at the mercy of the elements, the rain falling heavily, the flat blue calm of the lake transformed to choppy, treacherous greys.

'Look out!' Jean-Pierre yelled.

His warning was futile. A monstrous swell hit the side of the boat, lifting it high before flipping it like a child's toy. For Sonia, everything seemed to happen in slow motion: the terrifying roll as the wave connected with the hull; the way her feet lost contact with the solid wooden deck; a moment of weightlessness, almost like flying, before the icy slap of the water engulfed her, roaring in her ears, forcing its way inside her mouth, dragging her down to a place of darkness.

Instinctively, Sonia kicked out, though it was impossible to determine whether that would bring her to the surface or send her deeper into the malevolent lake. A horrifying sequence of thoughts flashed through her mind: was this it? Was there a God? Who would break the news to her mother?

A dull light pierced her consciousness and Sonia propelled herself towards it, pushing down her terror as her lungs screamed for oxygen. She broke through with a noisy inhalation, eyes bulging with fear as she gasped the air. The driving rain pummelled her skin, every droplet like a knife slash. Through choking coughs, she pushed handfuls of hair from her face, blinking water from her eyes.

Jean-Pierre surfaced beside her, gasping and spluttering, his limbs thrashing uncontrollably as he sought to stay afloat. Their eyes met for a second before he was gone, disappearing beneath the swell. Sonia remembered his earlier revelation that he didn't know how to swim.

'Jean-Pierre!' she screamed, her head whipping from side to side as she searched the spot where he'd vanished. 'Jean-Pierre, here's the boat. Hold on!'

A few feet away, a shock of dark hair emerged and Jean-Pierre came up once again. Sonia reached out and clutched his arm, guiding him towards the boat. His knuckles were white as he found a groove in the wood and clung on, panting with exhaustion, slumped against the upturned hull as he retched violently.

Sonia's clothes clung to her like an oppressive second skin, obstructing her movement. She'd already lost a sandal, claimed by the murky depths of the lake, and she kicked off the remaining one, which was hindering her progress. Now she turned her attention to the others, screaming Madeleine's name. Distantly, she heard an answering cry and fought her way to the other side of the boat where she found Madeleine and Paul attempting to swim towards it, buffeted by the relentless waves.

'I can't do it,' Madeleine panted, her face agonised as she kicked her legs ineffectually.

'Yes, you can, you're almost there!'

'Sonia, help me,' yelled Paul, as the two of them caught hold of the exhausted Madeleine and guided her towards the boat. Her teeth were chattering, eyes rolling in her head like a frightened horse.

'I'm so cold…' She shivered. '… So cold…'

'What are we going to do?' Paul shouted. The wind caught his words, tearing them from his lips and whipping them into the sky.

'Help me… Somebody please help me…' Madeleine begged. She was still screaming, taking in mouthfuls of water, struggling with Paul as he clung to the boat with one arm and tried to support her with the other.

Sonia twisted from side to side, looking for any signs of help; the churning lake appeared devoid of life, no other boats in sight. Not even the mountains were visible behind the dark thunderclouds, although Sonia could just make out the town of Neuchâtel on the far shore, the outlines of buildings through the grey mist. She estimated that the distance was about a mile.

'I can swim it,' Sonia told them. Her breathing had slowed and she was calmer now. The movement might warm her freezing limbs.

'You can't. It's too far.'

But Sonia was determined. 'I can do it. I have to. What choice do we have?'

Without giving her friends time to respond, Sonia turned and plunged into the swirling waters, fighting against the lake as though it were a living, breathing enemy she had to defeat. Every movement was a struggle; every inch forward required a supreme effort. Being out in the open water, with not even the relative safety of the boat to cling to, was terrifying, and Sonia pushed away all thoughts of what could be lurking beneath the surface, refusing to think about how foolhardy her mission might prove to be.

It didn't seem possible that less than an hour ago they'd been basking in the glorious sunshine, relaxed and carefree with no warning of the nightmare to come, no idea that—

A rogue wave blindsided her, knocking her off balance, lashing her face and leaving her spluttering. Sonia was barely a few hundred yards from the spot where they'd capsized and already she was exhausted, her muscles on fire, shoulders burning with every stroke. But she was their only hope, she knew that.

Summoning all her reserves of energy, Sonia took a deep breath and dived down beneath the swell, ploughing on in a frenetic front crawl. When she resurfaced, she heard Madeleine screaming.

It took Sonia a moment to refocus, to shake the water from her eyes and locate the upturned boat. It was drifting aimlessly, pushed along by the relentless wind. Sonia realised with mounting horror that there were now only two figures clinging to the hull.

'Paul!' she cried hopelessly. 'Where's Paul?'

Jean-Pierre shouted something in reply, but Sonia was too far away to make out the words. She could only watch helplessly as he and Madeleine battled to stay afloat before another ruthless wave shunted the boat and Madeleine slipped under the water.

'Madeleine!' Sonia howled. 'Madeleine, please!'

But her friend never resurfaced.

Instinctively, Sonia began swimming once again, this time heading towards the boat and away from the shore. Her body was running on pure adrenaline. Every part of her ached, every muscle burning, exhaustion threatening to overwhelm her.

Jean-Pierre was thrashing uncontrollably as she reached him. He'd become separated from the boat and was panicking, legs kicking, arms wheeling, desperate to keep his head above the water. As Sonia drew near he lunged for her, but he was too heavy and he pulled her down with him, refusing to let go as the pair sank lower beneath the black waters, the light fading from view.

Sonia kicked for the surface but Jean-Pierre clung on, clawing frantically at her body, his hands finding her thighs, her waist, her shoulders, his fingers grasping tightly. Sonia needed air. She fought the instinct to inhale, pushing against Jean-Pierre with all her strength, but her efforts were futile. Jean-Pierre refused to release her, his body jerking and convulsing, large hands gripping her chest and constricting her ribcage.

This was no longer a rescue mission; it was a fight.

Sonia knew that if Jean-Pierre didn't let go, she would drown. He was far stronger than her, his muscular body pressing down on hers in a suffocating embrace, their limbs entwined in some grotesque parody of a lovers' dance. Lake water had forced its way into Sonia's ears, her mouth, her nose, stinging her skin and slowing her movements. The pressure on her lungs was unbearable. She was acting purely on instinct now, quite literally fighting for her life. Kicking out as hard as she could, she felt the heel of her foot connect with bone – Jean-Pierre's knee, or his shoulder perhaps. His grip loosened a fraction and she kicked out again, connecting with his chin this time. One arm came away from where he held her waist and Sonia dug her nails deep into the remaining hand. The next moment, she was free.

She swam away, her body feeling light as air now that Jean-

Pierre's bulk no longer weighed it down. She rose swiftly to the surface and broke through, retching and choking but alive, thanking a God she'd professed to stop believing in.

The rain had almost stopped, the mist lifting and the lake settling. Sonia found that she was merely yards from the upturned boat and kicked lamely in its direction, drifting towards it as the life flowed back into her body. Her fingers found the edge of the wood and she laid her head against the battered hull, closing her eyes. She was shaking uncontrollably, her body spent, the water lapping against her exhausted frame.

Sonia was dimly aware that none of her friends were with her.

———

It felt as though she'd lain there for hours; drifting, depleted. In reality, it was no more than thirty minutes before a pleasure cruiser spotted the upturned craft, changing course and pulling alongside. Sonia was dimly aware of the passengers onboard, the crush of people pressed against the railings as they stared in horror at the unfolding drama. Women were turning away in shock, some of them crying, as their husbands tried to comfort them and children were led away from the scene.

Strong arms gripped Sonia, disturbingly reminiscent of Jean-Pierre's vice-like grip. But she was too exhausted to protest, limp and leaden as the men hauled her out, laying her on the deck like a fish ready for gutting. Curious faces rushed forwards to stare, the crew members trying their best to hold back the gawkers.

Sonia attempted to stand, momentarily confused by the fact everyone was speaking French.

'Please, don't move,' someone said, and then she was being picked up again, one arm around her waist, the other beneath her knees, like a lover carried over the threshold. Sonia stared blankly at a sky so blue and so cloudless it was impossible to believe that the afternoon's events were anything more than a bad dream. But as the crowd parted to let her through, Sonia heard gasps of shock and muffled sobs, saw hands flying to faces in distress.

Her head rolled to one side, straining to see, catching the briefest glimpse of a sight she knew she would never be able to forget – bloated limbs, bulging eyes, blue-tinged, waxen skin – as they pulled Madeleine's lifeless body out of the lake.

Chapter Fourteen

London, England

April 1938

Tregunter Road, straddling the border of Kensington and Chelsea, was a smart residential street in a well-to-do neighbourhood. From the outside, number 31 appeared much the same as its neighbours: well-kept and respectable, with lace curtains hanging uniformly and the front steps freshly scrubbed. Inside, the same veneer of respectability was maintained – good quality china on the dining room table, silver candlesticks, a vase of flowers on the mantlepiece and even an upright piano in the parlour. Yet despite Beatrice Dixon's best efforts, good-natured chaos reigned in the crowded household, the sound of children playing and fighting, crying and laughing, providing the noisy backdrop to daily life.

Sonia lay curled in her bed, the sheets pulled high and a pillow wedged over her head, as she attempted to ignore the morning mayhem. Feet pounded along the corridor outside, shrieks and giggles exploding from the next bedroom.

'Sonia!' Her sister's voice. 'You're going to be late.'

'I don't care!'

A beat, then Bay tried again. 'Sonia?'

'Go away!' Sonia threw back the covers in frustration, grabbing her robe from where it hung on the corner of her scuffed cheval mirror. Her reflection gave her cause to pause: there were dark shadows under her eyes, her complexion pallid. Then she checked the clock – almost eight o'clock. She was due at work in Holborn at nine. Swearing under her breath, she hastily brushed her hair and pinned it up, noticing last night's clothes slung on the wicker peacock chair in the corner. She'd spent the evening in town with friends, getting tight on cheap wine. Pulling on fresh underwear and stockings, Sonia opened her wardrobe and selected a simple grey skirt with a rather crumpled pussy-bow blouse, before crossing the hallway to the bathroom.

'Get out!' Sonia yelled, rattling the handle and finding it locked. 'Come on, hurry up. Who's in there?'

'It's Kitty,' came the sulky reply. 'I'm having a bath.'

Sonia swore again, rolling her eyes as she ran downstairs to the kitchen. She was greeted by a scene of disarray; half a dozen children of varying ages were clustered around the large wooden table as her sister attempted to get them all seated and orderly. Her mother, Beatrice, stood at the stove, eggs bubbling in the pan while she dished up fried mushrooms and tomatoes and slices of toast.

When Beatrice's divorce settlement had come through, she was finally able to end the cycle of moving her young family from place to place, one boarding house to the next, living in a different hotel every season. When Sonia came 'home' from Roehampton, she rarely came back to the same address twice. The money from Geoffrey Dixon enabled Beatrice to rent the house in Tregunter Road, setting up as a home from home for children of the Empire. Ably assisted by Bay, Beatrice acted *in loco parentis* for youngsters whose parents were hundreds of miles away, furthering British interests overseas, but who wanted their offspring educated back in England – just as Sonia (and, indeed, Vivian) had been.

'Kitty's in the bathroom again,' Sonia snapped. 'Why is she

bathing at this time of day? Using all the hot water. It's self-indulgent if you ask me.'

'Which nobody did.' Bay grinned good-naturedly as she poured out glasses of cold water from a large jug. Sonia scowled.

'Good morning to you too,' Beatrice greeted her. 'What time did you come in last night?'

'Late.' Sonia hastily washed her face in the kitchen sink, drying it on a tea towel.

'Don't do that!'

'Well, what am I supposed to do if Kitty's hogging the bathroom?' Sonia threw herself down on a chair, grabbing a glass of water and draining it in seconds. 'I'm so thirsty. And I've got a pounding headache. This noise is unbearable.'

Beatrice turned from the stove. 'Sonia, you can't carry on like this – staying out until the early hours, drinking alcohol, keeping company with all kinds of disreputable characters. Then you're tired and late every morning. I'm worried you're going to get the sack.'

'I don't care if I do. I hate my job.'

'Sonia...' Beatrice looked pained, whatever she was about to say lost to exasperation.

Bay watched the exchange with concern. 'Would you like some breakfast, Sonia?'

'No time.' Sonia reached across the table, stealing a piece of toast from the plate of a red-headed child sitting opposite.

'That was mine!' The boy squealed.

'Finders keepers, losers weepers,' Sonia shot back, taking a large bite.

'Darling, that's not fair.' Beatrice sounded angry.

'Well, make him some more. You never take my side, do you?'

'Sonia, he's eight years old. You're a grown woman – even if you don't act like one most of the time.'

Sonia jumped to her feet, eyes flashing in fury. 'I've had enough. I'm leaving.'

'What time will you be home tonight?'

'None of your business. I'm a grown woman, aren't I?' Sonia stormed out of the kitchen, grabbing her handbag, which she'd thrown under the hallway table late last night. It contained her purse, a red lipstick and a battered copy of *Mrs Dalloway*.

'Sonia?'

Sonia turned to see her sister standing nervously by the staircase.

'What?'

'Is everything… all right?'

'Everything is absolutely fucking marvellous. Thank you *so* much for asking.' Sonia's voice was thick with sarcasm, as she pulled a wide-brimmed dark green cloche hat fiercely down on her head.

Bay was shocked by her sister's vehemence. 'Look, I know you've had a tough time and we're all making allowances, but you're not being fair. I don't know if you realise just quite how badly you're behaving, but it's not fair to Mother, and it's not fair to the rest of us.'

Sonia knew that Bay was right, but tiredness and self-righteous anger conspired to make her dismiss her sister's feelings. She ploughed on regardless, her comments childish and cruel.

'Well, I'm sorry that I'm not the perfect daughter like you.'

'Sonia, that's not—'

'Fair? Life isn't fair, Bay! If life was fair, I wouldn't be living in this house with a bunch of other people's children I don't give a damn about. Father wouldn't be dead, my friends wouldn't be dead, I wouldn't have the world's dullest job and I wouldn't hate my life so much.'

'You sound like a child! You're getting worse and worse, and this last year has been intolerable. I don't know how Mother puts up with you. You're unbelievably selfish and—'

'Oh, do shut up. Shouldn't you be scrubbing floors or something?'

'Why are you being so horrible?'

'Because I hate it here. I hate all of you.' Sonia was

unrepentant. *No one* understood what she'd been through. She'd witnessed her friends die. She'd tried to save them but failed, and would have to live with that for the rest of her life. Every night she saw their innocent faces, haunting her dreams, tormented by visions of what had happened. When she closed her eyes, Jean-Pierre stared back at her, and she remembered his expression as he'd kissed her, a mixture of shyness and lust. He'd had less than an hour to live.

Sonia suffered from nightmares where she was drowning, feeling the weight of Jean-Pierre's body pressing down on hers as he clutched at her in desperation. Sometimes she dreamed that he'd finally succeeded, pushing free towards the light whilst Sonia sank beneath the water, spiralling to the depths. She welcomed the oblivion, feeling nothing but relief, her guilt at sending him to his death finally assuaged. It was only right that *she* should drown and this handsome, youthful, vital boy should survive and thrive. Sonia would toss and turn and cry out in her sleep, waking with tears on the pillow.

In the cold light of day, she tried to ease the pain with drinking, laughing, flirting, living every day as though it was her last because one day – perhaps sooner than she expected – it would be. Why had she been spared? Was it part of God's plan? It was perverse that He had allowed her to live and left her friends to die, Sonia thought furiously, wondering how the nuns of Roehampton would explain that.

She'd been serious when she said that she hated her job, and the obvious answer now seemed to be to resign. Her mother had paid for a secretarial course when she returned from Switzerland, hoping it might give her some purpose, but in fact it had done the opposite; Sonia was wasting her life in that dull, dingy office. She was certain God hadn't spared her for her administration skills. Yes, she should resign, make something of her life to atone for what had happened. Her Catholic upbringing was fully ingrained, she reflected ruefully; the rest of her life was to be viewed as a penance.

Sonia wanted to say all of this to her sister, to explain everything that was running through her mind, a constant dialogue that wouldn't switch off. But that felt impossible, and now it was too late because she'd said she hated everyone, and Sonia could only watch in dismay as Bay's face hardened.

'Why don't you move out then, if you hate us all so much? Go and live with your layabout friends, the ones you think are so much better than the rest of us.'

'Maybe I will.' Sonia walked out of the house and slammed the front door behind her.

Later that day, the lighter evening holding the promise of spring, Sonia walked into the Wheatsheaf on Rathbone Place. She called hello to familiar faces as she threaded her way through the early evening crowd, the dimly lit rooms and cosy leather armchairs offering a far more hospitable welcome than the house on Tregunter Road.

Sonia found her friends at their usual table; they were a disparate, bohemian bunch of writers and poets, penniless artists and titled aristocrats – impossible to tell who was who from outward appearance. Like most of the pub's clientele, they were creative and charismatic, enjoying nothing more than an impassioned debate over a bottle of cheap wine and a packet of Woodbines. Sonia loved their warmth and joie de vivre, how they accepted her without question or judgement.

'Sonia!' Serge Konovalov – a grizzled, heavy-set bear of a man – spotted her and rose to his feet. Russian by birth, he was a professor of the subject at Oxford University, and somewhat besotted with Sonia.

'Hello, darling,' she beamed, greeting him with a kiss on the cheek.

'Now there are no chairs left so you'll have to sit on my lap.'

'Thank you very much, but I'd rather sit on Caitlin,' Sonia

teased, warmly embracing the woman beside him – a pretty blonde with a neat waist and heavy, full breasts – before turning her attention to the barman. 'Tom, be a sweetheart and bring me a bottle of champagne, would you?'

There were cheers from the group and Sonia smiled, delighted by their reaction.

'What are we celebrating?'

'I've found a flat and I've left my job.' The announcement elicited another round of raucous applause and whistles. 'I finally had enough of typing and filing and saying, "Yes, Mr Perkins. No, Mr Perkins. Three bags full, Mr Perkins," to the world's dullest man. I genuinely thought I might explode with boredom, so I resigned. And it feels liberating!'

Serge nodded approvingly. 'Excellent news. You're far too pretty to work.'

'That's very sweet of you, but unfortunately pretty won't pay the rent.'

'Oh, I think you'll find it can. In fact, I know a number of women without gainful employment who manage to pay their rent every month and still have enough left over for silk stockings.' Serge wiggled his eyebrows suggestively.

'Why doesn't it surprise me that you're well acquainted with women of loose morals? But no, that route's not for me.'

'If you ever change your mind, I'll be your first customer.'

'Oh, leave her alone, Serge,' said Eugene Vinaver, shaking his head. Eugene was a Russian-born academic, fine-featured and softly spoken. Addressing Sonia, he asked, 'So you've gone the full Virginia Woolf have you? A room of one's own, and all that?'

'Yes, I rather suppose I have.'

'And are you going to write a literary masterpiece?'

Sonia laughed as she took a drag from the cigarette he was offering and passed it back, red lipstick coating the stub. 'Perhaps I will. I'll give it a bloody good go!'

'According to dear Virginia,' Caitlin interjected, 'a woman must have *money* and a room of her own, if she is to write fiction.'

'Well, that's rather fucked things up. Now that I've left my deathly dull job I'm rather short of the former. In fact, I can't really afford this bottle,' Sonia sighed, as the barman came over with a champagne bucket and half a dozen glasses.

'Put it on my tab, Tom,' yelled Serge.

'You don't have a tab, you broke Russki,' the barman retorted, to gales of laughter.

Serge turned puce with rage, but Sonia leaned over to kiss him once again. 'Thanks anyway, darling,' she murmured, squeezing back in between Caitlin and a woman with dyed red hair, wearing a thin slip of a dress beneath a heavy fur coat.

'Sonia, have you met Lilian?' asked Caitlin.

'No, I don't think I have. How do you do?'

'Oh, what beautiful manners,' Lilian exclaimed. Sonia's smile faltered, unsure whether the woman was making fun of her.

'Oh, she's a proper little princess is our darling Sonia.' Serge winked, as Sonia waved away his words in embarrassment.

'Lily used to be in the chorus line with me, at the Palladium,' Caitlin explained.

'I'm still a dancer. I work at the Windmill,' Lilian added, re-crossing her legs so that her skirt slipped higher.

'How thrilling. I must come and watch you perform sometime.'

Lilian smiled tightly, but didn't reply, leaning over to pour herself a glass of champagne from Sonia's bottle. 'You don't mind, do you?'

'Of course not,' Sonia lied.

'So where's your new digs?' asked Caitlin, sensing the tension and changing the subject. 'And how did all this come about?'

'Well, I spent this morning in the office circling adverts in the newspapers, then told Mr Perkins to stuff his job and went to view half a dozen places this afternoon. The best was on Grafton Mews. It's a tiny little attic room with barely enough room to swing a cat, and it's draughty as hell so it'll be freezing come winter time. But it's *mine*. No more sharing with my mother and sister and half the Empire's unwanted offspring.'

'Sounds perfect,' Caitlin grinned. 'Dylan and I have friends just around the corner on Fitzroy Street. Edward and Connie Wyndham. Do you know them? I'll have to introduce you. You'll throw a housewarming party, won't you?'

'Of course. You must come – and bring Dylan. How is he?'

Caitlin rolled her eyes. 'The same as ever. Working, working, always working. And drinking and smoking and then working some more. You know we've moved to Wales, to Laugharne? It's beautiful, you must come and stay.'

'That would be lovely.'

'Do come, don't just say that. There's bugger all happening in that tiny village and it can get awfully lonely. Dylan gets so absorbed when he's writing I think he completely forgets about me. Promise me you'll visit.'

'I promise. Although I—'

'Mind if I have a refill?' Lilian interrupted, topping up her glass without waiting for an answer. Caitlin turned to speak to her, as Eugene sat down in the chair Serge had just vacated, leaning across to Sonia.

'Seriously though, what will you do for money?'

'Find another job, I suppose. The problem is that the only thing I'm qualified for is secretarial work. And the thing I find dullest in the whole wide world is secretarial work.'

Eugene smiled. 'Why don't you help me out?'

'Doing what?'

'I'm working on the manuscript of Thomas Malory's *Morte d'Arthur*. Have you heard of it?'

'No,' Sonia admitted.

'I need someone to assist me with typing up the translation. How much is your rent?'

'Four shillings a week.'

'I'll pay you three pounds.'

Sonia's eyes lit up. 'Eugene, that's a fortune!'

'What are you talking about?' Serge demanded, striding back across the pub, annoyed to find Eugene in his seat. 'Are you telling Sonia about the adventure we've planned?'

Sonia frowned, looking to Eugene for an explanation. 'What adventure?'

'This madman has persuaded me to travel around Europe with him. We're going to explore Bulgaria and Romania and Yugoslavia, and drive to Poland to find my long-lost relatives.'

'But you can't drive!'

Eugene shrugged. 'How hard can it be?'

Sonia threw back her head and laughed uproariously. 'You're insane. Both of you.'

'Why don't you come with us?' Serge suggested. 'We could do with some female company.'

'Oh, now you really are insane!'

'Why not? You have no husband, no job, no commitments… Come and have an adventure.'

Sonia opened her mouth to say no. But then she hesitated. She thought of her dreary former job in a lifeless office. She imagined her sister's shock, her mother's anger, when they discovered she'd run off to the Continent with two men who were more than twice her age. And somehow, the word 'no' never came.

Chapter Fifteen

Hoia-Baciu, Romania

June 1938

'Where the hell are we?'

'How the fuck should I know?'

'Because you're the one with the bloody map!'

'I can't see the fucking map in the fucking dark, can I? You're the one who drove us into this fucking forest!'

'Just shut the fuck up and help me get out of here!'

Sonia sat curled up on the back seat of the rickety Wolseley Hornet, listening to the argument raging in the front, and sipping intermittently from a dangerously strong bottle of potato vodka they'd bought for a pittance from a farmer a few villages back. Everything was fuzzy. Everything was funny. She giggled delightedly to herself, attempting to roll a cigarette with her free hand, swearing under her breath as they hit a tree root and she dropped tobacco all over her skirt.

'Great! Now you've fucking stalled.'

'Because *you* directed me into a bloody tree!'

'You've been driving this heap of shit for a month now and you're still not getting any better.'

'Why don't *you* drive then? You can't be any worse at it than you are at navigating.'

'Right, that's it. That is *it*. Stop the car. STOP THE FUCKING CAR.'

Eugene slammed down on the brakes and the car stalled once again. The headlamps went off, plunging them into darkness, and Serge jumped out, utterly livid. After being cramped in the passenger seat for hours, his body uncoiled like a tightly wound spring as he made his bid for freedom.

'Where are you going?' Eugene yelled after him.

'I don't know, because I don't know where the fuck we are!' The tail-end of Serge's sentence was hard to make out, swallowed up by the dense forest as he stomped off into the trees. Within seconds he was gone, enveloped by a night as black as velvet, the silver sliver of crescent moon unable to penetrate the gloom.

Sonia took another gulp of vodka. 'Will he be okay?'

'He'll be fine. He has a tremendous homing instinct, like a pigeon. A fat, angry pigeon.'

Sonia giggled again, at the accuracy of the analogy. She wasn't concerned. She felt sure that everything would turn out just fine as it had all the way along this extraordinary, preposterous journey that had so far seen them traverse almost a dozen countries, encounter Nazis on the streets of Austria, eat boiled rat in a tiny village in Albania, and get stranded on a mountainside in Czechoslovakia. They'd spent a terrifying night sleeping in a crypt in Yugoslavia, and been separated and detained at the Hungarian border, but throughout it all Sonia had felt protected and safe with Eugene and Serge, confident that they would take care of her, whatever came their way.

'Do you think there are bears in this forest?' she asked suddenly.

'Perhaps. But my money's on Serge to beat one in a fight. Come on, let's stretch our legs while we're waiting for him to come to his senses.' Eugene got out, taking Sonia by the hand as she climbed unsteadily through the driver's-side door.

'*Merci beaucoup*,' she thanked him prettily.

'*Enchanté*,' he returned, softly kissing the back of her hand.

For a moment, neither of them said a word. The woods were alive with sound: the hoot of an owl and the shriek of a fox; a scurrying of feet in the undergrowth and a swooping of bats overhead.

'Drink?' Sonia asked, breaking the stillness and offering the bottle to Eugene. He took it from her, as Sonia walked round to the front of the car, leaning against the bonnet and throwing back her head to look up at the sky. High above, the branches of the trees laced together, a near-impenetrable cover through which she could just make out the tiny lights of thousands of stars, her eyes tracing the familiar constellations: Orion; Canis Major; Ursa Minor.

'Look at that,' she sighed. 'Doesn't it make you feel so small and insignificant? At school, we were taught that God created the heavens and the earth, but surely it's impossible that something so spectacular could be produced by design. Don't you agree?'

'You're not religious then?' Eugene came to stand beside her, so close that Sonia could feel the warmth of his body, his hip resting lightly against hers.

'Lapsed Catholic. All the best people are,' she grinned. 'You?'

'My father's Jewish.'

'Tell me about him. What's he like?'

Eugene took papers and tobacco from his pocket and began rolling a cigarette. 'He died just over a decade ago. He was a great man. He trained as a lawyer in Warsaw, then moved to St Petersburg and became a politician. He fought for civil rights, for the Jews. He believed in democracy, and he believed in people. But growing up, life was... difficult. The authorities... We moved often, spent time in hiding. My father was regularly arrested, flung into jail. So eventually we fled to Paris. Have you ever been?' Eugene struck a match, the flame temporarily illuminating his face. Sonia stared at him; all his features seemed more pronounced in the orange light – the hollows of his cheeks, the dome of his forehead. Then the match hissed and they were plunged into darkness once more.

'No, never. I'd love to, though.'

'I'll take you there. You'd adore it. It's my absolute favourite city. We lived in the Marais, the Jewish quarter, and had a great many friends there. There's something about the city that's so inspiring, as though creativity flows through the very waters. It was in Paris that I found the courage to tell my father that I didn't want to be a lawyer, like him, but to follow my passion for literature. I wanted to be a scholar, to study mediaeval texts and carve a different path for myself than the one expected of me.' Eugene turned to her, and Sonia inhaled the scent of tobacco on his breath.

The sentence resonated with her – to *carve a different path for myself than the one expected of me*. That was what Sonia longed for – to break free of the shackles of expectation, to turn her back on a safe but dull career as a secretary until a suitable husband came along and—

'I don't know why I'm telling you all this.' Eugene's voice interrupted her thoughts.

'The darkness invites confidences. I learnt that at boarding school.' Suddenly she longed to reach out and caress his face. 'It somehow becomes easier to share in the middle of the night, when no one can see your face, your expression. It's the same principle as the confessional.'

'So, go ahead. Confess.' Eugene dropped the cigarette butt on the floor, grinding it out beneath his shoe. 'What's your deepest, darkest secret?'

Sonia hesitated, pulling herself up onto the bonnet of the car and reclining against the windscreen. After a moment, Eugene did the same, coming to sit beside her.

'I don't think…' Sonia closed her eyes. She wanted to confide in him, to invite that closeness. 'I don't think that my father was really my father.' The words seemed to ring through the night air, whispered by the pine trees and carried on the breeze. She'd never said that out loud before. 'I have a sister, Bay. She was four years old when our father – Charles – died, and I was four months. My mother always said that he'd had a heart attack but… there were rumours. He shot himself. A year later, my mother remarried – only one week after she formally came out of mourning. His name was Geoffrey Dixon and he was a colleague of my father's – or, at least, the man I've always been told was my father.

'The following year, she and Geoffrey had my little brother, Michael. He's a wonderful boy, so intelligent, I've always been madly in love with him. He's at Ampleforth, on a scholarship. Michael and I have always had such a bond… we're so similar. Bay and I… It makes sense. It makes complete and utter sense that *her* father wasn't *my* father. And I think Charles realised that. And so I've always felt rather responsible, you see. Responsible for his death. I was the reason he shot himself. When he found out I wasn't his.'

'Sonia, you can't—'

'No, it's quite all right. I've never told anyone this before, you know. Although I think perhaps Bay might have her suspicions too. But I've been such a bitch to her, I really have. I'm a terrible person.'

'No. No, you're not.'

Sonia laughed humourlessly. 'Yes, I am. That's the problem with Catholicism, you see. Even if you renounce it, you can never quite escape the guilt.' She reached for the vodka and realised her hands were shaking. 'Do be a darling and roll me a cigarette.'

They sat in silence whilst Eugene did as she asked, hearing the indistinct howl of an animal in the distance. As he struck the match, Sonia found she couldn't meet his eyes. She hadn't even told him about Jean-Pierre, hadn't admitted that she was culpable in the death of both her alleged father and a beautiful, brilliant young man who'd been falling in love with her. Instead, she said, 'Have you ever read Freud?'

Eugene seemed surprised by the question. 'I'm aware of his writing, his ideas. I can't say it's my cup of tea.'

Sonia exhaled a long stream of smoke, the glowing tip of her cigarette winking red against the blackness. The howling came again, nearer this time. 'I think that's why I've always been attracted to older men,' she murmured, moving closer to Eugene as she spoke. Her breathing was light and shallow, her heart rate quickening. 'I've never really had a stable father figure, you see, so I long to be adored and protected and loved…' She tilted her head upwards, closing her eyes as their lips brushed and he drew her inevitably towards him.

'Fuuuuuuck! Start the fucking car!'

Sonia and Eugene sprang apart as they heard Serge's cry. He was crashing through the forest towards them, the air suddenly filled with a tremendous barking and yapping.

'Wolves! Fucking wolves! Get in the fucking car!'

Sonia scrambled down from the bonnet as Eugene wrenched open the door and she tumbled onto the back seat. He turned the key and the headlamps beamed into life, flooding the forest with yellow light as Serge came barrelling towards them, sheer terror on his face, the noise growing louder as he reached the car and hurled himself inside.

'Go! Go! Go! Fucking drive!'

Eugene floored the engine, managing not to stall, accelerating so quickly that Sonia flew off the seat and landed in the footwell behind Serge. The whole situation struck her as impossibly hilarious and she began to giggle once again, her laughter becoming hysterical as the battered Hornet sped away, deeper into the malignant forest.

Chapter Sixteen

Tokaj, Hungary

July 1938

The woman's waist was slender, swelling to softly rounded hips, the movement of her body hypnotic as she swayed in time to the music. Her hair was dark, thick and long, her eyes lined with black and her red mouth sensuous, her skirts flying as the men sang a traditional song, accompanied by guitars and violins and the clapping of the bar patrons.

'Do put your tongue back in, Serge,' Sonia commented archly. 'She's young enough to be your daughter.'

'So are you, and that's never stopped me trying,' he grinned. 'Where's Eugene anyway?'

Sonia jerked her head across the room. It was a cave-like cellar with stone walls and a bar made of pine from behind which foaming glasses of beer and lethally strong spirits were served. 'Mingling with the locals.'

'I hope he's not asking too many questions,' Serge muttered darkly, following her gaze to where Eugene sat surrounded by a small group of men, apparently deep in conversation.

'What do you mean?'

'Nothing. Nothing.' Serge shook his head, as though to clear it. 'Now, Miss Brownell, I think it's time that you and I danced together, don't you?'

Sonia smiled, finishing the last of her drink – a regional speciality that tasted like strong brandy – and getting to her feet. There were cheers and stamping as they took to the floor, Serge whirling Sonia in his arms as she let the music flow through her, the very opposite of the formal dances she'd learned as a child.

She was aware that the three of them were attracting a lot of attention; it had been that way throughout their travels. They made an unlikely trio – the beautiful English rose with the two older Russian men – and Sonia revelled in their incongruity. Almost everywhere they went, Eugene or Serge were able to find some commonality of language – a smattering of Russian, a dialect whose origins were Polish, occasionally even an English or French speaker – and thus they got by, Sonia relying on the men as both her translators and her protectors.

Tonight, they'd landed up in a small tavern not far from Tokaj in northern Hungary; Eugene believed some of his ancestors might have originated from the area and was keen to speak to the villagers to find out what they knew. Tomorrow, they would cross back into Czechoslovakia, then on into Poland, where he planned to introduce them all to his extended family in Warsaw. But that was tomorrow, and the night was still young…

'Serge!' Sonia squealed, as she spun away from him, only to fall into the arms of a dashing young man. Dark-haired and swarthy, his muscles were tight beneath her fingertips, his strong hands holding her waist. Sonia felt a thrill of excitement; the stranger was undoubtedly handsome and the alcohol was surging in her veins. She was warm and relaxed, her guard down as she allowed the man to manoeuvre her around the floor, aware of the stares and comments in a language she didn't understand.

Around them the crowd grew bigger and the man pressed closer, his hands holding tightly onto her wrists. She felt the first stirrings of discomfort and tried to pull away, but he refused to relinquish his grasp. Sonia's throat seemed to close, the room becoming a blur as her vision swam in and out of focus. Flashbacks of Jean-Pierre, the lake, a body stronger than her own pinning her down… She needed air, couldn't breathe, opened her mouth to scream—

And then she was free. Her eyes refocused and she saw Serge beside her, primed to throw a punch, the man she'd been dancing with stepping back, holding up his hands in a gesture of appeasement.

'Serge.' Sonia's voice was soft, but it cut through the noise around them. Serge looked at her and immediately dropped his stance, taking her by the hand and pulling her through the crowd.

'We need to get out of here.'

Sonia looked around for Eugene and noticed a group of men huddled together, watching them. She shivered involuntarily, unable to shake the sense that there was something sinister about them.

Seeing the commotion, Eugene excused himself from his conversation and followed them up the narrow staircase and out of the door. The night air was cool and refreshing, but it provided little relief, that same feeling of menace tailing them like a shadow.

The Hornet was parked just yards away, but before they could reach it two uniformed men stepped in front of them, blocking their path.

'What is it? What's happening?' Sonia demanded.

She didn't understand what they were saying, but as one of them stepped forward and roughly took hold of Eugene, she screamed. Serge tried to fight but two more men appeared, overpowering him, twisting his arms up behind his back. The other grabbed Sonia by the shoulder, shouting instructions, forcibly dragging her towards an open truck.

'Where are they taking us?'

'Try to stay calm and don't struggle. It's all a misunderstanding. We're being arrested.'

'Arrested? Why? What for?'

Serge turned to her, his expression grave. 'They think we're spies.'

The cell was small, damp and draughty – though she could hardly have expected it to be luxurious, Sonia thought wryly. The walls were exposed brick, with thick black bars across the narrow window, and there were long concrete benches on either side. A skeletally thin woman lay asleep on one, a rough blanket pulled over her, her face hidden from view by a nest of dyed hair. Apart from her, Sonia was alone, though Eugene and Serge were being held in the neighbouring cell. It felt comforting to have them close by.

'How are you holding up?' Eugene called across.

'Fine.' Sonia's voice was husky when she spoke and she coughed to clear it. The police had taken everything from her – money, handbag, cigarettes – and she still felt rather drunk.

'We'll get you out of here, Sonia,' Serge insisted, in gruff tones.

'I hope so.' Sonia tried to laugh, but it fell flat. She was reassured at least that they'd been taken to the local, provincial police station – not driven through the night to Budapest to an underground bunker of the secret police.

'Hey!' Serge yelled, banging on the door, rattling the bars of the cell. He let forth a stream of Russian.

The woman on the bench stirred. She muttered in her sleep and rolled over, but didn't wake.

No one responded to Serge's shouts, and Sonia heard him slam the wall in frustration. She sat down on the concrete bench. As expected, it was hard and uncomfortable. Shivering, she pulled her knees into her chest, picking up the scratchy woollen blanket that had been left for her use and wrapping it around herself. The discomfort and sense of unease reminded her of Roehampton – no doubt the nuns would have approved – and she wondered what her old schoolfriends would think if they could see her now.

It had seemed like such a jolly wheeze, setting off across the Continent with two older men and only the vaguest of plans. Sonia had always wanted to see the world, and revelled in the shock value of travelling this way. In truth, the idea was ridiculous, and at times downright dangerous. The atmosphere in Europe was febrile; Jews were being persecuted across the continent, and there were reports of German troops massing on the border with Czechoslovakia. They were on the brink of war, and Sonia felt like a fool. She wasn't some bohemian traveller, or a rebel defying convention; she was simply an ex-convent-schoolgirl who'd found herself in above her head.

She thought of Maureen O'Sullivan, who'd moved to America and was now a famous actress. Hollywood seemed so far away from Sonia's existence in grey, forbidding Europe that she could scarcely imagine it. Vivien Hartley was married, with a child, and was now a rising star of the London stage. Sonia felt insignificant in comparison, a failed secretary who had no idea what to do with her life and was currently imprisoned in a Hungarian police station.

She lay down on the bench and closed her eyes, hoping sleep might bring temporary relief. Jean-Pierre's face swam in front of her and she gasped, hastily sitting up, shaking her head to try and clear it. She wondered whether she'd ever be free of the memories, the nightmares. Perhaps it was a sign, a call to action – to stop wasting her own life when her friends had been deprived of theirs. She would start to make changes, just as soon as she got out of here, Sonia vowed.

If she got out of here.

She stood up, shivering, and walked to the wall that divided her from the neighbouring cell.

'Eugene?' she murmured.

'Yes?'

'I'm frightened.'

'Oh, Sonia,' he sighed. 'Please don't be, my darling. I'll get us out of here, I promise. I—'

'Hey!' Serge began kicking the bars, the door rattling as he began to shout once again, causing a commotion, demanding attention. 'Hey! You can't keep us locked up like animals. I demand to speak to someone! We've done nothing wrong, you fascist pigs!'

The shouting continued, in various languages. Eugene tried to placate him, but Serge paid him no heed.

Sonia jumped as she heard the rattle of keys, followed by the clunk of a heavy door and the sound of footsteps. A dour-looking man – short and slender, with dark curly hair and a neat moustache, dressed in uniform – walked past her and stood wordlessly in front of Serge and Eugene's cell. He folded his arms across his chest, a menacing-looking baton tucked in his belt.

'*Igen?*' He raised an eyebrow.

Sonia could only listen uncomprehendingly, her heart pounding, as Serge began to speak in a language she didn't understand. Unable to see her friends, she could only guess at the content of the conversation from the guard's reaction, and he looked distinctly unimpressed.

'What's he saying?' she asked Eugene.

'Wait a moment…'

Serge's stream of rapid speech continued. The guard shifted his weight from one foot to the other and sucked his teeth.

'Oh no,' Eugene groaned. 'Oh Serge, don't…'

'What's he doing?' Sonia asked urgently, unable to take her eyes from the man's face.

'He's offering him money,' Eugene hissed, in a loud whisper. 'Christ, Sonia, he's trying to bribe a policeman!'

Finally Serge ran out of steam, his monologue coming to an abrupt halt. The guard raised his eyebrows and shouted to a colleague.

'What the hell did you do that for?' Eugene berated Serge.

'You've made everything ten times worse. God only knows what they'll do now. What if they split us all up?' His voice was full of alarm as another uniformed officer entered the cell block, and the two men conferred in low tones.

The new arrival glanced across at Sonia. She saw the glint in his eye and quickly looked away, her stomach churning. She recognised that lascivious look in men and didn't like it, understanding that in this situation she was completely powerless.

'Eugene…' She spoke in low tones, trying not to draw attention to herself. 'What's happening?'

'I don't know,' he whispered, his anxiety evident in his voice.

Sonia exhaled, trying to slow her racing pulse. There it was again – that feeling of drowning, of disappearing beneath the waters, of being unable to catch her breath. No one back home knew where she was. *She* didn't even know where she was. These men could do whatever they wanted with her, and no one would ever find the evidence. She cursed her own stupidity, knowing all she could do was watch and wait to learn her fate.

PART III
The Star

Chapter Seventeen

MAUREEN

Los Angeles, USA

October 1933

Maureen inhaled sharply. 'Is that it?'

Dorothy Walker, the costume designer on *Tarzan and His Mate*, took in Maureen's expression and let out a peal of laughter. 'That's it. It's been green-lighted. It has Cedric's approval.'

'I bet it does,' Maureen muttered under her breath, as Dorothy laughed again.

She stared at the costume Dorothy was holding up – if it could be called a costume. There was so little material, it hardly constituted an outfit, with a skimpy bralette and a skirt that consisted of two small panels of leather tied together with what looked like string.

'Can I even wear underwear with that?' Maureen gasped.

'Best not to,' Dorothy advised. 'But that's authentic. Jane wouldn't have had undergarments in the jungle.'

'I didn't realise the role required so much commitment,' Maureen quipped.

In the back of her mind, she wondered what people would

think. Not the public *en masse* – the *Tarzan* fans would love it, she felt sure. But her family, her friends, the nuns of Roehampton. They'd be outraged, but the thought was exhilarating. Let them be shocked. The movie would undoubtedly cause a stir, but wasn't that what she'd always enjoyed doing? Ever since she was a child, she'd had a wild streak, with a desire to shock and rebel against convention. Now she was doing it on the world stage.

'Come on, let's get you into this costume,' Dorothy said. 'We'll need to see how it moves and how it looks on camera.'

Maureen nodded; she'd been in almost twenty films by now, and knew what was required. She peeled off the dress she was wearing, quickly stripping to her underwear. She wasn't shy about her body; on the contrary, she was proud of it and growing in confidence every day, determined not to be the cowed, unhappy girl she'd been in childhood.

After being fired by Fox and ending up at the bottom of the Hollywood heap, Maureen had sent out the headshots Ed Tucker had taken to every studio, producer and casting agency she could find, determined to make a success of herself. Incredibly, it had happened. It felt as though someone was looking out for her – perhaps there was a God after all, she thought cynically.

Irving Thalberg, a producer known as the Boy Wonder due to both his youthful appearance and the fact that everything he touched turned to gold, had cast her as Jane in *Tarzan the Ape Man*. The movie was based on the books by Edgar Rice Burroughs, and Johnny Weissmuller, a former Olympic swimmer, had won the role of Tarzan.

Released the previous year, it was MGM's biggest film of the season, banking two and a half million dollars and catapulting Maureen to international fame. Moviegoers across the world had fallen for this unlikely love story of a jungle man meeting a woman for the first time, and the unexpected chemistry between them. It had everything: adventure, drama, passion – and a mischievous chimpanzee.

Maureen was now hot property, squired around town by a

series of eligible men – James Dunn, Leslie Howard, John Farrow – and providing excellent copy for the gossip columns. She was enjoying playing the field, though she imagined the nuns of Roehampton would have been horrified by her lifestyle. She thought with a pang how Vivien had done the right thing – marriage, swiftly followed by a child. And Maureen *did* want to wed and have children eventually, but right now she was having too much fun. She wanted to find the right man – and there were so many to try!

Inevitably rumours had begun to circulate about Maureen and her co-star Johnny, with the studio encouraging the stories, even arranging dinner dates and dancing for the two of them, to fuel publicity for the film. Despite his tall, athletic frame and dark good looks, there had never been anything romantic between them, with Maureen viewing the fun, likeable Johnny as akin to an older brother. Besides, she knew he was serious about his latest girlfriend, Lupe Velez.

'Oh my,' Dorothy breathed. 'I'd say that's a perfect fit.'

Maureen stared at herself in the costume department's full-length mirror, excitement pulsing through her. The outfit was tiny, but she was a knock-out, even if she did say so herself. She'd been exercising since her arrival in Hollywood, and following a good diet, and her reflection showed the results – slim thighs, creamy skin, a handspan waist and breasts that strained against the minuscule costume. She looked sensational.

This *Tarzan* sequel would push the boundaries. Maureen knew it would be controversial, and she thrived on the sense of rebellion. It was implied in the movie that Tarzan and Jane were in a relationship, doing all the things that couples do, despite not being married. There were also several (simulated) nude scenes, including an underwater montage which had been shot two weeks earlier in a giant tank on the studio lot. Johnny, having been an Olympic swimmer, played himself, but Maureen had a body double.

She'd seen the footage and it was beautiful, a sensuous, aquatic ballet with Johnny wearing nothing but a loin cloth and Josephine McKim – Maureen's double – in a flesh-coloured one-piece which gave the appearance that she was wearing nothing at all. Their taut, youthful bodies dived and spun and somersaulted together, limbs intertwined, soft, pale flesh a delicious contrast to the darkness of the depths. Maureen knew that the audience would love it.

She dragged her eyes away from her reflection and smiled at Dorothy. 'Should we go show Cedric?'

Cedric Gibbons was the director who'd been brought on board for the second film, and he would ultimately have approval over every detail.

Dorothy nodded. 'Would you like a robe?'

Maureen hesitated. 'No, I'll be fine,' she replied, a grin spreading across her face.

She stepped out of the trailer and onto the lot, the warm sun slicing between the buildings and bathing her in golden light. It wasn't far to the set, but it seemed as though every man working on the production was there today, as she encountered electricians, cameramen, carpenters, extras and more on the short walk. They all stared, jaws dropping.

Maureen was causing a sensation, and Lord only knew what the paying public would make of it. Far from being embarrassed, she was thrilled by the reaction. Having spent her formative years at Roehampton being told that sexual feelings were wrong and should be repressed, that her body was an instrument of sin and should remain covered, Maureen was overjoyed to revel in her body and the effect it had on men.

Dorothy opened the door and they walked onto the set. Johnny happened to be there, speaking with Cedric, and both men turned as she entered.

Johnny let out a low whistle and Maureen giggled.

'Jesus Christ, Maggie,' he said, using his nickname for her. 'I've got a feeling this movie's going to be a hit.'

Maureen was standing by the Moorish arched windows, looking out over the vast San Simeon estate already teeming with beautiful people, when there was a knock at the door.

'Coming!' she called, dashing across the bedroom with a final glance in the mirror. She hoped that she was suitably attired for an upscale barbecue, casual and pretty in high-waisted shorts and a cap-sleeve broderie anglaise blouse.

She opened the door to find Hulbert – Hully – Burroughs standing there. He looked every inch the archetypal All-American hero, tall and broad-shouldered, with his Californian tan and sun-kissed blond hair, dressed smartly in a suit and tie. Hully's father was Edgar Rice Burroughs, the author of the original Tarzan books, and Maureen knew he had high hopes for her and Hully. But although she thought Hully was a great guy – perfectly nice, perfectly mannered, and the perfect companion for a weekend party – she didn't see her future with him. There was no chemistry, and besides, Maureen secretly longed for someone dominant to sweep her off her feet.

'You look swell,' he grinned, his gaze sweeping over her. 'Let's go.'

Maureen took his arm as they strolled together through Casa del Sol, one of the three magnificent guest houses in the grounds of Hearst Castle. She'd stayed here half a dozen times now but didn't think she'd ever get over her awe at the place. Built for William Randolph Hearst, who'd inherited a fortune and made another in publishing and media, *La Cuesta Encantada* was a colossal, fantastical property, built in the Spanish colonial style, and filled with art, antiques, silver, and Greek pottery.

Maureen and Hully were there as guests of William's eldest son, George, who was throwing a weekend-long shebang, starting with a Saturday afternoon barbecue followed by what promised to be a stellar party that night. Following a champagne brunch on Sunday morning, guests could depart at their leisure from the estate's private airfield, landing back in Los Angeles less than an hour later.

'George sure knows how to throw a party, huh?' Hully quipped, as they stepped outside and descended the grand staircase beside an elegant stone fountain. They could hear the music from the jazz band, conversation and laughter layered on top like a melody. Excitement rose in Maureen; twenty-four hours of fun and frolics and flirtation. What could be better?

'He certainly does.'

The grounds were extensive, the plot itself more than 40,000 acres, immaculately landscaped with a vast Romanesque swimming pool. Today the estate was decked out like a traditional fairground, with a Ferris wheel and swing boats and side stalls, and stands with popcorn and cotton candy. The party was already well underway; Maureen glanced round at familiar faces, calling 'hello' to those she recognised. It was like a Who's Who of the movie industry: Norma Shearer and Irving Thalberg, Laurence Olivier and his wife Jill Esmond, Clark Gable, Claudette Colbert, Tallulah Bankhead, Charlie Chaplin, Ginger Rogers, James Cagney. There wouldn't be a star left in the Hollywood hills tonight.

A waiter passed by, bearing cocktails on a silver tray. Maureen and Hully each took a martini, dry and delicious. Maureen waved as she spotted Johnny and his girlfriend Lupe approaching, the two of them beaming. Johnny looked smart in slacks and a white shirt, open at the neck. Lupe was positively glowing in a white silk dress, her dark hair falling in glossy waves, her lips painted a vampish red.

'Hey, Maggie.'

'Hi, Johnny. You know Hully, of course.'

'Sure, sure, good to see you. And may I introduce you to Lupe.'

Maureen frowned. 'Lupe and I have met several times before...'

'Or should I say, may I introduce you to my *wife*, Lupe Weissmuller.'

Maureen's mouth fell open in shock, but she recovered herself quickly. 'Congratulations! But how…? I mean, when…?'

'We flew to Las Vegas last night as soon as I got off set, put the ring on her finger and flew here this morning. I guess this is our honeymoon.'

'Well, congratulations again,' Maureen laughed, as Hully echoed her sentiments.

'Although if he thinks I'm calling myself Mrs Weissmuller, he's sorely mistaken,' Lupe jabbed, through pursed lips.

'Didn't I marry a firecracker?' Johnny grinned proudly. 'She'll come around.'

Maureen smiled politely. This was Johnny's second marriage; his first, to singer Bobbe Arnst, had lasted less than two years, and his relationship with Lupe was famously tempestuous. Lupe thrived on her reputation as a hot-tempered and passionate Latina, with the press dubbing her 'the Mexican Spitfire'. There'd been reports of their physical fights, and Maureen knew the make-up team on *Tarzan* were often required to cover up bruises or love bites on Johnny. As a friend, she couldn't help but be concerned about him, but she knew it wasn't her place to voice those concerns.

'Speaking of *le grand amour*,' Johnny lowered his voice and leaned in to Maureen, 'I spotted one of your old flames here today.'

'Really?' Maureen replied, with studied casualness. She'd dated a considerable number of Hollywood's most eligible bachelors – and some of its married men too – but there was something in Johnny's tone that piqued her interest. 'Who?'

'John Farrow,' he declared triumphantly.

Maureen tried not to react but could feel spots of colour suffusing her cheeks, her pulse quickening at the mention of his name. 'Ancient history,' she shrugged, affecting nonchalance.

'Well, in case you want to do a little excavation, he's right over there by the carousel.'

It was impossible not to look, her eyes seeking him out in the crowd. She found him in an instant, and it felt as though the air had been sucked from her lungs. She hated the way her body betrayed her when she tried to feign indifference, her heart racing, adrenaline pumping, blood rushing.

Almost as though he knew she was watching, John turned. He smiled lazily, then murmured something to the woman he was with, never taking his eyes off Maureen, before strolling towards her.

In the time it took for him to cross the lawn, it was as though their whole history flashed before her. She instantly recalled the first time they'd met, the first time they'd kissed, the first time they'd made love…

John Villiers Farrow was Australian by birth, had been educated in England, and spent years as a sailor, leaving him with an enduring love of the South Pacific. He was full of contradictions – a devout Catholic, and a legendary womaniser; a creative who had no respect for art – and he was the most fascinating man Maureen had ever met.

They'd first laid eyes on one another almost two years earlier at the Cotton Club in Culver City, and they'd dated on and off, with Maureen returning to Ireland for long periods to see her ailing father, and John running off to London where he almost married Diana Churchill, daughter of the Conservative politician Winston. One day, out of the blue, John called Maureen and asked her to fly to Tahiti with him. She turned him down flat and hadn't heard from him since, though she'd heard on the grapevine that he'd taken another woman, eventually leaving her for a local Tahitian goddess with dark hair down to her waist.

At the beginning of 1933, John had been arrested at the Cocoanut Grove nightclub for breach of his visa, part of a crackdown against illegal immigrants working in the film industry. But now he was back and standing in front of her, tall and blond and suave, and Maureen felt dazzled by his presence, oblivious to Hully Burroughs beside her. Oblivious to the rest of the world, in fact.

She stood up tall, throwing back her shoulders. 'So, they let you out of jail, huh?'

John threw back his head and laughed, his eyes dancing as they drank in her appearance. 'Hello, Maureen. I've missed you.'

'Oh really. You didn't think to call?' It sounded like a line from a bad movie, and she hated that she couldn't think straight when he was around.

'I didn't know if you'd pick up,' he said smoothly.

'Maureen?' Hully asked, stepping across, uncertainty in his voice. Maureen felt a pang of guilt; she'd never led him on, but equally he didn't deserve to be treated like this.

'Hully, this is John Farrow. He's a writer and an old friend of mine. John, this is Hully, Edgar's son.'

'And Maureen's escort for the weekend,' Hully said pointedly, offering his hand to John.

John looked him square in the eye. They were both over six feet tall, but John had a physical presence, a dominance, that Hully couldn't compete with. Maureen watched, wondering what would happen, as John briefly shook Hully's hand.

'Good to meet you. Say, do you mind if I borrow your date for a little while? We have a lot of catching up to do.'

Before Hully could even respond, John had wrapped his arm around Maureen's waist and steered her through the crowd, towards the seclusion of the gardens beyond.

Maureen felt bad for Hully, but the moment was forgotten almost instantly as she was swept up by John's presence, all the old feelings for him rushing back. There'd been times when she'd hated him, times when she'd wept over him. He'd cheated on her, lied to her, behaved like an absolute cad at times, but ultimately that pull was still there.

'I haven't stopped thinking about you. There's never been anyone like you,' John murmured into her ear, his breath hot on her neck and his lips brushing her skin. His large hands were on her hips, and she shivered with anticipation, her body coming to life beneath his touch. Being in his presence was like being on set with the spotlight focused solely on her.

When John pulled her into the rose garden and kissed her passionately, Maureen knew that there was no point pretending. She was head over heels for John Farrow.

Chapter Eighteen

Santa Catalina Island, California, USA

April 1934

Maureen felt his strong muscles ripple beneath her, felt the powerful curve of his shoulders as she gripped him tightly with her thighs, urging him on. The stallion responded, moving from a canter to a gallop, and Maureen raced ahead, her dark hair streaming out behind her in the warm breeze, laughing in exhilaration as they raced uphill.

They emerged from beneath the cover of the oak trees onto a narrow, open trail, the deep blue of the Pacific Ocean surrounding them on all sides, with views stretching to Huntington and Laguna thirty miles away across the channel. Maureen tugged gently on the reins, shifting her weight backwards and softening her stance, bringing the sleek bay horse back down to a trot.

John drew up alongside her, flushed with exhilaration, his blue eyes dazzling in the sunlight. He looked handsome in chino shorts and a short-sleeved Turnbull & Asser shirt, musky sweat patches soaking through the fabric, which Maureen found inexplicably, thrillingly masculine. The tattoos on his arms – a shamrock, and a black flag and skull, souvenirs of his Navy career – stood out darkly against his skin, a bracelet inked around his ankle with the words *Semper Fidelis* – Always Faithful. Maureen knew he had another tattoo as well, a snake that slid over his upper thigh before disappearing into his underwear.

'Looks like you've found the perfect spot for a picnic,' John smiled, slipping down from his mount, a 17-hand grey mare.

They walked their horses over to a shady copse and tied them to a tree, leaving them to crop the grass. A short distance away, John spread their picnic blanket on the ground, unpacking roast chicken, pitted olives, sourdough bread, mixed berries, wedges of coconut cake. A bottle of champagne had been packed in ice, but the ice had melted and the fizz was starting to grow warm.

All of the signs pointed to a proposal. Hollywood was awash with rumours, and columnist Louella Parsons had written, *'Maureen O'Sullivan and Johnny Farrow have had all the news hounds on their toes for months waiting for the grand elopement…'*

Their relationship was still volatile, but despite the arguments, the unfaithfulness, the screaming rows and the frequent break-ups, they always came back together. Maureen was irresistibly drawn to him, seemingly able to forgive him anything.

She liked that their relationship was unconventional, that they'd had sex before marriage, that her life was nothing like the future her parents, teachers and even her peers would have envisaged. Vivien would have understood, Maureen reflected, before doubt crept in. In fact, Vivien had married an older barrister and, as far as Maureen knew, settled down and done what was expected of her. The two women had fallen out of touch recently; Maureen was so busy with her career, and Vivien presumably occupied by her dual role as wife and mother, that they'd exchanged little more than hastily scribbled Christmas cards with the barest of news.

Perhaps she had misunderstood Vivien all along, Maureen thought sadly, and the two of them hadn't been kindred spirits after all, with Vivien's apparent ambitions merely tiding her over until a suitable match could be found. Although Maureen supposed she could hardly judge when she was desperate for a proposal today.

'It's so romantic, isn't it?' she beamed up at John, prompting. Their picnic spot was in the centre of the island, part-way up Blackjack Mountain. The scenery was magical, with sprawling pine and eucalyptus trees, a cluster of mountain peaks rising around them, hazy in the California heat. If this were a movie, John would have got down on one knee right now.

'Sure. If you like sitting in fox shit with seagulls squawking over you.'

Maureen laughed, but couldn't help but feel deflated. She'd dressed with extra care today – albeit limited by what she could wear for riding – and was wearing daringly short shorts that showed off her lithe legs, paired with a pretty pastel sweater. She wanted to look perfect when John popped the question – though she was starting to wonder if he ever would.

'How's *The Spectacle Maker* coming along?' she asked, helping herself to a boiled egg and dipping it in salt.

John pulled a face. 'I don't know. Sometimes I think it's all total junk and I'm wasting my time.'

'Of course you're not! You're so talented. And I think directing will be perfect for you. It'll give you a whole new appreciation of film-making.'

Maureen wasn't being disingenuous – she genuinely thought John was an incredible talent, if only he'd knuckle down and take his work seriously. He was a writer by trade, and a chance meeting with film producer David O. Selznick led to John moving to Los Angeles to try his hand at screenwriting. John had done well in Hollywood and was about to make his directorial debut with a short film. Maureen was proud of him, but she knew that there was no fiercer critic of John than John himself; he struggled to take art seriously, meaning he never really respected his own endeavours.

'Maybe...' He pulled a face, as he tore off a hunk of bread. 'Who's directing *Copperfield*?'

'George Cukor. I'd like to give Dora more fire, but he wants her meek and childlike.'

'He knows what he's doing. You can learn a lot from him.'

Maureen had landed the plum role of Dora in an adaptation of Charles Dickens' *David Copperfield*, and both the budget and expectations for the project were high. She'd fought hard for the role; the studio didn't think she was a good fit, but Maureen was determined to prove them wrong. In the minds of the public, she was indelibly associated with the character of Jane Parker from *Tarzan*, and she was eager to take on another high-profile role that might shift that perception.

During her time in Hollywood, Maureen had got used to fighting – for roles, for recognition, against stereotypes. She wasn't simply a sweet Irish girl with a lilting voice and a kind heart; nor was she just a jungle man's loyal and sexy companion. She was multi-faceted, and anyone who underestimated her would do so to their detriment.

'You know, I'm thinking of buying a yacht,' John mused, staring out to sea. 'We had so much fun on Joseph Schenck's, didn't we? I could call it *The Irish Enchantress*. How about it?'

'Sounds tremendous. Do you miss the Navy, darling?'

'Yeah, always. The sea captures your heart, and there's nothing quite like it, though she can be a cruel mistress. Maybe I need to grow up and settle down on land, find myself a different kind of mistress,' he said with a wink.

He reached into his knapsack and Maureen's heart began to race. As he pulled out a shiny red apple and crunched down on it with relish, Maureen bit back her disappointment.

'It's only a few weeks until I go back home,' she sighed melodramatically, hoping to prompt a reaction from him. 'Will you miss me?'

'Every damn day,' John grinned, in a tone that Maureen

couldn't quite read. In that moment, she hated him for being so flippant. It would be her first proper break in almost two years, since she'd started filming the Tarzan movies and, if the truth be told, she was worried about what he might get up to while she was away. John Farrow and fidelity were foreign concepts, despite the tattoo on his ankle, which was why a proposal would have been so reassuring.

Maureen wanted to ask if he'd be faithful while she was away, but she didn't want to hear the answer, or see the expression on his face as he lied to her.

'I was thinking you might like to come with me.' She forced herself to sound light-hearted. 'Meet my family. Meet my father.' Having Charles's approval was extremely important to Maureen, however much she was forging her own path in life. The two of them had always adored one another, her father's unconditional love almost making up for her mother's coldness. Maureen had always felt protective towards Charles, knowing how much pain – physical and mental – he'd suffered from his war injuries, with the crippled right arm that the doctors had recommended should be amputated, though her father had never agreed.

John wrinkled his nose. 'I'm not sure I'm that kind of guy. I don't do well with fathers – they take against me.'

'Maybe you need to try a little harder…' Maureen began then broke off, knowing it was a sore subject. It was Farrow family legend that John was the product of an illicit liaison between his mother, Lucy, and King Edward VII. Whatever the truth, Lucy had died giving birth to John and he'd never known his father, being raised by his aunt and sent to boarding school in England.

'You know, I've been thinking,' John continued, changing the subject. 'Why don't we get a place together?'

'What?' Maureen was equal parts shocked and elated. To live together before marriage was almost unheard of for a respectable couple, but she'd done her fair share of breaking the rules and the prospect was exhilarating. Plus, it was commitment of a sort –

perhaps not a ring on her finger, but a very public statement that they were a couple, living as man and wife.

'Maybe a little Spanish place up in the hills. Or a cottage by the ocean, in Santa Monica or Malibu. Think about it,' John murmured, moving closer, his fingers finding her bare thighs and dancing over them, her skin puckering into goosebumps as he painted a picture for her. 'You, me, together. All day, all night…'

Maureen was overcome with desire at the very thought of it. Oh Lord, she might never get out of bed again.

'But we wouldn't be married,' she clarified, through the haze of lust that threatened to envelop her. 'We'd be what my fellow Catholics call living in sin?'

'I'd say we've already done our fair share of sinning, don't you reckon? A little more couldn't hurt.'

'But what would my father say?'

'I don't really care. I'm not asking him.' John's body language was masterful, his confidence enthralling.

Right now, Maureen was living in a hotel, although that wasn't as dull as it sounded. From the early days of her arrival in Hollywood, she'd been put up by the studio in a bungalow at the Garden of Allah on Sunset Boulevard. The hotel, once the home of the legendary silent movie actress Alla Nazimova, was fast acquiring legendary status; everyone who was anyone had been a guest there – Marlene Dietrich, Clara Bow, Tallulah Bankhead, F. Scott Fitzgerald, Ernest Hemingway – and all kinds of scandalous happenings had taken place around its unique swimming pool, reputedly shaped like the Black Sea.

Maureen was no stranger to shocking behaviour. *Tarzan and His Mate* had been released last month – she'd attended the premiere with John – and, whilst it had been hugely successful it had proved controversial, implying sexual relations between the unmarried Tarzan and Jane, not to mention Maureen's barely-there costume. There was talk of bringing in a code to rate films according to their content, so that audiences wouldn't be offended, and Maureen hated that she might be indirectly responsible for bringing about censorship in Hollywood.

Living with John before they were married, or even engaged, would be scandalous – heaven alone knew what her family back home would say. Well, she simply wouldn't tell them. It felt progressive and exciting. It felt *right*. She knew John was the man for her, regardless of his faults; it was just taking him a little longer to realise that she was the one for him.

'All right,' she giggled. 'Why not?'

John leaned across to kiss her, long, lingering, and sensual, the kind of kiss that made her want to surrender to him right there and then. If he'd wanted to make love in that secluded spot, Maureen would have agreed without hesitation.

Instead, he stood up, dusting the crumbs from his shorts and beginning to pack up the picnic. 'Come on, time to get going. We don't want to miss the ferry.'

'Right,' Maureen said quietly, desire and disappointment mingling. Was that it? Had he brought her all the way here just for a picnic? She watched him hopefully for tell-tale signs of an imminent proposal, for signs of nerves, or somewhere he might hide a ring box. John looked his usual calm, confident self as he folded up the picnic blanket, placing everything back in the leather saddle bag.

Maureen was never usually needy in relationships, but John wasn't like any man she'd met before. She was deeply in love with him. Despite his many faults, she wanted to be his wife, for them to be together for the rest of their lives. That he didn't seem to feel the same urgency was devastating.

'Is that it?' Maureen burst out in frustration.

John was striding back over to the horses. He stopped and turned around, squinting in the sunlight. 'Is *what* it?'

Maureen stared hard at him for a long moment, willing him to understand everything she was thinking and feeling. Was she being an idiot, holding out for him like this? She wasn't the only one expecting their engagement to be imminent – the gossip columns were rife with rumours, so John couldn't be blind and deaf to the speculation. Nor did he seem commitment-shy. In fact, John had been engaged twice before, and married once, with a seven-year-old daughter from his short marriage to Felice Lewin, the daughter of a millionaire mining tycoon; when she found out she was pregnant, her father forced John to marry her, but they'd divorced a couple of years later. In 1928, he'd become engaged to the silent film actress Lila Lee, but she broke it off after discovering he'd been unfaithful.

'Nothing.' Maureen narrowed her eyes, returning to the horses. She put her foot in the stirrup and pulled herself up, swinging her leg over and seating herself in the saddle. She nudged the eager stallion in the flanks and cantered off before John had a chance to respond.

The journey from Santa Catalina Island back to West Hollywood was a long one; the horseback ride to Two Harbours, the boat to Marina del Rey, the drive east along Venice Boulevard. Maureen was subdued, trying not to sulk; John hated it when she was downbeat.

As they drove through Culver City, they stopped at a gas station. As the attendant filled the Chrysler, John rested his arm casually along the back of Maureen's seat. She sat primly with her hands in her lap, looking straight ahead. John turned his head to look at her.

'I've been thinking, and I guess I'd better marry you.'

Maureen gasped, her excitement quickly replaced with suspicion. Was this a joke? She stared at him, unsure how to respond.

The gas attendant watched them both with interest.

'Why?' Maureen burst out.

'Because you make me happier than anyone else,' John said simply.

Maureen burst out laughing, a mixture of elation and relief. She threw her arms around him and kissed him, whilst the attendant stared at them as though they were crazy.

'If that's a proposal, John Villiers Farrow, then I say yes!'

Chapter Nineteen

VIVIEN

London, England

May 1935

London in the small hours was silent and slumbering, a nocturnal world where the birds had fallen quiet and the gas street lamps strained to penetrate the gloom. A tomcat prowled the pavement, concealed by the shadows as he sidled down an alleyway and disappeared into the darkness beyond. In the grand houses, blinds were down and curtains drawn, shutting out the city until daybreak.

Leigh and Vivien were in the back of a taxicab, heading eastward through the empty streets of Mayfair. They emerged at Piccadilly, mere moments from John Gliddon's office on Regent Street, passing the giant advertisements for Bovril and Guinness, Schweppes tonic water and Wrigley's gum that illuminated the side of the London Pavilion, before skirting Leicester Square and traversing Covent Garden. The street hawkers and flower sellers had long since gone home, and the city felt almost deserted: the theatres were dark; the shops closed and shuttered; the liveried doormen yawning idly outside the smart hotels.

The car turned onto Fleet Street and came to a stop. Leigh jumped out, purchasing half a dozen newspapers from the sellers outside the printing presses. They were the first editions and felt warm to the touch, the ink smearing on his hands.

'You look, darling. I just can't bear it,' Vivien told him as he rejoined her in the car. Her body was taut with anticipation, her velvet slip falling from her shoulders to reveal the milk-white skin beneath. She wore a Schiaparelli evening dress, upon which the scent of Arpège and cigarette smoke still lingered.

The *News Chronicle* lay on the top of the pile and Leigh flicked quickly to the review section, his eyes skirting over the critics' opinions of films and books and concerts. Then he turned the page and inhaled sharply, shocked to find his wife staring back at him.

'Oh, Leigh!' Vivien gasped, grasping his wrist as she leaned across to look. The publicity photograph took up almost a quarter of a page and showed her from the waist upwards in full eighteenth-century costume, corseted and bewigged, her dress cut low on the décolletage and a white silk bow encircling her neck. She looked elegant and poised, startlingly young. The heavy stage make-up accentuated her cheekbones, but it was her thickly kohled eyes that arrested the reader, the camera capturing that mesmeric quality which had so utterly beguiled reviewers and theatregoers alike.

Vivien pulled the paper from Leigh's hands, wanting to drink in everything they'd said, savour every word.

VIVIEN LEIGH SHINES IN NEW PLAY screamed the headline, in bold black capitals. *'Vivien Leigh is the name of a young actress whose distinguished beauty and sense of style in acting will astonish all London as they astonished the audience last night...'*

The other papers were similarly effusive. Leigh rifled through the *Daily Express* before reading aloud: *'A ravishing stage debutante whose beauty will be the talk of the town, Miss Leigh was the success of the evening...'* He finished the rest silently before Vivien handed him the *Daily Mail*: *'A new young British star... arose on the British stage last night with a spectacular suddenness which set playgoers cheering with surprised delight…'*

'They've put that I'm nineteen, how funny! Oh, look – you get a mention in this one: *"Vivien Leigh, who is married with one child…"'*

'That's hardly a mention.' Leigh forced a laugh, trying not to sound churlish, but Vivien was too preoccupied to notice.

She reached out to grab his hands, kissing him impulsively. 'Leigh, darling, can you believe it? I'm so happy, I truly am.'

'I'm glad,' he replied honestly, but there was a melancholy that belied his words, borne of the sudden realisation that their lives were about to change irreparably. Already he sensed a fracturing of their relationship, understanding now that Vivien could never be satisfied with being merely his wife, merely Suzanne's mother. However hard he tried, she would always want more than he could possibly give her.

Last night had been the opening of *The Mask of Virtue* at the Ambassadors Theatre, where Vivien was playing Henriette Duquesnoy – a prostitute presented as an innocent girl of good reputation to lure the Marquis D'Arcy into a marriage that would disgrace him – and she had triumphed in the role. Afterwards, at the cast party at the Florida Club, Leigh had been bursting with pride to be by her side, to be introduced as her husband to this motley crew of actors and stagehands and assorted theatre types. It was an entirely different world from his own, and he felt his irrelevance. Here, no one deferred to him because he was a barrister. He was treated politely, yet indifferently; tolerated because he was Vivien's husband. Vivien, by contrast, was in her element. Leigh saw the effect she had on people, captivating the crowd just as she'd captivated him at the Devon Hunt Ball.

The taxi rumbled on, turning back across the city towards Mayfair as Vivien pored over the papers, excited as a child opening a stocking on Christmas morning. Dawn was breaking, the earliest shafts of pale light filtering through the city gloom and falling across her face. It gave her the appearance of being lit from within, and Leigh didn't think he'd ever seen her so happy or so radiant – not even on their wedding day.

As the car pulled up outside their house in Little Stanhope Street, Leigh stifled a yawn. Vivien would be awake for hours, he knew, but he would go directly to bed. He had to be in court by nine o'clock, and he had a full day ahead of him.

———————

'I'm sorry, John, but this simply isn't good enough.' Vivien burst into John Gliddon's office in a fury.

John looked up in surprise as his secretary followed in Vivien's wake, her expression apologetic. John nodded to her and she left the room, closing the door behind her.

'Do sit down, Vivien. To what do I owe the pleasure?'

Vivien declined his invitation and remained standing. 'It's been five months since *The Mask of Virtue* opened. Five! I had reporters outside my front door, there was a blaze of publicity and then – nothing!'

'Nothing apart from a fifty-thousand-pound deal with Alexander Korda.'

Vivien gave a rather unladylike snort of derision. 'Not that anything's materialised from it. I need to be busy, John. I *need* to act.'

John regarded his client, exquisite as always in a long-sleeved green dress with a button front and cinched-in waistband. The anger leant a focus to her features, her blue-green eyes ablaze, her jawline defined as she jutted her chin. He understood her frustration. *The Mask of Virtue* had turned her into a sensation, quite literally overnight, and the morning after the play opened every newspaper editor in London had sent a journalist to her house to request an interview. Vivien had graciously consented, agreeing to be pictured in a variety of outfits and even being photographed with Suzanne, leading to a slew of pieces about 'having it all' with Vivien hailed as the epitome of womanhood for acquiring a husband, a young child and a career, all whilst managing 'a small staff of servants' in her Mayfair home.

Then came the lucrative contract with Alexander Korda, one of the most powerful men in films, which made Vivien the country's highest-paid film actress at the stroke of a pen. But Korda was notorious for signing up-and-coming talent purely in order to prevent his rivals from securing them, without having suitable projects available, and that fate appeared to have befallen Vivien. Leslie Howard had cabled from Broadway requesting that she appear with him in *Hamlet*, but while Korda dithered on whether to release her, the part was given to another actress. A mooted film of Cyrano de Bergerac, with Vivien opposite Charles Laughton, had also frustratingly failed to materialise.

'I'm waiting for the right role,' John explained, smiling in a way he hoped would appease her. 'We have to be patient, to make sure your next move is the right one.'

'I don't have time to be patient.' Vivien was not one to sit around and wait for opportunities to come to her. She believed in creating her own luck.

'Look, keep yourself busy. Make sure you're seen around town. Go to lunches, nightclubs, the latest plays – anywhere you might be seen by casting directors. Something will happen soon, I promise you.'

Vivien had taken John's advice to heart, launching herself onto London's social scene with her customary zeal. She lunched regularly at the Ivy and the Savoy Grill, took supper at the Ritz and the Criterion, dragged Leigh to parties and premieres every evening – and if Leigh wouldn't go, Vivien certainly wasn't short of willing companions to squire her around town. She ensured she was seen in all the right places, attended exhibitions and gallery openings, and – most importantly – kept up with the latest West End shows.

In the autumn of 1935, the hottest ticket in town was a production of *Romeo and Juliet* at the New Theatre. In a novel twist, the roles of Romeo and Mercutio were to be alternated between John Gielgud and Laurence Olivier, with Olivier taking the first stint as Romeo and Gielgud taking over five weeks later.

Vivien purchased two tickets for a matinée performance and invited her actress friend Beryl Samson to join her. As they took their seats in the stalls, only a few rows back from the centre of the action, Vivien was fizzing with energy.

'It's had the most wonderful reviews. I can't wait to see it,' she confided to Beryl.

'Laurence Olivier's supposed to be sensational,' Beryl agreed. 'Did I tell you I met him last week at the Colony Club? Peggy introduced us. He was a total delight – utterly charming.'

'What did he—' Vivien began, but then the house lights went down and she fell quiet, eyes wide with anticipation. The prologue was spoken and the Capulets took to the stage, followed by the Montagues, their long-standing feud swiftly established and the opening scenes energetic and bold, full of action as swords were drawn and a fierce fight ensued. Vivien was on the edge of her seat, wincing with every blow. Then came Olivier's lovelorn Romeo, pining for the affections of Rosaline. He was young and vital, unquestionably good-looking, with a commanding voice and a powerful presence. He moved with a raw athleticism, physically impressive and bold in his use of the space as he pushed himself to his limits. Vivien was unable to tear her eyes away from him. There was something magnetic in his performance, a raw sexuality that she'd never seen on stage before, and it stirred something within her, a sense of exhilaration and energy, as though the world had been brought into sharper focus by this incredible performance, this incredible man. It was ground-breaking, and electrifying to witness. When the lights came up, Vivien was breathless.

'Let's go backstage,' she told Beryl. 'You can introduce me.'

'If you want.' Beryl was amused but not surprised by Vivien's reaction; she knew that her friend was audacious and impulsive, instinctively drawn to talent and good looks.

Beryl spoke to the staff and the two of them were led to Larry's dressing room. It was a cramped, rather messy space, with a large mirror and a dressing table filled with cards and flowers, half a dozen books and a dog-eared, heavily annotated script. Costumes hung from a rail, with discarded props leaning against a wall, and there was a small leather sofa draped with a cashmere throw. Larry was surrounded by a group of admirers, everyone in high spirits as they congratulated him on his performance. He'd removed his shirt and was bare-chested, a fine sheen of sweat on his skin.

Vivien stood just inside the door, waiting for her moment. Outwardly, she remained as poised and collected as ever, but inwardly she was bubbling with excitement, overflowing with impatience, using this time to drink in every detail. Her eyes traced the perfectly pronounced cupid's bow of his upper lip, the distinctive cleft of his chin, the heavy eyebrows that added a broodiness to his expression, and the softly rounded curves of his cheekbones. His torso was smooth and lightly muscled, with a line of dark hair below his navel.

One by one, the others said their goodbyes and melted away. Larry looked up and his eyes met Vivien's. She didn't wait for Beryl to introduce them.

'Hello,' she said, stepping towards him. It was a warm autumnal day, and she was wearing an emerald-green wrap dress with a button front, the colour perfectly complementing the vivid blue-green of her eyes, with a thick belt emphasising her tiny waist. Her long dark hair was loose, with the sides pinned up in a way that drew attention to her extraordinary cheekbones, a slick of mascara highlighting those feline eyes. 'I'm Vivien Leigh.'

Larry got up from his seat, kissing her on each cheek. 'I know. I saw you in *The Mask of Virtue*. You were quite the revelation.'

Vivien smiled, but there was nothing calculated or contrived in the gesture – she was utterly thrilled by his praise, and the knowledge that he'd seen her perform. Being so close to him was intoxicating. 'Thank you,' she managed.

'What are you working on next?'

'I've been offered Jenny Mere in *The Happy Hypocrite* with Ivor Novello, but I haven't made a decision yet.'

'I think you should do it.'

'Then I will,' Vivien responded instantly. They hadn't taken their eyes off each other since the conversation began.

'There's a production of *Richard II* coming up, with John Gielgud. You should audition for it. You'd make the most marvellous Queen.'

'I've always rather suspected I would,' Vivien replied, with a delightful giggle. 'And thank you for the tip, I'll speak to my agent.'

'Well, if you need any further advice we should have lunch some time.'

'I'd like that.'

The two of them locked eyes for a long moment. Vivien's heart was beating rapidly, her chest rising and falling as her breath came quick and shallow. Beryl coughed awkwardly.

'We should get going. Leave you to get changed.'

'It was nice to see you again, Beryl,' Larry smiled. 'And wonderful to meet you, Vivien. I hope to see you again soon.'

'I'm sure you will.' As Vivien turned to go, she impulsively kissed his bare shoulder, before hurrying out of the door. As they left the theatre, she was positively giddy. Beryl followed in shock, astonished by the scene she'd just witnessed.

'What on earth did you do that for?'

'I don't know.' Vivien shrugged delightedly. 'I wanted to kiss him.'

Beryl stared at her, uncomprehendingly.

'In fact,' Vivien ran on, the words spilling freely and honestly, 'I'd like to marry him.'

'He's already married,' Beryl stated, as though that was an end to the matter, before remembering: 'And so are you!'

Vivien said nothing. She merely smiled enigmatically, the taste of Larry's skin still on her lips.

Single reported defeat for alter ego (4,4).

Vivien was sitting in the parlour in her favourite armchair, a copy of *The Times* folded on her knee and open at the crossword. The house was quiet; Nanny had taken Suzanne for a walk in Green Park and Mrs Bradley, the housekeeper who'd come with them when they moved from St John's Wood, was out running errands.

Single reported defeat…

Vivien mulled over the clue, tapping her fountain pen rhythmically against the paper. Whilst she adored being busy and surrounded by people, she also loved to sit quietly and read a novel or a script, to immerse herself in another world just as she could do when acting. Completing the daily crossword kept her mind active and alert, and she enjoyed the rigorous mental challenge.

Soul mate, she realised, triumphantly. As she entered the letters, in her small, neat handwriting, the telephone in the hallway began to ring. Vivien ignored it, reading the next clue, but the ringing was insistent and she realised there was no one else in the house to answer it.

'Hello?'

'Vivien? It's John.'

'Ah, good morning, Mr Gliddon. I do hope you have some good news for me.'

'I do, as a matter of fact. I've just come from a meeting with Alexander Korda. He's producing a new film, called *Fire Over England*, with Flora Robson as Queen Elizabeth. He thinks you'd be perfect for the role of Cynthia – one of her ladies in waiting, and the granddaughter of her advisor Lord Burleigh.'

At the other end of the line, Vivien pulled a face. 'It sounds rather dull, if I'm being honest. But do tell me more. Is there a script? Has anyone else been cast?'

'Korda's promised to send the script over first thing tomorrow. I do know of at least one other actor that's signed a contract, and I believe you're familiar with his work.' John paused to clear his throat. When he spoke again, he sounded amused. 'The man they've cast as your lover is Laurence Olivier.'

Chapter Twenty

Capri, Italy

October 1936

'By Jove, you've outdone yourself this time, Vivling. It's superb!'

'It does look rather marvellous, doesn't it?'

Vivien stepped out of the taxi, smiling graciously at the uniformed porter who had opened the door. Her eyes were shielded behind tortoiseshell sunglasses as she gazed up at the stately hotel, its grand facade soft yellow as though ripened by the Italian sun.

'Tell me again how you heard about this place?' Oswald Frewen asked, fresh in a miraculously uncrumpled white shirt and linen trousers, as he emerged from the other side of the car and followed Vivien up the steps. At fifty years old, with greying hair and an aristocratic face, he cut a distinguished figure, his shoulders broad and his posture upright as befitted a former Royal Navy Commander.

The trip had originally been planned for Vivien and Leigh, a relaxing break after filming *Fire Over England*, but at the last moment Leigh had been unable to go due to work commitments so he suggested that his old friend Oswald accompany his wife. Oswald and Leigh had known one another for many years. He was the first person Leigh had confided in when intending to propose to Vivien, and he was affable and charming and from a very well-connected family: his sister was the sculptor Clare Sheridan, and their first cousin was the politician Winston Churchill.

'I was talking to a gentleman on the train to Rome, and he told me that the *only* place to stay in Capri was the Quisisana,' Vivien explained.

'I can understand why,' Oswald agreed, looking round appreciatively at the lavish interior, with its gilded bronze statues and rococo chandeliers. 'And to think, Capri wasn't even on our original itinerary.'

'I know, but I'd always longed to visit, and when I found out how easy it was to take the seaplane to Naples, my mind was made up.'

'And was the flight worth it?' Oswald teased. Always a nervous flyer, Vivien had been terrified on the noisy, turbulent journey, praying fervently in a way she hadn't for years.

'Oh yes,' Vivien smiled. 'I'm sure it will all be worth it.'

The two of them crossed the marble floor towards the reception desk. Vivien seemed somewhat nervy, glancing skittishly around her, but Oswald assumed she was still on edge following the difficult flight. They'd been touring Italy for almost a week now, travelling down through the country to Sicily, before this whim of Vivien's to see Capri took hold.

'Darling!' Vivien cried, her voice ringing out across the lobby. The other guests turned to stare, trying to discover the source of the commotion.

Oswald did the same. Following Vivien's gaze, he was startled to see Laurence Olivier and his wife, Jill Esmond, walking towards them.

'Vivien!' Larry exclaimed.

Jill looked just as shocked as he did, Oswald noted, but quickly recovered herself, calling out joyfully, 'Vivling!'

The three of them came together, kissing one another on both cheeks and professing delight, as Viven made the introductions and Oswald looked on in bewilderment.

'What a splendid coincidence!'

'Such a wonderful surprise.'

'How lovely to see you, Vivien.'

'It's terribly funny because we weren't even supposed to *be* in Capri, were we, Oswald?'

'No, last-minute change to the itinerary,' he agreed, looking somewhat bemused.

'Well, what a serendipitous addition,' Jill smiled. Dark-haired, with patrician features, she was from a wealthy theatrical family – her father was the actor and playwright Henry Esmond, and her mother, Eva Moore, a respected veteran of stage and screen. Jill herself had enjoyed considerable acting success – West End, Broadway, Hollywood – and her talent was undeniable; her joy at seeing Vivien would have convinced all but the most astute of observers.

'Oh Jilli, you're just too adorable. And you're looking so well! You've almost lost the baby weight, and this glorious Italian sunshine will soon clear up your complexion. Who's looking after little Tarquin?'

'He's in London with Nanny,' Jill replied, bearing up in the face of Vivien's assault. 'Larry and I are having a romantic week away, just the two of us. He's been working so hard recently.'

'You're not breastfeeding then? It's probably for the best. I hated it, and it absolutely ruined my figure.'

Involuntarily, the three of them looked at Vivien, three gazes running in unison over her slender frame and pert bosom, shown to best advantage in a close-fitting blouse and navy sailor shorts. She looked completely at ease in the glamorous surroundings of the Quisisana, polished and flawless, with her hair swept up in a neat roll, her flat pumps emphasising her diminutive stature. Her immaculate appearance was in marked contrast to Jill, who had given birth just ten weeks ago. It had been a difficult pregnancy, followed by a long and complicated labour, and Jill's body was still recovering. Her limbs were swollen and her face was covered with unsightly red blemishes, her heavy frame swathed in a rather frumpy polka-dot dress.

'Shall we check in?' Oswald suggested breezily, breaking the awkward silence.

'Would you? That would be just darling of you. Jill, would you keep Oswald company? I'd love to look around, I've heard there's the most beautiful view from the gardens. Larry, would you show me?'

'Of course.'

'Splendid!' Vivien tucked her arm through his, and the two of them set off without looking back.

'And of course you were quite brilliant as Romeo…'

'Thank you, that's very kind.' Larry inclined his head faux-modestly. 'But you see the difficulty with Romeo is that one's trying to play him for sympathy when his main character drive is an erection.'

Oswald guffawed and Vivien let out a peal of outraged laughter. Jill smiled politely, with the air of one who'd heard that line a number of times before, as she scooped up a mouthful of *spaghetti alle vongole*.

The four of them were dining al fresco on the hotel's terrace, with Jill and Larry opposite one another and Vivien between them, across from Oswald. The restaurant hummed with lively conversation and the discreet strains of a string quartet, and the group were in high spirits, a second bottle of *piedirosso* open on the table. The setting couldn't have been more perfect: the gardens of the Quisisana were teeming with oversized roses, delicate freesias and lisianthus blooming in a dozen different shades. Pine and cypress trees swept down to the sapphire-blue sea, lit golden as the sun began its descent, the dramatic *faraglioni* rock formations rising high above the waves. The evening held a faint chill, the autumnal temperature reminding them all that summer was over and change was in the air.

'We were planning our own production of *Romeo and Juliet*, weren't we darling?' Jill said conversationally. 'Until Johnny cast you in his show and that put the kibosh on our idea.'

'Larry's just so knowledgeable about the classics, isn't he?' Vivien gushed. She'd ordered a salad, a regional speciality with juicy tomatoes and fresh basil, but it lay, barely touched, in front of her. 'I've learned so much from him already, it'll be such a delight to work with him again.'

Jill blanched. The food was suddenly dry as sawdust in her mouth, balling like concrete in her stomach. 'I don't understand… I thought the film was finished?'

'Larry's offered me the role of Ophelia in *Hamlet*. Isn't it thrilling?'

Jill blinked. Once, twice. The noise from the other guests seemed to heighten and warp, her vision swimming as she struggled to bring her husband's face into focus. 'I thought we'd discussed me playing that role.'

'Yes, but…' He had the good grace to look ashamed. 'Well, nothing was finalised, was it?'

'Oh, Jilli, darling it's far too soon for you to even *think* about getting back on stage again. You need to recuperate after having a baby. Spend time with little Tarquin and enjoy the domestic life for a while. *I'll* take care of Larry in Denmark.' Vivien reached across, placing a proprietorial hand on his arm.

Jill gripped the edge of the table as she waited for Larry to speak, to contradict Vivien and defend his wife. But he said nothing, seemingly absorbed in devouring a broth-soaked mussel as he speared the meat and discarded the shell. Fury and humiliation and helplessness raged through Jill, as she fantasised briefly about depositing the entire bowl in his lap.

She wasn't stupid; she'd heard the rumours about her husband and Vivien during the filming of *Fire Over England*. The signs had been impossible to ignore: Vivien's slip during Jill's pregnancy, when she'd referred to the unborn baby by the name that Jill and Larry had vowed to keep a secret; the two of them sloping off together at a mutual friend's dinner party, Larry returning covered in lipstick; when Jill went into labour and Larry raced to her bedside, Vivien's scent all over him like a cheap suit.

Jill had hoped that now filming had finished, time alone together – and time away from Vivien – would make Larry forget this passing infatuation and remember that his loyalties lay with his wife and newborn son. But now Vivien was here and everything was slipping away and Jill feared she'd lost him. It was simply impossible to compete with this beautiful, vivacious creature who'd set her sights on Larry and wasn't going to stop until she had him. The feeling was clearly reciprocated; Larry had barely taken his eyes off Vivien since she'd arrived.

'Do excuse me, Oswald.' Jill stood up. Her face was steely, her voice controlled. 'I have a sudden headache. I'm going to return to my room.'

Oswald frowned, oblivious to the cause of Jill's distress, as she threw down her napkin and rushed out of the restaurant. 'Oh dear, what a shame. I do hope she'll be all right.'

'Perhaps a little too much sun today,' Larry suggested. 'I'm sure she'll be right as rain in the morning.'

After coffee, followed by grappa, Oswald said goodnight and retired to his room. Vivien and Larry decided to take a walk in the hotel grounds. The sun had sunk below the horizon, the silvery moon high above the bay, with the majestic bulk of the Quisisana silhouetted against a purple sky and the heady scent of orchids and lilies perfuming the twilight air. The pathways were quiet and Vivien and Larry walked closely beside one another, their shoulders almost touching, fingers occasionally brushing.

'I still can't believe you're here,' Larry smiled, his eyes soft.

'Was it terribly naughty of me? I couldn't rest knowing that you were here and I was in Sicily and it was only a short plane ride away. So I developed a sudden longing to see Capri and told Oswald we simply had to go. He's such a darling, he agreed to whatever I wanted.'

'Who could blame him?'

They walked on, wordlessly, the only sound coming from the whispering sea beyond the trees. Eventually, Vivien spoke: 'When I get back to London, I'm going to leave Leigh.'

'Don't say that, Viv.'

'Why not? I mean it. This last week without you has been utterly unbearable. I can't be apart from you ever again, my darling.' Vivien went to embrace him but Larry stopped her, his hands gently enveloping hers.

'It's not that simple.'

'Of course it is. I want to be with you and I know you want to be with me.' There was a desperation to Vivien's tone. She'd thrown down the gauntlet and offered to leave her husband, but instead of Larry being delighted, she could feel him pulling away from her. She'd always known he would take some persuading; religion and morality were even more deeply rooted in him than they were in Vivien. Larry's father had been an Anglican priest, and despite father and son having a difficult relationship, Gerard Kerr Olivier had managed to press guilt and honour irreversibly into his youngest child's psyche.

'We can't just abandon everyone and pretend we have no responsibilities. You have a child. *I* have a child. I can't simply leave Jill. She's been a wonderful wife to me and I owe her so much.'

'Do you love her?'

'Yes! And you love Leigh, I know you do.'

'I love him, yes, in the same way one loves one's favourite uncle or the family Labrador—'

'*Vivien!*'

'But I'm not *in love* with him. And yes, I'm aware that's such a terribly dull cliché. But I love *you*, and I know you love me. Don't try and deny it.'

'I'm not going to deny it. I've fallen madly in love with you and I want nothing more than for us to be together. But it can't happen.'

'Why not?'

Larry closed his eyes, rubbing a hand wearily across his face. 'Think of our careers, our reputations. The scandal would be colossal.'

'I don't care about any of that! All I care about is you!'

Vivien's heart was racing, her tone shrill and her movements agitated. She knew that she was behaving irrationally, but Larry had become her whole world, her need for him bordering on obsession. He was everything she wanted, everything she craved in a man – passionate, inspirational, devastatingly handsome, and he understood her in a way that Leigh never had and never would. Larry recognised her talent, saw that her ambitions matched his own, and Vivien longed to learn all he had to teach her.

During the making of *Fire Over England*, they had fallen hopelessly, inevitably, in love. Once they'd acknowledged their feelings for one another, the relationship had quickly turned physical. They made love two, three, times a day, slipping away whenever they found a spare moment. Vivien had barely slept for weeks, for if she was sleeping, she wasn't with Larry. Her whole world revolved around him, and she was going half mad from trying to live a double life: successful actress and Larry's lover on the one hand, wife and mother on the other. She'd made very little attempt to conceal their affair, but Leigh barely seemed to notice, unable to conceive that anyone should act so dishonourably.

In the heady surroundings of the film set, Vivien hadn't

doubted the sincerity of Larry's feelings, certain that he loved her just as deeply as she loved him. But now shooting had finished and Vivien was terrified of losing him. If she couldn't be with Larry, it would destroy her.

'Don't you feel guilty?' His voice was little more than a whisper. 'I lie awake at night, with Jill sleeping soundly beside me, and I can't stop thinking about you. I hold my son in my arms and the only thought in my head is when I'm going to see you again, and the guilt and shame are so overwhelming that I feel I might suffocate from the sheer weight of them.'

'Of course I feel guilty.' Vivien moved towards him, gently cupping his cheek in the palm of her hand. She laughed softly. 'I was raised Roman Catholic, guilt is all I know. But don't we deserve happiness too?'

Larry didn't respond and the silence seemed never-ending. Vivien tried to make out the expression on his face, but clouds now covered the moon and the darkness was impenetrable.

Sometimes she felt as though she were going insane from the never-ending cycle of thoughts in her head: guilt, lust, shame, desire.

But it would all be worth it, she assured herself, when they were finally together. Their future would be idyllic: the two of them learning lines together beside the fire, deliberating over roles and character motivations, riding high in the London theatre – for Larry had told her there was no medium greater than the theatre, no genre superior to the classics – falling in and out of bed every spare moment they had.

'Darling?' She put her hand on his arm, realising with concern that he hadn't responded. To her alarm, he shook her hand off.

'I'm sorry,' Larry said finally. 'I love you desperately, but we can't do this. *I* can't do this. We have to do the right thing.'

He hugged her stiffly then walked away.

Chapter Twenty-One

MAUREEN

Los Angeles, USA

December 1936

Maureen and John were married on a glorious day in September of 1936, at St Monica's Church in Santa Monica. The bride's family hadn't been able to travel from Ireland for the wedding – with so many relatives to coordinate, and Maureen only granted a few days' break from her hectic filming schedule, it simply wasn't feasible for them to make the long journey – so the O'Sullivan clan descended on Maureen and John's new marital home in Bel Air shortly before Christmas. The Spanish-style house was beautiful, with lush gardens and a swimming pool and three permanent staff – a cook, a chauffeur and a dresser. Maureen was proud for her family to see it, eager to show them who she'd become and what she'd created with her life.

The day after they arrived, Maureen threw a party in their honour, amused to see her mother chatting animatedly with Bing Crosby, her sisters starstruck at the sight of Gary Cooper.

'Do you like him, Pa?' Maureen asked, as she linked her arm through her father's and nodded discreetly in John's direction.

'At least he's Catholic,' Charles replied, his voice thin and quavering. His bouts of ill health were becoming more frequent of late, though he'd been well enough to make the journey across the Atlantic, rallying at the thought of seeing his eldest daughter, his favourite child. 'The Holy Father saw fit to grant you permission, and that's the most important thing.'

As John had been married before, and to a Jewish woman, they'd needed a dispensation from Pope Pius XII to allow him to marry in a Catholic church. It had taken two years to be granted, but Maureen had emphasised to her father how devout John was, how a plethora of priests and even the Archbishop of Los Angeles were regular guests at their home, and how he'd lived amongst lepers on Tahiti, writing a book about the community priest, Father Damien, which he'd been told would likely see him made a Papal Knight the following year. She *hadn't* told Charles about the other book John had written, a rather more racy tome called *Laughter Ends*, on the subject of Polynesian prostitutes.

'I know, Pa, but what about—' Maureen wanted to press him further – even though they were very different characters, it was important to her that her father approved of John – but then her younger sister, sixteen-year-old Sheila, bounced over. Her cheeks were flushed with excitement, her dark hair coming loose around her face.

'Maureen, Clark Gable is *right over there*!'

'I know, my darling, I invited him! Come on, let's go talk to him.'

'Oh no, I couldn't possibly,' Sheila squealed, turning an even deeper shade of puce. She had a pretty, heart-shaped face and pale Irish skin, but she lacked the star quality of her older sister.

'So, what do you think of our Sheila's chances of making it in the movies?' Mary O'Sullivan asked, as she sidled over. She'd put on weight over the years, her hips wide and thickly padded, her greying hair styled in a centre parting and looped up over each ear, giving her a somewhat eccentric appearance.

'She'll have to lose weight,' John Farrow interjected, overhearing their conversation.

'I've been trying!' Sheila protested. 'I was living on nothing but cream crackers 'til I got so hungry I thought I'd faint.'

'Well, we can help you with that,' Maureen said, with a warning look at John. 'You must swim every day in our pool, and I'll set you up with some tennis lessons too. It's a terrific way to keep trim.'

'Thank you,' Sheila replied gratefully.

'We thought you could put in a good word with the studio,' Mary ran on. 'Set up some screen tests and castings and whatnot.'

'I'll see what I can do.' Maureen eyed her little sister critically. 'But you must grow out your eyebrows – they're over-plucked, and it's not the fashion. Grow your hair too, and make sure not to sit out in the sun. A tan doesn't look good on camera.'

'I'll try, I promise,' Sheila said earnestly. She was all of five-foot nothing, wearing a beautiful dress that Charles had paid a considerable sum for, but its ruffles and lace looked out of place in sophisticated Bel Air.

'We'll need to get you properly fitted for a bra – they prefer them a different shape here. And I'll take you on a tour of the studio, introduce you to people and show you the sets.'

'Imagine that!' Mary exclaimed gleefully. '*Two* stars in the O'Sullivan house!'

'How long are you thinking of staying?' John asked bluntly, as Maureen shot him another look.

'Charles and the others will return soon – they're booked on the *Queen Mary* in two weeks' time,' Mary explained, 'But Sheila and I will stay for a month or two at least. Longer, if her career takes off.'

Although John looked appalled at the prospect, feigning horror, Maureen knew that he and Mary got on well. Whilst Mary had never made much of an effort with her eldest child – Maureen had witnessed her dark side too many times to be truly comfortable around her, dealing with the mood swings, the rages, the cruel words – outwardly she was convivial and charming, a great Irish raconteur.

'Pa, I'll miss you.' Maureen turned to her father. She was worried about him; he seemed to grow increasingly frail with every season that passed, his frame slender, his hair almost gone, his moustache thinning. 'Although you might see more of me next year. I've signed up for a picture that's to be filmed in London, so I'll only be a short hop across the sea. Mother, do you remember my friend from Roehampton, Vivian Hartley?'

'Oh yes, such a pretty little thing. Whatever happened to her?'

'She married a London barrister, but she's an actress too – isn't that a coincidence? She always longed to be, even when we were in school together, and she was terribly good.'

'She didn't get banned from the school plays then?' Charles thundered, his brow furrowed.

'No, Pa,' Maureen smiled. 'But we've both been cast in the same film, *A Yank at Oxford*.'

'How funny, the two of you actresses. Won't that be lovely, to see one another again.'

'Oh yes,' Maureen beamed. 'I can't wait.'

Vivien stared at her face in the dressing-room mirror. Beneath the exposed bulbs she looked cold and hard, almost trashy, her eyes lined with kohl and her dark lashes coated with several layers of mascara. Her lips were painted an attention-seeking red, her black jacket trimmed at the collar and cuffs with a garish leopard print. She looked like a harlot, like a woman who would betray her husband with another man.

Vivien frowned at her reflection, feeling her image was uncomfortably close to her real-life situation. She had asked George B. Seitz, the director, to tone down the look and make it less obvious, but he had outright refused.

Picking up a pot of cold cream, Vivien unscrewed the lid and scooped the thick concoction onto her fingertips, working it into her alabaster skin to remove all traces of the heavy make-up her role required. Vivien's character, Elsa Craddock, was something of a man-eater, married to an older, dull bookseller in Oxford but with a particular fondness for seducing young male students.

She was wiping the last of the cream from her cheeks when there was a knock on the door. Opening it, her hand flew to her mouth in surprise and delight.

'Maureen!'

'Oh, it's so good to see you, Vivling!'

Maureen threw her arms around Vivien, and the two women hugged tightly, before standing back and taking in one another.

'You look wonderful,' Vivien gushed. Maureen was pretty and petite, in a cream dress with a cinched-in waist and pussy-bow neck. 'I can't believe it's been so long. What is it? Ten years?'

'At least. We've both been rather busy,' Maureen joked. 'And you look more beautiful than ever.'

'Hardly. This hair style's terribly unflattering, not to mention the awful make-up.'

The two women stared at each other, years disappearing in seconds, as they reflected on everything that had happened in the decade since they'd been schoolgirls together at Roehampton – relationships, marriages, families, roles won, contracts signed, ambitions fulfilled.

They'd kept in touch sporadically, with invitations to significant events that were declined due to clashing schedules, but by pure coincidence they'd both been cast in this film. They only had one scene together; Vivien, as Elsa, was having an affair with the brother of Maureen's character, and the two women had a brief, bad-tempered exchange.

'When did you arrive in England?'

'Yesterday. I thought I'd come down to the set today and take a look around. I start filming on Monday.'

'Well, the timing couldn't be more perfect. I've finished for the day, so we can have a jolly old catch-up. Can I get you a tea or coffee? Or I've got a bottle of gin and some Schweppes tonic water if you fancy something stronger?'

'Oh, you've twisted my arm, I'll have a proper drink.' Maureen settled herself in one of the chintz armchairs, whilst Vivien was all too aware of the deficiencies of her small dressing room as she busied herself with the glasses and the bottles.

'Could you imagine what Mother Lennox would say if she could see us now?' she smiled.

'Oh, she was a wicked old cat, wasn't she?'

'She certainly was.'

'She'd have a coronary if she saw us drinking hard liquor in the afternoon, both of us *actresses*.'

Vivien smiled, playing along. 'Yes, we were supposed to make good marriages and settle down to a terribly dull future and be happy with our lot.'

'Cheers to escaping provincial life,' Maureen toasted, as Vivien handed her a highball glass.

'To defying expectations,' Vivien returned, taking a sip.

'You always did want to be an actress, didn't you?'

'Well, I'm little more than an extra in this film. *You're* the star, darling.'

'Don't be silly.'

'It's true. You're world famous now, thanks to *Tarzan*.'

An awkwardness descended on the room, and Vivien realised her words sounded more bitter than she'd intended. In truth, she *did* feel envious of her old friend. As Maureen had noted, Vivien had been the one with acting aspirations, and now here was Maureen achieving everything Vivien had longed for. Although Vivien's role in *A Yank at Oxford* was substantial, Maureen had higher billing. That was to be expected – she had more than thirty films under her belt by now, whilst Vivien had just half a dozen and was mostly unknown outside Britain – but it still rankled.

Vivien took a slug of her drink; the tonic was bitter, the lemon sharp. 'I'm sorry if that sounded...' She trailed off. 'I didn't mean—'

'Don't worry. Tell me everything that's happening with you,' Maureen beamed, a deliberate attempt to change the subject. 'You're a married woman now! I'm so sorry I couldn't make the wedding. It must have been a wonderful day.'

'It was lovely but—'

'And you're a mother now, too?'

'Yes, to Suzanne.'

'Oh! A little girl, how heavenly. How old is she?'

'Almost four.'

'I bet she's just the sweetest thing. Do you have a photograph of her? I'd love to have a daughter. John and I hope to be blessed with children very soon.'

'Oh, of course, you were married last year, weren't you? Do tell me all about him.'

'His name's John Farrow, and he's a screenwriter. Australian,' Maureen gushed, and it seemed suddenly that they'd been transported back to the dormitories of Roehampton, trading confidences, and giggling about a handsome boy they'd met in the holidays. 'And he's Catholic, so the Reverend Mother Ashton Case would have approved,' Maureen joked.

'Well, my husband and I are separated and I'm begging him for a divorce, so I doubt very much the Reverend Mother Ashton Case would have approved of *me*.'

'Oh...' Maureen faltered. 'I'm sorry, I didn't... I didn't know.'

'No need to be sorry, but you must be just about the only person who doesn't know, darling. I'm with Larry now – Olivier. We're going to get married, just as soon as my husband and his wife will grant us a divorce, which neither of them will do, so we're locked in this horrible stalemate. Larry and I are desperately in love, but we can't openly be together.'

Maureen's eyes were wide, unsure how to respond to Vivien's revelations.

'I'm sorry, darling. Have I shocked you?'

'No, not at all. It's rather a surprise, that's all. John had been married before, and we had to get a Papal dispensation to allow us marry in the Catholic church. My father would have had kittens if we'd done anything else.'

'It's impossible to escape the guilt, isn't it? Religion is always there, hanging over us, pointing its judgemental finger. Larry feels it more keenly than I do – his father was a vicar and his upbringing was even stricter than mine. And he has a son – Tarquin's just turned one – whom he misses dreadfully.'

'You must love him desperately. I can see it in your face.'

'Oh, darling, I do,' Vivien gushed. She looked radiant as she spoke of her lover, relieved to finally have someone she could confide in. 'It's all-consuming. Every moment I'm not with him, I'm desperate to be back with him. I'm barely sleeping because I want to spend every spare minute with him.'

'Are you living together?' Maureen asked, thrilling to the romance of it all.

Vivien nodded, her eyes sparkling. 'Larry's found us a darling little house in Chelsea. We've committed adultery and we're living in sin and it's quite glorious! But we're having to keep it quiet because of *public opinion*.' Vivien rolled her eyes. 'It's all so silly. I'm sure the public get up to heaven knows what behind their net curtains, yet Larry and I are expected to be squeaky clean. It's like Edward and Mrs Simpson. But I don't care about the scandal, I just want to be with Larry.'

'Does... Does your daughter live with the two of you?' Maureen ventured.

Vivien's ecstatic expression faltered for a moment. 'No, she... she stayed with Leigh. It's not terribly practical to have a child around – I'm travelling and working so much. She adores her nanny, and my mother visits regularly. As do I, of course.' Her voice dropped to a whisper, her eyes wide. 'Do you think I'm a terrible person?'

'Oh, darling, of course not!' Maureen took Vivien's hands,

squeezing them reassuringly. 'It sounds frightfully complicated, and I'm sure you're doing your best.'

Vivien nodded, buoyed by the reassurance. 'My love for Larry eclipses everything. I can't explain it. Do you feel like that about John? I love him, but… I sometimes feel I should die without him.'

'Oh, Vivling,' Maureen's expression was sympathetic. Vivien slipped her hands from Maureen's, embarrassed by how much she'd revealed, as she turned away and took a moment to compose herself. She drained her drink and began to undress, taking off the trashy costume she wore as Elsa Craddock. 'You don't mind, do you?'

'Of course not. Go ahead.' Maureen averted her eyes to give Vivien some privacy. 'Oh, are you reading this?' she exclaimed, as her gaze fell on a copy of *Gone with the Wind*.

'Yes, for about the twentieth time. I adore it.'

Maureen picked it up, noticing the underlinings and annotations Vivien had made in her small, neat handwriting. 'You know they're casting the film adaptation?'

'Of course.'

Maureen's eyes were dancing. 'It's not official yet, but I'm being lined up for the role of Melanie Wilkes. John's great friends with the producer, David O. Selznick – he was the one who encouraged John to come to Hollywood and try his luck – and I've been told, off the record, that he was very happy with my screen test. Obviously they have to agree on the other cast members, but I'm quietly confident. Scarlett O'Hara is the part that's causing a real headache. I think every actress in Hollywood has tried out for it.'

'So I've heard,' Vivien smiled. 'Larry's been suggested for Rhett Butler. He won't play him, but I intend to play Scarlett.'

Maureen burst into laughter, but the look on Vivien's face told her the comment wasn't intended as a joke, and Maureen quickly fell quiet. 'I'm so sorry, I didn't realise you… I mean, it's the role of the decade. They've already turned down Bette Davis, Joan

Crawford, Katharine Hepburn... I've heard Norma Shearer's already been cast. And aren't you under contract to Korda?'

Vivien turned around, one perfectly arched eyebrow raised as she regarded Maureen levelly. 'Anything's possible if you want it badly enough. You've known me since I was a child – you should know not to underestimate me.'

'I do,' Maureen agreed, noting the steely demeanour and realising that Vivien was deadly serious. 'I wish you all the luck in the world, darling.'

Chapter Twenty-Two

VIVIEN

Los Angeles, USA

December 1938

Vivien landed at Los Angeles' Clover Field airport and swept outside to the car that was waiting for her. A clamour of reporters was waiting too, shouting questions as flashbulbs popped in her face. One voice stood out above the melee: 'Miss Leigh, why are you in Los Angeles?'

Vivien bestowed a cat-like smile on the reporter who'd asked the question. 'To see Mr Laurence Olivier,' she declared. A fresh round of camera flashes exploded, as she slipped into the waiting Cadillac which pulled smoothly away into the traffic.

'It's all right, darling, you can come out now.'

Crouched in the footwell of the back seat, Larry popped his head up. In a second, they were in one another's arms, but Larry seemed angry with her.

'What is it, darling?' Vivien stroked his face, drinking him in. It had been weeks since she'd seen him, and it had felt as though she were missing a limb.

'Why did you tell the reporter you were here to see me?'

'Why not? It's hardly a secret.'

'Not amongst our friends, no. But the public don't know. And the American public are the most puritanical and hypocritical of all.'

Vivien was too excited to be chastened. She and Larry were in love – madly, deeply, undeniably – and she wanted to tell the whole world.

She looked out of the window as the car pulled onto the freeway. It was her first time in the States, and she was wide-eyed at the vast roads and enormous buildings and the freshness of the city compared with grey, wintry London. To Vivien, Los Angeles lacked a charm and a history, though she admitted to herself that she was predisposed to dislike America. It was the country that had taken Larry away from her, the country where he'd spent miserable weeks and months separated from her.

At least if the press thought she was here to visit Larry – currently filming *Wuthering Heights* opposite Merle Oberon – then they would likely overlook the real reason for her trip: to audition for the role of Scarlett O'Hara in *Gone with the Wind*. Excitement rose in Vivien at the prospect, along with a fierce desperation, a burning intensity at how badly she wanted this role.

Larry's American agent was Myron Selznick – fortuitously, the brother of David O. Selznick, producer of *Gone with the Wind* – and the instant Myron saw Vivien he'd been convinced that she needed to meet his brother. She was by far the outsider. No one had mentioned her name amongst the slew of actresses fighting it out for the coveted role: Bette Davis, Barbara Stanwyck, Paulette Goddard. But Vivien was determined to win the part, the same way she'd been determined to have Larry.

She rested one hand on his knee, the other on her crocodile-skin handbag in which she carried her copy of *Gone with the Wind* everywhere she went, like a talisman. She'd read it countless times, and the hardback book was tattered and well-thumbed.

But now they were arriving at the Beverly Hills Hotel where Larry had a room. Vivien, overwrought with anticipation and adrenaline, needed an outlet. She turned to him and saw her desire mirrored in his eyes. Everything else – even Scarlett – could wait until later.

'Nervous?'

Myron Selznick couldn't resist a sly sideways glance at Vivien, who looked exquisite in a full-length mink fur coat that was hiding a taupe-coloured silk dress, emphasising her tiny waist. Her dark hair hung loose beneath a wide-brimmed hat, and her make-up emphasised those cat-like eyes and her extraordinary smile.

Vivien laughed, as though the idea was an impossibility, though in reality her heart was racing, her breathing shallow as though her lungs couldn't take in enough air.

It was more than two years since David O. Selznick had bought the rights to *Gone with the Wind* for $50,000. Despite his exhaustive search, he still hadn't found the right actress to portray Scarlett, but Vivien intended to be the answer to his prayers. She offered up a hasty one of her own, willing to try all avenues, even the long-neglected Almighty, as she stepped onto the set of *Gone with the Wind* on the lot of Selznick International Pictures.

She caught her breath as she took in the scene in front of her: flames reaching up to the sky, shards of red and orange dancing wickedly against the black night, buildings crashing into ash and cinders. Atlanta was burning and Vivien was exhilarated, the fire on set reflecting her own.

She watched, mesmerised, as a man and woman in a horse-drawn buggy picked their way across the set. Myron had explained to her that, despite the role of Scarlett not yet being cast, nervous executives wanted filming to get underway, so the cameras had begun rolling on these dramatic shots of the burning city, with background artists portraying Rhett and Scarlett.

Vivien felt the significance of the moment, the sheer

impossibility of what she was trying to do making itself known as nerves flared unexpectedly. Even if she were to win the role, could she successfully, convincingly, play the daughter of a plantation owner caught up in the American Civil War, with a life so very different to Vivien's own? It was a rare moment of doubt, and Vivien exhaled slowly, attempting to control her emotions.

Myron waited for a break in filming and they approached David. He was a heavyset man, with slicked-back dark hair and round, rimless glasses. Standing beside him was George Cukor, the director, wearing a pale grey suit and trilby hat, physically very similar in appearance to David.

'Hey, genius,' Myron called to his brother. 'Meet your Scarlett O'Hara.'

Vivien stepped forward. The night sky burned around her, the flames reflected in her blue-green eyes as her coat fell open, revealing her youthful, perfectly proportioned figure.

'Good evening, Mr Selznick.' She smiled prettily, in her best approximation of a Southern belle.

David didn't speak, simply staring at her, his mouth open. Then he recovered himself, glancing briefly at George.

'Why don't you come into my office. Let's set up a screen test.'

The Buick Roadmaster crawled up the winding streets of the Hollywood Hills, nestled high above the Sunset Strip. The gate to 9166 Cordell Drive had been left open and Larry drove straight through, pulling to a stop outside the sprawling white stucco Spanish-style house. Vivien thought it rather showy and excessive, but there was no denying it was an impressive property, surrounded by tall trees and sitting in almost an acre of land.

Larry opened the door for her and she climbed out. She was dressed in a red velvet gown trimmed with fur, in a nod to the season, and Larry squeezed her hand reassuringly as they walked up the steps and rang the doorbell.

'Merry Christmas, darling,' Vivien exclaimed, kissing George Cukor on both cheeks. He looked relaxed and off-duty, in an open-necked shirt with a V-neck sweater and slacks.

'A little different to the weather you're used to, huh?' he grinned, as he led the couple through the lavishly decorated house and out onto the poolside terrace, where a well-stocked drinks trolley resided. The smell of turkey drifted out through the open windows, as he handed them both a glass of eggnog.

'It feels odd not to be freezing in a British winter, but I could get used to it,' Vivien joked. 'Thanks awfully for having us.'

'Couldn't leave you to celebrate Christmas on your own. Now, have you met Tallulah Bankhead?'

Everyone said their hellos, but Vivien struggled to concentrate. Since she'd been introduced to George and David O. Selznick earlier that month, she'd embarked on a gruelling round of screen tests, costume fittings, photography sessions, dialect lessons and – perhaps the most testing of all – waiting. She knew she was a serious contender for the role, but had she done enough? The long hours kept her busy and gave her a focus, but worse were the interminable days when Larry was wrapping up filming on *Wuthering Heights* and all Vivien could do was obsess over Scarlett, wondering whether the decision had been made yet, and what on earth she would do if she wasn't successful.

She was scheduled to appear in *A Midsummer Night's Dream* in London in the New Year, but had begged the director, Tyrone Guthrie, to postpone the start of rehearsals. In truth, she'd completely lost interest in reprising Titania. All she could think about was Scarlett.

'How are you finding Hollywood?' Katharine Hepburn sidled up to the group. She was tall and elegant, in tailored trousers and a silk blouse, a cigarette languishing between her fingers. She gave off an air of confidence, of taking no bullshit, and Vivien liked her immediately.

'Well, I'm rather hoping I might stay,' Vivien quipped, and Katharine laughed. If Vivien was being honest with herself, however, she didn't like L.A. Yes, it was big and it was exciting, but there was something artificial about it that she found distasteful. She had learned from Larry that the stage was the pinnacle of the acting experience, not the screen. But when all was said and done, films paid far more money and could catapult her to global fame.

Vivien did her best to follow the small talk, but as Cole Porter regaled them with an anecdote about his latest Broadway show, she felt a hand on her arm and looked over to see George standing beside her.

'Vivien, could I have a word?'

Her stomach lurched and she almost dropped her eggnog. 'Of course,' she said brightly, though her heart was racing like an express train.

George steered her to the far corner of the terrace beside the swimming pool, where they could talk privately. It was impossible to tell from his body language what news he was about to impart. One moment Vivien was certain she had it, the next convinced it would be a no.

'The part's been cast,' George said gravely, not meeting her eyes.

Vivien swallowed, her insides feeling as though they'd tumbled to the bottom of the pool in front of them. The water seemed to bend and warp in front of her eyes, and the heat of the day felt suddenly unnatural. There was a pounding in her ears that kept time with her heartbeat, a rushing sound inside her head. Distantly, she wondered who'd claimed the victory: Paulette Goddard? Joan Bennett? Jean Arthur? She would wrap up the conversation as quickly as possible, excuse herself politely – a sudden headache perhaps – then gather Larry and return to the hotel.

Vivien inclined her head gracefully. 'I see.'

There was a moment's pause, a shift in the atmosphere. Vivien narrowed her eyes as she studied George's face. He stared at her intently from behind his glasses, and the hint of a smile crossed his face. 'So I guess we're stuck with you.'

It took a second for understanding to register, then Vivien let out a small cry, tears springing to her eyes. For a moment, she almost lost her composure. She wanted to scream, to cry, to kiss him. It was almost too much to take in.

Realisation washed over her in waves: the role was hers; she would play Scarlett O'Hara; she had won the most coveted part in film history. She had wanted it so much, worked so hard for it, dreamed about it, even prayed for it – her Catholic roots ran deep. In this industry, you were at the mercy of others; she'd had to take risks, to be bold and defy expectations, but it had finally paid off. She was going to be Scarlett, the character she adored, whom she knew inside and out. Vivien genuinely believed that there was no one who could play Scarlett as well as she could.

And now she longed to tell Larry her good news, wanting him to share in her excitement.

'Thank you,' she said sincerely to George, clasping his hands, tears shining in her eyes. 'I'm overwhelmed, but so very, very grateful. I won't let you down, I promise.'

George was beaming from ear to ear, confident he'd made the right decision. 'I know you won't. Merry Christmas, Vivien.'

One month later, Vivien signed the contract to play Scarlett O'Hara at a ceremony beside her co-stars Olivia de Havilland and Leslie Howard, director George Cukor and an ecstatic David O. Selznick. His epic search – two years, $92,000, 1,400 candidates, 90 screen tests – had finally ended.

'Darling, I miss you so much.'

It was late at night, and Vivien's car had dropped her off minutes earlier at 520 North Crescent Drive in Beverly Hills, the house she and Larry had rented when they were both in Los Angeles. The studios were putting pressure on journalists not to leak the story – that two of their major stars had been living as a married couple when both were, in fact, married to other people. Vivien was torn between her desire to shout about her love to the whole world, and her fears of causing a backlash against the movie before it had even been released.

'I miss you too.' Larry's longing was clear down the line, from two and a half thousand miles away in New York where he was performing *No Time for Comedy* on Broadway. He and Vivien suspected that they'd been deliberately separated to avoid scandal, with Larry's agent, Myron, conspiring to find him work on the other side of the country.

'They've sacked Victor,' Vivien burst out.

'What?'

'And appointed Sam Wood. I thought Victor was bad but at least he knew what he was doing. Sam's completely a puppet of Selznick's. All David cares about is *his* film, *his* story, *his* version of Scarlett.' Vivien paced the room as far as the telephone cord would allow. Her eyes flashed dangerously; an onlooker would have taken her for Scarlett right then.

'How many directors now?'

'Three. It's a fucking joke,' Vivien swore, the word sounding odd in her cut-glass accent.

'Are you still seeing George?'

'Yes. Do you know what's terribly funny? I discovered the other day that Olivia's seeing him too – he's coaching her for Melanie.'

Larry roared with laughter, enjoying the joke. George Cukor had been the first director on *Gone with the Wind*, and Vivien had adored him. He was known as a women's director, able to get the best out of the actresses he worked with, and he understood Vivien's classical theatre training. He'd resigned after two weeks, though no one was quite sure of the reasons; some said he'd clashed with Selznick, others said Clark Gable had got him fired due to him prioritising the female roles.

George had been replaced by Victor Fleming, fresh off the set of *The Wizard of Oz*, and whilst Vivien had disliked him at first – his admission that he'd never even read Margaret Mitchell's novel went down like a lead balloon – she'd learned to work with him. And now David O. Selznick had had *him* replaced.

'And Gable's being a nightmare, swanning about like he owns the place. He's unbelievably arrogant.'

'Viv, darling, you need to stay strong and get through it.'

'I told David I was going to quit.'

'Vivien!' Larry was shocked. 'What did he say?'

'He said he'd sue me and I'd never work again in Hollywood.'

Larry sighed. 'He's probably right. I know how much you wanted this role, but I think we need to be honest and accept it's going to be a colossal failure.'

'Oh, darling, I know you're right. But what can I do?'

'You must make sure that you're utterly perfect. Then when the film flops, no one can blame you and your career won't be tarnished.'

Vivien felt close to tears. She was exhausted, miles away from Larry and having a miserable time on set. 'I just want it to be over. I want it to end.'

'Oh, Puss, I hate to think of you so unhappy.'

'I'm only happy when I'm with you.'

'I'll try and get back for a weekend,' Larry promised. 'We won't leave the bed.'

'Do try, you're all I can think about. Everything would be bearable if only I was with you.'

There were long declarations of love before they finally hung up the phone. Vivien sat alone in her bedroom, staring at the script for the next day's scenes, wondering how her dream job had turned into one she despised.

Chapter Twenty-Three

Los Angeles, USA

December 1939

'I won't do it without him.'

'Vivien—'

'I swear, David, I'm not going to Atlanta without Larry.'

David O. Selznick rubbed his hand tiredly across his face. They were in his vast office on the lot of Selznick International Pictures, with the cast and crew due to fly to Atlanta in two days' time for the world premiere of *Gone with the Wind*. Principal photography had been completed in June, then Vivien and Larry had taken a well-deserved holiday in France, stopping off in London, where war appeared to be imminent, to catch up with friends and family. Contractual obligations meant they had to return to America – Larry to begin filming *Rebecca*, and Vivien to publicise *Gone with the Wind*.

'We can't have *Gone with the Wind* without Scarlett O'Hara,' David argued, his tone irate.

'And you can't have Vivien Leigh without Laurence Olivier,' she snapped back.

'I don't think you quite understand. The premiere is in Atlanta, Georgia, the heart of the Bible belt. The American public are not going to countenance you – a married woman – appearing on the arm of a man who is not your husband and is, in fact, married to someone else. There'll be outrage. Do you want to tank this film before it's even been released?'

Vivien was chastened, but the fire in her eyes and determination in her expression were pure Scarlett. She wasn't being deliberately difficult, but this premiere would be one of the biggest nights of her life – certainly the biggest of her career – and she wanted Larry with her. She needed his support, his comfort, his guidance, but more than that, she simply wanted to share the experience with him. They hated to be apart from one another at the best of times, so why should this premiere be any different?

War had broken out in Europe, and Vivien was terrified that Larry was going to be called up any day now. Leigh had already joined up, being posted to Ramsgate as a Sub-Lieutenant in the Royal Navy, and Vivien's mother, Gertrude, had stepped in to take care of Suzanne. As though the war had focused everyone's minds on what was important, both Leigh and Larry's wife Jill had agreed to grant the lovers a divorce. It would take six months from filing until it was official, but their agreement lifted a huge weight off all of their shoulders, and Vivien didn't want to waste another second.

She'd shed blood, sweat and tears for the studio over the past year. By the time she'd finished filming she was physically and mentally broken, her mind unsettled as she felt unable to fully shake off the role for weeks afterwards. Now that they had their movie in the can, Vivien wasn't going to dance to the studio's tune for a moment longer. For once, she felt as though she had the upper hand; like David said, they couldn't have the premiere without Scarlett.

She smiled sweetly, endearingly, the corners of her mouth turning upwards. 'Do what you have to, darling, but I won't be there without Larry.'

CAROLINE LAMOND

Vivien stood up, perfectly poised as she turned and left David's office. She was going home to her husband-to-be, and no one could tell her otherwise.

The plane banked as it came in over Atlanta, and Vivien was treated to a glimpse of the entire city from the window of the American Airlines plane, specially decorated with the name of the film above its wing. It was almost unheard of for an American film premiere to take place outside New York or Los Angeles, and the move had caused considerable excitement. Vivien had to give credit to Selznick's publicity department – they'd certainly whipped theatregoers into a frenzy of anticipation. Far from being the flop Vivien and Larry had feared, it looked as though *Gone with the Wind* might prove a success after all.

The plane flew lower over the sprawling city, the main roads running like arteries through its heart, though the buildings were laid out less formally than the stark gridlines of New York or central Los Angeles.

Vivien turned to Larry, seated beside her, and smiled.

'Everything all right?' he asked, his eyes warm. He knew that she was afraid of flying, and the nerves were heightened on this trip in anticipation of the punishing schedule ahead. It was to be a three-day extravaganza and, despite the presence of her co-stars, all eyes would be on Vivien.

She nodded, exhilaration triumphing over anxiety, as the plane made its final descent and touched down on the runway.

David winked at Vivien as she made her way towards the exit. 'Knock 'em dead, kid,' he grinned.

They descended the steps to be swarmed by well-wishers who'd come to greet them, with reporters shouting questions as cameras rolled and flashbulbs exploded. Vivien's heart was racing, and she knew there was no turning back now. Whether *Gone with the Wind* was a triumph or a disaster, she was inextricably linked

208

with it; Vivien Leigh was Scarlett O'Hara, and Scarlett O'Hara was Vivien Leigh. But the signs were positive, and a buzz was building. This was a foretaste of how her life might be from now on: mobbed by an adoring public; strangers shouting her name; pens and paper thrust under her nose as fans begged for autographs. And throughout it all, Vivien beamed and waved, the smile coming naturally to her lips.

'Oh, they're playing our song,' Vivien exclaimed, as the band struck up 'Dixie'. The tune was omnipresent in the movie, as the unofficial song of the South. She turned round, looking for Larry, wanting to share the moment, but he remained in the background, debonair in a dark suit and tie. Despite his efforts not to draw attention to himself, his presence was soon noticed by journalists.

'Why is Mr Laurence Olivier here?' called a reporter from the *Atlanta Journal*.

'Production has recently begun on *Rebecca*, in which Mr Olivier is starring with Joan Fontaine, so this is a little pre-publicity for our next picture,' Howard Dietz, MGM's publicity director, explained hastily.

Vivien smiled wider when she heard the justification, delighted that she'd got her way. David O. Selznick had agreed to her request on the proviso that the two of them were in no way linked as a couple; Larry was in Atlanta on official duties only. But despite the prescribed conditions, the studio seemed to be softening in their stance towards the two of them. Now that Leigh and Jill had agreed to the respective divorces, it was surely only a matter of time until Vivien and Larry made it official. The studios had therefore agreed to a number of press interviews and articles intended to paint them in a positive light: as young lovers, successful actors, beautiful people who had battled the odds to be together, with true love conquering all. It was a romanticised, sympathetic picture of the two of them, taking the focus away from the failed marriages and small children they'd left in their wake.

In the melee, Vivien felt Larry's hand on her waist and thrilled to his touch, a burning point of heat beneath the fur coat she was wearing. A stolen moment in a very public setting. They were booked to stay in separate rooms, naturally, at the Georgian Terrace Hotel, but they planned to sneak away and stay with friends who had a house locally, where they could openly be together.

'This way, Miss Leigh,' Howard said respectfully, steering her through the crowd towards the waiting motorcade. Vivien dutifully followed, fulfilling every duty like the professional she was. They would tour the city, accompanied by a police escort, before Vivien would finally have the opportunity to meet the reclusive Margaret Mitchell – author of *Gone with the Wind* and creator of Scarlett O'Hara. There were to be balls and parties and luncheons, with the celebrations culminating in the premiere at Loew's theatre.

As Vivien settled herself in the open-top car, with the crowds cheering and calling her name, she felt determined to take in every single moment of this wonderful adventure. Right now, it was worth all the hard work, the long days and the lack of sleep. It was almost worth the enforced absence from Larry.

Vivien was on the edge of a precipice, and she was ready to fly.

'Vivien, you're a vision!'

'I'm pleased to see you're not letting the side down, darling,' she joked, as she air-kissed David O. Selznick.

Tonight was the 12th Academy Awards, and *Gone with the Wind* had been nominated in thirteen categories, including Best Actress for Vivien, and Best Picture. David was throwing a pre-Oscars party at his incredible house on Summit Drive in Beverly Hills, and Vivien was the guest of honour. She'd certainly dressed for the occasion, wearing a floral silk slip dress by Irene Gibbons, with an enormous aquamarine pendant – a gift from Larry from Van Cleef & Arpels – around her neck.

Larry, handsome in black tie, was nominated for Best Actor, for his role as Heathcliff in *Wuthering Heights*, and both he and Vivien hoped for a double victory this evening.

'I just adore your home,' Vivien told David sincerely, as they passed through to the large reception rooms where the party was already in full swing. She and Larry had visited a number of times before, but never had there been such a glamorous crowd, the air abuzz with anticipation and the expectation of victory.

There was a spontaneous round of applause as Vivien entered the room, and she accepted gracefully, as she was handed a glass of champagne. Looking around, she spotted her co-stars – Clark Gable, Olivia de Havilland, Hattie McDaniel – and was about to go over to speak to them when there was a sudden commotion by the door.

'We've won!' A young man Vivien recognised as one of David's assistants came running in, waving a newspaper, his face alive with excitement.

David frowned, moving towards him. 'What do you mean?'

'The *Los Angeles Times* printed the results already – I guess it was a mistake, but everyone's talking about it. I managed to get a copy. Look!'

Vivien's heart leapt as David took the paper and hastily looked through it.

'Best Picture – oh my God!' he exclaimed. 'Best Screenplay… Best Art Direction…'

Vivien could barely breathe as he ran through the list, each win being greeted with ecstatic cheers.

'Hattie – Best Supporting Actress.'

A ripple ran through the room at this announcement, before heartfelt cheers and congratulations rang out. Vivien turned to look at Hattie, who was resplendent in a turquoise dress and matching bolero jacket, a corsage of white gardenias at her collar and in her hair, her hands clasped over her mouth in delight and shock. Hattie had been banned from attending the film's premiere in Atlanta; the state's Jim Crow laws mandated racial segregation, and on this occasion no exceptions would be made. And now she'd become not only the first Black actor to be nominated for an Academy Award, but the first Black actor to win. It was a truly astonishing moment.

'And Vivien...'

She turned back to David as he called her name, so tightly wound with anticipation that she thought she might burst.

'You did it. Best Actress. Congratulations.'

The cast and crew piled into the fleet of limos which had been booked to take them to the awards ceremony. Inevitably, the celebrations had begun early, and everyone was in high spirits, a sense of victory in the air.

The biggest disappointment of the night, for Vivien at least, was that Larry had lost out on the Best Actor award. Jimmy Stewart had taken the prize for *The Philadelphia Story*, but Larry was gracious in defeat and outwardly thrilled for Vivien.

'Your time will come, darling, I'm sure of it,' she assured him, snuggling up to him in the back of the sleek, black limousine, the lights of the mansions flashing past in the darkness as they swept through Beverly Hills on their way to the Ambassador Hotel.

The ceremony was to be held in the Cocoanut Grove nightclub within the hotel, with guests seated at tables and enjoying a banquet whilst the awards were presented. The spectacular room, decorated with palm trees and Chinese lanterns, awash with red velvet and gold leaf, was crammed with the great and good of the film industry, and it wasn't long before Vivien spotted Maureen, looking incredible in a white column gown with gold detailing.

'Congratulations!' Maureen called, looking genuinely excited for her friend.

'Thank you. Good news travels fast,' Vivien laughed, as Larry greeted Maureen. The two of them were filming *Pride and Prejudice* together, with Maureen playing Jane Bennet and Larry as Mr Darcy, but there was no time to catch up as Vivien was ushered to her seat near the front of the stage.

She was sharing a table with her co-stars, with one notable, shameful, exception: Hattie McDaniel was seated at the back of the room on a segregated table beside her agent. The Ambassador Hotel had a no-Blacks policy and, whilst they'd allowed Hattie to attend the ceremony, it was on the condition that she sat separately. Not even her impending victory, or a threatened boycott of the Awards by Clark Gable, could change the minds of the faceless policymakers.

The lights dimmed, the host, Bob Hope, came on stage, and the ceremony began.

'*And the nominees for the Academy Award for Best Actress are... Bette Davis for* Dark Victory... *Irene Dunne,* Love Affair... *Greta Garbo in* Ninotchka... *Greer Garson,* Goodbye, Mr Chips... *Vivien Leigh in* Gone with the Wind...

'*Need I say, it is a privilege and an honour to announce this winner... Miss Vivien Leigh in* Gone with the Wind.'

Even though she knew she'd won, nothing could have prepared Vivien for this moment. She was barely aware of the thunderous applause, the cheers of excitement, as she floated up to the stage to collect the iconic gold statue. Her acceptance speech was poised and gracious, although her heart was racing as she looked out over the room, full of her peers and Hollywood's most important figures. Then she found what she was looking for: Larry. Her eyes locked on his and she felt her heart swell with pride and love.

Vivien had put all she had into winning both Larry and her Oscar, and right now she had everything she'd ever wanted. In that moment, life was perfect.

Chapter Twenty-Four

SONIA

London, England

May 1939

Sonia's slender fingers danced over the typewriter keys, the rhythmic clacking a hypnotic drumbeat that filled the small room.

It was approaching midnight and she was tired, a low lamp burning in the corner as she sat at the small wooden desk, hunched over a sheaf of paper covered in sprawling, almost illegible handwriting.

That was enough for this evening, she decided, sitting up and stretching, yawning as she removed the pencil from her long blonde hair so it unfurled and spilled down her back. Sonia was typing up a manuscript for Eugene, and she was back living in her little attic room in Grafton Mews, with its threadbare rugs and lumpy mattress.

She'd kept the room on during her adventures in Eastern Europe, where the path to freedom had opened up rapidly once silver had crossed palms. Sonia and Eugene had underestimated the guards' ability to be swayed by a bribe, terrified that Serge's attempt would see them marched outside and lined up against a wall, shot as spies without a second's hesitation. But sufficient *pengő* had greased the wheels and the trio had been released, reunited with their belongings and the Wolseley Hornet in which they fled, not stopping until they reached the Czechoslovakian border, before pressing on to Poland and Eugene's long-lost family where they were received warmly with *pierogi* and pear vodka.

Sonia and Eugene had, perhaps inevitably, begun a love affair, but in recent weeks he'd grown distant, his phone calls infrequent, his letters focusing on professional matters. Now that he was based in Manchester, as a professor at the university, the geographical distance, at least, was unavoidable, but Sonia had heard that he was courting a woman named Alice Elizabeth Malet, and the rumours were that it was serious. Sonia felt his behaviour was rather unchivalrous, not having the good manners to tell her himself and to let their fling fizzle out, but she'd always known Eugene wasn't to be the love of her life. She was still searching for the man to bear that honour.

Sonia was in a reflective mood as she brushed her hair, with long, slow strokes that made her scalp tingle. The window was open a crack and she listened to the sounds of the city: traffic drifting up from the Euston Road; revellers on their way home from the pub; a yowling cat on the prowl. The area was popular with students and academics, and during the day Sonia liked to watch the buzz of life happening beneath her window four storeys below.

She slipped off her cardigan and began to unbutton her blouse, when a tap on the window made her jump in alarm. She whirled round, staring into the darkness of the night, seeing only her own reflection lit by the lamp. As Sonia stepped closer, she realised there was a man perched on her window-ledge, and he was grinning at her.

Anger overtook her. Pulling her blouse tightly around her, she marched over to the window. 'What the hell are you doing?'

The man didn't stop smiling, though he did at least look a little apologetic. She could see now that he was around thirty, a decade older than her, lean and wiry, with thinning hair and an aristocratic face.

'I'm so sorry, I didn't mean to scare you,' he said, in a well-spoken voice, as Sonia scoffed in reply.

'Well, what did you ex—' She broke off as she realised he wasn't listening, but had turned round and was giving a thumbs-up to someone below.

'What on earth…?'

'My friends,' the man explained. 'We were talking about you and, well, it was something of a dare, you see. I thought I'd come up here and introduce myself. I'm William Coldstream. But you can call me Bill.'

'I have no intention of calling you anything,' Sonia retorted hotly. But, despite herself, she was intrigued. There was something romantic and reckless in the gesture; her room was four floors from the ground, and reaching it required shimmying up a drainpipe, inching along a sloping, tiled roof with a steep drop, and negotiating a cluster of chimney pots. Sonia almost admired his tenacity.

Besides, Bill didn't seem threatening; he seemed like a charming, self-possessed English gentleman. If he'd been a genuine Peeping Tom, he would have kept quiet and watched her take her blouse off, Sonia reasoned.

'Perhaps I should explain. I'm not some madman, honestly,' he continued, with a roguish smile that threatened to undermine his argument. 'I'm one of the founders of the Euston Road School. We're a group of painters, based just over there.' He waved vaguely into the darkness behind him. 'My colleagues and I have often admired the girl in the window, unreachable in her ivory tower, looking like a Renoir muse.'

Whether it was the late hour, or the sensuous images he evoked, Sonia felt herself weaken at the flattery.

'What I wanted to ask was… could I paint you sometime?' He

looked somewhat abashed, embarrassed that the culmination of his dramatic gesture was this simple request.

Sonia considered him, unsure what to make of it all. The sentiment was trite, but Bill delivered it with sincerity.

'And it's bloody uncomfortable on this ledge, not to mention rather terrifying, so if you're going to say no, I'd appreciate it if you'd put me out of my misery sooner rather than later.'

Sonia laughed, realising the ridiculousness of the situation, with Bill clinging to her window ledge as the church bells chimed twelve, his friends presumably still waiting below, or perhaps having got bored and wandered off.

'Well then,' she smiled, pulling up the sash and offering her hand to help him, 'I suppose you'd better come in.'

Sonia was sitting languidly in an armchair, the radio playing low on the sideboard, Bing Crosby crooning 'What's New?' It was a sweltering afternoon at the end of summer, the day before her twenty-first birthday; a party was planned tomorrow at a nightclub off Tottenham Court Road.

She watched Bill as he worked, her gaze flickering over the face she'd come to know so well: the furrow between his eyebrows as he concentrated; the way his lips pursed as the brush stroked the canvas.

They were on Howland Street, a few minutes away from her place on Grafton Street. Bill and his friend Graham Bell had rented rooms there and Graham would often paint his lover, Anne Olivier Popham – a distant relative of the actor Laurence Olivier. Sonia had heard rumours that he'd left his wife for her old school friend Vivien, and she was both astonished and envious of Vivien for living such a thrilling, scandalous life.

The news had broken earlier that year that she had been cast as Scarlett O'Hara, and since then hardly a day had gone by without Sonia seeing Vivien's face in the newspapers as she made headlines around the world. She remembered Vivien's great beauty, even as a child, and recalled her talent for acting. Sonia had sat in the darkness of the Great Hall, staring up at the stage, mesmerised along with the rest of the school as they watched the annual productions, Vivien's scenes a joy amidst the tedium.

Sonia had no gift for performing, and her ambitions didn't tend that way, so she wasn't jealous of Vivien's success in that arena. Rather, she found it incomprehensible that one of her contemporaries could be so ambitious and accomplished, when Sonia had very little idea of her own vocation.

Since agreeing to sit for Bill, the two of them had begun a relationship, and he'd introduced her to a world she'd yearned to be part of, mixing in bohemian circles with the creatives that inhabited the bars and cafés of Charlotte Street. Earlier that year, a group of them had visited Paris, and Sonia had fallen in love with the city just as Eugene had told her she would, revelling in its effortless glamour and ubiquitous creativity, where writers and painters and artists of all kinds could flourish.

Sonia stretched luxuriously, enjoying the slight breeze from the wide-open windows.

'Do you want to take a break?' Bill asked.

'Not yet. But soon.'

'All right. I'll put the kettle on.' He crossed the studio, dropping a kiss on her forehead as he passed. 'When it's boiled, we'll stop.'

Sonia watched him, his rangy, shambling figure as he fumbled for the tap, his long neck and elegant hands. The gold ring on his wedding finger.

'My wife and I are like houses in the suburbs,' Bill had told her in one of their earliest meetings, as they drank wine together in the Fitzroy Tavern. Sonia had frowned, and he'd continued with a smile, 'Semi-detached. She's having an affair with a young poet.'

'Are you planning to divorce?'

'There's no real hurry. Although if either of us wanted to marry again, then we probably should.'

Sonia shrugged, unconcerned – perhaps even a little thrilled – at the prospect of a married lover. Though she didn't know them personally, friends of Sonia's were tight with the lauded Bloomsbury Set – Virginia Woolf, Vanessa Bell, Lytton Strachey and others – and Sonia had heard all kinds of tales of infidelity and partner-swapping and same-sex couplings. It felt deliciously rebellious and liberated.

'My mother divorced my stepfather,' she told him.

'Then she sounds like a very enlightened woman.'

Sonia smiled, thinking how wonderful it was to be so free of judgement, how different Bill was from the people she'd encountered in her early life – her family, and the convent girls, and the hated nuns.

'Have I ever told you what we call you?' Bill asked from across the room, as he lit a match and the flames on the stove flickered into life.

Pulled from her reminiscing, Sonia shook her head.

'The Euston Road Venus.'

Sonia snorted with laughter, equal parts self-conscious and delighted.

'It's true,' Bill went on, coming back behind the easel and picking up his palate. 'Everyone notices you on the way to the studio. The beautiful maiden in her tower. Creamy skin, rosy cheeks, golden hair. We're all fascinated by you.'

'Don't be ridiculous.' But Sonia felt gratified, nonetheless. She adored being part of this world and was fascinated by creative people. She'd long feared that she wasn't a skilful enough writer or poet, and if her talent alone wasn't sufficient to enter this rarefied life – if her youth and beauty were what would secure her entry – then it was a trade Sonia was content to make.

Bill worked in silence, the only sound being the low whistle of the kettle as it began to boil. Sonia shifted in her seat, regretting her choice of a high-necked, navy-blue blouse on this hot day. She would have been far cooler had she chosen to pose nude, like many of the Euston Road muses, but it seemed too clichéd. Or perhaps her Catholic schooling had affected her more than she'd realised.

Bing Crosby finished singing and a news bulletin came on.

'… Reports are being received of an agreement signed between Germany and the Soviet Union. A non-aggression pact between the countries was apparently agreed in Moscow earlier this month. The BBC has seen photographs of the Soviet leader, Joseph Stalin, shaking hands with the German Foreign Minister, Joachim von Ribbentrop, shortly after the signing which took place in the Kremlin…'

They were both quiet, taking in what they'd heard. Bill put down his paintbrush and lit two cigarettes, passing one to Sonia.

'I thought Hitler hated the Russians,' she frowned, taking a drag. 'Didn't everyone expect him to invade the Soviet Union?'

'Now he's free to do what he wants,' Bill said quietly. 'It means the Soviets won't interfere, as long as he leaves them alone.'

'So war's inevitable?'

Bill's grim expression told her all she needed to know. 'I'd say it's a question of when, not if. Britain can't stand by if Hitler makes another land grab. Chamberlain's already committed to defending Poland if Germany invades.'

'Will you fight?' Sonia asked, her expression sombre.

'Of course – if they'll have me. It's my duty as an Englishman, to fight for King and Country.'

Sonia briefly wondered if he was being ironic, but Bill seemed completely serious. The whistling of the kettle filled the silence, now loud and shrill. Bill rose and took it off the hob.

It felt as though they were standing on the edge of a precipice, and everything that had been so solid and certain was collapsing around them. It had been a long yet seemingly inevitable march to war, bound up in fear and uncertainty. Sonia wondered what she would do. The world she inhabited – one of literature, creativity, frivolity – was not made for war. There was no place for artistry amidst bombs and death.

Bill returned with two cups of sweet tea and two shortbread

biscuits. 'Let's talk about something more fun,' he suggested. 'Have you heard that Cyril Connolly's starting a magazine?'

Sonia shrugged disinterestedly, unable to shake off her bleak mood.

'He's planning to launch in January – a journal dedicated to art and literature. I thought it might appeal to you. You could see if they have any vacancies.'

'As what? A typist?' The translation work Sonia received from Eugene was increasingly sporadic these days; he was now engaged to Alice, and they planned to marry later that year, which explained his withdrawal from Sonia. She'd found some part-time work tutoring the daughter of a wealthy family in Hampstead, but knew that wasn't what she wanted to do with her life.

'Darling,' Bill reproached her teasingly. 'I had thought you might show a little more ambition than that.' Sonia raised an eyebrow questioningly, and Bill continued, 'Why not write for them?'

'Write?'

'Yes! You're certainly not short on brains, and you know more about art than most of the men at the Euston School – even if I did teach you everything you know,' he added with a grin.

Sonia thought about it, her pulse beginning to race. As soon as Bill made the suggestion, she knew she wanted to do it. It was true that she and Bill had long discussions about art, and she considered herself an authority on the subject, imagining that her taste – refined under Bill's tutelage – was little short of impeccable. Perhaps it was merely a question of self-belief on Sonia's part, of finding the confidence to take the leap and pursue a path that scared her.

'What do you want from life? What are your ambitions?' Bill pressed.

'I...' Sonia trailed off, alarmed to find that there was nothing specific beyond a vague, unstructured desire to be involved with art and literature, to be around creative people, even if she didn't possess the talent to be one herself. But that was impossible to pinpoint or articulate. 'I don't know, exactly,' she admitted, embarrassed.

'Look, you're twenty-one tomorrow,' Bill reminded her softly. 'Old enough to vote.'

Sonia mustered a smile, but she understood the point he was making. She would be an adult and should behave accordingly. In truth, she still bore the scars – mental if not physical – of the boating accident three years ago. She was drifting aimlessly, without purpose, haunted by a sense of restlessness and rootlessness. Yet if she stopped to reflect on this, Sonia felt an overwhelming guilt, a conviction that she was betraying her friends; she was the only survivor, and should be living her life to the full. Jean-Pierre, Paul and Madeleine would never have that opportunity.

'You're extraordinary,' Bill insisted, his gaze so intense that Sonia looked away. 'You need to believe that.'

'You're very sweet.' She shook her head at his words, unable to shake the feeling that she was destined to be always in the shadows and never the star – a typist for Eugene, a model for Bill. An artist's muse. 'I'll think about it,' she promised, standing up and moving over to the window, gazing out over the rooftops of Fitzrovia as she tried not to show how excited she was, or how perfect a job at Cyril Connolly's magazine sounded. All she needed to do was find the courage.

Chapter Twenty-Five

London, England

April 1940

'... And I thought reprinting Winston Churchill's essay "Painting as a Pastime" would give historical context to this new movement, as well as providing a sense of gravity, and a wider world view, extending beyond the art community.'

Sonia was almost breathless as she outlined her vision, speaking nineteen to the dozen in her haste to expound her ideas. Her eyes were sparkling, her enthusiasm for the subject matter of Young English Painters evident for all to see.

She reminded herself to take a breath, looking in turn at each of the three men seated round the table. They were all older than her, in Charvet ties and tweed suits to which the scent of cigar smoke lingered thickly. They held the power.

They were certainly meeting in style, in the glamorous surroundings of the Café Royal on Regent Street. The decor was opulent, a profusion of red velvet and gilt, and the clientele were well-heeled and well-connected. Were it not for the limited menu

– the lack of entrecôte, the scraping of butter in the pomme purée – it would have been almost impossible to tell that war had broken out. Sonia willed herself not to be intimidated.

Peter Watson, dark-haired and slender, with heavy-lidded eyes, screwed up his elegant face. 'This is all very impressive, Sonia, and you undoubtedly have some good ideas. My problem, gentlemen, is that I agreed to finance a literary review, not an art magazine. Particularly not one that focuses on this rather drab, unoriginal style. If you look at the work of de Chirico, for example, and what they're doing in Paris right now...'

Sonia stopped listening, fighting her growing frustration. She'd spent hours on this presentation, and a sea of paper, neatly typed and illustrated, lay strewn across the table for their inspection and critique.

Stephen Spender, curly-haired and dishevelled, the co-editor of the newly named *Horizon*, had suggested Sonia might like to edit a special edition of the magazine, on the subject of Young English Painters. Nothing could have been more suited to her talents; she was impeccably well organised and had an in-depth knowledge of the most exciting developments in the art world. But she was also twenty-one years old with no experience of editing a magazine, so the odds were stacked against her.

Sonia turned to look at Stephen and his co-founder, Cyril Connolly, hoping they might have a more favourable reaction than Peter's. Peter was the money man, the financial backer, but Stephen and Cyril were the ones with the cachet and the connections – to Ernest Hemingway, Virginia Woolf, Evelyn Waugh and others of their ilk.

Cyril was a god in Sonia's world. Charismatic and radiating natural authority, she saw him as a genius, his intellect impressive, his mind expansive. Sonia didn't find him physically attractive, although Cyril always had a string of pretty young things hanging off him, despite his stocky and balding appearance. Rather, he represented entry to the life that Sonia wanted, one inhabited by writers and artists and intellectuals.

'How old are you?'

Peter was addressing her. Sonia bristled but forced herself to stay calm. She wanted this badly.

'Twenty-one. A perfect age, wouldn't you say? I'm fresh, full of energy, and I know what's going on in the art scene. These people are my contemporaries.'

'And remind me of your credentials?'

Sonia's fury rose. She felt like a fool, wondering whether Stephen's invitation had been a joke, cruelly and inexplicably designed to waste her time.

'I might not have a degree in art history, but I know Victor Pasmore, William Coldstream, Graham Bell, Rodrigo Moynihan, all of the most important figures on the London art scene. It's all in here.' She drummed her fingers on the sheets on the table, making eye contact with each of them in turn. 'Give me a chance to prove it to you. One chance. That's all I need.'

Dear Sonia,

Thank you for meeting with us the other day. Whilst we admired your effort and applaud your accomplishment, we have ultimately decided to take a different direction, and will not be proceeding with the Young Painters issue.

I, personally, was extremely impressed by your ideas and your enthusiasm, and feel that you could make a strong contribution to the future of Horizon. *Whilst we can't offer you a formal role (with a formal salary!), we'd love to have you on board; we can always find secretarial work and odd jobs for talented young ladies, for which we can offer occasional recompense.*

Fondest regards,
Stephen

. . .

'I can't believe I didn't get it.' Sonia, hurt and angry, threw the letter across the table of the café on Shaftesbury Avenue. Her sister, Bay, picked it up, her expression sympathetic.

'Do you know how much work I put into that proposal?' Sonia continued. 'I wouldn't trust Connolly *or* Spender's views on art, to be quite frank. And Peter Watson's too distracted by the scene in Paris to pay any attention to all the exciting changes that are happening *here*, right under his nose. It's simply too frustrating.'

'Oh, Sonia,' Bay sighed, pulling a face as she handed back the disappointing letter, now apprised of its contents.

'And I don't want your sympathy either,' Sonia snapped, aware she was being unfair, but wanting to take her frustration out on someone. Bill was stationed in Dover and she'd dashed off a long, disgruntled letter, full of underscorings and expletives. She longed to see him in person but, for now, her sister would have to do.

Sonia and Bay had arranged a long overdue catch-up, an early supper and a visit to the pictures. Bay lived in Islington and worked as a nurse; she was devoted to caring for others in a way Sonia couldn't quite fathom, and she rarely had time off.

'You'd have been perfect for it. They're idiots,' Bay assured her, as she sliced an enormous currant bun in two and slid half across the table to her sister. 'This Stephen chap said how impressed he was with you. Your time will come, mark my words.'

'Will it?' Sonia's eyes pleaded for reassurance. The bun remained, ignored, on the table. 'I'm not so sure. I've wanted to be a writer for so long – whether poetry, or literature, or journalism – but perhaps I'm not cut out for it. I've always thought that writers were the cleverest people in the world, so perhaps I need to accept that typing work is all that I'm good for.'

'Oh, do buck up, darling,' Bay teased. 'You're twenty-one years old and you're a woman. Of course those fusty middle-aged men aren't going to let you come in and prove you can do it better than them. Feminism might have brought us a long way, but there's still an awful lot further to go.'

Bay's comment didn't raise a smile.

'It's beastly unfair! All around me, I see women getting married, having children, giving up their fledgling careers as writers and artists. The men get to carry on exactly as they did before – creating art, getting drunk, chasing women, staying up all night, whilst the women are stuck with... Well, that's the point, isn't it? They're stuck. Their lives don't progress and they... Oh, I don't even know what I'm trying to say.'

Bay looked sympathetic. Sonia knew she was trying to understand, but she and her sister were from two different worlds. Bay no more understood the tribulations of bohemian Fitzrovia than Sonia understood the workings of the cardiovascular system.

'What are you going to do for money?'

Sonia half-snorted, half-laughed. 'Oh, darling, I do adore you. You're so terribly practical.' She sighed, resigning herself to the inevitable. 'Swallow my pride and take the typing job, I expect. Stephen's a darling, though rather intimidating. I can learn an awful lot from him. And *Horizon* is such a thrilling prospect that I'm flattered to be involved in any capacity, even if it is a lowly secretary and not guest editor.'

Bay frowned. 'Can you really pay your rent on "occasional recompense"? Look, I'm not trying to pooh-pooh this opportunity, but you have to be realistic. Have you thought about taking up nursing instead?'

Sonia roared with laughter. 'No, never.'

'Only as a stopgap. University College Hospital are looking for staff for their Mobile First Aid Unit. So it's not nursing as such, but you'd be helping the war effort considerably more than working for a magazine.'

Sonia bit back a smart retort and drained her cup of tea. 'Come on. Let's go or else we'll be late.'

The two women stepped out into the steady drizzle of a London evening. The light was beginning to fade, the theatres and restaurants drab without their usual illuminated signs, prohibited due to the blackout. Sandbags were stacked in front of buildings, road signs removed to confuse the Germans in the event of an invasion, and the posters on billboards issued stern advice about always carrying your gas mask and sending your children to the countryside. Despite the precautions, very little had happened in the seven months since Chamberlain's declaration, and the public were calling it the 'Bore War'.

Sonia and Bay cut through the seedy environs of Soho, hurrying to Leicester Square. The cinemas and theatres had closed when war was first declared, but within a month they were allowed to open again. Despite her recent disappointment, Sonia felt a faint tingle of excitement. There'd been so much anticipation around *Gone with the Wind*; it had opened in England mere days ago but had been out in America for a few months now. The critics and public alike adored it, and it had swept the board at the Academy Awards, winning a record haul of eight statues.

'I'm so looking forward to seeing this,' Bay gushed. 'I can't believe that Vivien's such a huge star now.'

'I wonder what the Reverend Mother Brace-Hall would have to say about it,' Sonia said, with a wry smile.

They reached the Ritz cinema, joining the queue of people snaking round the square. It looked as though the auditorium would be full, and there was a palpable sense of expectation in the air. The crowd were dressed in their finery; a night out at the pictures was an occasion worthy of dressing up, and this movie in particular felt like an occasion.

Sonia and Bay took their seats, pleased to be out of the drizzle in the glamorous surroundings of the cinema. The lights went down and the reel started up. The introduction was long, with orchestral music playing over a scene of a plantation in the Deep South. When Vivien's name came on screen, the audience gave a spontaneous cheer, London claiming her as one of their own.

Sonia stared at the words as they scrolled upwards: Vivien Leigh as Scarlett O'Hara. No longer Vivian Hartley, as she had been at school, or even Vivian Holman, her married name. She had reinvented herself, as a movie star no less, only a few years Sonia's senior. Yet here was Sonia, a secretary, being told that an editorial role at a minor literary magazine was beyond her grasp.

Vivien appeared on screen, young and fresh and utterly beautiful. She'd always been striking, but she'd grown into an exceptional woman. Sonia found it hard to reconcile the memory of the schoolgirl she'd known with the actress up there on the big screen, playing the most coveted role in Hollywood's history. And she played it perfectly. Like everyone else, Sonia had read the book (she could see its appeal, but personally found it long-winded and mawkish), and there was no doubt that Vivien was born to play Scarlett.

Sonia examined her feelings and found that yes, she was undoubtedly envious of Vivien. Not simply because of her wealth and fame, but because Vivien had found her place in the world. Even back at Roehampton, she'd expressed her desire to act; she'd discovered her talent and was being lauded for it, whilst Sonia barely knew where to start. But she found Vivien's success inspiring too, buoyed by the knowledge that one of her contemporaries had broken the mould. And it wasn't just Vivien – Maureen O'Sullivan had also become a huge movie star, discovered back home in her native Ireland.

Sonia glanced at Bay beside her, noticing that she was completely engrossed in the film. She doubted Bay would be wrestling with such angst; likely she was admiring Scarlett's dress, or swooning over Rhett Butler's easy charm, or simply wrapped up in the story with no inner critic to spoil her enjoyment. Sometimes Sonia wondered whether it would be easier if she could be satisfied with less. To be like Bay and live a small life – a good life – with a steady job and a dull but dependable man.

But as she watched Vivien on screen, bewitching every man she met and frustrated by her inability to snare Ashley Wilkes,

Sonia knew that a small life would never be enough for her either. She vowed that she would achieve success in her own right too. She was intelligent, she was talented, and she was determined to prove to the men at *Horizon* that they'd been fools to turn her down.

Chapter Twenty-Six

London, England

May 1941

Forty-nine Bedford Square was the centre of Sonia's universe right now. The genteel garden square had not been spared the ravages of the war, with the pristine lawn dug up to make way for allotments, the iron railings melted down to make Spitfires. But inside number 49, a different atmosphere prevailed.

The apartment belonged to Cyril Connolly, editor of *Horizon*, and almost every night he would host a dinner party, a casual supper, cocktails or a moveable feast. Cyril knew everyone who was anyone in literary London; Sonia had encountered Nancy Mitford, Aldous Huxley, Peter Quennell, TS Eliot, to name but a few such luminaries, in his drawing room.

'Sonia, darling.' Cyril kissed her on both cheeks as she made her entrance. 'You brighten up a room as always.'

She was wearing a lavender twinset with a cream pencil skirt, her blonde hair somewhat dishevelled after a long day in the office. Cyril was resplendent in his habitual tweed.

'Yes, I'm sure it was deathly dull before I arrived,' Sonia said wryly, glancing round at the party that was in full swing.

Walking into Cyril's was like entering another world; outside war was raging, but inside it was entirely possible to forget the death and privations. The 'Bore War' had ended abruptly a year and a half earlier, with the Luftwaffe bombing London for more than fifty consecutive days and nights. Within months, swathes of the city had been destroyed, and the nightly – sometimes hourly – air-raid siren had become a bleak reality. Sonia had got used to trooping down into the nearest underground station, with a flask of tea and a book, until it passed.

Cyril lived as though none of this was happening. In his apartment, though the music was turned low and blackout curtains hung at the windows, life was civilised and beautiful. Here there was no rationing or shortages, no terror and destruction. He surrounded himself with pretty girls, most of whom Sonia had become good friends with – Lys Lubbock, Janetta Woolley, Diana Witherby – and a few she hadn't.

'By the way, how's that chap of yours?' Cyril asked, as he led her into the melee. He'd previously made intimations that he was interested in Sonia – at the very least, that she'd make an excellent wife – but although she was flattered and admired his intellect and charisma, she had no interest in him sexually.

'We broke up,' Sonia said shortly.

'Oh, I'm terribly sorry to hear that,' Cyril said, not sounding the least bit sorry.

'C'est la vie,' Sonia quipped, deflecting. She had no intention of going into the details of her breakup with Bill, but the truth was that the two of them had barely seen each other in recent months. What with Bill being posted to Dover and Sonia busy in London, they had drifted inexorably apart. The final straw had come when Bill had named Sonia in his divorce papers, after he'd promised that he wouldn't. Given that Bill had assured her his marriage was all but over when they met, citing his wife's lover, Sonia thought it bitterly unfair that she should be dragged into it. Perhaps it had provided the excuse she needed to break it off, Sonia reflected as she moved through the apartment, swallowed up by the throng, waving hello to Evelyn Waugh as she accepted a glass of an excellent Chablis which it was almost impossible to procure these days.

'Hello there,' Sonia smiled, as the artist Francis Bacon approached, kissing her on both cheeks.

'Sonia,' Francis replied delightedly. 'When are you going to let me paint you?'

'Never,' she replied with a shudder. 'No doubt you'll turn me into a monster, or something equally grotesque.'

'Perhaps,' Francis grinned impishly. 'But wouldn't it be more fun than those dull realist portraits your friends are so fond of?'

Sonia raised her eyebrows, giving him her best schoolmarm expression. 'Well, the world would be terribly dull if we all had the same taste, wouldn't it? Anyway, what are you working on at the moment, darling?'

Francis screwed up his face. He was moon-faced and dark-haired, a shabby character whose general air of dishevelment hinted at his chaotic life and his love of alcohol. 'I'm experimenting,' he confessed. 'I have an idea for...' he hesitated, and Sonia understood that he didn't want to jinx it. 'For a triptych. Based on some of my earlier work. I want to explore the Furies some more, and other themes too. I'm obsessed with Picasso's work – all that incredible biomorphic shit.'

'He's fascinating,' Sonia agreed. '*Guernica* was a fucking triumph. The world would be a better place if politicians paid more attention to artists, don't you agree? Ah, here's someone who's bound to have an opinion.'

She beckoned over a young man who looked as though he was still a teenager. Lucian Freud was undoubtedly handsome, with strong features and a shock of dark hair. He moved through the room with an irresistible magnetism, kissing Sonia and clapping Francis on the back heartily. He looked delighted to see them both.

'We were talking about Picasso,' she explained.

'Old hat,' Lucian said with a sly look at Francis, knowing how much the dismissal would rile him. 'Bring on something new.'

'Going to change the world, are you, Lucian?' Francis sniped good-naturedly.

'Yes, I rather think I might.'

'Stop bickering, boys,' Sonia told them. 'I have every confidence that you'll *both* go on to achieve great things. I wouldn't waste my time on you otherwise,' she laughed, as the dinner gong sounded and they were shepherded through to the dining room. Here, again, the privations of war seemed far away, as courses oozing with butter and cream were brought out, plates piled high with tender meat. Cyril had even been known to offer a cheese plate at the end of a meal. It was largely black-market produce, but Sonia and the other girls would sometimes offer their own ration books to make these evenings happen; it was worth living on bread and dripping for a week in return for the feast – both literal and cultural – that Cyril's gatherings offered.

Sonia took her place at the long walnut dinner table, which was beautifully dressed with candles, fine china and Sheffield silver cutlery. Lucian switched place cards and sat down on one side of her, whilst on the other was a tall, gaunt man who smelt strongly – and rather unpleasantly – of shag tobacco. He had a shock of unkempt dark hair and a small moustache, his appearance somewhat moth-eaten and dishevelled.

'Sonia, have you met Eric? We were at prep school together in Eastbourne, then I followed him to Eton,' Cyril explained as he swung past. 'Although I believe he mostly calls himself George these days.'

'George Orwell, pleased to meet you,' the man said, extending his hand formally.

'Sonia Brownell, likewise,' she smiled, shaking it, noticing his slender fingers and bony wrists. 'I've heard a lot about you – and read a lot of your work.'

'Thank you. Someone has to,' George replied, his face inscrutable. He reached into the pocket of his tweed jacket, and

Sonia noticed how the leather elbows were almost worn through. 'Cigarette?'

She stared at the tin he'd opened, tightly packed with hand-rolled cigarettes. The smell was pungent, the offer unappealing.

'No, thank you.'

He seemed unperturbed by her response, lighting one for himself and slipping the tin back inside his jacket. He took a drag and began coughing heavily.

'Are you all right?' Sonia was suddenly concerned for this pale, thin man who was clearly unwell.

'Quite all right,' he insisted. 'Throat's not been quite the same since a sniper's bullet went through it.'

'In Spain?'

'Yes.' He looked surprised.

'I read *Homage to Catalonia*,' she told him, by way of explanation.

'You and half a dozen others,' he grinned, showing crooked, yellow teeth, though behind the self-deprecating remark Sonia sensed his embarrassment. The account of his time fighting with the Republicans in the Spanish Civil War had sold fewer than a thousand copies.

'You're heavily critical of Stalin and the Soviets.'

'Soviet *communism*,' he corrected her. 'Not the Soviet people.'

'I rather admire communism,' Sonia said airily, determined to be controversial.

George merely looked amused. 'As do I – just not the Soviet kind. But when you've fought in a war and experienced it first hand, then perhaps I'll respect your opinion.'

Sonia bristled at his arrogance. 'Lots of people fought in Spain and have a different opinion to yours. Ernest Hemingway for example.'

'Hemingway.' George shook his head dismissively, stifling a laugh which turned into a cough. When he recovered, he said, 'So, tell me more about yourself, Miss Brownell. What do you do with your time? Other than give ill-informed opinions at dinner parties?'

Sonia's hackles rose, then she saw the teasing glint in his eye. 'I work for the Ministry of War Transport.'

His eyebrows rose infinitesimally. 'And what do you do there?'

'It's classified. I couldn't possibly tell a mere civilian.'

Sonia's curriculum vitae had grown over the last year or two. Whilst she'd accepted Stephen Spender's offer of occasional secretarial work for *Horizon*, she'd also – rather more surprisingly – taken up Bay's suggestion of nursing for UCH. Sonia had been gratified to contribute to the war effort, but in all honesty was glad to be out of it now; the shift work, accompanying rescue crews digging corpses from the rubble, was exhausting and traumatising. Occasionally the lifeless body of a young woman would give her such vivid flashbacks of Madeleine in Switzerland that she had to walk away. Sonia was much better suited to the desk-based civil service work in Berkeley Square, and the regular salary enabled her to rent a flat in Percy Street.

'Churchill's right-hand woman, are you?' George asked archly.

'Quite,' Sonia shot back. 'No, in fact I'm bound to a desk and spend my days poring over shipping routes and bills of lading. What I don't know about requisitioning liners, quite frankly, isn't worth knowing.'

Her smart comments raised a wry smile from George. 'And how do you know Cyril?' he asked, as he topped up her wine glass.

'I've done some work for *Horizon* – mostly administrative, but some editorial.'

'I see. So he hasn't asked you to marry him?'

'Not yet,' Sonia laughed. She regarded this man critically, with his rather shambolic appearance and impenetrable expression, finding herself intrigued by him. She knew that Cyril considered him a superb writer who had yet to fulfil his potential, and Sonia's interest was always piqued by anyone Cyril admired. So far, however, George Orwell was proving to be something of a disappointment. Sonia had imagined a strapping war hero, handsome and charming, a skilled wordsmith with witty anecdotes and sparkling conversation. Instead, he seemed rather dour, socially and physically awkward. But if Cyril revered his talent, then Sonia was willing to believe that there was more to George Orwell than first impressions might suggest. 'Cyril speaks very highly of you,' she said, watching his reaction.

'Well, that's very kind of him. He's always supported my work, even if he hasn't always agreed with it.'

'What are you working on at the moment?'

'Essays, reviews... I'm writing for *Tribune* and the *Partisan Review* in America, as well as *Horizon*. And I'm mulling over ideas for a new novel. Perhaps even something based on Soviet communism.'

Sonia narrowed her eyes. 'I can't tell whether you're being serious.'

George shrugged, his expression giving nothing away.

'If you fought in Spain, why aren't you fighting in France?'

'I'm *"unfit for any kind of military service"*. It's official. The Medical Board say so.'

'The sniper in the throat?'

'Amongst other things. I'm working for the BBC – the Eastern Service – so contributing to the war effort, just like you.'

'Through propaganda?'

'Absolutely. It's essential in wartime. And I've joined the Home Guard, so I'm practically the first line of defence if the Germans land.'

Sonia smiled. 'Are you married?' It was more a way of making conversation than a genuine interest in the answer.

'Yes. For almost six years. My wife's name is Eileen and she works for the Ministry of Food.'

'Sounds delicious. Where is she tonight?'

'Greenwich. She's gone to visit her parents.'

'And do you have children?'

'No, we... No.'

As their plates were cleared, Sonia excused herself to use the bathroom. She realised that she was a little drunk and found herself wondering whether George had found her attractive, or whether he was as much of a cold fish as he appeared. Oh, she knew it was shallow to even consider the question, but Sonia was astute enough to understand that sexuality was currency for a woman, and flirtation greased the wheels. Yet it was fair to say that whatever Cyril admired about George was a mystery to Sonia, she reflected, as she re-applied her lipstick and headed back to the dining room.

When she returned to the table, George had struck up conversation with the glamorous Barbara Skelton, seated on his other side, and Sonia turned gratefully to Lucian, whom she knew from experience to be far more fun as a dinner party guest. They were soon conversing about realism versus surrealism, their voices growing louder as each fought to make their point.

There'd been nothing memorable about her first encounter with George Orwell, and Sonia promptly forgot all about him.

PART IV
The Mother

Chapter Twenty-Seven

MAUREEN

Los Angeles, USA

January 1939

Maureen strolled into her expansive house in Bel Air, dropping her handbag onto the entry table before heading through to the wide, low-ceilinged lounge. She slipped off her shoes and lay down on one of the Chesterfield sofas, calling out, 'John?'

Moments later, John Farrow appeared in the doorway, striding over to greet his wife. He knelt down on the rug beside her, leaning in to kiss the gently rounded bump of her stomach.

'I'm exhausted,' Maureen groaned. 'Why did I ever let Edgar talk me into another Tarzan film?'

'You have to take care. Make sure you don't overwork.' John sat down on the other end of the sofa, settling her stockinged feet in his lap and gently rubbing the soles as Maureen sighed with pleasure.

'I won't. They're going to try and film most of my scenes first, because soon there'll be no hiding this.'

Maureen was currently five months along with their first baby, and she and John were overjoyed. She'd already signed up to another Tarzan film – *Tarzan Finds a Son*, the fourth in the franchise – and in this one, rather appropriately, Jane and Tarzan become parents to a baby they find in the jungle, the sole survivor of a plane crash.

'I've told them I want to die. At the end of this film,' Maureen explained with a smile, as John looked at her quizzically. 'Death by spear, or perhaps mauled by Cheeta. Something suitably dramatic. That way, I won't be able to go against my better judgement and say yes to another *Tarzan*.'

'The audience won't like that,' John said sagely, working his thumb into the arch of her foot. 'And I'll be surprised if the studio agrees. America always wants a happy ending – especially with everything that's going on in the world right now.' It was a reference to the unstable situation in Europe, with the rising tensions and Hitler's evident territorial ambitions.

'Edgar agrees,' Maureen nodded, referring to the creator of the Tarzan books. 'He's written to MGM telling them it would be a huge mistake to kill off Jane, so perhaps they'll simply replace me.'

'Ah, but you're irreplaceable.'

'Thank you, darling,' Maureen smiled. 'Anyway, tell me about your day.'

'Work's going well. I've got a good feeling about this one.' John was in pre-production for a film he was about to direct, called *Five Came Back*. It was a disaster movie about a plane crash in the Amazon jungle, and Lucille Ball was starring. 'I can visualise the final scene. It's going to be incredibly dramatic and heart-wrenching. The survivors finally get the plane fixed but only five of them can leave. The rest have to stay behind and take their chances with the hostile natives.'

Maureen shuddered. 'I'm sorry, darling, but it sounds terribly depressing to me. How strange that we're both working on films involving aeroplanes crashing. I can't bear to think of it, it upsets me terribly.' Instinctively, Maureen put a protective hand over the gentle swell of her stomach. Her bump was still small –

fortunately for the lengthy filming schedule – but Maureen could feel an unexpected firmness in her abdomen, noticing how her body was changing. Her breasts were full and swollen, which could only be good for the film, although this time Maureen had insisted that the costumes be less risqué. She was older now, a married woman and a mother-to-be; it didn't feel appropriate to be swimming naked or baring so much flesh. Besides, now the Hays Code had come into force – a set of guidelines for the self-censorship of the motion picture industry – it seemed unlikely such an insubstantial costume would be allowed. 'Have you eaten?' Maureen wondered, changing the subject. 'I'll ask Nellie to make a light supper and have it on a tray in my room.'

'Sounds good. I'll join you.'

John held out his hand, pulling Maureen up from the sofa, and she groaned as she got to her feet. 'I've never felt as tired as I have during pregnancy. Honestly, it's like a fog that envelops you, and you simply can't see straight.'

'You're a real trouper.'

'I'm not complaining,' Maureen insisted. 'I feel like the luckiest woman in the world. And you should see the baby that's playing my son on set – he's adorable, and so well behaved. I just want to eat him right up.'

'You know, I've been thinking,' John began, as they made their way up the L-shaped wooden staircase. 'About the baby's name. We should call him Damien.'

It was all Maureen could do not to roll her eyes; her husband's fascination with Father Damien, the priest who'd dedicated his life to working with lepers on the Pacific island of Molokai, was bordering on obsession.

'Perhaps,' she said softly. 'There's still a few months to go. Let's wait and see.'

'Oh my goodness!' Maureen's hands flew to her face in surprise.

'Happy baby shower,' exclaimed Norma Shearer.

'Norma, it looks beautiful,' Maureen gushed, embracing her friend as she glanced round the living room of Norma's chic Beverly Hills home, which had been decorated in a profusion of yellow and white especially for the occasion. There were bunches of yellow and white balloons, a banner reading 'Welcome, Baby Farrow', and even a life-sized model of a stork with a beautifully wrapped gift hanging from the swaddle in its beak. A table was spread with finger sandwiches and iced biscuits, and decorated with bunches of yellow flowers.

Norma ushered Maureen into the small circle of women. There was Myrna Loy, Carmelita Geraghty, Pat Paterson and Louella Parsons, as well as Maureen's mother Mary and her sister Sheila.

'I didn't invite too many people,' Norma murmured. 'I didn't want it to be overwhelming for you.'

Maureen smiled gratefully. At eight months pregnant she felt enormous; her bump entered the room well before she did, her face and ankles were swollen and puffy, and she'd developed a decidedly unappealing waddle when she walked. 'Thank you. I feel like a baby elephant.'

'Oh no, you look radiant,' Norma insisted, as the two of them were enveloped in a cloud of the Blue Grass perfume that Mary O'Sullivan had taken to wearing since she'd been living in Los Angeles.

'Isn't this just grand?' Mary beamed, gazing around. 'Aren't you just the luckiest?'

'Yes, Mother, I am,' Maureen said, humouring her. She sat down, eager to take the weight off her feet. She'd been expecting a relaxed catch-up over tea with Norma – nothing too strenuous to tax her pregnant body and tired mind – and had been stunned to see her close friends waiting for her. 'By the way, how did Sheila's screen test go?'

They turned to look at Maureen's younger sister, who was standing next to the tray of sponge cakes, clearly battling with herself.

'She said it went well, but I'm not so sure,' Mary replied, in a loud whisper, her voice carrying across the room. 'Between you and me, I'm not sure she's got the talent for it.'

The O'Sullivan family's latest trip to Los Angeles – ostensibly to help Maureen when the new baby arrived – had been Sheila's second attempt to crack Hollywood. Two studios had offered her screen tests, and there were rumours that a small role would be written into *Tarzan Finds a Son* for her, but so far it had all come to nothing.

'No, if we haven't heard anything by the time the baby's born, then it'll be time for us to go back home,' Mary insisted, and Maureen tried to hide her sigh of relief. 'California's all very well, but I miss Ireland.'

'Yes, all the sunshine and parties can get rather dull after a while,' Maureen empathised, her tongue very firmly in her cheek.

'I'm terribly sorry I'm late, I had to pop by the studio on my way here.'

Maureen stood up as she heard the newcomer's voice. 'Vivien!' She felt a stab of envy at how good Vivien looked, tinier than ever in an elegant royal blue Schiaparelli dress with a cinched waist and butterfly sleeves.

'Maureen, darling, you look wonderful,' Vivien complimented her friend, as she strode across Norma Shearer's living room, her court heels sinking into the thick pile carpet.

Maureen waved away the compliment disbelievingly. She was surely the size of a house and had never looked worse in her life. 'I didn't know if you were still in the country.'

'I'm returning to London tomorrow, so I can't stay long, but I wanted to pop in.'

'How sweet of you.'

'I wouldn't have missed it for the world,' Vivien beamed. 'So, how are you feeling about everything? Excited? Scared? In denial?'

'All of the above,' Maureen laughed. 'But I keep telling myself that my mother gave birth eight times so surely it can't be *too* terrible…'

Vivien pulled a face and Maureen laughed.

'Thought she certainly seemed to resent us for it afterwards,' Maureen continued, *sotto voce*, glancing over at Mary, who was holding forth by the canapes. 'She didn't set the greatest example for motherhood…'

'Yes, I remember,' Vivien replied discreetly, and Maureen knew she was remembering their private conversations at Roehampton, confided after lights out, when Maureen would tearfully confess how upset she was by her mother's coldness, her callous behaviour, her heartless comments. As a child, she couldn't understand why her own mother didn't even seem to like her, and she was confused by what she'd done wrong.

'What if I'm the same as her?' Maureen whispered, cradling her baby bump anxiously. 'What if, when the baby comes, I'm distant and dismissive? What if we don't bond? What if we—' She broke off, remembering that Vivien's relationship with her daughter was far from ideal, that little Suzanne was back in England being cared for by her father and grandmother whilst Vivien lived the life of a movie star in Hollywood with her married lover.

'I'm sure you'll be a wonderful mother,' Vivien assured her, placing her hand on her arm. 'You're warm and loving and empathetic. I'm not going to lie – having a baby is life-changing, physically and emotionally. You suddenly have someone else to consider every time you make a decision. Even though I'm over here, and Suzanne's with Leigh,' Vivien continued, as though she'd read Maureen's mind, 'I'm always thinking of her. But then I wonder, is it too late? Have I already damaged her in some way by leaving, or would it have been worse if I'd stayed? If she'd seen me unhappy, frustrated, resenting Leigh…' Vivien trailed off, her eyes shining wet.

Maureen could see that she was weighed down with guilt and

uncertainty, but she knew that, ultimately, Vivien had done what was right for her.

'I'm sorry, darling,' Vivien apologised, dabbing her eyes with a handkerchief she produced from her handbag. 'This is supposed to be your day and I'm rabbiting on about myself.'

'Don't be silly, darling. I'm always here if you need me.'

'Thank you,' Vivien sniffed, pulling herself together. 'Tell me about John. Is he excited? Looking forward to becoming a father?'

'Well, he already *is* a father, but he's hoping for a boy this time around.'

Vivien frowned in confusion.

'I told you he was married before, didn't I? He got someone in the family way, as they say, and her father forced John to marry her. It didn't last long. Felice, the daughter, lives in San Francisco with her mother, so John rarely sees her…'

Vivien looked shocked, her ruby lips a perfect O, and Maureen couldn't help but laugh.

'So you see, darling, you're not the only one in an unusual situation.'

'And here was I thinking you had a perfect life and a perfect husband, that you were following every cardinal rule of the Catholic Church. I felt sure you must be looking down on Larry and me for behaving so sinfully.'

Maureen looked hurt. 'Did you really think that? Of course I wouldn't. Look, life certainly isn't black and white, like the nuns told us it would be. We all have to navigate our own path, and we can't set store by other people's opinions.'

There was a beat of silence as Vivien absorbed her words, then she smiled. 'I think you're going to do just fine as a mother, darling.'

The two clasped hands and Maureen felt a rush of warmth towards Vivien, reflecting how the bond they'd shared from their school days would never truly be broken.

Louella Parsons, the gossip columnist, came bustling up to them, a lemon-coloured hat on her head in a nod to the theme. She and Maureen were great friends, and Maureen was thinking of asking her to be the baby's godmother. 'I thought this was a baby shower?' she demanded, in her no-nonsense Midwest accent. 'So let's do some showering.'

She handed Maureen a large gift, exquisitely wrapped with an enormous yellow bow. Maureen opened it to find a white mohair Steiff teddy bear, with a red ribbon around his neck.

'Oh, he's adorable,' Maureen exclaimed, giving the bear a cuddle. The presents continued to come: clothes, blankets, bootees, rattles. Mary had bought her daughter a large hamper of cloth diapers.

'Mark my words,' she said with a nod. 'They'll be the most useful present you receive here today.'

'Thank you, Ma. Practical as always.'

'What do you think you're having?' asked Myrna.

'Do you have a preference?' added Carmelita.

'I'd like a girl, but of course John wants a boy. So I suppose I don't really mind.'

'It's a boy,' Mary insisted, nodding at Maureen's stomach. 'I can tell from the way you're carrying. Low and large means it's a boy.'

'Perhaps,' Maureen smiled, rubbing her belly affectionately.

'Mark my words,' Mary continued. 'I've had eight babies – though not all of them are still with us, God rest their souls – and I couldn't be more certain. It's a boy.'

On the 30th of May 1939, Maureen gave birth to her first child: a son, named Michael Damien Villiers Farrow. The baby was serene and good-natured, fair like John, brown-eyed like Maureen. And he was perfect.

Chapter Twenty-Eight

Los Angeles, USA

January 1942

'Catch me, Mamma! Catch me!'

Little Michael toddled across the lawn on sturdy legs as fast as he could go, looking back over his shoulder and screeching with delight. Maureen ran after him, her arms outstretched, before scooping him up and swinging him round. His giggle was infectious, and Maureen experienced a moment of pure joy as she cradled him in her arms, burying her face in his neck as he clung to her, inhaling the familiar scent of her boy.

Reluctantly, she set him down on his feet – he would be three in a matter of months and was growing heavy – and he dropped to his knees to examine a bug crawling in the grass. Maureen watched him, marvelling at his ability to find such pleasure in the mundane. Then her thoughts turned, as ever, to her husband and a weight came over her, a familiar wave of sadness that he wasn't here to experience these moments. John had missed out on so much of Michael's childhood.

'Look, Mamma. Look!' Michael entreated her, as he picked up

a maple bug and watched it crawl over his hand. The winter day was mild, the sun filtering through the leafy garden and bathing him in a shaft of light that caught his blond hair. Her golden child.

She loved him beyond measure, the strength of her feelings like nothing she'd ever experienced before. But motherhood evoked a mixture of emotions for Maureen. She'd engaged a string of governesses and nannies to look after Michael and, in truth, she'd been glad to get back to work, to focus on something other than this little person who'd taken over her life. But she adored this time with Michael, these special, precious moments. If John came home – *when* he came home, she corrected herself – she wanted more children.

'Mrs Farrow?'

She looked up to see Nanny Croft emerge from the house. She was smart and well presented, kind but disciplined. Maureen had made sure to hire well-reputed staff from a good agency; she didn't want Michael to experience the torments she had as a child.

'Would you like me to take Michael inside for lunch now?'

'Yes, thank you. Remember to wash your hands, darling,' she addressed Michael, who leapt to his feet, letting the bug fly away as he raced towards the house. 'Steady, darling,' she called after him. 'No need to run.' Maureen followed him; she had work to do whilst Michael ate and napped.

Inside the house, she was surprised to see that Michael had stopped, and was standing by the mahogany side table with its cluster of silver-framed photographs, staring intently at one of them.

'Daddy,' he said, pointing at it.

Maureen felt her heart flip. She sank down beside him on the plush carpet, and he sat on her lap, cuddling into her. 'Yes, that's Daddy,' she encouraged him.

'Daddy on boat,' Michael continued, his bright voice high and cheery.

'Yes,' Maureen smiled sadly. 'Daddy's on a boat. Your daddy is so brave and so handsome, and you're going to grow up to be just like him, aren't you?'

Michael was watching her face as she spoke, and nodded sombrely. 'Michael on boat,' he told her, before turning back to the picture. It showed John in his naval uniform, a dazzling white jacket and trousers, with the epaulettes of a Commander. It had been taken in Nova Scotia, when he'd first joined up, more than two years ago now.

Although the US wasn't at war at that time, John's native Australia was fighting alongside the Allies, and both he and Maureen felt that they should be supporting the war effort. John, with his naval background, had enlisted in the Canadian Navy in November of 1939. Maureen had initially given up her film career – she'd recently made *Pride and Prejudice* with Greer Garson and Laurence Olivier, and the movie had been very well received – and gone to join her husband in Canada. After a few months of sitting round, idle, with John still having not been despatched, she'd gone back to Hollywood with baby Michael to make the comedy-drama *Maisie Was a Lady*.

He'd been posted in December 1940, on minesweeper duty in the South Pacific, and every single day Maureen was terrified that he might not come back to her. She prayed, more fervently than she had for years, that he would be returned to her unharmed. She couldn't help but think of her father's injuries in the war, how it had changed him and affected everything about their household, especially his relationship with Mary.

In many ways, Maureen knew that she was privileged – she wasn't overly worried about making ends meet, although she'd had to go back to work as John's naval salary was significantly less than he'd been making in the movies, and they'd become accustomed to a certain lifestyle. It was a great leveller, knowing that she was in the same position as so many women across the world, waiting for news of their loved ones. It felt as though life was on hold; Maureen and Michael were living in a rented house in Los Angeles, but had got rid of their furniture and their dogs when they'd moved to Canada, not knowing where they'd end up or what the future held. Now, it didn't seem right to put down roots until the war was over and John was safely back with them in California.

Michael was a huge comfort to Maureen, a piece of John that couldn't be taken from her. She had to keep the atmosphere light and playful for him, couldn't let herself sink into melancholy for his sake. Now, she held him tight and planted a kiss on the top of his head, before reaching up to put the photograph of John back on the side table.

'Run along now, Michael, darling. It's lunch time. Mamma will see you later.'

He scampered off happily, following Nanny Croft. Maureen watched him go, assailed by a tumult of emotions, then went to get her script.

Maureen was sitting in the garden, a blanket round her shoulders as the weather was still cool at this time of year. She was reading scripts; she'd been sent a vast number of them, and was trying to decide on her next project when Nanny Croft came running across the lawn, an anxious look on her face.

'There's a phone call for you, Mrs Farrow.'

Maureen's stomach plummeted, nausea overwhelming her. 'Is it…?'

'It's the Canadian War Department,' Nanny Croft confirmed, and her face was ashen.

A cold sweat broke out all over Maureen's body. She ran into the house, carried by adrenaline, and snatched up the phone, trying to sound composed.

'Hello?'

'Mrs Farrow?'

'Yes. This is she.' Maureen tried to swallow but her throat felt thick and swollen.

'I'm calling from the Canadian War Department about your husband, John Farrow.'

Our Father, who art in heaven… Please let him be alive. Please God, don't take John from me…

Maureen thought she might pass out. 'Yes?'

'I'm afraid your husband has contracted typhoid.'

Oh, thank God, thank you. He's still alive, thank you, he —

'He's not expected to live. I'm very sorry, Mrs Farrow. He's being repatriated to our base in Ottawa. I believe you're in the United States, so if you could make arrangements to have him admitted to a hospital near you, so that he's nearby when—'

'No.' The word came out instinctively. The revelation that John was still alive brought with it joy and relief and resolution.

'I'm sorry?'

Maureen glanced back at the framed photo of her husband on the hallway table. 'John is a terrible patient. He'll never recover in a hospital, and I wouldn't want to inflict him on those poor nurses. Send him home to me. I'll look after him.'

'Mrs Farrow, I would strongly advise—'

'He'll get the best medical treatment here, but I want him by my side.' Maureen knew in an instant that she would give up her career – would give up everything, in fact – for John. Being with him, for however long he had left, was all that mattered.

'Very well. If you could make the arrangements at your side and we'll be in touch later today.'

'I will. And thank you.'

Maureen put the receiver down and burst into tears. She was overjoyed that he was still alive, but terrified about what state he might be in. She gave herself a minute to cry, then wiped her eyes on a handkerchief, taking deep, gulping breaths. There were arrangements to be made, practicalities to be seen to, and there was no time to waste.

'Oh, my darling,' Maureen exclaimed, shocked as she laid eyes on John for the first time in over a year. The private ambulance had driven slowly up the long driveway towards the house, with John's inert, wasted body moved onto a gurney to be wheeled inside. Maureen was beside him instantly, self-conscious in front of the medical staff who accompanied John as they were reunited. It certainly wasn't the way Maureen had expected her husband to return home.

It felt surreal. She'd spent the last few days preparing for this moment, rearranging the house, hiring staff and reading up about his condition. Maureen had had one of the reception rooms converted to a bedroom, and employed a small army of nurses so that a medical professional was always on hand, though she intended to undertake the bulk of John's care herself. And now he was finally here, covered with a pristine white sheet, his face pale, his eyes closed. Maureen couldn't shake the images of bodies she'd seen covered with shrouds, newsreels of fallen soldiers in Europe and Asia. She knew she should be grateful that John was coming back to her at all.

She thanked the ambulance staff profusely as they settled him in his room, but then they were gone, and husband and wife were alone. Maureen smothered John in soft kisses, trying to hide her distress at his appearance. His eyelids flickered open and he seemed to recognise her, but his cheeks were hollow and sunken, his lips dry. He'd lost so much weight that his once-powerful frame seemed haggard, the bloom of a fierce red rash emerging from beneath his night shirt.

Maureen blinked back tears, trying to push the doctor's words from her mind: *He's not expected to live… I'm very sorry… Not expected to live…*

John looked like a corpse, his skin ashen, dark shadows ringing his eyes. She couldn't lose him… Not now, not after everything they'd been through. Michael needed a father; *she* needed a husband.

Maureen was well aware that she was being selfish. Right

across the world, wives were losing husbands, children losing parents and parents losing children, as this damn war rolled on endlessly. Now that the United States had entered the fray, Maureen hoped there'd be a swift conclusion, though it meant neighbours, friends, colleagues were all signing up to be shipped off to fight. It was such a waste, she thought angrily, not ashamed to admit she wished John had never signed up. It had seemed a noble gesture at the time, but now she'd give anything to turn back the clock, to try to change his mind, to keep him safe at home with her and Michael.

The tears rose again, and for a second, Maureen almost gave in to the comfort of breaking down. But she'd sobbed solidly these past few days, and now that John was finally here, she needed to stay strong for his sake.

She sat beside him on the bed, taking his limp hand in hers, stroking it softly.

'You're going to get better, darling,' she murmured. 'I promise you. I'm going to be the best nurse – oh, I know you probably think I'm useless at that kind of thing, but you'd be surprised what I can turn my hand to.

'And Michael's been missing you dreadfully. Just as soon as you're feeling better, I'll bring him in to visit you. You should see him, darling, he's such a bright, happy little boy, and he's the spitting image of you. I'd like us to have more children, just as soon as you've recovered. God, I've missed you dreadfully. I've thought about you every night. Perhaps that can be an incentive.' Maureen laughed softly. 'I'm ready and willing whenever you are.'

She fell silent for a moment, watching for any flicker of reaction from John. His body was hot with fever, his breath rattling in his lungs.

'And I'm not going to let you lie here all day, being idle and growing bored,' Maureen teased, wiping away a tear. 'You need to finish the book you're writing, for a start. And I'm going to find you a script to direct... You're going to be such a success, my darling. You're so talented and so clever, there's nothing you can't do. But you have to get better, John… Promise me, darling,' Maureen begged, bringing his hand to her lips and kissing it. She was crying freely now. 'I'll pray for you every night but you have to get better… I need you… Don't leave me, John… I love you so much… Please, don't leave me…'

Chapter Twenty-Nine

Los Angeles, USA

May 1945

'Too-ra, Loo-ra, Loo-ral…'

Maureen awoke to the distant sound of singing. For a moment, she couldn't work out where she was. Was she back in Roscommon, her mother crooning a lullaby?

As she was slowly pulled from sleep and her eyes adjusted to the darkness, Maureen realised that she was in her bedroom, the song made famous by Bing Crosby drifting along the corridor to reach her.

She took a sip of water from the glass by her bed and got up, pulling her robe around her before setting off along the shadowy passage to the nursery. Maureen's bedroom was at the back of the house, the nursery at the front.

She passed Michael's room, her firstborn, about to turn six and the most happy, lively child. Then came Patrick, her second child, now two and a half. He'd been born ten months after John came home. Maureen had known her husband was on the road to

257

recovery when she'd seen that twinkle in his eye and – slowly, gently – they'd made love for the first time in almost two years.

At the far end of the corridor, a low light spilled out from under the door and the singing grew louder. Gently, Maureen pushed open the door and went inside.

Her daughter's room was neat and tidy, painted in palest pink, with a white wooden cot surrounded by lace drapes that hung from the ceiling. A rocking horse stood in one corner, a collection of teddy bears and dolls keeping guard from the shelves behind. Over by the window was Mia's night nurse, Jean, a stout, capable woman in her early sixties, gently rocking the three-month-old baby in her arms. Mia was almost asleep, making gentle, snuffling noises and Maureen padded quietly towards them.

'How is she?' she murmured.

The nurse jumped, stepping away from the window, a guilty expression flitting across her face. Mia, disturbed in her arms, let out a small cry.

'She's fine, Mrs Farrow. I've just given her a feed – she took four ounces.'

'Thank you, Jean. I'll take her,' Maureen said, reaching out for her beloved daughter. She adored her two boys, but had prayed for a girl and her supplication had been heard. Maria de Lourdes Villiers Farrow, known as Mia, had been born on the 9th of February 1945, and both Maureen and John were smitten.

Maureen rocked the baby, who stared up at her with drowsy eyes, ignoring the look of surprise from the nurse who hovered nearby. Maureen had employed a small army of nannies and governesses to look after her children, and it was true to say that she was not a hands-on mother. Whilst she adored her children, and enjoyed being pregnant, she wasn't sure what to *do* with them. Maureen herself had been raised by a succession of nannies and, whilst she'd hated it, both she and John had busy careers and the pattern looked set to continue.

Maureen traced her finger over Mia's soft skin, stroking her nose to encourage her to close her eyes. The curtains were open a crack, a shaft of moonlight falling into the room. Maureen went to close them when she heard a noise outside, the low rumble of her husband's voice followed by a woman's laughter. Throaty and flirtatious. Maureen tensed and the baby stirred.

'All right, Jean, you can go now. I'll put Mia to bed.'

'Very good, Mrs Farrow.'

Jean turned and left, and Maureen's cheeks burned with shame as she realised why the nurse had been looking out of the window. She wondered how many other nights Jean had stood here, looking out over the gardens, seeing John Farrow arrive home with another woman.

Maureen moved closer to the window, balancing Mia in the crook of her arm, pulling the curtain aside with her free hand. It took a moment for her to find them, hidden by the bushes in the lush garden, pressed up against the trunk of a palm tree. Then John took the woman by the hand and pulled her along the path. They were laughing, drunk, hanging off one another, his hands roaming over her body, squeezing her buttocks in the clinging dress she was wearing.

The woman was glamorous, in a cheap way; her dyed blonde hair hung loose in tonged waves, her red dress low cut and riding up her thighs. Maureen wondered briefly if she was a prostitute and the thought made her feel sick.

She glanced down at her own flannelette nightgown, aware of the rollers in her hair and the cold cream on her face, feeling dowdy and old-fashioned. She knew she should move away from the window but she couldn't stop watching.

They made their way down the path towards the house, John looking tall and broad and handsome. He'd always been attractive to women, and Maureen had known he wasn't a saint, but having his infidelity thrown in her face like this was overwhelming. She was aware of his reputation when she'd married him, but she'd hoped he would change. Now she found herself wondering if he'd ever been faithful, even for a short period.

Something bubbled deep inside her – bile, nausea, but anger

and shame too. He wasn't even trying to hide it, she thought, fury and sadness coursing through her.

Wasn't she enough for him, Maureen wondered? She'd borne his children, she had a stellar, highly lucrative career, she was regularly named one of the most beautiful women in the world. Yet still John Farrow wasn't satisfied.

Was it the variety that stimulated him? The thrill of the chase? Some kink that he didn't feel comfortable requesting from his wife? Maureen would never understand men, she realised. They were always restless, always searching for something better, some cruel quirk of biology engaging them in an endless quest to fornicate and procreate.

She thought of her own parents, how her mother would disappear into her father's room every Wednesday afternoon and lock the door. Whatever happened inside was conducted in absolute silence, and neither of their moods seemed to be improved afterwards.

Mia was now sleeping soundly in Maureen's arms. Maureen let the curtain drop and crossed the room to the cot, laying her down gently. Mia stirred but didn't wake.

'Don't ever let a man treat you that way, my darling,' Maureen whispered into the darkness. She hoped for better for her daughter. She wondered how John would feel if someone ever treated Mia the way he treated Maureen. Had he ever stopped to consider his daughter, to think what it would be like for Mia growing up and meeting women who'd slept with her father, making friends whose mothers had conducted affairs with John Farrow? But Maureen knew those thoughts had never crossed John's mind – he was thinking only of himself, as he always did.

She moved back to the window but her husband and his mystery woman had disappeared from view. Maureen knew exactly where they'd gone. On the west side of the sprawling house was John's bedroom; he and Maureen had slept separately for some time now, and John had even gone so far as to have a separate entrance put in for his room.

'When I get back late from my boys' nights, a little drunk and smelling of alcohol and cigars, I won't wake up the rest of the house,' he'd said casually, when he first suggested the idea. 'You can be near the children, and if you have an early call on set, I won't disturb you.'

There was a whole litany of invented reasons, which were somehow more humiliating than if he'd simply told her the truth.

Maureen had agreed to the request, her face bright but resentment and sadness balling in her stomach. Days later, the builders arrived and work commenced. She felt culpable, though she'd done nothing wrong; they both knew what he was asking, and her silence was her tacit consent.

Outside it was still and silent, the moon a sliver, the stars invisible. John and his tart had moved indoors to continue their liaison, but Maureen wouldn't forget what she'd seen, the images printed indelibly on her mind.

She wouldn't go in there tonight, wouldn't lower herself to interrupt them *in flagrante* and embarrass herself by making a scene. But this was a humiliation too far, and Maureen was determined not to put up with it any longer.

The following morning John rose late. He sloped down to the breakfast table just before midday and seemed surprised when Maureen sat down opposite him. She was calm and composed, her lips pursed and her back erect.

'Good morning,' John said. His voice was gravelly after a night's heavy drinking and Lord knew what else.

'Good morning,' Maureen replied tightly, her eyes blazing.

'Everything all right?'

She'd barely slept last night, going over this conversation a thousand times in her head with all its possible iterations. When it came to it, she blurted out the words unplanned. 'No, everything is not all right. I saw you last night, John. I *saw* you.'

'And?' He looked unconcerned.

'I saw you with *her*.' Maureen was shaking with fury by now. How *dare* he treat her like this. She had quite literally nursed him back to life when the doctors had written him off with typhoid, and *this* was how he repaid her?

His face remained unchanged, though he paused, clearly weighing up how to reply. 'Well, she's gone now,' he said casually. 'She won't be back.' He reached for a slice of toast and began to butter it, as though they were conversing about the weather. 'She didn't mean anything to me, if that's what you're worried about.'

Maureen was incandescent. 'That's not the point! It's humiliating for me, John. Jean saw you too. I can't imagine what she thinks.'

'Why do you care what some nurse thinks? It's none of her damn business.'

'It's *my* business, John. You're married to *me*. You're not supposed to be running around with every tart in town. I've put up with it for long enough and now I'm sick of it.'

John crunched down on his toast, crumbs scattering across the tablecloth. 'Well, I'm sorry that you're upset but, quite frankly, you knew what I was like before you married me. And it's not like you've been a saint.'

'I beg your pardon! I've never been unfaithful to you. Never!'

'Perhaps not since we were married. But you were hardly a virgin back then, were you? Running around Hollywood, sleeping with married men. The sanctity of marriage didn't seem to concern you then, did it? Your morals went straight out of the window.'

'Don't you dare try to put this on me! You've cheated on me repeatedly – more times than I know – and you don't even seem to care.'

'This is just how I am.' John shrugged. 'I can't promise it won't happen again.'

Maureen felt as though she'd been slapped. This was far from the reaction she'd been expecting – she'd imagined that John would at least pretend to be contrite and apologetic, even if he didn't mean it, but this was brazen.

'So what was so special about her?' Maureen demanded, her voice quavering as tears threatened to fall. 'What's she got that I haven't?'

John shrugged. 'Nothing. But she was there, she was available. You were at home with the kids, cold cream on your face and wearing a nightgown that looked like it belonged to my grandmother. Can you blame me?'

Maureen burst into tears, horrified to recognise herself in his description, and disgusted that he was making her feel as though it was her fault. She'd been feeling old and unattractive after giving birth to three children, and John's cruel words had only confirmed Maureen's worst fears. The war had changed her, their separation and his illness had had a profound effect on her, and she was no longer the carefree girl she'd been in her youth. But she was his loyal wife of almost a decade – surely she deserved better? She'd nursed him back from the brink of death; didn't he owe her some loyalty, some respect?

'Do you know how many thousands of men would cut their right arm off for a chance to sleep with me? You saw the letters I got after *Tarzan*. Hell, the industry brought in censorship because of me!'

'Exactly! Men are fickle creatures, easily distracted by a shapely leg or a generous bosom. How many of those guys fantasising about you had a wife at home who'd stopped making an effort? Who'd quit paying attention to them since the kids arrived? You built your career out of titillation so don't come all high and mighty and moral with me, Maureen, it won't wash.'

Maureen was sobbing now, her head pounding as she realised the truth. She understood now why she'd never confronted him before; she'd been wilfully blind. She'd always known what John was like, and she was a fool if she expected him to change.

'Do you want a divorce?' she whispered.

'No, do you?' John laughed as though the idea was

unthinkable. 'I love you and you love me. Why on earth would we divorce? But I'm not going to change, Maureen. You know I'm not. I didn't want to have this conversation, and I don't want to have it ever again. So either you accept how things are, or I'm gone.'

Maureen gasped as John issued his ultimatum, seeing the harsh reality of her situation. He loved her, but not *enough*. Not enough to give up the other women. *She* wasn't enough for him. She could hardly see through her tears, as she took in choking gulps of air.

Was this just what everyone did? Especially in Hollywood. Even Vivien had left her husband for a married man; they'd both cheated on their partners. Perhaps Maureen was naïve to think that her marriage would be different. John was right when he'd accused her of sleeping with married men. Sure, she'd been young and foolish, but it hadn't seemed to matter at the time. She realised with a stab of guilt that in every instance she'd dismissed the wife as irrelevant, a dull, distant figure, out of sight and out of mind.

Right now Maureen felt utterly broken. She wouldn't do this anymore, she promised herself, would never again put herself through such humiliation. But she had to make a decision – stay with John, or tell him to leave?

Maureen was thirty-four years old with three children – she was terrified that no one else would want her, and she was afraid of being by herself. Their lives had been intertwined for more than a decade and, despite everything, she still loved him. He fascinated her more than any man she'd ever met, and their sexual chemistry was undeniable. She wanted to be a good wife, didn't want their relationship to deteriorate into cold indifference, the way her parents' marriage had.

It was going to be hard, and it was going to hurt but, regretfully, Maureen knew which path she would take.

Chapter Thirty

VIVIEN

Denham, England

September 1944

'I am a queen. A real, real queen!' Vivien declared, her eyes flashing dangerously as she raised her arms aloft, her voice high and girlish. She ran across the polished floor of the Memphis Palace and leapt onto the dais, her chiffon robe floating around her, her black bobbed wig and winged eyes instantly recognisable as the famed Egyptian leader. 'Cleopatra, the queen,' she finished, watched by her coterie of Nubian slaves as she revelled in her power.

'Cut,' yelled the director. Gabriel Pascal was Hungarian by birth, with slicked-back hair and hooded eyes, his frame stocky in his well-tailored suits.

The crew sprang into action, resetting the scene on the set of *Caesar and Cleopatra*. Vivien stood, shivering, rooted to the spot as everything happened around her. She seemed to shrink when the camera wasn't on her, a petite figure lost in the cavernous space. She was freezing too, dressed for the Egyptian heat but standing in a draughty aircraft hangar on a cool autumn day in

Buckinghamshire. They were filming at Denham Studios, where the making of the motion picture was occasionally interrupted by the whistle of bombs landing nearby. Vivien longed to be back in her dressing room, where she had a warm robe and a four-bar electric fire.

'Let's go again,' said Gabriel. 'Vivien, I need more passion, more exuberance.'

Vivien nodded obediently but couldn't seem to summon her enthusiasm. She felt flat inside, assailed by the memory that mere weeks ago she'd been here, filming this same scene, full of life – quite literally. Back then, she'd had Larry's child growing inside her.

There had been an accident. Vivien had slipped on set, and days later she lost the baby. It was the second time it had happened; she'd miscarried two years earlier, and it had been devastating for them both. More than anything in the world, Vivien longed to have a baby with Larry. A child would complete them, would cement their relationship. And it would give them the opportunity to make up for previous failings with their own children; this time they would be dedicated, present, free of guilt.

She'd been on bed rest for the past few weeks but, bored and frustrated, she'd returned to work as soon as the doctor had allowed it, thinking that might be the tonic she needed. Now that she was back on set, she felt flat and listless, disenchanted with the film. The script was poor, the direction was bad; Vivien suspected that this movie would not be one of her finest.

Waiting for her cue, she pulled awkwardly at her costume, an Egyptian dress called a kalasiris. It felt too large around the midriff. She'd asked her dresser to have all her costumes taken in, now that her stomach was no longer full and swollen. She'd lost weight too, her birdlike appetite vanishing altogether during her convalescence. Now her robes seemed to mock her, the gaping material a visible reminder of what she'd lost. Had the woman done it on purpose? Had she deliberately disobeyed Vivien's instructions?

The clapperboard snapped shut, marking the take, but Vivien was oblivious.

'Action,' the director called. Vivien remained still and silent, as though she hadn't heard his words. 'Action,' Gabriel called again, a note of confusion in his voice.

This time, Vivien sprang to life, the cameras capturing everything as she played the scene flawlessly, word-perfect, her kohl-lined eyes flashing. She was playful one moment, menacing the next, in a dark wig with a gold diadem, her arched eyebrows thickly pencilled.

Unexpectedly, she stopped. The actors around her – Flora Robson as her nurse, Ftatateeta; the extras dressed as slaves – faltered. Was this intentional? Was it part of the performance?

Vivien turned, her gaze like ice, her mouth pressed into an angry line. 'Where is Mrs Edwards?' she demanded, naming her dresser.

Cast and crew alike stared in confusion. 'Cut,' yelled Gabriel, in frustration. 'Vivien, is there a problem with—'

'Where is she?' Vivien spat. Her voice was low and rasping, white-hot anger etched on her face. 'My costume. She hasn't taken in my costume! I told her to and she's purposely ignored me. Look,' Vivien insisted, balling handfuls of the material in her palms, thrusting it towards her director.

'Let's take a break,' Gabriel suggested, walking carefully towards Vivien, his arms outstretched. The cast stood down, the crew re-setting for the next take.

'Get your fucking hands off me,' Vivien hissed. She lashed out like a cat swiping with its claws.

'I'm sorry,' Gabriel apologised carefully. 'Let's go and find Mrs Edwards, perhaps she can explain.'

'Where is she? I want her fired! How can I work when my costume isn't right? The incompetent bitch.'

'Vivien, please, I'm sure it's a misunderstanding. Let's speak to her and resolve it.'

She turned on him, her mesmerising eyes now cold and dark,

her expression blank. Gabriel had never seen anything like it, and it terrified him. When she spoke, her voice was harsh and rasping. 'Don't you dare take her side! Are you fucking her? Is that why you're defending her?'

Gabriel was shocked, but he could see that something was seriously wrong; he knew Vivien wasn't herself. Glancing around, he met the horrified eyes of Brian Hurst, the first assistant director. 'Call the doctor,' Gabriel mouthed discreetly, but Vivien overheard him.

'I don't need a doctor,' she raged, her small voice echoing through the large space. 'I don't—' Vivien screamed and fell to the floor, her body convulsing, her limbs jerking. Her eyes were closed as she cried out in pain and alarm.

Gabriel was horrified, panic enveloping him. Brian could only stare, shocked at what he was witnessing, as Gabriel yelled, 'Get the doctor. *Now.*'

Vivien was sitting up in bed, *The Times* crossword open on her lap and a pen between her fingers. She hadn't yet solved a single clue as she stared blankly ahead, lost in her thoughts. Outside it was a blustery autumn day, the trees slowly turning bare as though they were losing themselves, piece by piece. In springtime they would bloom again, but would they be the same tree they once were? Vivien wondered distractedly. Or when they shed their leaves each year did they lose something essential, imperceptibly altered with the passing of every season?

Vivien tucked the quilt more tightly around her; the rickety old windows let in a cool breeze, and she was always chilly these days. Despite its faults, she adored this house, tucked away in a quiet street in Chelsea not far from the river. Durham Cottage was the first home she and Larry had made together; Larry had bought it for them seven years ago, and since then Vivien had set about decorating it and perfecting it, exactly to her tastes. It was her idyllic retreat from the world.

Vivien heard footsteps creak on the stairs and her heart leapt. It wasn't the maid; it was Larry's tread, she would have recognised it anywhere. She waited expectantly, hastily smoothing her hair and rearranging her bedjacket.

Vivien and Larry been married for four years now. They'd held the wedding as soon as they could – quite literally on the stroke of midnight once their respective divorces were finalised. The ceremony took place at San Ysidro ranch in Santa Barbara, attended only by their hosts and two witnesses – Katharine Hepburn, and the writer Garson Kanin. Vivien and Larry had no interest in throwing a huge party and inviting all of their acquaintances; all they needed was one another.

'Puss,' he greeted her, as he stuck his head around the door. Vivien saw the relief in his eyes that she was sitting up, that she was smiling at him. She hated the fact that he sometimes eyed her warily these days, that his adoration was tempered with hesitation. It was only a flash, and he tried his best to conceal it, but Vivien knew him too well. He might have been the greatest stage actor in the world, but he couldn't hide anything from her.

'How was your day, darling? I hoped you'd be home soon.'

Larry came over to the bed and embraced her. 'I missed you. But I've almost finished – a few more days and then we'll be there.' Larry was currently editing *Henry V*, a film version of the Shakespeare play in which he starred as the eponymous king. It was also his directorial debut, an extremely ambitious project that was also intended to boost morale during wartime, and Larry had high hopes for its success.

'You've worked so hard on this film, I know it's going to be a triumph.'

'Thank you. I dearly hope so.'

'Any news on a preview date?'

'Yes, it was confirmed today – next Thursday.'

'Oh, that's wonderful!' Vivien absent-mindedly played with a loose thread on the counterpane, picking at the cotton though she knew it would only make it worse. 'When do you think *I'll* be able to go back to work? I do get so bored lying here.'

'As soon as the doctors say you're well enough, my love.'

'But I feel well enough now.'

'I think you should rest a little longer…'

Vivien cast her gaze down. 'I'm so terribly ashamed of my behaviour.'

'Don't be. Besides, you've apologised to everyone a dozen times. They all understand.'

Vivien had written letters to every person she might have offended, humbly begging their forgiveness. They had all been gracious and understanding, but Vivien couldn't shake her embarrassment. 'I don't understand why I feel like this sometimes.' There was a note of desperation in her voice, as though pleading with Larry to provide the answer.

'It's because you're not well. It's not your fault.'

'What if it is? What if it's penance for something?'

'That's Catholic bullshit,' Larry smiled. 'Are you sure you don't want to go to hospital? They could run some tests, see if they can find anything…'

Vivien was shaking her head before he'd even finished his sentence. 'No, I'm all right. It won't happen again, I promise you.' In truth, Vivien was terrified of going into hospital. She was worried she might not come out again, afraid of what they might discover. Deep down, she knew that there was something wrong with her – she had periods of depression, yet at other times her moods were manic – and she lived in fear of a diagnosis, a label that would define her regardless of her actions.

Larry looked relieved by her reassurance, and Vivien felt guilty that she was putting him through this. She adored her husband and wanted him to adore her too, the way he always had. She didn't want to cause a problem for him, to be less than perfect. 'I'm scared,' she admitted quietly. 'Don't leave me.'

'Of course I won't.' Larry took her in his arms, planting a

tender kiss on her forehead as she leaned into his chest. 'I'll look after you. I love you. Just rest and get better.'

Vivien clung to him, nuzzling into his neck. She felt desire sparking within her and raised her lips to his, pulling him closer.

'Vivien…' Larry seemed reluctant, moving away.

'I want us to have a baby,' she murmured. 'Don't you?'

'Of course I do, but I want you to get better first. You're the most precious thing in the world to me.'

Vivien was persistent, her hands snaking round his body, pressing herself against him. She couldn't shake the notion that if they didn't have a baby, he would leave her.

'I'm tired, Puss, and you need to rest.' Larry disentangled himself and Vivien bit back her feelings of rejection. She hated to be vulgar, but Larry's sex drive didn't match her own. Of course they were sexually attracted to one another, but Vivien's urges were far more frequent, more intense. She adored the physical act, especially during one of her episodes; it seemed to reset her. An orgasm pushed everything out of her head, giving her a few moments of blissful oblivion.

'Do you still love me?' Vivien asked quietly, her eyes limpid as she searched his face for reassurance.

'Of course, my darling,' Larry assured her. 'Whatever happens, I'll always love you.'

Chapter Thirty-One

Indian Ocean

October 1948

The Captain's table on the *Corinthic* was abuzz with conversation and laughter, the envious eyes of the other passengers turning to the lively table with its glamorous guests. Vivien was seated beside Captain Hart, looking incredible in a gold evening gown, her beauty luminous and her eyes sparkling – perhaps a little too brightly. Larry, sitting on her other side, was exhausted and homesick, as were the other actors at the table.

The Old Vic theatre company had just completed a gruelling nine-month tour of Australia and New Zealand, sponsored by the British Council, to thank the countries for their efforts in the war. The actors had played shows in rep – *The School for Scandal*, *The Skin of Our Teeth*, *Richard III* – in cities across the Antipodes, and it had taken its toll on all of them.

Vivien and Larry – now Lord and Lady Olivier, after his investiture at Buckingham Palace the previous year – had been treated like royalty during the tour, with a hectic schedule of visits and receptions and speeches, crowds of well-wishers turning out to greet them at every event. King George VI and Queen Elizabeth were scheduled to tour the following spring, along with their youngest daughter, Princess Margaret, and the Oliviers' trip felt very much like a dress rehearsal.

The reviews had been superb, but excellence came at a price. For Larry, the cost was physical; he injured his knee, necessitating an operation to remove the cartilage, and forcing him to spend the first two weeks of their voyage home in their capacious stateroom, barely able to move. Tonight was the first night he'd left their cabin; he was still recuperating, but Vivien was wild with excitement. For her, the strain had been psychological, taxing her already fragile mental health. She'd experienced a number of 'episodes' during the tour and was barely sleeping, surviving on a few hours a night.

'So, Captain, if you're here with us, who's driving the boat?' she said, and everyone laughed.

'I have a very capable team,' Captain Hart smiled.

'Some of them are very handsome too,' Vivien observed, with a coquettish smile at the waiter who was refilling her glass. She took a sip; she'd scarcely touched her food.

'Vivien…' Her name, uttered softly by Larry, was a warning.

She stared at him, heedless, her eyes wide with innocence. 'Just like that chap we met in Sydney. What was his name again, darling?'

'Finch,' Larry said, through pursed lips.

'That's him!' Vivien clapped her hands together in delight. 'Peter Finch. He was so talented and good-looking, and simply wonderful in Le Mulade Imaginaire. He rather reminded me of you in your younger days.'

Whether it was a throwaway observation or meant as an insult, Larry clearly took it as the latter.

They'd met 31-year-old Peter in Sydney, having heard his name feted in the weeks beforehand. They'd gone to watch his show, an adaptation of the Molière classic, then taken him and his wife, Tamara, out to dinner. Larry had been deeply impressed by his talent and urged him to move to London for the sake of his career, insisting that he would mentor him and introduce him to the right people. Vivien, too, had been charmed by the young actor; she'd talked about him so incessantly that Larry was beginning to regret having extended the invitation.

'You know, Captain,' she turned to him, letting the strap of her gown slip off one shoulder, highlighting the flawless skin that had acquired a light tan during her time Down Under. 'My husband's been out of action for quite some time now, and—'

'Vivien!' Larry threw down his knife and fork, and discomfort rippled across the table. 'That's enough.'

'Whatever's the matter? Everyone knows you've been confined to our cabin for weeks because of your poor knee.'

'Yes, and I think I'm going to go back there right now. I rather think you should come too.'

'What? But the evening's just getting started. Besides, tonight I should like to play dominoes!'

'Dominoes?' Larry was incredulous, staring at her in bewilderment and frustration.

Vivien had had a number of manic episodes whilst on tour, becoming more and more tightly wound, like a coiled spring. Sex was a stress reliever for her, an antidepressant, almost a form of self-medication to calm and relax her. Larry had been ill and exhausted; he'd turned a blind eye if, on occasion, Vivien had found solace elsewhere. But he wouldn't be publicly humiliated like this.

'Darling, we have a long day tomorrow.' Larry tried a different approach, conciliatory and understanding. 'We'll be in intensive rehearsals for *Antigone*.'

'Oh, to hell with *Antigone*,' Vivien exclaimed, her voice loud and guttural. 'All I care about is Blanche. Captain Hart, I've discovered the most wonderful new play. In fact, it was Cecil Beaton who discovered it for me. He saw it on Broadway – *A Streetcar Named Desire*, by Tennessee Williams – and he said to me, "Vivien, you simply must play Blanche DuBois when it opens in

London." And I intend to. Critics said I'd never play Scarlett, but I proved them all wrong, didn't I?'

'You certainly did.' Captain Hart was kind and understanding.

'And I intend to prove them wrong again. I *will* play Blanche.'

'Well, you'd better get some rest if you want to conquer the world,' Larry drawled, unable to keep the note of sarcasm from his voice. He adored Vivien, of course he did, but right now she was trying his patience. When she was in this kind of mood – fiery, provocative – she was very hard to deal with.

'You go to bed if you want. I know you need your sleep, *old man*.' The words were perfectly enunciated, designed to needle and wound. 'But I intend to stay awake and have fun. If you don't want to join me, I'm sure I'll find someone who will.'

Larry stared hard at her then threw down his napkin, struggling to his feet and limping off across the dining room.

Vivien laughed lightly, looking round at her fellow diners, her gaze lingering on the younger, most attractive men. 'Now, who's going to ask me to dance?'

It was a dull, spring day a few months after their return from Australia. Vivien and Larry were having lunch in the dining room at Durham Cottage, listening to the rain patter on the windows, dripping from the budding trees onto the roof.

Larry had recently overseen production of *Daphne Laureola* at Wyndham's Theatre; it starred Peter Finch, who had taken the Oliviers' advice and moved to London, where Larry had made good on his word and immediately cast him in his next play. Vivien had been lobbying hard for the role of Blanche in *Streetcar* and was thrilled to discover her efforts had been successful; Larry would direct, and rehearsals would begin later that year, with the production slated to open in October. Professionally, life was busier than ever for the two of them.

'This is delicious,' Larry commented, tucking into his ham salad with gusto.

'Yes, quite,' Vivien said distractedly. She had little appetite, as ever. 'I see Peter's receiving excellent reviews for *Daphne*.'

'The whole cast are,' Larry agreed. 'Anna Turner's a delight. It was lucky that her Broadway show was cancelled.'

'Ah yes, "the most beautiful woman in Cheshire",' Vivien responded, her voice heavy with sarcasm.

'She *is* very beautiful. Talented too.'

Vivien stared at him, taking in the face that she knew so well. Larry was almost forty-two and starting to feel his age, unable to be as physical in his acting as he had once been; the days of leaping around the stage as Romeo were long gone. Yet for men, Vivien reflected, ageing wasn't the same curse as it was for women. Men grew in experience and authority, age lines and grey hair conferring a gravitas upon them that was attractive to the opposite sex. Vivien had noticed that her husband regularly spoke about other women lately, casting girls in their twenties where Vivien was dismissed as too old for the role. At times, it felt as though his cruelty was deliberate.

Vivien watched him chewing his lunch, pulling a face to extricate a piece of food stuck in his back teeth. He chased it out with his tongue and Vivien was suddenly so repulsed that she had to look away.

'I don't love you anymore.' The words were unexpected, but now Vivien had said them, they made complete sense.

Larry frowned, his forehead creasing in confusion.

'I mean, I do still love you in a way. But more like a brother.'

Larry resumed chewing in silence. It took him some time to swallow, as though the food were stuck in his throat, and he took a long drink of water before he spoke.

'I see. And what are we to do about that?'

'Oh, I don't think we need to *do* anything as such.' Vivien's tone was matter of fact. 'We'll carry on as before, but it will be purely a work arrangement.'

'All right.' Larry stared at her, and she could see the cogs whirring as he tried to determine whether she meant it, or whether she was in the midst of a breakdown. In truth, Vivien had been struggling in recent weeks, but it felt imperative that she should be honest and say what she was feeling. 'Do you want a divorce?'

'God, no,' Vivien laughed. 'Could you imagine, after everything we've been through? We fought so hard to be together, we can't possibly separate. Besides, it's not just about us. We're "The Oliviers". Lord and Lady Olivier. We need to consider the public too.'

'I remember a time when you didn't care what the public thought.'

'Oh, don't be facetious, Larry. This is just the kind of thing I'm talking about.'

Larry smiled sadly, putting down his cutlery and sitting back in his chair. 'Is there someone else?'

'Oh, no. Well, no one important,' Vivien added blithely. They both understood the situation; neither had been faithful in recent years. Sometimes it was easier to find comfort and understanding elsewhere, with no strings and few emotions.

'I see.'

'Good.' Vivien looked pleased, as though everything were settled, but Larry hadn't finished.

'Do you mean it, Vivien? Are you quite well, right now? I've put up with a lot over the years, you know.' He sounded angry and resentful.

'I know you have, and I'm grateful for your support. I'm aware that I haven't always been easy. But our relationship isn't the same as it was, is it? Back when we were young lovers, taking on the world…'

'Yes, but—'

Their housekeeper came in to clear the plates, bringing a fresh pot of tea and two slices of cherry cake.

Vivien thought about his words. She knew she wasn't the

easiest person to be with; her episodes had become more frequent, more intense, and she knew Larry was exhausted from having to deal with them. But *she* was the one having to live through them, to have her sanity questioned and her physical health deteriorate. For better, for worse; in sickness and in health; wasn't that what they'd said? It felt like such a long time since they'd made those vows. Their bond ran deep, but Vivien found herself wondering if it was unbreakable.

She poured out two cups of tea, adding milk and sugar, and pushed one across to Larry. 'Cake?'

'I seem to have lost my appetite.'

'Oh, darling, now you're sulking.'

'Well, can you blame me? This is all rather unexpected. I need time to adjust to my new status as a sibling, not a husband.'

Vivien rolled her eyes as Larry got to his feet.

'Aren't you going to kiss me goodbye? On the forehead, like a good brother,' she teased, quoting Scarlett in *Gone with the Wind*.

Larry looked furious.

'It was only a joke, darling.'

'Well, I don't find it funny.'

Larry stalked out of the room as Vivien sipped her tea, leaving the cake untouched. She felt bad that she'd upset him. All they seemed to do these days was bicker, but at least she'd got her feelings off her chest. What had she said again? Vivien screwed up her face, trying to recall her words, but the memory was cloudy and she couldn't seem to remember. It was probably something trivial. She would go to her room and study her lines for *Streetcar*. Her work, after all, was what was truly important, a crutch that never failed her, and this part felt as though it could have been written for her.

She was surprised to hear the front door slam, surmising that Larry must have gone out. She could apologise later if she'd said something out of turn, but right now, she needed to focus on Blanche.

Chapter Thirty-Two

SONIA

London, England

August 1945

'Hot off the press.' Cyril Connolly swung past Sonia's desk in the *Horizon* office and placed a small hardback book in front of her, its dust-jacket grey and green.

Sonia picked it up and looked at it curiously. '*Animal Farm*,' she read aloud.

'George's latest,' explained Cyril.

'Have you read it?'

Cyril nodded, his small, dark eyes alight with enthusiasm. Sonia recognised the familiar expression when Cyril had read a particularly accomplished piece of work or discovered a promising new talent. 'It's marvellous. I think George might have a hit on his hands.'

'Really? What's it about?' Sonia turned the book back and forth in her hands, flicking through the pages, frowning in confusion as she read the subtitle: *A Fairy Story*. 'It looks like a children's book.'

'That's the clever part. It's a fable, set on a farm with a cast of animals, but it's actually the most wonderful allegory for the Russian Revolution.'

A memory tugged at the back of Sonia's brain, and she began to laugh.

'What?'

'Do you know, some years ago – I think it was the first time I met him, at a dinner party at your flat – he told me he was thinking of writing something about Soviet communism. I thought he was making a joke.'

'George never jokes. He has the most terrible sense of humour,' Cyril said wickedly.

'Cyril!' Sonia chastised him. 'He's writing for *The Observer* now, isn't he?'

'Yes – or at least he was. Reporting on the war. Astor sent him all over Europe. But then he's had a rather difficult time of it – his wife died a few months ago.'

'Oh, how terrible.' Sonia's hand flew to her mouth in shock.

'Yes, awful business. It was a routine operation, I believe – for "women's troubles" – but she never woke up from the anaesthetic. They'd adopted a baby boy, Richard, a year or so earlier. So now it's a lot tougher for George. He's engaged a nanny, of course, but it's a terrible business, looking after that young boy and trying to sustain a career.'

Sonia looked at the novel in her hand. 'But if this is as good as you say it is, then George *must* continue to write. It's imperative that he has the time and the space to do so.'

Sonia had encountered George Orwell a few times since that first dinner, whether at Cyril's place or at other literary functions, and her overriding impression remained of a tall, gaunt man with an air of sadness and vulnerability. His writing talent was undeniable, and her heartstrings were tugged when she thought of this poor widower, caring for his young son whilst trying to pursue his art.

'Do you have his address?' she asked, her voice full of concern.

'Of course.' Cyril tore a piece of paper from his notebook and scribbled it down in his florid hand.

Sonia tucked it inside her copy of *Animal Farm*, a thoughtful expression on her youthful, pretty face. 'I think I might pay him a visit.'

'Look, Richard – Daddy's home!'

The dark-haired, chubby child, almost two years old now, toddled delightedly towards his father as the beanpole figure bent down and scooped him up, swinging him into the air as the boy giggled gleefully. The motion set off an attack of coughing, and George settled him back on his feet as Sonia looked on anxiously.

'How was your day, darling?' she asked, her voice ringing with cynicism, as she bustled around the apartment in Canonbury Square, inexpertly preparing a dinner of beef stew and mashed potatoes. Sonia had done her best to make the little flat feel homely, arranging his books neatly on the shelves instead of scattered in piles, and plumping up the chair cushions. In an ironic gesture, she'd even bought an aspidistra plant which sat limply on the flaking windowsill. But, overall, the apartment felt bare and bleak. The damp spring day was chilly, and Sonia had managed to get a fire going in the grate with the little fuel she'd found. Despite the privations, little Richard was a happy child who adored his father.

'Productive. I wrote in a café – I thought it was rather fitting – and I got a few hundred words down. Then I spoke to a chef friend of mine, to get a few recipes I thought I might add.'

'Wonderful. I can type it all up for you later, if you'd like.'

'Thank you,' George smiled gratefully, sitting down at the table and rolling a cigarette. He'd been commissioned by the British Council to write an essay on British food, with the aim of promoting British relations abroad, although he was finding it difficult to work up sufficient enthusiasm while rationing was still very much in force. His most recent novel, *Animal Farm*, had caused something of a stir and sold solidly in the UK; it was due to be published later in the year in America, and he'd been in demand in recent months. Being busy was a welcome distraction since the death of his wife.

'You're welcome.' Since reading *Animal Farm*, Sonia had been swept away by George's talent, as Cyril had been. It was a brilliant book, clever and satirical, deceptively simplistic and wholly original. Sonia had been overwhelmed by the certainty that George *must* continue to write, and that she should help him in any way she could. It felt like a calling of sorts; she would be an artist's helpmate, as she'd long envisaged.

Sonia had volunteered to look after Richard when his nanny was unavailable, and George had gladly taken her up on the offer. For Sonia, it was a world away from the routine of office work and, whilst she didn't consider herself maternal, she'd inherited her mother's organisation and efficiency when it came to taking care of other people's children. They'd fallen into a routine where Sonia watched Richard once a fortnight or so, an arrangement that had been going on for a few months now.

'Richard and I had a good day, didn't we, darling? We went to the park and saw the ducks and the sailboats, then we went to the shops. There wasn't very much in at the butcher, I'm afraid, though this braising steak looked passable,' Sonia said, as she plated up the meal and put it on the table.

'You know, you really must learn to make dumplings,' George commented, picking up his napkin.

'I prefer potatoes,' she replied evenly. 'Now, tuck in before it gets cold.'

'Sonia, you're a marvel,' George said admiringly, as he began to eat. 'You'll make someone an excellent wife, you know.'

'I'm sure I will, when it suits me. Richard, darling, it's bath time.' Sonia pulled the tin tub in front of the stove and filled it with jugs of hot water; it was far pleasanter than bathing the child in the cold, unheated bathroom.

'You'll make an excellent mother too,' George continued, watching her admiringly.

'Well, I'm not so sure about that. To be truthful, I'm not even sure whether I want children.'

'I thought every woman wanted children.'

'And I thought every man had moved on from such clichéd views,' she shot back, as George smiled. 'I don't think I'm cut out for it, in all honesty. It's such a responsibility,' she continued, as she stripped Richard and began to wash him briskly. 'You're going to shape someone's whole life, and there's a very high chance you'll fuck it up – pardon my language, darling.'

'I'd like him to grow up with a wide vocabulary,' George laughed, though Richard seemed oblivious to the profanity. 'Well, you never know what life has in store for you. And how's everything at *Horizon*?' George changed the subject.

'Busy. We're getting more submissions than ever. I can barely keep up with all the queries and rejections, but I run a pretty tight ship. There's some wonderful young talent coming through though,' Sonia added, as she plucked Richard from the water and dried him on a threadbare towel.

She was an editorial secretary now, but in practice did most of the day-to-day running of the *Horizon* office, working closely with Cyril and Peter. Decisions were made in tandem, and Sonia believed the two men respected her opinions and trusted her judgement. 'Though half the time Cyril's in Paris, or the South of France, and Peter's always off on one of his jaunts. Sometimes I feel as though I'm running that place single-handedly,' Sonia ran on, dressing Richard in his pyjamas that had been warmed in front of the stove. 'And the abuse I get from some of the writers who've submitted… *Men* who are incandescent that a *woman* has dared to reject them for publication… Now, say goodnight to Daddy, Richard.'

The toddler crawled onto George's knee, snuggling into him as his father told a story about a fierce dragon and a brave knight. Richard listened, wide-eyed, with his thumb planted in his mouth, as Sonia cleared up, washing and drying the plates, wiping the table and the kitchen surfaces.

He was a delightful boy, Sonia thought, with a rush of affection and sympathy. George and his wife had adopted him when he was just three weeks old, but Eileen had died a mere nine months later whilst under anaesthetic for a hysterectomy. With George left in sole charge of Richard, Sonia had fallen into the habit of looking after him on his nanny's days off, so that George could continue to write. Sonia believed that his work was important, that he had the potential to be a great writer, and she wanted to assist him by offering practical help.

When the story finished, Richard gave his father a kiss and reached for Sonia. She picked him up, carried him through to his room and laid him in his cot. The evening was cold and she added an extra blanket, softly singing a lullaby as she stroked his head. The boy was tired and fell asleep quickly, fortunately not kept awake by his father coughing uncontrollably in the next room.

Sonia walked through to the lounge in time to see George wiping his mouth with a handkerchief, a red stain blooming through the white cotton.

'You must see a doctor,' she insisted, but he waved her words away.

'I'm fine. I'm tired after a long day, that's all, and the dampness aggravated my lungs.'

Sonia gave him a look but didn't press the matter. She knew he'd been treated for tuberculosis in the past, and suffered regularly with bouts of bronchitis, but was reluctant to seek medical help. In Sonia's opinion, it was pure pig-headedness.

She drew the moth-eaten curtains, switched on the lamp on the side table and poured them both a glass of red wine. She'd been invited to supper at Lucian Freud's house, but it was growing dark and drizzling outside, and she didn't feel like leaving the warmth of the fireside to travel all the way back to Percy Street.

'Thank you,' George said, as she sat down in the armchair

beside him. 'I really am so very grateful to you, Sonia. For everything you do.'

'You're welcome. Just write something exceptional for *Horizon*, that's all I ask in return.' Sonia smiled, but George looked serious.

'Richard adores you, and you're so good with him. He needs a mother figure.'

'Well, I wouldn't say I'm that to him, but he's a lovely boy. You're doing a sterling job, without Eileen.'

'I've been terribly lonely without her. Being a writer's a solitary life, as you know. I can't tell you how good it was to come home tonight and see the lights at the window, to feel the warmth of the fire when I came in, and to have a delicious meal waiting for me.'

Sonia bit back a smart retort and smiled at him. She'd grown fond of him, and couldn't help but admire his fierce intellect and his talent with words. Physically, she didn't find him attractive – he was over six foot tall, lean and increasingly hollow-cheeked, with a narrow, bristling moustache, and all things considered he cut a shambolic figure. But there was something deeply appealing about him.

George cleared his throat. 'Sonia, I wondered if you might like to marry me. I'm not much of a catch, I know, but I could offer a degree of stability and intelligent conversation. I like you very much, and I find you very attractive.'

Sonia stifled her laughter at his inelegant proposal. She knew it wasn't out of love – they were hardly in love with one another; he hadn't even moved in his chair, let alone got down on one knee – and that the gesture was more motivated by practicality. She appreciated his offer, but it wasn't for her.

'I'm sorry, darling.' Sonia shook her head. 'Anyway, didn't you propose to Celia Kirwan a few weeks ago? And to Anne, in the flat downstairs?'

George didn't look embarrassed, just rather sad. 'I'm going to Jura in a few weeks. Will you at least come and visit me?'

Sonia pulled a face. George was planning to spend a few

months living in a cottage called Barnhill on the remote Scottish island of Jura, along with Richard and the nanny. Even just getting to the isle, where his friend David Astor had an estate, required a tremendous effort – taking the train to Glasgow, then the car to the west coast, then the boat across the sea. George loved the simplicity of life in the Hebrides, and the solitude would be ideal for his writing, but Sonia couldn't think of anything worse than being stuck in the back of beyond without the diversions of the city on her doorstep.

'Another no, I'm afraid, darling. Besides, I'm going to Paris next month, and I'm not sure how long I shall stay.'

'Oh. Who with?' George didn't sound jealous, merely conversational.

'I'm travelling by myself, but I'll see Jean-Paul and Simone, and Michel Leiris – do you know him? And whoever else I happen to meet. Cyril's already suggested a few people I might like to spend time with.'

'I see.'

The clock on the mantelpiece ticked loudly, filling the silence.

'Well if you won't marry me, and you won't come to visit me in Scotland, would you at least go to bed with me?'

Sonia burst out laughing. She liked George's bluntness, his direct manner. He looked so earnest; there was something melancholy and hangdog in his expression. She felt a rush of sympathy for him, and longed to cheer him up.

'All right. Why not?' Sonia drained her wine and stood up, holding out her hand. 'Lead the way, darling.'

Chapter Thirty-Three

Paris, France

June 1946

The lights from the Café de Flore glittered in the reflection from the puddles, the pavements wet from a sudden downpour that had stopped as suddenly as it had begun. Raindrops dripped from the awning, and the city felt fresh again, as though cleansed.

Sonia adored Paris. Her love affair with the city had begun before the war, when she'd visited with Bill and her friends from the Euston Road School, a gaggle of them spending their days around the Boulevard Saint-Germain. They lived the life of louche intellectuals, discussing art and life and literature, concerning themselves with drinking and dancing. Sonia had crossed the Channel many times since that first visit; she adored the city's vitality and civility, declaring it her spiritual home. It had undoubtedly changed in the intervening years, physically and mentally scarred by the Nazi occupation. But it had fought and won, emerging defiantly and somehow *more* resolutely French, as though determined to recapture what had been lost during those long months.

A fog of cigarette smoke drifted out into the night air above the sixth arrondissement, as Jean-Paul Sartre held forth on the meaning of existence. Beside him sat his lover, Simone de Beauvoir, a celebrated philosopher and a good friend of Sonia's, along with the poet Michel Leiris and the writer Marguerite Duras, all huddled around the table, glasses of Pastis in front of them. Sonia listened to the conversation, occasionally contributing where she felt she could offer something, but mostly she enjoyed being part of the fray, the earnest discussion of ideas and ideals. These people were free thinkers, defying the conventional boundaries of what relationships should be, their views borne out of war and a *carpe diem* mentality. Jean-Paul and Simone had been part of the resistance, co-founding the underground group *Socialisme et Liberté*, and they now felt vindicated by their stance, galvanised by victory.

'I'll never marry,' Simone was saying, the smoke from her cigarette curling into air. 'It's a trick, a trap for the woman. And there's very little in it for the man too – both locked together, trapped for ever.'

'There's always divorce,' Sonia posited. They conversed in French; Sonia was fluent. 'My mother's first husband killed himself, and she divorced the second, so it's not an irreversible situation.' She was aware she was using black humour, but she wasn't afraid to be controversial.

'Well, I'm sorry to hear that, but if you're not married at all then it's much easier to extricate oneself than it is to divorce. You can't deny that.' Simone tilted her head to one side, as though she were examining Sonia. Sonia stared back, trying not to feel intimidated. There was no doubt that Simone was fiercely intellectual, but Sonia enjoyed the mental gymnastics as she determined and defended her own opinions.

'No, but surely it's a question of female choice? As feminists, don't we agree that women should be able to do whatever they want – and if that's to get married, then so be it?'

'But if women were educated about what it involved, then none of them would want to get married.' Simone's answers were rapid-fire. She was eccentric-looking, with thick plaited hair pulled up on either side of her head, and whilst she wasn't conventionally attractive, she was certainly charismatic.

'Write an article about it for *Horizon*,' Sonia smiled, and Simone laughed.

'If I'm writing for anyone, it'll be *Les Temps Modernes*,' she shot back, naming the magazine that Sartre had founded.

'Of course,' Sonia acknowledged. 'How's everything going?' She was keen to know more. Sonia was now an editorial assistant at *Horizon*, wielding power and commissioning pieces, and *Les Temps Modernes* appealed to a similar reader: the young left-wing idealist.

Sartre turned to her. 'It's going very well. We're preparing an issue about the US, and I'm writing an article on the myths that Americans hold about the French. Ah, here he is, in fact. The very person you need to speak to.' A tall, heavy-set man approached the café. He was in his thirties, around a decade older than Sonia, and he wore a tweed jacket over a black polo shirt and crisp trousers. His dark hair was beginning to recede, revealing a prominent forehead, but that only served to give him a sense of gravitas. 'Sonia, you've met Maurice, yes?'

'No, actually, though it seems impossible.' She rose from her seat as he kissed her on both cheeks. He smelt of French cigarettes and soap, and his intense, dark eyes were fixed on her with interest. It was an expression Sonia was used to seeing; she wasn't being arrogant, it was simply a fact. She was twenty-seven years old, attractive and buxom, with an obvious intelligence and an energy that seemed to draw men to her.

'*Enchanté* to finally meet you. I appreciate your support for our magazine.' Maurice Merleau-Ponty was the editor of *Les Temps Modernes*, and *Horizon* had published its manifesto when it had launched the previous year.

'Of course. I'm simply mesmerised by your ideas. Paris feels so energised and alive compared with stuffy old London.'

He smiled. 'I'm not going to disagree with you. I think we're at a very important moment in our history, an opportunity to build a new civilisation.'

'You're a professor, aren't you?'

'Yes. I teach philosophy at the University of Lyon.'

'What discipline?'

Maurice seemed amused by Sonia's direct line of questioning. 'My specialism is phenomenology. Do you know what that is?'

'No,' Sonia said, without embarrassment.

'It's the philosophy of experience. Perception is key in our experience of the world; everything is subjective, based on our judgements, our emotions, our perceptions. Right now, I'm experiencing this conversation in a certain way, and you may be experiencing it rather differently. To me, we're having a delightful first meeting where I'm conversing with a charming young woman on a subject I'm passionate about. You may view me as a dull, unattractive man droning on about a topic in which you couldn't be less interested.'

'Not at all. It's fascinating.'

'Well, they do say the English are known for their politeness.' He grinned, as Sonia laughed. 'Would you like to dance?'

'Here?'

'Why not?'

He pulled Sonia to her feet and she felt a rush of uncertainty and excitement. They were outside in the street, but swing music spilled out from the café, and she was charmed and intrigued by his spontaneity.

'Not the dancing again, Maurice,' Jean-Paul groaned.

'You dance with every pretty girl that comes in here,' Michel jeered.

'You're all jealous,' Maurice retorted good-naturedly, 'because none of you have my panache.'

Sonia laughed as she reached up to put a hand on his shoulder, his right hand finding her waist, resting neatly in the curve above her hip as they began to move together. He led her along the pavement to a chorus of wolf-whistles and cheers, but Sonia paid no attention, her eyes fixed on his. She enjoyed the feel of his hands on her body; he moved with assurance, leading her with confidence, so that all she needed to do was follow.

Her low-heeled brogues sloshed wetly in the puddles, but Sonia found that she didn't care. She threw her head back, looking up at the handful of stars scattered across the dark sky. She was in Paris, in the arms of an attractive man; life was beautiful, and the night was full of possibilities.

It briefly crossed her mind that she could have been on Jura right now. She'd received a letter from George before she left London, telling her that he missed her and asking her to join him on the Hebridean island, with advice to bring a raincoat and stout walking boots. Instead, she was wearing a pretty floral tea-dress and luxuriating in the warmth of a Parisian evening in early summer. She felt glad that she had declined George's invitation.

'Why are you sad?' Maurice murmured in her ear.

'I'm not. In fact, I was just thinking how delighted I am to be here.'

'Perhaps you're not sad at this moment, but there's a melancholy in your soul. On the surface, you're vivacious and dazzling, but there's something deeper, I can tell.'

Sonia's heart was beating fast, but she didn't reply, and they carried on dancing. She was disconcerted by this man who seemed to see right to the core of her, past the facade she presented and deep into her soul. Wasn't that what everyone wanted? To be truly seen and understood and accepted for one's true self? His comments were a revelation and she felt overwhelmed by him.

Sonia had always believed she carried a sadness within her, as though her very existence was a bad luck charm to those around her: the death of the man purported to be her father; the uncertainty over her parentage; the boat accident in which her friends had died and she was the sole survivor. And all the men she fell in love with seemed to marry someone else…

'Are you married?' she asked. Her tone was urgent, breathless.

'Yes.'

Maurice didn't say anything further, his grip tightening imperceptibly on her waist. Sonia fought the fierce waves of disappointment, the deep, irrational jealousy at this unknown woman. She pressed herself closer to him, fancying that she could feel his heartbeat beneath his shirt.

They talked nonstop, discussing philosophy, art, politics, religion. Maurice had also been raised Roman Catholic, rejecting it as it didn't align with his socialist values. Sonia was vociferous on the hypocrisy of the Catholic church, and the cruelty of the nuns of Roehampton. They spoke about the prominent writers of the day – Ernest Hemingway, Albert Camus, George Orwell – and Sonia was determined that Maurice should pen an article for *Horizon*.

He walked her home that evening, back to her rented apartment on the rue des Beaux Arts. It was past 2 a.m. and Paris was sleeping, the City of Light now a place of shadows.

'I have to go back to London soon,' Sonia told him, as they stood facing one another beneath the pale glow of a streetlamp. The road was deserted, sashes pulled down and curtains drawn. She stepped closer, tilting her face up towards him. 'Will you come and visit me there?'

He took her hands in his and slowly raised them to his mouth, kissing them softly, her fingertips tracing his lips. She felt the heat of his breath, the roughness of his stubble, the sensation faintly erotic. She longed for him to sweep her into his arms and kiss her passionately, but he didn't and she couldn't hide her disappointment.

'Yes, I will, I promise.'

'Soon?'

He nodded. 'Good night, Sonia.'

Then he turned and walked away, and the sense of loss was immediate and powerful. Sonia had never felt this way about anyone, she realised, but it seemed as though the feeling hadn't been mutual. Perhaps, as Maurice had said, it was all a matter of perception.

Chapter Thirty-Four

London, England

September 1947

Sonia and Maurice were strolling along the South Bank, the walkway slippery with autumn leaves, the air crisp with the changing of the seasons.

'*Incroyable*,' he breathed, as they stopped for a moment beside Waterloo Bridge, watching the boats churn through the muddy water. Ahead of them was the gothic splendour of the Palace of Westminster; behind was the iconic dome of St Paul's Cathedral, both still standing despite the wartime efforts of the Luftwaffe.

It was Maurice's first visit to London to see Sonia, and he was in awe of the city. Though Sonia was charmed to see it through fresh eyes, she found it all rather dull and backward compared with Paris. But all she cared about was that Maurice was here with her.

For the past year, she'd been travelling back and forth regularly between England and France, seeing Maurice every time she was on the continent. They would meet in a café and while away the afternoon, discussing politics and religion and other, more inconsequential, topics. She was certain that she was falling in love with him, but he hadn't so much as kissed her – beyond the traditional French greeting. Sonia knew that he had a wife and daughter, but for most of the men in her circle that was no barrier; the intellectuals of the Left Bank and the literary London set were forever falling in and out of bed with one another, regardless of marital status. This felt like an extended courtship, which could have no satisfactory outcome.

'So, what do you think of our humble city?' Sonia asked. She watched the light play across Maurice's face, his expression one of almost childlike wonder as he took in the view.

'I love it.' He turned to her, his dark eyes soft.

'I prefer Paris. I wish I could stay there.'

'I know. I'm sorry.'

Maurice had been trying to find her a permanent role in France, but so far nothing was available, so she stayed in London, dissatisfied at *Horizon*.

'Perhaps you can come to England more often?' she suggested, trying not to sound too hopeful. 'That would make it bearable.'

'I will, though it can be hard to get away...' Both thought inadvertently of his wife and child, though Sonia didn't ask about them and Maurice didn't speak of them. 'But I think it's good for me to be around you.'

'You do?' Sonia's heart leapt.

'*Absolument*. When I'm with you I'm calmer, more focused. I adore speaking with you – I feel as though no one else in the world understands me as well as you do. You have such life, Sonia, such energy. You make me think about the world completely differently.'

'I adore you. You know I do.' Perhaps the confession was too much, but Sonia was tired of repressing her feelings.

'When we're together, it's as though all the things I'm worrying about don't matter – the petty squabbles at work, and fighting for professional recognition, and the internal politics at the university. You make me feel that I'm... enough...'

'You are. You're more than enough. You're one of the cleverest, most fascinating people I know,' Sonia said breathlessly. It was true, and it felt as though they were stuck in this horrible stalemate where neither of them would take the next step. Sonia wasn't saving herself for him – she'd still been seeing, and sleeping with, other men. But no one measured up to Maurice, and her thoughts were always drawn back to him. It wasn't simply his Gallic charm; he was old-fashioned, courteous, exceptionally intelligent and a deep thinker. Despite her many love affairs, Sonia had never felt like this about anyone.

Maurice didn't reply immediately, looking thoughtfully into the distance. The evening was perfect, the streetlamps illuminating the twilight as the mildness of the day gave way to crisper temperatures.

'You have a friend at University College, *n'est-ce pas*?'

They spoke to one another in a mix of languages, as Maurice was keen to improve his English.

'Freddie Ayer? Yes, he runs the philosophy department. I saw him the other week, actually, at the Gargoyle Club.'

'Do you think he might have any positions available? Any jobs for a professor of phenomenology?'

Sonia's heart leapt. 'Would you consider… You'd move here?'

Maurice nodded slowly. 'I think so, yes…'

'For work?'

'Not just work…' he said carefully.

They turned to one another. Sonia's heart was racing, hope rising irrepressibly within her. She tilted her face up to his and then she was in his arms, and finally his lips were on hers. It was everything she'd been waiting for, after months of longing, of dreaming of this moment. She was overwhelmed by the scent of his skin and the feel of his body on hers, the taste of his lips, his strong arms around her. It felt like coming home.

'Would you really move to London for me?' Sonia asked, as they broke apart.

Maurice nodded. 'I'd have to travel back and forth but…' He

let the sentence trail off. Sonia didn't want to think about his reasons for that, about the wife and child he'd left back in France. For now, he was here, with her. He was willing to move to London for her. In time, she felt sure, he would see that Sonia could offer him more than his life in France. He would divorce his wife, propose to her, and their life would be idyllic, with Sonia ministering to his every need whilst he rose to ever greater intellectual heights…

But she was getting ahead of herself. Maurice wrapped his arms around her and she snuggled against him as they walked on, her heart singing, her body fizzing, her mind alive with possibilities and happiness. She'd thought she'd misread the signals somehow, fearing that the attachment was one-sided, but he *did* want to be with her. He was going to be hers, she felt sure of it.

Big Ben struck the hour, the familiar chimes ringing out across the city, but right now Sonia felt as though they had all the time in the world.

The affair continued for two years. It swiftly became physical, as they made love for the first time in Sonia's flat in Percy Street, the same evening they'd shared their first kiss. Despite their efforts, Maurice was unable to find a suitable job in England, or Sonia in France, so they crossed the Channel as often as time allowed, delighting in the snatched moments and the heightened passion.

Maurice had fallen in love with London, and with Sonia, and she'd relished seeing the grey, gloomy capital anew as they explored its hidden corners, feeling as though it belonged to them and them alone. They would return to Sonia's flat and stay up into the small hours, discussing and debating, drinking wine and making love.

Between their cross-Channel visits, they kept up a regular correspondence, their letters filled with ideas and theories, books they'd read and everyday happenings they were eager to tell one another, along with outpourings of love and expressions of devotion. His wife and child were kept mercifully in the background, but their very existence was a constant, invisible form of torture for Sonia, an insuperable barrier to her happiness. She believed that Maurice would have married her, were it not for Suzanne and little Marianne. Sonia had never wanted anyone the way she longed for him.

But then they'd started arguing. Not the passionate disputes of their early relationship, clashing over theories and beliefs and *amour*, but petty, unhappy spats. Late at night, they'd engaged in long, tearful, emotional conversations that lasted for hours and took their toll. Sonia had slammed plates and thrown glasses.

Now it was mid-December 1948, the last time they'd see one another before Christmas. Sonia had cooked – she wanted them to have an intimate meal at home, rather than going out and sharing him with the world – and she'd made a traditional Christmas dinner, saving her ration books for weeks in order to get a good-sized turkey with all the trimmings. They moved on to their second bottle of red, French jazz playing on the gramophone.

'I have something for you.' Sonia's eyes were sparkling as she jumped up from her chair, opening the drawer of the dresser and pulling out a festively wrapped gift. Her flat was warm and comfortable, the windows steamed up from the residual heat from the oven. Paintings – gifts from her friends – hung on every wall, and books were stacked floor to ceiling, overflowing the shelves.

'Open it,' she said, excitedly, handing the present across.

'Sonia, that's… it's so thoughtful,' Maurice said softly, holding the first edition of *Sentimental Education* by Gustave Flaubert in his large hands, flicking through the yellowed pages as Sonia looked on with delight. 'I have a gift for you, too.' Maurice reached into his bag and pulled out a small box.

Sonia took it eagerly, rushing to unwrap it. It was a small bottle of Chanel Nº5 and she couldn't help but feel underwhelmed, despite knowing what it would have cost him.

Sonia had spent hours thinking of what Maurice might like, sourcing the book itself, lovingly wrapping it. There was something in this gift that felt… impersonal. She wondered if he'd bought an identical bottle for his wife. Two birds with one stone.

'Thank you,' she said quietly, not trying to hide her disappointment. Her frustration was building as she took a long slug of wine, feeling bitter and resentful that he wouldn't be with her at Christmas. That he was never with her for Christmas. Oh, she wouldn't be alone – she'd been invited to spend the day at Cyril's – but she was tired of spending every holiday without her lover. She was thirty years old and sick of playing second fiddle to his family.

'What did you buy for Suzanne?' Her eyes were hard, and she was clearly spoiling for a fight.

Maurice winced. 'Don't do this, Sonia.'

'Oh, I'm sure that would suit you, wouldn't it. Why don't you ever mention her? Are you hoping we can forget about her, pretend she doesn't exist?'

'I don't want to throw my marriage in your face, Sonia. But yes, Suzanne exists. Marianne exists. What do you want me to do about it?'

Sonia drained her glass. 'I want you to leave them for me.'

There it was, her last throw of the dice. The words had been said and couldn't be taken back. Sonia had acted out of desperation and hated herself for that – it was far from the calm, rational, persuasive conversation she'd always planned.

The record had finished, the gramophone crackling on an endless loop. In the silence, they could hear the neighbours in the downstairs flat laughing and shrieking. It sounded as though they were having a party.

Maurice remained silent, his head bowed, and Sonia flew into a rage.

'Why won't you do it? Why don't you love me enough? Is it my cooking, hmm? Is it not good enough?' Sonia leapt to her feet, picked up Maurice's empty plate and hurled it to the floor. Gravy splashed across the rug as the crockery splintered.

'Sonia…' Maurice stood up and stepped towards her, taking hold of her wrists, wrapping his arms around her. The gesture was more restraining than loving but the fight went out of Sonia and she collapsed against him. All she wanted was to be held by him.

'I love you,' she told him as she began to cry. 'I've never felt this way about anyone. All I want is to be with you. Why don't you want the same? What's wrong with me?'

Maurice let go of her and took a step backwards. Sonia instantly felt cold without his embrace, a feeling of panic beginning to take hold. She searched his face and he looked at her briefly, warily, then looked away.

'What?' she demanded. 'What is it?' In truth, she wasn't sure she wanted to hear the answer. In her gut, she knew it was the kind of conversation that, once started, could not be taken back.

Maurice ran his hands through his hair and winced once again. 'We must end this, Sonia.'

'End what?' Sonia was in denial, as though by asking such a silly question she could hold off the inevitable for a few more moments.

'Us,' he said gently. 'It was a beautiful affair, but now it's over. I'm not going to leave my wife for you, and we have no way forward.'

'But we're destined to be together,' Sonia protested. 'We're made for one another.'

'No,' Maurice said, sadness etched in the droop of his shoulders, the slope of his mouth. 'We're not.'

Sonia felt a growing sense of panic; it was like the boat accident all over again. She couldn't catch her breath, she was going to drown without him, lost beneath the dark waters. 'I need you. You can't leave me. I love you, and you love me.'

'*Mon amour*, I do not regret one second of this, but you must understand the difference between *un amour* and *love*. I wish I could explain more – there are so many things I want to talk about and discover with you.'

'Then do it! I want to do that too. Christ, Maurice, I want to have your babies. I never wanted to be a mother, but I want to have children with you. I want to be your wife, the mother of your children.'

'No. It must end here. It is for the best.'

'You tricked me,' Sonia raged. 'Stringing me along all this time. You made me believe you wanted to marry me, that you were going to leave Suzanne.'

'That's not fair. I never said that. I was never going to leave her, Sonia.'

Sonia realised it was true, but that didn't make it any less painful. She'd planned her future around Maurice, wilfully blind to the fact that he'd never been a participant in those plans. 'I hate you,' Sonia whispered fiercely, tears spilling down her cheeks.

'No, you don't.' Maurice shook his head.

He was right. Sonia wanted to hate him, but it was impossible. All she really wanted was for him to change his mind.

'Get out,' she told him.

'Sonia, I—'

'Get out!' she screamed. The noise dipped in the flat below. She knew the neighbours could hear them, but that was nothing unusual. They'd been party to enough screaming rows over the past few months. 'Get out or else I'll call the police,' she hissed.

Maurice turned and went to the bedroom, retrieving his small suitcase and coming back to the kitchen to pick up his bag. He hesitated for a moment, then walked out of the door. He'd left the unwrapped book on the kitchen table and the sight of it made Sonia feel sick. She wanted to howl, like a dog abandoned by its owner.

Maurice was the love of her life, she was sure of it. And now she had lost him.

Sonia spent Christmas in her apartment, reeling and raging at the loss of her lover. No festive parties could tempt her, and she had her correspondence despatched from the *Horizon* offices, unwilling to leave the house. Not even her work could cheer her; she was utterly unable to concentrate, and it was no exaggeration to say that she was heartbroken.

They'd split before, but this had an air of finality. Sonia had written letters, trying desperately to change his mind, but she didn't want to lose her dignity and had gracefully withdrawn from the fray. The hope that he would eventually leave Suzanne for her had sustained her for months but, as with her other love affairs over the years, the wife had won and Sonia had lost out. She'd never felt about anyone the way she'd felt about Maurice, and she'd believed he felt the same. But she'd been wrong, and the realisation brought with it shame and anger.

In her pragmatic manner, Sonia told herself that enough was enough. On a Monday morning in January 1949, she stepped out into the frosty morning and began the short walk to the *Horizon* office. The world felt flat without Maurice. Everything reminded her of him: her apartment on Percy Street where they'd first made love; the café where he'd had his first cup of English tea; the bookshop on the corner where they'd attended a terrible poetry evening. They'd roamed the streets of Fitzrovia and Soho together, and every corner held shadows of their former selves.

Sonia sat down at her desk. It was early; no one else had arrived yet and for that she was grateful. She worked through her pile of post and picked up a heavy parcel wrapped in brown paper. It looked like a manuscript, and Sonia sighed. It was one thing when budding writers sent articles for her consideration, quite another when they sent whole books.

She was about to throw it directly in the bin when she noticed the sender's details: George Orwell, Jura. They'd kept in touch periodically over the years, meeting at literary events and corresponding through his work for *Horizon*, but she hadn't seen him for some months due to his self-imposed exile on the Hebridean island. Intrigued, Sonia tore the package open.

Inside, on the back of a postcard of Scotland, was a note written in George's spidery handwriting:

> *Dearest Julia,*
> *I finally finished it. I'm rather proud. I do hope you like it.*
> *Yours,*
> *George.*

Julia? Sonia frowned, wondering what he meant. Had he sent the package to the wrong person? She couldn't think of a Julia amongst their acquaintance.

The cover contained only a number, written out in full: *Nineteen Eighty-Four.*

Despite herself, Sonia felt a flicker of excitement. She sat back in her chair, slipped the string from the manuscript and began to read.

Chapter Thirty-Five

Cranham, England

March 1949

'Well, this is hardly the fucking Ritz,' Sonia declared breezily, as she strode into the room.

George was lying in bed wearing a pair of blue and white striped pyjamas, but he laughed at her comment, his eyes lighting up at the sight of her.

It was Sonia's first time visiting him since he'd been admitted to the sanatorium in Cranham, and she was shocked by his appearance though she tried not to show it. He was thinner than ever and, as he tried to sit upright, he convulsed in a fit of coughing. Sonia busied herself with filling his water cup and opening the blinds to reveal the pretty view of the Cotswolds countryside outside his window. Illness made her uneasy, an uncomfortable reminder of her own mortality, but she wanted to cheer him up and knew his mind was still as sharp as ever. *Animal Farm* had been a critical and commercial success, transforming both George's career prospects and his bank balance, and *Nineteen Eighty-Four* was a masterpiece. It was scheduled to be published later that year, and Sonia had no doubt it would be a triumph.

'How's the recovery going? Will we be seeing you in the Wheatsheaf soon?'

George smiled, though there was a trace of sadness in his expression. 'It's taking longer than expected. Unfortunately I developed rather severe side effects from the medication I was on. A rather unpleasant skin condition that can prove fatal. It's quite rare apparently.'

'Good to see you're as contrary as ever,' Sonia quipped.

'Indeed.'

'So what are you taking now?' she asked, picking up the pile of notes on the table beside his bed and leafing through.

'Well, I'm back on the streptomycin, despite the side effects.'

'But that's madness! Can't they give you something else?'

'They're trying penicillin too.'

'But I thought your complaint was tubercular? Penicillin is ineffective against tuberculosis, even I know that and I'm hardly a doctor.'

George shrugged, nonplussed. 'They know what they're doing.'

'Do they?'

Back in London, Sonia had heard the disquiet amongst George's friends that his treatment was ineffective, and that they were concerned for his health and how rapidly it was deteriorating. Sonia could see exactly what they meant, but she didn't share her anxieties with George. Instead, she smiled brightly, sitting him forwards and plumping up his pillows.

'Well, if you're not going to come to London to take me for a night on the town, I suppose I'll just have to keep visiting you here.'

'Please do, Sonia. I can't tell you how much I've enjoyed seeing you.'

Sonia was as good as her word, visiting George regularly in the wooden chalet-like accommodation at Cranham Lodge. Visitors were only supposed to stay for twenty minutes, to avoid tiring him, but Sonia charmed the nurses and they often let her sit with George for almost an hour. Rather than exhausting him, Sonia's visits seemed to leave him with a renewed energy and purpose; she suspected that was part of the reason they turned a blind eye to the length of her stay. She was determined to keep him focused on the future, to give him a sense of purpose.

'What's the plan for when you get out of here?' Sonia asked, one summer's day when the sun was high in the sky and the fields outside were turning brown with drought. 'What do you still want to achieve?'

'I won't recover fully. My health's shot. I have a fifty-fifty chance of dying.' George's tone was matter of fact; he wasn't looking for sympathy. 'My doctors say that if I go somewhere with a better climate – Switzerland, for example – then I might be able to manage the TB and eke out a few more years.'

'Then you must do it.' Sonia was adamant. 'You must keep writing, your work is so important.'

'I need someone to take care of me. I can't do it alone.'

Sonia thought about it. She walked over to the window and opened it, letting in the thick, cloying air and the scent of grass being mowed. She sensed that her time at *Horizon* was drawing to a close; Cyril was far less interested in being at the office, spending most of his time travelling, or working on other projects, and Sonia felt she'd climbed as high as she could within the organisation. She was all but editing the magazine herself, but she would never be given that title, and the publication no longer felt fresh and relevant. She needed a new challenge.

The idea of being a helpmate to a gifted artist had always appealed to her, and it would play to her strengths. Sonia was organised, thorough and conscientious, and she would take care of everything day to day. The income from *Animal Farm* meant that George would be untroubled by financial concerns; all he had to do was write.

'I'll do it,' she offered.

'Really?'

Sonia nodded before she changed her mind.

'And will you marry me? Please, Sonia. I truly think I might get better if you did.'

'All right. Why not?' she said, with a giggle that was almost hysterical. 'Yes, I'll marry you.'

And she meant it. Maurice didn't want her; she was convinced that he was the love of her life and, although she'd seen him occasionally since their break-up, he'd made it clear that they were now finished for good. To keep having affairs, and to keep having her heart broken, was a tiresome prospect and one she didn't relish.

Sonia truly believed that George was one of the greatest writers of the twentieth century, perhaps even one of the greatest literary minds of all time. She would do everything for him, she vowed. She would quite literally keep him alive.

'Good. Good.' He nodded delightedly, his tired eyes sparkling with happiness. 'But you must learn how to make dumplings.'

'Oh, George,' Sonia laughed. She sat down on the bed beside him, then patted his arm fondly. It was thin and bony and she quickly withdrew, trying not to show her distaste.

On 13th October 1949, Sonia was standing nervously outside room 65, in the long white corridor of University College Hospital, as the hustle and bustle of life and death carried on around her. She exhaled slowly, trying to slow her racing heart. However much she told herself that it was just a bourgeois piece of paper, she couldn't help but feel the gravity of what she was about to do.

She was wearing a cream suit with a pale blue blouse and a matching teardrop hat, and she carried a small posy of flowers in her gloved hands. George's friend, the writer and journalist Richard Kee, stood beside her. He'd agreed to give her away.

The door to George's room opened and his Irish nurse, Mary,

gave her a nod. Sonia thought briefly of her family – her mother, Beatrice, and her siblings Bay and Michael – and wondered whether she should have invited them, but it was too late now. She linked her arm through Richard's and he escorted her into the room.

Sonia wanted to laugh when she saw George. He was sitting up in bed, propped up by his pillows, and wearing a crimson corduroy jacket over his striped pyjamas, like a dandy. He looked pleased and proud, and Sonia felt a wave of affection for him.

She glanced around the tiny room, which was crammed with their closest friends: Richard's wife, Janetta, with whom Sonia had worked at *Horizon*, and David Astor, his best man, suave and broad-shouldered in a dark suit, next to Malcolm Muggeridge and Anthony Powell.

'Shove up a bit, darling,' Sonia said affectionately, making everyone laugh. She perched on the bed beside George as they said their vows, the UCH chaplain, Reverend Braine, officiating. It felt surreal as George slipped the plain gold band onto her finger, beside the pretty Italian engagement ring she'd chosen herself, decorated with rubies and diamonds around a central emerald. George had chosen not to wear a ring; she doubted it would stay on his skeletal finger anyway.

As the Reverend Braine declared them man and wife, Sonia and George shared a kiss. It was impossible not to notice how bony his body felt beneath the dazzling jacket, his face drawn, his breath unpleasant due to the medication he was taking.

David Astor picked up a bottle of champagne from beside George's medical equipment and popped the cork; George took a few sips, though he wasn't supposed to drink as the dry bubbles irritated his coughing.

Sonia was speaking with Janetta when someone touched her lightly on the elbow, and she turned to see Mary, the nurse, standing beside her, proffering a card.

'We all signed it,' she explained. 'All of the nurses. To say congratulations.'

'Thank you.' Sonia felt unexpectedly touched.

'He's been so much happier since you two got engaged,' Mary confided. 'We're hoping that will give him extra strength and keep him going.'

Sonia blinked back tears, squeezing her hand. David cleared his throat, and Sonia was grateful for the distraction.

'We're here today to celebrate the marriage of George and Sonia. We all know how much George wanted to get married, and we're thrilled that someone finally said yes.'

The speech raised guffaws of laughter, but Sonia smiled tightly, feeling that the comment was a little too close to the bone. She was well aware that George had proposed to a number of women since the death of his first wife; indeed, he'd popped the question to Sonia more than once over the years.

'And of course we're thrilled that *Sonia* said yes. We can all see how close the two of you have grown over the past few months, how much your visits mean to George, and how much you care for him.'

'Hear hear,' echoed Richard.

'So let's raise our glasses – well, our paper cups – to George and Sonia.'

'Mr and Mrs Orwell,' everyone echoed.

They mingled for a few more minutes, until Sonia said, 'Right, shall we get going? Richard, am I going in your car?' She went over to the bed and kissed George goodbye.

'Have fun, Mrs Orwell,' he waved cheerily. 'Have a cocktail for me. And a cream scone.'

'I'll bring one back for you,' she promised, blowing him a kiss, as everyone piled out of the room, heading for the Ritz in London to celebrate the wedding, leaving the frail groom alone in his hospital bed.

'And are all the arrangements finalised?'

'Yes, darling. We fly to Switzerland in five days' time – the 25th of January.'

'Yes, yes, I may be an invalid but I'm not an imbecile. I know what day it is.'

'And then we'll be transferred by car to the sanatorium in the Alps,' Sonia continued, ignoring her husband's outburst as she bustled round his hospital room, making a mental note of items that still needed to be packed.

'I want to take my fishing rods. That's why I had David bring them in.' George nodded to the poles propped up in the corner, incongruous amongst the medical paraphernalia.

'All right,' Sonia agreed.

'When's Richard coming to say goodbye?'

'Tuesday – the day before we leave.'

George's young son, Richard Horatio, was now five years old, and had spent half of his life being looked after by his aunt, George's younger sister, Avril. *Nineteen Eighty-Four* had done well – even better than *Animal Farm* – selling out its print runs in the UK and US, and the royalties would cover Richard's upkeep.

'Are you all right?' George asked, peering closely at Sonia. She looked exhausted, pale and washed out.

'Quite all right. I'm just getting over this wretched flu.'

'I missed you this past couple of weeks.'

'I missed you too, but I didn't think it wise to visit when I was so ill. I'm feeling much better today, honestly.'

'Perhaps you should go home and rest. We don't want two invalids on the journey.'

Sonia smiled. 'I'd like to spend this time with you, and go over the arrangements before we leave.'

'I thought you said everything was finalised?'

'The practicalities, yes. But I thought it might be nice to think about what our days might look like, and how I might best assist you. Do you have any ideas for what you're going to write next? Secker & Warburg are clamouring for your next book. Oh, and is there anything in particular you'd like me to pick up? I've got a dozen boxes of your tea from Fortnum's to take with us, I know how grumpy you get if you don't have it.'

'You're wonderful, Sonia. I'm glad I married you. I'm in the best hands.'

'You're very sweet.' Sonia came across to the bed and stroked his hair affectionately.

'You've done enough for today. Go home and rest.'

'I think I shall go home, but I might not rest. Lucian and Ann have invited me for farewell drinks; I'll just pop to the Bricklayers for a glass or two, and I can fill him on the travel arrangements. I'll give him the fishing rods to deal with,' Sonia laughed.

Their mutual friend, the artist, Lucian Freud, had agreed to accompany them to Switzerland, to act as a porter. George was obviously too unwell, and Sonia was unable to carry all their luggage and bags by herself.

'Of course, you must go. Have a wonderful time.'

'Thank you, darling. I'll be back tomorrow.'

George waved her off as Sonia blew him a kiss.

It was the last time she would see him. A few hours later, sometime after midnight, an artery burst in his lungs. Just three months after marrying George, Sonia Orwell was a widow.

Chapter Thirty-Six

VIVIEN

London, England

March 1950

'I don't know you… I want to be left alone… please!'

Vivien screamed as hands fought to grab her and she lashed out in fright, the sounds she was making guttural and inhuman. The doctor appeared in front of her, talking to her gently, calming her down as he said her name – 'Blanche… Miss DuBois…' – in a soft voice. Vivien focused on his face, consenting to accompany him as he placed a hand on her elbow, steering her across the stage, onto the porch, off into the wings.

As the final moments played out in the Aldwych Theatre, Vivien stumbled behind the set, her eyes wild, her breathing coming fast. She was alone – the doctor who'd been with her had now left – and she couldn't seem to remember where she was, but she was strangely comforted by the darkness.

Don't turn the light on!

She tried to remember who she was and where she was going. Then it came to her – she needed to escape. Stanley, he was chasing her, he was going to—

'Miss Leigh? Is everything all right?' The young woman's voice was a whisper. Vivien squinted, trying to make out her face in the dull light. She vaguely recognised her; perhaps it was a friend of her sister, Stella. No, that wasn't right. Vivien didn't have a sister, and Stella was a character in the play. This woman was—

'Yes, I'm quite all right, thank you.' When Vivien spoke, it was with a Mississippi accent, her mannerisms those of a Southern belle.

'Why don't you come with me, Miss Leigh?' the woman said kindly. 'I'll take you back to your dressing room.'

'Why, that's mighty good of you,' Vivien simpered. She clutched her arm, letting the young woman guide her through the narrow, dimly lit corridors. 'You know,' Vivien ran on, 'I have always relied on the kindness of strangers.'

The young woman smiled worriedly. Vivien could see now that she was rather plain, with mousy brown hair tied back in a ponytail, and her name was Rachel. Yes, that was it.

'Here we are,' Rachel said. 'This is yours. Is there anything I can get you, Miss Leigh? Would you like me to call anyone?'

Vivien's eyes flickered around the room, alighting on her familiar possessions: the bottle of Joy perfume; the bunch of white roses; the triumphant press cuttings; the pots of make-up; the photograph of her director. Of Larry. Her husband.

She sank down into the chair, her head in her hands. 'No, I'm quite all right, thank you,' she insisted, waving the woman away. Her voice was her own now. She stared at herself in the mirror, suddenly frightened and confused. It was as though she'd been dreaming and had woken with a start, the bright lights of her dressing room illuminating who she really was.

She was Vivian Hartley. Vivien Leigh. Scarlett O'Hara. Lady Olivier. Blanche DuBois.

Blanche. Yes, she was Blanche.

Her breathing came easier now and she felt calmer. She was Blanche DuBois, and she had always relied on the kindness of strangers.

The woman in the mirror was older than she remembered, with troubled eyes and hollow cheeks. She'd once been so beautiful, but now her looks were fading, her charms wearing thin. She turned around to ask Rachel to stay – she was scared to be on her own – but the young woman had already gone. She wanted Larry, but she was afraid that he didn't want her.

Vivien was alone, she was confused, and she was frightened.

There was a knock at the door. Vivien looked up, startled, unsure how long she'd been sitting in her dressing room. Was it minutes? Hours?

'Come in.'

A man. She recognised his face. He was aristocratic-looking and urbane, with slender features and wavy hair. And he was with a woman. There was something familiar about her too, but Vivien couldn't place her. She'd met so many people over the years, it was hard to keep track. But she wasn't scared. They seemed warm and kind, and she was confident they didn't mean her harm.

'Vivien, darling, you were simply marvellous as ever.' The man sashayed over and kissed her effusively on both cheeks. The scent of his cologne triggered a flicker of recognition.

'Cecil,' she said carefully. He was Cecil Beaton, and she remembered him. 'You're a photographer.' They had worked together many times throughout her career; as a costume designer, he'd dressed Vivien for both stage and screen, and his work behind the camera had seen him shoot everyone who was anyone, from film stars to royalty. His black and white shots of Vivien and Larry were amongst the most stunning in her collection.

The flicker of a frown crossed Cecil's prominent forehead. 'Yes, that's right. And do you remember this young lady?'

The woman shook her head, waving away his words. 'It's

quite all right, I'm sure you won't. We were at school together, in Roehampton. I'm Sonia. I was Sonia Brownell back then.'

Vivien's face lit up in recognition. It was strange, often these days she couldn't recall what she'd had for supper the night before, yet she had the clearest memories of the Sacred Heart, her mind wandering to her school days with increasing frequency of late. It was often sensory; a dressing-room mirror scrubbed clean with vinegar would transport her right back to her dorm room in the cutting depths of winter, the fear and the cruelty ever present. On the edge of her memory hovered images of Darjeeling and Calcutta; there was something about Sonia she associated with India too.

'Yes, of course I remember you, darling.' Vivien stood up to greet her, and suddenly her mind felt clearer, the terror of moments earlier forgotten like a bad dream.

'Although she goes by Sonia Orwell these days,' Cecil added, with a meaningful look.

It took Vivien a moment to put the pieces together. She remembered the articles she'd read, and the obituary in *The Times*. Vivien had heard of George Orwell, although politics – and communism in particular – held little interest or appeal. 'Oh yes, of course.'

'My husband died two months ago,' Sonia explained.

'I'm terribly sorry. I read about it in the newspaper. I didn't realise you… He was a great friend of yours, wasn't he, Cecil?'

'Yes. I miss him terribly. Poor Sonia's been having an awful time of it.'

'I wasn't going to come tonight. I've hardly been out since he… I couldn't bear it. But Cecil persuaded me and I'm so glad he did. Your performance was exquisite, and terrifically moving. I can't imagine what it must take to do that on stage every evening.'

'Yes, it is rather… taxing.' Vivien smiled brightly, unwilling to think about the toll of pouring her heart and soul into Blanche night after night. 'Oh!' she exclaimed suddenly. 'We must all go out for supper.'

'I'm terribly sorry, darling, I can't.' Cecil shook his head ruefully. 'Prior engagement, I'm afraid. I only popped in to say hello, and to reintroduce you to Sonia.'

'Can you come?' Vivien turned to Sonia, her expression hopeful. She was always flying high after a performance, and the adrenaline ensured she was still awake long after midnight. Theatre people kept different hours to the rest of the world, going to bed in the early hours and rising late in the morning.

Vivien felt strongly that she wanted to reacquaint herself with Sonia. From her school friend's exhausted expression, her face puffy from alcohol, her eyes haunted by sadness, Vivien identified a kindred spirit. 'Do say you will,' Vivien pressed, taking hold of her hands.

'Of course,' Sonia smiled. 'I'd be delighted.'

Fifteen minutes later, the two women were sitting at a discreet corner table at The Ivy, a bottle of wine open in front of them, two cigarettes resting in the ashtray. They'd ordered a light meal for the sake of it; neither had much of an appetite.

'So, darling, tell me everything you've been doing since we last saw one another. When *did* we last see one another?'

'What year did you leave?'

'Nineteen twenty-seven. I couldn't get out of there fast enough,' Vivien laughed.

'It was hellish. That place scarred me for life, I swear.'

They lapsed into silence, both contemplating the effect that their Sacred Heart schooling had had upon them. Wrenched from their families at a tender age, to contend with the physical hardship, the psychological cruelty, the hated rituals and the perverse morality. Sonia reached for her cigarette, and Vivien did the same.

'You heard that it was hit during an air raid? The pupils had been evacuated to the countryside, but the buildings were razed to the ground.'

'I did hear, yes,' Vivien said, her eyes lighting up. 'I didn't know whether to laugh or cry.'

'I thought it extremely fitting. Blow the place to smithereens! Perhaps there is a God after all…' Sonia said archly, and Vivien laughed heartily, her voice low and throaty. A few other diners turned around; Sonia noticed their surreptitious glances at the star in their midst.

'I do like you, Sonia. What a marvellous sense of humour! You simply must tell me all about yourself,' Vivien pressed. 'I'm sure you've led a fascinating life.'

'I'm not so sure I have… Most of my work has been bound up with *Horizon*. Do you know it?'

'Cyril Connolly's magazine?'

Sonia smiled ruefully. 'Yes, that's the one. Although most days it feels as though I'm putting in all of the work and Cyril's getting all of the credit whilst sunning himself in the South of France.'

'Ah. I understand.' Vivien nodded, and Sonia believed her. She felt sure that Vivien, like every successful woman, would have experienced what it was like to have a man take credit for her achievements. 'Did you never think of writing yourself?' Vivien asked.

'I did, once upon a time, but I swiftly found out that I wasn't good enough. I'm destined to always be a handmaiden to those who *do* write.'

'Oh, tosh, darling. I'm certain you're clever and talented enough. Why don't you write a play? Or a film? Do you know, there's so much appalling shit out there – mostly written by men. I'm sure you'd be a hundred times better.'

'Thank you,' Sonia smiled, though scriptwriting had never crossed her mind. She would never have admitted it to Vivien, but Sonia considered the novel the highest form of art, with playwriting merely a distant (and inferior) cousin.

'How did you end up married to George Orwell? I heard he was the most dry old stick.'

'I'm not entirely sure,' Sonia laughed. 'He asked me – a number of times, in fact – and eventually I said yes.'

'But did you love him?'

'In a way, yes. I came to care for him deeply. I wouldn't say he was the love of my life, but… I found my *grand amour* before and it worked out rather badly. Perhaps I was tired of getting my heart broken.'

Sonia topped up their glasses, as Vivien thought of her passionate, tempestuous marriage to Larry, of how much they'd sacrificed to be together. There'd been great highs – she'd been utterly spellbound by him, head over heels – but then came the great lows, like a star that burned so brightly it couldn't sustain its brilliance, burning out and collapsing in on itself, crushing its own core. Would it have been better to have a calmer, more stable relationship, akin to the life she'd shared with Leigh? She might not have experienced overwhelming passion, but neither would she have had to live through the volatility, the emotional instability, the mental torture that were her daily companions.

'Do you have children?' Vivien wondered, deliberately changing the subject.

Sonia shook her head. 'I was a stepmother briefly, I suppose. But Richard – George's son – lives with his aunt and I rarely see him. It's better that way, I think. What about you, do you have children?'

'A daughter, with my ex-husband. She's sixteen now. I don't know where the years have gone… I haven't been the best mother, you know,' Vivien confided, as she stubbed out her cigarette. 'I never had the natural inclination. But I should like to try again, now that I'm less young and foolish. Less selfish, I hope. Larry and I are trying for a baby.'

Sonia looked surprised, and Vivien pursed her lips. 'Yes, I know, I'm thirty-six now and far too old. I've been pregnant twice over the past few years, but never… never to term.'

'I'm sorry.' Sonia was genuinely sympathetic. 'And you're not old. I'm thirty-one and you've given me hope that one day I might... I had an abortion, a few years ago. Oh, it wasn't George's,' she clarified, noting Vivien's expression. 'I never told the father. The baby would be three by now. I don't even know if it was a boy or a girl. I've been thinking about it a lot recently, wondering what would have happened if I hadn't... Silly, isn't it?'

'No. No, it's not silly.'

The food arrived – lobster cocktail for Vivien, herb omelette for Sonia – but neither woman felt like eating. Sonia dutifully speared a forkful of egg and said, 'Anyway, let's not talk about me. Your life is far more interesting. I can't believe all the things that have happened to you.'

'Oh, it all seems like so long ago. I was a different woman back then.'

'But you're still doing incredible work. Tonight, for example – I can't imagine what it must be like to go out on stage, night after night, as Blanche. Does it take its toll?'

Vivien paled, looking distraught, and Sonia regretted asking the question.

'I'm sorry, I shouldn't have—'

'No, it's quite all right. Sometimes I think I should never have taken the role. I was desperate to play her, but it's too much for me, I can't... I've always had problems, and this has made them worse. It's as though I feel the character too deeply, I can't seem to shake her off. And now I've signed up for the film...'

'Should you have done that?' Sonia pressed gently.

'Perhaps not, but it's like she has a hold over me. Blanche, that is. Besides, we need the money.'

Sonia remained silent, letting Vivien speak.

'I feel like I have to keep it a secret, as though it's something to be ashamed of. All the chaos, in here.' Vivien tapped her temple. 'The press would have a field day. I don't care about them, but it could end my career. No studio could get insurance, so no one would employ me. I feel like I'm fighting a battle every day, yet I can't tell anyone about it.'

'I understand. More than you know,' Sonia said with feeling, and Vivien believed her. 'Especially since George died. I can't seem to pull myself together. At times I feel I'm going mad.'

'This is rather cathartic, isn't it?' Vivien smiled, as she pushed a piece of lettuce around her bowl. 'Like the confessional. Do you know, I can't remember the last time I even set foot in a church.'

'Nor me. Nothing like a Catholic education to make you renounce your faith,' Sonia joked, but Vivien was distracted, her eyes glittering.

'Darling, do you want to know a secret? I'm in love,' she finished triumphantly.

Sonia frowned. 'With… Sir Laurence?'

Vivien shook her head irritably. 'No, no. With Peter Finch.'

'Who?'

'He's an actor, and a damn fine one. Better than Larry even – or at least, he has the potential to be. He's Australian, but now he's moved to London.'

'Oh.' Sonia didn't know what to say. 'Are you having an affair?'

'Not yet. But I adore him.' She seemed full of light suddenly, her face radiant as she spoke of Peter. 'The problem with Larry,' she continued, her voice loud and indiscreet, 'aside from his lack of prowess in the bedroom, is his fucking God-like reputation. I can never match up to him on the stage – at least, not in the minds of the public and the critics. Fucking critics.'

'It's because he's a man,' Sonia said simply. 'I know that if I ever *did* try to write again, I'd be compared to Hemingway, to Waugh, to Camus… and of course to George, and I'd be found wanting. The next best thing – for me, at least – is to assist them. To play a part in their success and know they couldn't have achieved what they did without me.'

'Frustrating, isn't it, darling? But I think you should just fucking do it. You might surprise yourself. Now, shall we get the bill?'

Their food was almost untouched, the bottle of wine empty.

'Of course,' Sonia nodded, trying to keep up with Vivien's capricious moods.

Vivien signalled for the waiter, and said to Sonia, 'Thank you so much, darling, I've had a wonderful evening. It's been quite the tonic.'

'For me too. I almost didn't come out tonight, but Cecil was so persuasive, and I'm glad of that. It's been so lovely seeing you.'

'Well, we must do it again. And let's not leave it so long next time,' Vivien quipped, settling the bill despite Sonia's protests. She'd meant what she said – it had been lovely to catch up with Sonia, to unburden herself to someone who seemed to understand. She'd found a sense of peace temporarily but tomorrow, Vivien knew, the demons would return.

Chapter Thirty-Seven

London, England

January 1953

Peter Finch stirred in his sleep; he knew that something had disturbed him, but he wasn't sure what. Beside him, his wife, Tamara, shook his arm vigorously, then came a long, insistent ringing.

'Someone's at the door,' she hissed.

'What? What time is it?'

'Almost one.'

'Hold on.' Peter climbed out of bed and pulled on his dressing gown, blearily running his hands through his dark hair, blinking in the brightness as Tamara switched on the bedside lamp. He jogged down the stairs of the red-brick townhouse in South Kensington, where he lived with his wife, a Romanian-born ballerina, and their young daughter, Anita.

Peter hesitated as he reached the front door. He considered taking the poker from the fireplace but decided against it. Surely burglars and other criminals didn't ring the doorbell and wait for admittance?

He pulled open the door to see Vivien standing there. She was wearing a full-length mink coat that fell open to expose a revealing silk slip dress. Her lips curled into a smile the moment she saw him, her blue-green eyes sparkling.

'Peter, darling! I had to come and see you right away.'

'Vivien, do you know what time it is?'

'No,' she said, without guile. 'All I know is that I had to tell you as soon as I had the idea.'

'Come in,' Peter said, ushering her inside, the bitter wind blowing through the open door. It was London in early January, and the temperature was below freezing, but Vivien didn't seem cold.

'Who is it?' Tamara appeared at the top of the stairs. Tall, dark-haired and slender, she looked like a ghost in her white nightgown.

'It's Vivien.' In those two words, Peter tried to convey his surprise and confusion, an undertone of apology. 'Go back to bed. I'll be up shortly.'

Tamara frowned, but did as she was bid; Vivien waved at her distractedly, following Peter through to the reception room. He sat down on the chintz sofa and Vivien joined him, taking hold of his hands.

'Peter, darling, I've had the most tremendous idea. I simply had to tell you straightaway. I've accepted a role in a film called *Elephant Walk*. They're filming in Ceylon, and it's the story of the owner of a tea plantation and his new bride. They wanted Larry to play my husband, but he's filming *The Beggar's Opera*, and then he's committed to other projects for almost the whole of the year. So I suggested you! Don't you think it would be perfect?'

Peter's head was spinning. Surely he must still be dreaming. How else was it possible that an incredibly glamorous Vivien Leigh had turned up at his house in the early hours and offered him a role in a movie? She looked impossibly beautiful, and Peter was in awe of her. Even at this time in the morning she was ravishing. He'd adored her since the very first time they'd met in

Sydney and, more than four years later she was still utterly fascinating to him, completely irresistible.

When Peter had won his first role on the West End stage, playing Ernest Piaste in *Daphne Laureola*, they'd found they were performing in theatres next door to one another – he at Wyndham's, Vivien in *Antigone* at the New Theatre. The two of them had become lovers, their affair continuing on and off in the intervening years, as Vivien went to America to film *A Streetcar Named Desire*, for which she won her second Academy Award.

Peter sometimes wondered whether her husband knew what had happened between them. Larry wasn't an idiot, and likely had his suspicions, but seemed happy to turn a blind eye. Peter loved his wife, but he worshipped Vivien – she was glamorous, vivacious, and had a voracious sexual appetite.

'So what do you say?' Vivien asked, looking at him beseechingly. 'I've already told them I won't work with anyone else. We fly out in a fortnight's time, and they'll pay you fifty thousand dollars. Plus, you get to be my husband for two months.' Her cheeks dimpled as she smiled, the scent of her perfume intoxicating.

Peter stared at her. There could only be one possible answer to her question and they both knew it.

Colombo in Sri Lanka was hot and humid, colourful and exotic, with its temples and markets, macaques and smiling locals. The heat barely let up at night, and neither did Vivien; instead of sleeping, she'd taken to walking around the city, or following the paths through the dark jungle. Often, Peter Finch accompanied her. Tonight it was past midnight as the two of them strolled down to the beach, the air thick with warmth and promise, the tropical noises of insects and animals and the distant whisper of the sea.

'It reminds me of my childhood,' Vivien murmured, and her voice was husky and reflective. 'Half-remembered memories and glimpses of something familiar. It's the most curious thing, as though the past and the present coexist, yet neither are solid. Neither have a tangible form that I can fully grasp and keep hold of.'

'I can imagine you as a child,' Peter smiled. 'Scampering about the hillside.'

Vivien laughed delightedly. 'I'm not sure I scampered. It was all very prim and proper. I don't have many clear memories of India – I left when I was six, your daughter's age. I was sent to England to a terribly strict convent school on the outskirts of London. Can you imagine doing that to your child?'

'I suppose not.' Peter's tone was non-committal, all too aware that he'd left his wife and child back in Britain whilst he cavorted in Colombo with Vivien. He knew, too, that Vivien's daughter, Suzanne, had mostly been brought up by her father and grandmother.

He stifled a yawn. Checking his wristwatch in the moonlight, he saw that it was almost 2 a.m. 'Aren't you getting tired, Vivien?'

'Oh no, Larry, I'm never tired.'

'Larry?'

'Hmm?' Vivien seemed unaware she'd just called him by her husband's name. 'Sometimes, when I'm walking around like this, I feel that the night belongs to me. That there's magic, but it will only reveal itself when the rest of the world is sleeping.'

'Perhaps we should head back,' Peter suggested gently.

'Back? We've hardly started. I want to go to the beach. I want to feel the sand beneath my toes and the water on my body. Don't you?'

'Yes, but we have an early call tomorrow,' Peter said carefully. 'I know William wants to re-shoot some of your close-ups. He's concerned that you look tired.'

'Of course I look tired. I'm forty this year. I'm not some ingenue with unlined skin and raven hair. If I look *old*, if that's what you're delicately trying to tell me, it's because I *am* fucking old!'

'Vivien—'

'You don't think that, do you, darling?' She wrapped her arms around him as they walked, her hands roaming over his chest, slipping beneath his shirt.

'I think you're the most incredible woman I've ever met,' Peter said truthfully. 'I worship you. Which is why I don't want you to get fired.'

'They won't fire me. They're paying me too much, and besides, the cost of re-shooting would be extortionate. Oh, darling, look how wonderful this is! Have you ever seen anything so magical? Oh! Quickly! Take off your shoes.'

They emerged onto the pristine white sand, the full moon overhead illuminating the scene in spectacular fashion and shimmering on the water, like an ethereal beacon lighting the way to the horizon. The jungle stopped abruptly, a strip of black that spilled onto the beach, leading to a calm sea whose gentle ripples kissed the shoreline.

Vivien danced across the sand, shrieking with delight. Peter pulled off his canvas shoes; they dangled from his hand as he followed her, his laughter echoing across the cloudless heavens.

As she neared the water's edge, Vivien pulled her white slip over her head, flinging it recklessly onto the sand. Underneath she wore nothing.

'Vivien…' Peter said warningly. He glanced around, but the beach appeared deserted.

'What?' Her gaze was challenging. She walked away from him, her body pale and inviting in the moonlight. The water embraced her as she stepped into the ocean. When it had reached her waist, she turned around. 'Well?' She arched an eyebrow. 'Aren't you coming in with me?'

Peter hesitated, but only for a moment. He unbuttoned his shirt, slipped off his shorts and his underwear, and strode naked into the Indian Ocean to join her.

'Larry? It's Peter Finch.'

'I can't hear you very well, the line's bad.'

There were more than six thousand miles between Peter in Los Angeles, where production of *Elephant Walk* had moved, and Larry in Italy. Larry had finished work on *The Beggar's Opera* but was taking a few days' holiday with friends before launching into a punishing schedule of rehearsals and filming that would last for almost a year.

'It's Peter Finch.'

'Ah, Peter. Everything okay? I assume not, or else you wouldn't be calling me.'

'It's Vivien...' Peter paused. Now that he'd finally got hold of Larry, he couldn't seem to find the words.

'Go on.'

Peter stared out of the window of his rented house in the Hollywood Hills. It was another beautiful L.A. day, and he supposed he'd better make the most of it whilst he wasn't due on set; production had been forced to take an unscheduled break, which was the reason for his call. 'She's not well. They're going to replace her.'

Larry's exhalation echoed down the line all the way from Ischia, loaded with concern and sadness. 'Who with?'

'Elizabeth Taylor. They're making the announcement tomorrow.'

'Fuck.' Elizabeth Taylor was twenty-two years old, seventeen years younger than Vivien, and dubbed a 'raven-haired siren' by the press. Larry understood immediately that Liz's casting would be like a red rag to Vivien's insecurities. Once it was announced, the whole world would know that she was unable to fulfil her commitments. There would be speculation – much of it unpleasant and inaccurate – about why she'd effectively been fired, and Larry wouldn't be able to get to her before that started. 'What happened?'

'There've been a number of... incidents. She keeps messing up scenes, forgetting her lines—'

'Vivien *never* forgets her lines.'

'She's not herself at all, and she's been getting worse. I thought perhaps that when we finished in Ceylon and moved to Los Angeles, she might rally. That it would feel more familiar – less exotic – and might calm her down, but if anything it's the opposite. No one knew what to do, and the studio's had enough. They called a doctor – he had to sedate her. She threw the pills he gave her into the swimming pool, so they had to hold her down and inject her...'

'Oh my God. My poor Vivien.'

'She's in a bad way, Larry. There've been so many... I don't even know where to start. The other night she flew at me, clawing at my face and screaming. She was speaking in a Southern accent – I think she thought she was Blanche.'

'I'm... sorry you had to experience that.'

There was an awkwardness between the two men, brought on not merely by the circumstances of the conversation. Larry was her husband, but it seemed evident that there'd been an affair – physical *and* emotional – between Vivien and Peter Finch. Neither alluded to it, but Peter was almost certain that Larry knew.

'Something happened the other night. Something serious,' Peter continued. It felt cathartic to share these harrowing stories, to finally be able to tell someone who might understand. 'The cast were invited to a party at the Garden of Allah. Vivien said that she was tired, that she had a headache, and needed to rest. We left my daughter, Anita, with a babysitter and we'd almost reached the hotel when Tamara insisted that the cab driver turn around. She said she had a bad feeling and wanted to go back. When we returned to the house, Vivien had dismissed the babysitter. She was in Anita's room, by her bed, and she...' Peter's voice caught in his throat and he broke off. 'She had a pillow in her hand and she... I really think she was trying to smother her.'

'Jesus Christ.'

'She didn't know what she was doing, or even who she was. It was horrific.' Peter was on the verge of tears. 'We were letting her stay with us because she seemed so fragile, but we had to ask her to leave… Can you get here?'

'To L.A.? It'll take a few days.' Larry would need to take a boat to the Italian mainland then fly to Rome; Rome to London; London to New York; New York to Los Angeles. He was literally half a world away from Vivien, though the distance between them now felt further than ever, impossible to breach.

'I'll make all the arrangements,' he promised, and Peter understood the sentiment, if not the detail. In fact, Larry intended to book her into Netherne Hospital in Surrey, which specialised in psychiatric disorders. He'd made enquiries previously but could never quite bring himself to institutionalise his wife. This time there was no choice. He'd heard of the merits of electric shock therapy too; it wasn't pleasant, to say the least, but they were desperate. 'I'll be there as soon as I can.'

'Thank you.' The relief in Peter's voice was obvious. 'She needs you.'

PART V
The Grande Dame

Chapter Thirty-Eight

MAUREEN

Benidorm, Spain

August 1958

The air was stifling, the mercury barely dropping even as the day slid into evening. Maureen was sitting on the porch of their large rented house by the sea, sipping local lemonade, which was tangy and refreshing. Her eldest daughter, Mia, was a ball of energy, dancing around in front of her.

'"From our petticoats, sir,"' Mia said seriously, with a frown. Her face changed, and she repeated cheekily, '"From our petticoats, sir." How was that, Mom?'

'Perfect, my love,' Maureen beamed, as Mia continued to repeat the line a dozen times, changing her intonation and expression. Now thirteen years old, Mia was tall and willowy, her legs long and tanned in white shorts, teamed with a ruffled peasant blouse bought from a local market. Her sweeping hair was the palest blonde, her face scattered with freckles, and she had the most extraordinary blue, soulful eyes. She'd been given a line in her father's film, and she was determined that her performance would be flawless.

'Daddy, watch me,' Mia called, as her father stepped out onto the terrace, a large glass of dark rum in one hand, the bottle in the other. She recited the line again and John smiled distractedly.

'That's great, honey. Now run along and find your sister.'

Mia did as she was told – her father had a terrible temper, and the entire family did their best not to anger him – and headed into the house to find Prudence, three years her junior. There was rarely 'family time' in the Farrow household; as the children were growing up, they'd had dinner with their parents only once a week, a succession of nannies and governesses employed to fill the void. John and Maureen had lived very separate lives from their children, busy with their careers and their friends. It was a source of regret for Maureen now, but at the time she hadn't known how to do anything different, following the path her parents had laid out. She'd found herself thinking a lot about her regrets in recent months, dwelling on the mistakes she'd made, the choices she'd taken that had led her to this moment.

John sat down in a wicker chair beside Maureen, taking a large gulp from his glass and topping it up from the bottle.

'How was filming today?' Maureen asked primly. She wore a pretty navy and white dress, with a straw sunhat perched on her head.

'It's going well. I'm pleased.' John was directing a movie called *John Paul Jones*, an adventure on the high seas. They'd filmed earlier scenes in Madrid and then the cast and crew moved to the quiet, picturesque town of Benidorm on the Costa Blanca to film the naval battle along the coast.

At forty-seven, Maureen was now semi-retired from acting, although that wasn't entirely by choice. Parts for women of her age were thin on the ground. She'd kept her slender figure, but giving birth to seven children took its toll, and the producers' eyes were critical. In recent years, she'd increasingly found work on television and had embraced the new medium, with guest roles on popular shows and meatier parts in teleplays.

'Have you decided?' John asked, with a nod to where Mia had just been standing.

'About…?'

'Boarding school.'

Maureen pulled a face.

'It could be a great experience for the girls,' John insisted. 'And it would keep them out from under your feet. They've had all this time here with you, and soon you'll all be in Ireland for the rest of the summer. They'll probably be glad to get away from you when term starts.'

Maureen smiled uncertainly, wondering whether he'd meant to sound so cruel. The family were scheduled to move to London in the autumn, where John would begin editing *John Paul Jones*, and the issue of schooling for all the children had to be decided. John was keen to send Mia and Prudence to a convent boarding school, to be educated as Maureen had been, but Maureen had her reservations, for obvious reasons.

'I worry about Mia,' Maureen sighed. 'After everything she's been through.'

John shrugged. 'She's recovered. No lasting scars.'

'I'm not so sure…'

Over three years ago, the day after Mia's ninth birthday, she'd been diagnosed with polio, a frightening, highly contagious disease that affected the spinal cord and the brain. A terrifying epidemic had swept through the country, paralysing and killing tens of thousands of children. Mia had been wrenched from the family home, bundled into an ambulance and driven straight to Los Angeles General Hospital. There'd been no time to say goodbye to her siblings, and her clothes and belongings had been burned lest they be contaminated. The house had been cleaned from top to bottom, the carpets replaced, the walls repainted, the swimming pool drained.

Mia had spent three weeks on an isolation ward, seeing her parents for just twenty minutes, three times a week, from behind a window. Maureen had been distraught, desperate to see her daughter but knowing the risk any contact presented to the rest of her family. She cancelled her work commitments, unable to concentrate on anything else whilst Mia was gravely ill. The idea of losing a child was unthinkable.

When Mia finally came home, weeks later, she was a different person – knowing, mature, frightened. The ordeal had changed her – by her own admission, it had marked the end of her childhood – and Maureen was wary of inflicting another such experience on her.

'She'll be fine,' John assured her blithely.

'I'll think about it some more,' Maureen replied, remembering Roehampton: the coldness, the cruelty of the nuns, the ridiculous bathing shifts. Yet time and distance had eased the pain, and she found herself thinking that surely it hadn't been that bad? Perhaps she'd simply been a precocious, unhappy, hormonal teenager, going through a normal phase of rebellion. Perhaps the discipline had been necessary. After all, she'd gone on to lead a mostly happy, extremely successful life. And she'd made great friendships at school, revelling in the camaraderie of the girls. The experience had undoubtedly been character-forming. She and John were working and travelling so much that it would be good for her children to have some stability. The younger ones could attend a day school, perhaps, but the older ones could board, although the Sacred Heart of Roehampton was no longer an option; the school had relocated to the countryside during the Second World War, and the original buildings had been destroyed in a bombing raid.

Their eldest child, Michael, hadn't come on the trip at all. He was almost nineteen now and had chosen to remain at home in California, enjoying his first real taste of independence. He was tall and handsome and intelligent – Mia always joked that he'd be President one day – and, like his father, he was extremely popular with women. Maureen found herself missing Michael dreadfully, but she supposed that was what happened when your children flew the nest. All you could do was ensure that you'd equipped them with everything they needed to navigate the world.

'I was just thinking about Mike,' she said to John. 'It feels strange not having him here.'

'He'll be having a ball at home by himself. Think about what you were doing at nineteen.'

'That's what I'm afraid of,' she laughed. 'At that age I'd just moved to Los Angeles and was making my first movie. Everything was so exciting. My life was full of possibilities.'

Maureen smiled wistfully, lost in nostalgia, reflecting on everything that had happened in the intervening years. She could never have imagined that Michael would be joined by six siblings, nor that her marriage to John could have deteriorated so badly. 'Perhaps I'll call him this evening. It would be good to hear his voice, get his news.'

John pulled a face. 'Leave the kid alone. You need to cut the apron strings.'

Maureen's face fell, stung by the implicit criticism.

'Besides, the international call will cost a fortune. And you're not working, so that's money we don't have.' John drained his glass and got to his feet. 'Right, time for me to go.'

Maureen's annoyance was replaced by frustration. 'I thought you might stay for dinner tonight.'

'Sorry, honey. I have too much work to do. Say bye to the kids for me.'

John got up and kissed her, squeezing her waist rather roughly. Maureen couldn't help but notice how he'd changed over the years. He was still handsome, but there were hard lines around his mouth, his face bloated by drink.

Maureen didn't accompany him to the door, instead remaining in her seat as she listened to the sound of a car starting then driving away. Inside the house, she could hear the children shouting as they came down for dinner, the nanny and housekeeper taking charge. She stared out at the sparkling Mediterranean, the cresting white waves on the dazzling blue sea, the boats in the distance and the fine yellow sand that came almost to their back door.

Whilst Maureen and the family were staying in this large house on the outskirts of Benidorm, John was staying in a hotel in town, with the rest of the cast and crew. He said it was because he needed to concentrate, to stay focused on the movie, but Maureen wasn't so sure.

She wasn't blind to her husband's dalliances; they'd been going on for years, and he was hardly discreet about it. At one time John had been romancing Ava Gardner, and their passionate affair had been the talk of Hollywood. Maureen had always found herself unable to countenance divorce, no matter how unhappy she was. Her own parents had endured a miserable marriage, staying together long after the love had departed, and that was the example Maureen was led by. But it was something that had flitted through her mind of late, a musing if not a serious consideration.

She and John were increasingly distant, worried about money and drawn into vicious arguments. She was ashamed to say that she was almost relieved when John went away; she was protected from his moods, able to live her life without walking on eggshells. In truth, she was desperately unhappy and didn't know which way to turn. She couldn't imagine life without him – he was all she'd known for more than a quarter of a century, and at her age, would any other man want her? Maureen couldn't shake the feeling that she was past her prime, with a washed-up career, clinging to John like a life raft. It felt like a long time since she'd been a young starlet in Hollywood, clicking her fingers and having men fall at her feet.

So she remained in her marriage due to… what, exactly? Respectability? Habit? Catholic guilt? Maureen had always thought of herself as a brave woman, a trailblazer, but now found herself paralysed by indecision. She admired Vivien, who'd left her first husband when the relationship wasn't working – although having fallen deeply in love with someone else helped to cushion the blow. There was no other man in Maureen's life and, despite there being potentially dozens of other women in John's, she was confident that there was no one special, no one he loved better than her.

They'd raised seven wonderful children together, but now that they were beginning to grow up and make their own way in life, where did that leave Maureen and John? She exhaled deeply, sitting back in her chair, drinking her lemonade and staring out at the view.

Two months later, the Farrows moved to London, and into a suite at the Park Lane Hotel in Mayfair. Whilst John spent his days editing *John Paul Jones*, Maureen led the life of a lady of leisure, lunching with friends, shopping on Bond Street, visiting the theatre and cinema. While it was not unenjoyable, Maureen suspected that the endless rounds of dining and frivolous buying, spending money they didn't have on items they didn't need, were to distract from something far bigger: namely, the unhappiness in her marriage, the stalling of her career, a general lack of purpose and direction. A malaise had settled upon her that she could never quite shake off these days, finding herself weeping unexpectedly, or lying listlessly in bed until well past noon.

Maureen longed to act again but didn't know how to pick up the remnants of her career; despite finding sporadic work in television and radio, it was a far cry from the heady days of her early movie stardom. There were moments when she despised John whole-heartedly, but underneath it all she wanted him to love her like he had in the early days. She missed the children terribly, but couldn't bear to be around them when they came home; their exuberance and need for her attention were too much to cope with.

John and Maureen had made the decision to send Mia and Prudence to a convent boarding school in Surrey, whilst the two boys, Patrick and Johnny, were at school in Bournemouth on the south coast of England. The youngest girls, Tisa and Steffi, attended a day school in London, not far from the hotel.

It was mid-afternoon when Maureen returned to her suite, laden with bags from her spree in Harrods. They certainly weren't as wealthy as they had been in the heyday of the 1930s and '40s, but John had been paid well for *John Paul Jones*, and Maureen needed to keep herself occupied. Besides, the children needed new things; they were growing out of clothes so quickly, and Maureen liked to send parcels to Mia and Prudence. She remembered the excitement at Roehampton when someone received a parcel from home, a trunk of goodies to be shared amongst the friends in the dorm.

Mia had called Maureen at the hotel a few times, begging to be allowed home for the weekend, but John and Maureen had decided against it. It would only make things worse in the long run, and the separation would be harder when they had to endure it once again.

Maureen decided to run a bath to freshen up. Tisa and Steffi would be home soon, and perhaps she would read them a story and put them to bed after Barbara, the Scottish nanny, had got them ready. John wouldn't be home for hours. She rarely saw him these days, and she was glad of it. After editing until late at night, he would often go out to a nightclub, coming back in the early hours – if he bothered to come home at all.

Maureen walked through to the luxurious bathroom, ran the water and added Floris bath oil. When the telephone began to ring, she strolled back through to the living room and picked it up.

'Good afternoon, Miss O'Sullivan, I have a call for you from California. Will you take it?'

'Yes, of course. Thank you.' As the line was connected, Maureen found herself idly wondering what it could be. Perhaps an offer of work – hopefully not another Tarzan film. She'd sworn she wouldn't do any more, and she'd been replaced by another actress in the role of Jane, but with their current financial situation she might have no option but to agree to a cameo or—

'Mrs Farrow?'

'Yes.'

'This is Officer Ryan calling from the Los Angeles County Sheriff's Department.'

Maureen almost rolled her eyes, wondering what Michael had been doing to get himself in trouble with the law. She hoped he hadn't got into a fight, or been driving under the influence.

'Yes, Officer, what's happened?'

'I'm afraid there's been an accident.'

There was a pause, and in that moment Maureen felt white-hot fear shoot through her, her stomach dropping as though she were on a rollercoaster, falling from a great height.

'Your son Michael was taking flying lessons, we believe. There was a mid-air collision over the San Fernando Valley. I'm very sorry, ma'am. We're doing our best to retrieve the body.'

The phone dropped from Maureen's hand with a crash. She opened her mouth to scream but no sound came out. Michael. Her firstborn. Her baby. They were trying to find his body.

The scream finally found its release, echoing round the hotel room walls, bringing the butler running. The bathwater spilled over onto the tiles, and Maureen's world was ripped apart.

Chapter Thirty-Nine

London, England

December 1958

The quaint red-brick house on Swan Walk in Chelsea was lit up for the festive season, with fairy lights twinkling, candles aglow, and a large tree dominating the living room window. Inside, though, there was little Christmas cheer.

Maureen and John had flown back to Los Angeles for Michael's funeral, before returning to London. John needed to finish editing *John Paul Jones*, but had shown little enthusiasm for the task, spending his days drifting and drinking. They'd moved out of the Hyde Park Hotel, renting this grand property in Chelsea, and the children were due home for the holidays from their respective schools over the next few days.

Maureen was still numb. Life had been reduced to mindlessly putting one foot in front of the other whilst trying to shield oneself from feeling. She couldn't believe that Michael was gone. Her eldest, her firstborn, her beloved son. She tortured herself imagining what he must have gone through in the moments before his death – the realisation, the terror, the impact. She prayed it had been quick, that he hadn't suffered; in the same breath, she berated the Almighty for taking Michael away from her, questioning the existence of a god who could allow such suffering.

She and John found no solace in one another, each locked in their own grief, dealing with it in their separate ways: John through alcohol and a fierce, irrepressible rage; Maureen oscillating between stupor and uncontrollable weeping. She was at her lowest ebb. Not only had she failed in the most basic requirement of parenting – to keep her children safe – but her career was non-existent and her marriage was essentially over. She was expected to be festive for the sake of her other children, but she couldn't have felt less like celebrating.

Mia and Prudence had already returned from Surrey; Prudence was out with a friend, and Maureen and Mia were cooking, inexpertly. John was sat at the kitchen table, drinking a large glass of rum, leafing through *The Times* and scanning the obituaries. Recently he'd become obsessed with death, pondering his own mortality, seeing which of his contemporaries had died and at what age. John looked up as Maureen sliced the roast chicken she'd made. It had spent too long in the oven, and looked dry and flavourless.

'What's this shit?' John snarled. 'Where's the cook?'

'I gave her the evening off. If you're not going to work then we need to tighten our belts.'

'If you're going to feed me this rubbish then maybe I will.'

'Yes, you bloody should,' Maureen hissed. 'To provide for me and this family. Otherwise how are we going to eat? We have seven children, for heaven's sake.'

'Six!' John roared, getting to his feet. He was drunk and angry, unstable on his feet. 'We just buried one, remember? We buried my son.' His voice caught on the final word and he hung his head, close to tears.

'He was *my* son too,' Maureen hissed back. She looked pale

and thin, the devastation wrought by Michael's death painfully obvious.

'Stop it!' Mia screamed, holding her hands over her ears. But her parents ignored her.

'Some mother you were. You were supposed to be looking after him. You should have stayed with him in L.A., not followed me across the world. Flying to Spain to sit on your ass whilst I busted a gut working.'

'You did your best to pretend we weren't there, didn't you? Too busy running round with your whores as always.'

John's eyes were cold and black. 'Can you blame me?'

The crockery smashed as it hit the floor. Maureen didn't even realise what she'd done until she picked up the second plate, holding it aloft.

'Stop it!' Mia screamed again.

'Crazy bitch,' yelled John. 'We can't afford new plates.'

'Then go back to goddamn work!'

'*You* go back to work,' John roared. 'I'm *done*. And I'm done with *you*.' His gaze swept maniacally round the kitchen, alighting on the carving knife Maureen had been using moments ago. He lunged for it and Maureen screamed, fear flooding through her, believing John capable of anything right now. She launched the plate in his direction then ran from the kitchen with Mia following, crockery crashing in their wake as they raced up the stairs to the very top of the house, past the furniture that wasn't theirs, rented and temporary like everything in their lives.

John was slower, less agile, hampered by alcohol, but they could hear his thumping footsteps behind them. Maureen fled into the main bathroom, pulling Mia in behind her, fumbling with shaking hands as she slid the bolt across. They clung to one another, terrified, as John hammered on the door, shouting and swearing.

'I'll kill you,' he raged. The hinges shook as he kicked it with the sole of his shoe, the force of his six-foot frame behind it. 'Come out here and I'll fucking kill you!'

Maureen held Mia close, smoothing her hair with shaking hands, her whole body trembling. Maureen genuinely believed that John would make good on his threats if he was given the chance, through anger and inebriation. She was living through a nightmare, one she'd helped create, and the grief and trauma were too much to bear. She could feel her body shutting down, her mind closing off, unable to think, unable to function. Overcome by some long-buried instinct, she closed her eyes and began to pray. Wrapped in her arms, Mia joined in.

'Lead us not into temptation, but deliver us from evil…'

Time was meaningless, the waiting interminable. Finally the yelling slowed, the banging stopped. Maureen unclasped Mia, the two of them hot and clammy despite the freezing temperatures outside. Moonlight glinted through the window, the horror in Mia's doe eyes reflected in Maureen's own. On the other side of the splintered door, footsteps retreated. Moments later they heard the front door close. The silence was deafening, the hammering of Maureen's heart louder than anything. She let out a breath she didn't know she'd been holding and stood up on shaky legs.

'Stay here,' Maureen whispered to Mia, as she noiselessly unlatched the door, crossing the hallway to look out of the window. In the glow of the streetlamp, she saw John striding off down the street, knife still in hand. A handful of snowflakes drifted in the blackness.

There was a moment of stillness, of relief, as Mia appeared at her shoulder.

'I think we should go to bed,' Maureen said. She felt strangely numb, her thoughts opaque.

Mia nodded, heading wordlessly towards her room, but Maureen stopped her.

'Darling, I think you should sleep in here tonight,' Maureen said, indicating the room she shared with her husband.

Mia's breath caught in her throat. 'Why? I'm scared, Mom. What if Daddy comes back? What if he stabs me while I'm sleeping?'

Maureen reached out to stroke her cheek. 'Your father adores you. When he comes back and sees you lying there, he'll stop being angry because he loves you so much.'

'What if he doesn't see me?'

'Oh, darling,' Maureen gave a hysterical laugh. Her eyes were glazed, her expression distant. 'God will watch over you.'

'Where will you be, Mom?'

'I'll sleep on the couch in my study. I'll lock the door. Sweet dreams, darling.' Maureen tucked Mia into bed, then turned off the light and walked away.

The Farrows had moved back to Los Angeles. They now lived in a much smaller house than they had before, unpretty and unloved, on North Roxbury Drive. It reflected their diminished status and their precarious financial position; the heady days of the 1930s and '40s seemed like a lifetime ago. Neither of them were working. John spent his days drinking, Maureen passed hers crying in her room. If they ever encountered one another, in the kitchen or lounge, an argument would ensue – usually about money – where each blamed the other for their current situation.

Mia came in from the garden where she'd been enjoying the sunshine to find her father entertaining. These days, the Farrows no longer threw wonderful parties attended by the great and good of Hollywood. The only people who visited now were Jesuit priests, who debated with John and made their way steadily through his drinks cabinet, the discussions becoming increasingly bad-tempered as the evenings wore on.

Mia went through to the reception room where her father sat with the clerics. Silently, she made for the bar in the corner, taking a bottle of Scotch from the shelf before making her way round the room, pouring two fingers in each glass.

'Thanks, honey,' John slurred. Despite it being only early

afternoon, he'd already made a substantial dent in the bottle. 'You're a good girl.'

Mia could feel the eyes of the men of the cloth following her as she moved. She was sixteen years old, dressed for the heat in a light cotton dress, her bathing costume underneath.

'Have a good evening, Daddy,' she said, before retreating.

Upstairs, she passed her mother's room. Her parents had begun sleeping separately again now that they had the space to do so. Her mother had set up an easel and talked of painting. In reality, she spent her days crying, and today was no exception.

Mia paused, tapping gently on the door. 'Mom?'

She heard her mother blow her nose. 'Just a minute.' Moments later, Maureen unlocked the door. Her eyes were red, her hair dishevelled, and she was wearing her nightgown. Whether she'd changed early for bed, or simply hadn't taken it off from the night before, Mia didn't know.

'Mom...' Mia began. She bit back the instinct to ask if she was all right; they were beyond pleasantries, and it was evident that Maureen was desperately unhappy. The easel stood, untouched, in the corner, the side table littered with discarded tissues. 'What are we going to do?'

Maureen frowned. 'About what?'

'This.' Mia gestured around her, at the state of the room, the state of their lives. 'I want to go to college, but I don't know if you can afford it. I heard Yolanda complaining that she hasn't been paid for two months. She said she's going to quit housekeeping for us unless she gets her pay check. There's no groceries in the cupboards.'

A flicker of annoyance crossed Maureen's brow, as though she didn't want to face up to the reality of their situation.

'Where's your father?'

'Downstairs. The priests are here.'

Maureen rolled her eyes. 'Drinking his Scotch, I bet. He always finds money for *that*.'

'Don't you want to go back to work, Mom?'

Maureen laughed hollowly. 'You think anyone wants to see a fifty-year-old Jane Parker?'

'Well, if not the movies, what about the theatre?'

'Theatre? I don't think I've been in a play since school.'

'Why not? You're an incredible actress, you're so talented. I'd like to act myself, but everyone would compare me to you and I couldn't take it,' Mia smiled.

'Oh, you'd forge your own path,' Maureen snuffled. The two of them sat down on the bed, and Maureen stroked her daughter's waist-length blonde hair affectionately. 'But you're right, far better to become a doctor. Now *that* would be a fulfilling career.'

'Stop changing the subject,' Mia teased. 'Picture it: New York. Broadway. Your name in lights.'

Maureen thought about it, realising that Mia might be right. The theatre would be exciting and challenging; at the very least it would pay the bills. And it would get her out of this horrible house, across the country, far away from John and his moods and his drinking and his philandering.

Broadway was beginning to seem more appealing by the minute.

'Pass me my address book, would you, darling?' Maureen gestured towards her desk in the corner. Mia skipped across the room obligingly and brought the bulging leather-bound tome to her mother. 'Now,' Maureen continued, eagerly leafing through it. 'What time is it in England?'

'I'm so sorry, darling, is it a bad time for you?'

'Maureen? Oh, my goodness, no, not at all. I have a few friends here, but they can wait—'

'I can call back if you'd like me to—'

'No, don't worry, they're entertaining one another without me. What is it? Is everything all right?'

Thousands of miles away, across the Atlantic, Maureen could

hear the sounds of a party in the background. It was past ten o'clock in the UK, but Maureen had suspected that Vivien would still be awake; it was unlike her to go to bed early, and she loved to entertain. Maureen had dialled a London number – Eaton Square, according to her address book, which she knew was in Belgravia, one of the chicest, wealthiest areas of the capital.

'I suspect it will all sound rather silly,' Maureen apologised. 'But I wanted to pick your brains about something.'

'Pick away,' Vivien laughed. Maureen could imagine her dressed immaculately, sitting in a Louis XIV chair beside the phone table, in a lavishly decorated apartment filled with fresh flowers and gilt-framed paintings.

'I wanted to ask about the theatre – Broadway in particular.'

'Of course. What about it?'

Maureen was straight to the point. 'Do you think I could do it?'

Vivien laughed at Maureen's earnestness, then rushed to reassure her. 'Of course, darling, I'm sure you could. Why ever not? But what's all this about? Has someone made you an offer?'

'No, not yet. I'm not certain that anyone would. I'm just thinking… about a career change. Or rather, a revitalisation of my career, and I thought this might be a good way to go about it.'

'Well…' Vivien began carefully, 'in my experience, I've found there are more opportunities in the theatre for…'

'… *Les femmes d'un certain âge*?' Maureen interjected, as Vivien burst out laughing.

'Exactly that, darling. God, getting older is hellish, isn't it?'

Maureen sighed. 'Nature's cruellest trick.'

'Did you know that I'm a grandmother now?' Vivien continued. 'Suzanne had a baby – a boy called Neville.'

'Congratulations!'

'Well, I'm not entirely sure it's a reason for celebration. There was one newspaper that ran the headline "Scarlett O'Hara Now Granny". I mean the baby's adorable, but me, a grandmother?'

'I suppose not all of us have the privilege of ageing,' Maureen said sombrely, thinking of Michael. 'But it doesn't always feel like good fortune, does it?'

'Quite.' They lapsed into silence, and Maureen heard laughter in the background.

'I'd better let you get back to your party.'

'I'm all right for a little longer. It's so nice to catch up. Might I ask what's prompted all of this?' Vivien pressed gently.

'It was my daughter's idea, but what's prompted it... Money – or the lack thereof. And a terrible marriage and a husband I want to escape. And a desire to prove to myself that I'm not a washed-up old has-been.'

'Oh, darling, of course you're not. But I understand completely, on every count,' Vivien said with feeling, and Maureen believed her. 'I used to think that it was lonely at the top – that there are so very few who understand what you're going through. But there are other compensations – the success, the wealth, the good feeling from the public. Now it's so much harder. You can't help but feel that your best years are behind you, in every sense. Your husband doesn't look at you the way he once did, and everyone's shocked that you no longer look the same as a character you played in a film almost thirty years ago. I'm sorry, this is terribly depressing. Here you are ringing me for advice, and instead I'm the one who's pouring my heart out.'

'I don't mind at all. It's reassuring,' Maureen insisted. 'To know that I'm not alone. That I'm not the only one who feels like this.'

'No, you're not,' Vivien said quietly. 'Look, I must go – hostess duty calls. But do ring me again soon. I'd love for us to talk more. And I want to be the first to hear when you've landed an award-winning role on Broadway.'

'Do you really think I can do it? I don't know if I have the stamina – physical or mental. It's so different from anything I've ever done.'

'Of course you can. You've come a long way since Caliban,' Vivien teased. 'It's true, it's an entirely different beast to film acting. A different muscle to flex. But there's nothing like the adrenaline rush of the stage, the thrill of live performance, the applause of the audience...' Vivien trailed off, but Maureen could hear the passion in her voice.

'Good night, Vivien,' she said, softly. 'Thank you.'

'My pleasure, darling,' Vivien replied before ringing off.

Maureen replaced the receiver, looking around at the detritus of her room, ashamed by how she was living, that she'd let herself sink to such depths. But for the first time in a very long time, she felt optimistic about the future.

Chapter Forty

New York, USA

January 1963

The audience applauded wildly, giving Maureen a standing ovation as she took her bows, her gaze sweeping over the sold-out auditorium of The Playhouse on Broadway. She couldn't have imagined that the aptly named *Never Too Late* would be such a success, but the reviews were superb – particularly for Maureen – and the audiences kept on coming, with full houses night after night.

She was playing Edith Lambert, a middle-aged woman who unexpectedly becomes pregnant later in life, and the plot was warm and funny. In the weeks leading up to her Broadway debut, Maureen had been fizzing with excitement, eager to prove her acting chops, but the overriding sensation was one of fear. She'd woken up night after night, heart racing, following a variation on a nightmare where she found herself centre stage and unable to remember her lines, the audience pointing and sniggering whilst she burned with shame. Or she'd forgotten to wear her costume, making her grand entrance in her underwear, trying to flee to the safety of the wings with the audience's laughter ringing in her ears. No scenario was too clichéd for her subconscious, it seemed.

John had hardly been supportive; he was keen to get her out of the house and eager to have her earning money, but had no qualms about casting doubt on her abilities. 'Are you sure you want to do this? You'll end up a laughing stock,' was his unwelcome advice.

But Maureen had proved him wrong. She had won over the critics, pulled the role off with aplomb, and proven she could still act, even without the safety net of multiple retakes offered by film and television. When it worked, with the audience spellbound in the palm of her hand, it felt like flying.

'Congratulations, Mom. They couldn't get enough of you.'

Back in Maureen's dressing room, Mia was waiting for her mother. She was seventeen years old now and living with Maureen in New York. They'd been staying at the Algonquin Hotel just off Times Square, but when it became clear that the show would extend its run, Maureen had rented an apartment in Manhattan. She and Mia had been having a wonderful time exploring the city, enjoying parties and premieres, dinner with friends after the show, then on to a nightclub. The lifestyle was fast-paced and exciting, and Mia was dazzled by her mother's new world.

Right now Maureen was bursting with post-show adrenaline, unable to settle to anything as she read the cards on the flowers that had arrived, placing them beside the wonderful, effusive letter Vivien had sent her for opening night. 'Thank you, darling.' Maureen changed out of her costume, slipping on a Christian Dior dress and spritzing herself with perfume. 'Oh look, how sweet, Frank Sinatra has sent a telegram. He'll be in town next week and is hoping to come and see the show.'

'Frank Sinatra?' Mia's eyes were wide.

'You met him once, a few years ago at Romanoff's when we were all out for dinner. You were only twelve or thirteen, I think. You probably don't remember.'

Mia shook her head. 'So what's the plan for tonight? Where are we going?' she asked eagerly.

Maureen blushed, not meeting Mia's gaze. 'Actually George has invited me for dinner,' she said, trying to sound casual as she mentioned her director. 'I think it might be just the two of us, so that we can discuss the show without interruptions. It probably wouldn't be so interesting for you – shop talk, you know,' Maureen explained, as she removed her heavy stage make-up and put on something lighter and fresher.

Mia nodded in understanding. 'That's fine. I might go out with the guys from *Cuckoo* – Gene invited me to dinner with them.'

Across the street, at the Cort Theatre, *One Flew Over the Cuckoo's Nest* was playing and the two casts had become good friends, with Maureen and Mia often meeting up with Kirk Douglas and Gene Wilder after their shows were finished, exploring late-night Manhattan.

'Have a wonderful time, honey. You look so pretty tonight.' Maureen glanced at her daughter through the reflection in the mirror. Mia had left her long hair loose, and was wearing a sleeveless shift dress in a vibrant yellow print that sat daringly just above the knee. Going out and having a good time was exactly what Mia should be doing at her age, Maureen reflected, remembering how she'd been attending a strait-laced finishing school in Paris when she was seventeen.

Now it felt as though she was in a period of rediscovery. It was delightful to have this revival of her career at a time when she thought it was all but over. She hoped it would lead to more work, and she'd discovered a newfound respect for the theatre, after so long doing film and television. She adored the lifestyle too, and she was earning money, and doing what she loved. She could almost forget about the dark cloud on the horizon – out of sight and out of mind, as the saying went.

Maureen was now the sole breadwinner in the family and was sending money to John, back in Los Angeles, in the unhappy house on North Roxbury Drive. The two of them barely communicated anymore, bar the occasional terse phone call when practical matters needed to be sorted. Their other children were still in L.A., the youngest two attending the local high school, and Maureen had learned from Prudence that their father was still drinking heavily, still reading obituaries daily, still visited by the Jesuit priests. She wondered how many women he'd invited into their marital bed, then pushed the thought away, determined not to think about it.

Her director, George Abbott, was taking more than a professional interest in her and Maureen welcomed it. He was kind and funny, polite and charming. Physically, he reminded her of John in many ways, and she felt as though she were being courted in the old-fashioned style. They went for dinner, to museums and galleries, for walks in the park. Their fledgling relationship wasn't serious – Maureen certainly wasn't intending to divorce John for him – but after so many years of neglect she was enjoying a moment of happiness, and she felt she deserved it.

'Thanks, Mom. You look pretty too.' Mia smiled, a look of understanding passing between them. 'I'll see you at home later. I love you.'

'I love you too. Don't wait up.'

Mia returned to the apartment shortly after 1 a.m. It was dark and felt deserted. The door to her mother's room was open, so Mia realised that she was still out with George. She didn't resent Maureen spending time with another man; if anything, it was nice to see her happy. Mia had spent so many years watching her parents argue, seeing her father rage and her mother cry, that she could forgive this indiscretion.

Mia knew that her father had had affairs for years. She remembered, as a child, walking in on him and Ava Gardner. She hadn't seen anything graphic, but there was something in the way they moved, a shift in the atmosphere when she entered the room, as though the air itself was vibrating with something she didn't understand. Growing up in Hollywood, Mia had spent her whole life receiving knowing looks from women once they found out who her father was, leaving her with the uncomfortable knowledge that they'd likely slept with him.

Mia showered quickly and put on her pyjamas. She was about to go to bed when the phone in the hall began to ring. Her stomach twisted as she realised who it might be; it was 10.30 p.m. on the West Coast, and her father would be halfway down a bottle of rum by now.

'Hello?'

'Mia?'

'Yes, Daddy.'

'Can you put your mother on the phone, honey?'

'Um…' Mia's heart was racing. Her father sounded drunk, belligerent, slurring his words. 'She… I… She's not here right now.'

'Where is she?' He was instantly suspicious.

Mia closed her eyes. 'She went out after the show. She'll be back soon. I'll ask her to call you.' She twisted the phone cord round her wrist and prayed it was true.

'Out? Who'd she go out with?'

'Just some people from the play. The cast and crew. They went for dinner. I'm sure she'll be back soon.'

There was silence on the other end of the line. Mia heard the chink of ice, followed by the splash of liquid in a glass. 'Daddy?'

'Mmm?' John mumbled.

Mia heard him take a gulp, heard the wetness smacking against his lips. 'I'll ask her to call you when she's back, okay?'

John didn't respond.

'Okay, Daddy? Try and get some sleep, okay? I'm putting the receiver down now. I love you.'

Mia hung up and exhaled in relief, staring at the phone as though it were a ticking bomb. Moments later, it rang again, the shrill noise ringing out through the apartment.

'Hello?'

'Is she there?'

'No, Daddy, Mom's still not back yet. I'll ask her to call you.'

'Who's she with?'

'I told you, she—'

'Is she with a man? That director of hers? George something. What's his fucking name…?'

'I… He might be there, Daddy, I'm not sure. I—'

'Tell your whore of a mother to get back here and call me!' John yelled.

Mia held the phone away from her ear. Tears prickled at her eyelids. She felt guilty for lying to her father, but she knew she couldn't tell him where her mother was. She was stuck in the middle, and her father was still yelling, his words slurred and unintelligible.

'Goodnight, Daddy,' Mia said tearfully. She put the receiver down. Within seconds, it rang again. Mia hesitated, but this time she didn't answer. The phone continued to ring, and Mia walked away into her bedroom. She closed the door and switched off the light. She could still hear it as she climbed into bed and put the pillow over her head, clamping it tightly around her ears and closing her eyes.

The phone continued to ring.

Chapter Forty-One

New York, USA

January 1963

Maureen stretched languorously as the sun crept round the curtains and fell across her bedspread. She'd had a wonderful night with George, having gone back to his apartment for the first time, but she'd drawn the line at staying overnight in his bed.

She glanced at the clock: 11 a.m. She would usually have slept for longer, but this morning she didn't feel tired. Instead, she felt clear-headed and light-hearted. It was a long time since a man had looked at her with desire in his eyes, and George's attentions had made her feel alive for the first time in years. It was such a delight to flirt and have fun with a man, with no pressure and no expectations.

Maureen climbed out of bed and ran through her morning ablutions, humming to herself. The apartment was chic and modern, and she relished having this space of her own, after so long cooped up in the toxic atmosphere of the family home. She truly felt as though things were on the up. She'd somehow lost herself after so many pregnancies, the demands of motherhood and marriage and career. Now she was rebuilding her life.

She went through to the kitchenette to fix herself half a grapefruit for breakfast, staring out of the window at New York City, the soaring skyscrapers and the people scurrying far below, like ants. She remembered how she'd first sailed into this city in 1929, how extraordinary it had seemed, and how impossibly young and naïve she'd been back then. It felt like a lifetime ago.

Maureen turned as Mia sloped into the kitchen, looking anxious and guilty.

'Morning, darling,' Maureen said brightly. 'Everything all right?'

The telephone began to ring and Mia jumped in fright, her face pale and haunted.

'Daddy tried to call last night,' Mia explained. 'A lot of times. I didn't tell him where you were.'

'All right.' Maureen digested the information. 'Perhaps that's him now.' The phone was still ringing insistently, echoing throughout the apartment. Bracing herself, Maureen strolled through to the hallway and picked up the receiver. 'Hello?'

'Mommy?' It was Tisa, her eleven-year-old. She was in floods of tears and Maureen could barely make out what she was saying.

'Darling, what is it?'

'It's Daddy… He's… He's dead.'

A shiver ran down Maureen's spine, goosebumps prickling on her skin. It was impossible. John was a young man, just fifty-eight years old. He couldn't be dead.

'What?'

'I found him this morning,' Tisa hiccoughed. 'I came downstairs and he was in his chair, slumped over. It looked like he was reaching for the phone. I called an ambulance. The doctors said he had a heart attack.'

'Oh my darling, my poor darling.' Maureen could hear the agony in Tisa's voice.

'Can you get here, Mom? Can you come, please? I need you…'

'Of course, honey. Of course. I'll come right away.'

Maureen's head was spinning. She would need to make the arrangements, she would need to contact George and the show's producers – they would give her time off, surely? She had an understudy after all. She would make the next flight. She had to tell Mia, standing behind her, her eyes wide and shining wet – though it seemed that she had gleaned enough from the overheard phone call.

The two of them clung to one another. Mia was sobbing but Maureen was in shock, her mind racing. She'd spent more than half her life with John Farrow and had been deeply in love with him. But for the past few years they'd been terribly unhappy, and she was ashamed to find that part of her was relieved. Neither of them would have countenanced a divorce, but they were both utterly miserable, their marriage clearly over. Now it was done, it was finished.

Maureen was suddenly assailed by memories: the first time she'd laid eyes on John at the Cotton Club; their first date at Cocoanut Grove; seeing him at the barbecue at Hearst Castle; his inelegant proposal at a gas station. Their wedding day, Michael's birth, Michael's funeral… Oh God, it was too much to bear.

Her heart broke for Tisa that she'd been the one to find him; so sad for all their children that they'd lost their father today. Tisa had said he was reaching for the phone. Mia had said he was trying to call. Was he calling Maureen? Or had he given up, and tried to call one of his other women? Maureen would never know the answer to the question and knew it would haunt her for the rest of her days: the image of her husband, trying to call for help, but no one answering.

It was a typical February day in California, the weather mild and the sky a piercing blue with a wisp of cloud. For Maureen, the contrast with a freezing New York winter, where she'd been mere days earlier, was unfathomable, adding to the surreal nature of her situation.

She was standing by John's graveside at the Holy Cross Cemetery in Culver City, the priest intoning the familiar words of the funeral rites as her husband's coffin was lowered into the earth. She didn't cry. She hadn't cried since she'd heard the news of John's death. She felt numb. She supposed she was still in shock, swept up on a wave of organising and comforting and *doing what needed to be done*, all of which ensured there was no time for emotion.

Maureen looked at her children alongside her, all of them in black, tears rolling down their cheeks. There were six of them, but there should have been seven, and losing John just a few years after the accident that had claimed her eldest boy felt like a double blow of grief. Now Maureen was solely responsible for Patrick, Mia, John, Prudence, Stephanie and Theresa. She had to provide for them all – John had barely a cent to his name, and she knew there would be nothing substantial in his will.

The alcohol had changed him. In recent years, John Farrow had become almost unrecognisable from the handsome man with the roguish charm who'd captured her heart three decades earlier. Had it not been for his passing, they would most likely have continued in their grim stalemate – him drunk and belligerent, her refusing to countenance a divorce, both of them deeply unhappy and breaking their marriage vows with alarming regularity. His death had released them from years of misery.

All Maureen could do now was look to the future, to keep putting one foot in front of the other as she always had. She would need to work to provide for herself and her children, and she felt lucky that she had a job to return to. She'd been given time off to arrange and attend the funeral, but in truth Maureen was looking forward to flying back to New York, to her fashionable apartment, and to the cast and crew who'd become her friends. She adored her job, and the Broadway lifestyle – rising late, performing in the evenings, before hitting the town to explore all that the city had to offer. Now that John had gone and her children were almost grown, there was very little left for her in Los Angeles.

A plane flew high overhead, its contrails marking the sky. Oh, she knew it was too early to be making plans, but the stiff-upper-lip mentality had saved Maureen over the years and she instinctively looked to the future. Her life as she knew it had been shattered. Like a kaleidoscope, the pieces were in flux, but the fragments were bright and beautiful, only the final formation still unknown. She would continue to act, revitalised by her newfound love of the theatre, open to whatever opportunities might come her way. And she had six wonderful children, their futures wide open and brimming with possibilities. Perhaps, like Vivien, Maureen would have the good fortune to be a grandmother.

Perhaps, too, she might find love again one day. Maureen didn't think her fling with George was anything serious, but she believed she still had love to give, and she wanted to *be* loved, after being starved of tenderness and intimacy in recent years. She knew it was too soon to think seriously about anything like that; she was still mourning her husband, and their relationship, and the life they'd built together. But on this bright, clear afternoon, she felt a stirring sense of optimism.

Maureen would survive, and she would thrive. She was determined to make it so.

Chapter Forty-Two

VIVIEN

Buckinghamshire, England

August 1955

Rock-and-roll music was playing on the turntable, the champagne was flowing, and there were shrieks of laughter at the outrageous antics of the guests. The Oliviers were throwing a party.

Larry was striding round in his smoking jacket, whilst Vivien looked regal in a couture gown designed by her good friend Victor Stiebel. Lady Diana Cooper had donned a suit of chain mail she'd found in the attic, whilst Sir John Gielgud was inexplicably clad in a toga. Noel Coward gossiped with Danny Kaye, and Maxine Audley danced on the dining table with Anthony Quayle. It was almost four in the morning, and the party was still in full swing.

Last night had been the premiere of *Titus Andronicus* in Stratford-upon-Avon, the third Shakespeare production starring the couple, following *Twelfth Night* and *Macbeth* earlier in the season. After the performance, Larry and Vivien had arranged for coaches to bring the entire cast and crew, along with dozens of the couple's friends, to their country home, Notley Abbey, for a celebration.

'Cecil, darling!' shrieked Vivien, as she caught sight of Cecil Beaton wearing a crown of flowers taken from the enormous bouquet on the marquetry table. 'How wonderful of you to come. Tell me, did you bring Sonia?'

A frown flickered across Cecil's face. For a moment, he was unsure who she was referring to. 'Ah, Sonia Orwell – or Brownell, as you knew her. No, Vivling, I didn't.'

'Oh you're terribly naughty,' Vivien pouted. 'We had such a lovely supper after the show. I should have liked to speak to her again.'

'Well, that was, what, five years ago? She's living in France now.'

'Is she? How marvellous. Five years, you say? Golly, how time flies. Well, you must promise to bring her next time. Do you have a drink?'

'Yes, yes,' Cecil raised his glass of champagne. 'I'm quite all right, thank you, Vivling. Don't worry about me – go and enjoy yourself.'

Vivien blew him a kiss before whirling into the throng, thinking how marvellous the house looked tonight, decorated in her tasteful style and filled to the brim with people having a wonderful time. They'd first seen Notley Abbey twelve years ago and Vivien had hated it on sight, but Larry adored it. A large grey stone building set in seventy acres of grounds beside the River Thames, it dated back to the thirteenth century and appealed to Larry's sense of history and grandeur and Englishness. They had owned it for a decade now, and Vivien had grown to love it and everything it represented.

Notley had become a refuge for them, away from London and the pressures of work, where they could simply be themselves and not the esteemed entity that was 'The Oliviers'. It was also where they entertained, a country retreat full of guests where Vivien was forever hosting suppers and soirées and cocktail parties. She liked to be kept busy; when it was just the two of them, alone, the cracks were all too evident.

Yet, even on a night like tonight, tensions simmered under the surface, and the partygoers felt it, despite the gaiety and the music and the free-flowing champagne. The legend of 'The Oliviers' endured; they were bound together by professional duty, shared history and a long-standing, deep affection. But their marriage was falling apart and they weren't even trying to hide it any longer, openly rowing and sniping.

Vivien and Larry had been riding high for twenty years now, but their godlike reputation had become a gilded cage, trapping them in their own mythology. At times Vivien blamed herself, taking responsibility for her mental health problems which continued to put their relationship under unsustainable pressure. But Larry was no saint either, his behaviour often selfish and self-absorbed, a narcissistic youth in the declining body of a middle-aged man. Their recent run of Shakespeare plays had brought their professional differences to the fore; Vivien couldn't match her husband on stage, as the reviews made all too clear, and that perceived inferiority bred jealousy and contempt.

'... Second word... Idiot?'

'Imbecile? Ass!'

Larry was acting out a charade, waving his hands in the air and pulling silly faces, bending over then kicking his legs in the air.

'Dunce?'

'Dolt?'

'Pillock! Bastard!' Vivien threw out the suggestions, delighting in the insults she was throwing at her husband.

'Booby?' tried Noël Coward. 'Nincompoop?'

'Cunt!' Vivien yelled gleefully, seeing how angry Larry was becoming.

'That's enough, Vivien.' He turned to her in fury, discomfort rippling through the room. 'You always go too far. There was no need to—'

'Fool?' She raised an eyebrow, her expression triumphant.

365

'Phrase, eight words. Hmm… "A fool and his money are soon parted"?'

Larry looked ready to explode.

'You're so predictable, darling,' Vivien drawled, turning away.

Larry grabbed her arm and spun her towards him. 'I'm a fucking good actor, that's what made it easy. I made you look good, as always.'

The barb was designed to wound, and it did. Throughout their relationship, Vivien had been conscious that, in both her own mind and the public's, she was considered a lesser talent to her husband. That she had won two Oscars to his zero was immaterial; the theatre would always be superior to film, and it was on stage that Larry was unparalleled.

The recent reviews had only cemented that perception. Kenneth Tynan, the esteemed critic for *The Observer*, had written that whilst *'Sir Laurence shook hands with greatness… Vivien Leigh's Lady Macbeth is more niminy-piminy than thundery-blundery, more viper than anaconda, but still quite competent in its own small way.'*

Unease rippled through the room, the guests clearly discomfited. The music continued to play but everyone had fallen silent, watching the exchange. It was as though Vivien and Larry were on stage with an audience, the lines blurred between performance and reality.

'Your turn, darling,' Larry said, his voice laden with sarcasm.

'Phrase, two words.' Vivien extended her middle finger. 'Fuck you.'

Larry's dismissive laughter provoked a rage in Vivien. Through the red mist she noticed Peter Finch observing the exchange. Her lips curling upwards, she smiled at him.

'Peter, darling,' she called across the room, holding out her hand.

He moved through the crowd towards her as though she'd cast a spell, unable to resist her summons. Vivien felt a surge of power, a rush of desire as his large hand closed around hers and she pulled him through the crowd, knowing everyone was watching them.

The wood-panelled corridors were busy, the library and drawing rooms filled with people who were taking a rest from the festivities, or those embarking on trysts in a quieter spot. Defiantly, Vivien led Peter up the stairs, pushing open the door to the bedroom she shared with Larry. She'd never taken him in here before, and she was suddenly assailed by emotions – regret and guilt and sadness – at what their relationship had become.

'I hate him,' Vivien declared, closing the door behind them. The room was elegant and ornate, boasting a mahogany four-poster bed with a floral silk canopy, and matching curtains at the mullioned windows.

'Vivien...' Peter's tone was reproachful.

'I mean it...' And right at that moment she did, though she knew if Larry said the word she'd come running.

Vivien was still desperate to have Larry's baby though, at almost forty-two years of age, it was increasingly unlikely. She'd believed from the beginning that a child would cement their union, and she was still convinced it could fix their fractured relationship. Sometimes, on a sunny afternoon when it was just the two of them, Larry would look out over the wide lawns and sprawling gardens of Notley, and Vivien would know exactly what he was thinking – he'd voiced it often enough. He wanted a child, to swing high onto his shoulders and run joyfully across the grass together, to play cricket and hunt for birds' nests and build dens from old bedsheets. Tarquin was now twenty-one, and Suzanne a year older, but a baby would allow Vivien and Larry to make up for their parental failings. It would wipe the slate clean in every sense.

Most of all, though, Vivien wanted Larry to fall back in love with her, to look at her the way he used to, as though he'd move heaven and earth if she asked him to. Now he looked at her with uninterest at best, contempt at the worst.

Both of them had had affairs – sometimes one-night stands,

others more serious and long-standing. Peter was a constant presence in Vivien's life; she'd cast a spell over him the way she once had over Larry, and she adored him for his devotion. If her husband didn't want her, she would show him that there were plenty of other men who did.

She reached for Peter and the next moment they were kissing passionately, Larry's presence simultaneously forgotten and all-encompassing in the room that smelt of his aftershave, where his pyjamas lay discarded on the armchair.

From downstairs, the noises of the party drifted up to the bedroom: Bill Haley on the record player; peals of laughter; cheers as a champagne cork was popped.

Peter broke away and looked at Vivien. 'Run away with me.'

'What?'

'I mean it. If you really hate him, then leave. Run away with me.'

Vivien's eyes were dancing. She and Peter thrived on drama, and this was exactly the kind of grand, romantic gesture that appealed to them both.

'But where would we go?' It was less an objection, more an invitation for Peter to paint an exquisite vision of their future.

'Anywhere we like. Europe? America? We can catch a boat, a plane… Wherever the fancy takes us.'

'Oh, let's! Tomorrow, after the show. I'll pack a bag tonight, and you can come and meet me at the stage door. We'll be halfway to France by the time anyone realises.'

Right now, Vivien was completely serious, wrapped up in the idea of leaving her life behind and starting anew. Her and Peter, in a picturesque cottage deep in the Provencal countryside, where they would eat good food and drink fine wine and make love night and day. She wrapped her arms around him, losing herself in his embrace, when the door flew open and they guiltily broke apart.

Larry was standing there, a pile of newspapers clutched in his arms. A flicker of emotion crossed his face as he took in their flushed cheeks and guilty expressions, but then it was gone, his self-control restored.

'Ah, Peter, enjoying my bedroom? Anyway, I won't keep you. I thought you might like to know that the first editions have arrived.'

'Oh!' Vivien leapt towards him, Peter temporarily forgotten as she took the papers from Larry, laid them out on the bed and leafed through them.

'Well, I'll leave you to it,' Larry said, with a mock bow, before retreating.

Vivien was paying little attention as she riffled through *The Observer*, her heart pounding in her chest as she hastily skimmed the words of Kenneth Tynan's review:

'Sir Laurence Olivier's Titus… is a performance which ushers us into the presence of one who is pound for pound the greatest actor alive… Maxine Audley is a glittering Tamora. As Lavinia, Vivien Leigh received the news that she is about to be ravished on her husband's corpse with little more than the mild annoyance of one who would have preferred foam rubber.'

Vivien let out a scream of rage, balling the papers and throwing them down in fury, tearing the review itself to literal shreds for good measure. Then she flew at Peter, pounding on his chest. 'I hate him! I hate him,' she screamed, her rage turning to sobs as Peter held her tight until her body went limp against his, clinging to him in desperation and despair.

Downstairs, Larry drank his champagne and the party continued.

Vivien's smile was radiant as she waved at the cameras, conscious that any hint of negativity would be picked up by the press and speculated upon a hundredfold. To her right was Larry, looking dapper and relaxed in a suit and tie; to her left was Marilyn Monroe, luminous and legendary, in a high-necked, figure-hugging dress and white trench coat. On Marilyn's other side was her new husband, the playwright Arthur Miller, gawky and incongruous in his spectacles and mismatching suit.

It was an overcast July day in 1956, and this trip to London was effectively Marilyn and Arthur's honeymoon – although the primary reason they were here was for Marilyn to shoot a movie, *The Prince and the Showgirl*. Larry would direct and produce the film, as well as playing the fictional Prince Regent of Carpathia, with Marilyn as the seductive music hall performer, Elsie Marina, who catches his eye.

Vivien had originated the role of 'the showgirl' in the West End two years earlier, when the production had been called *The Sleeping Prince*, her character the less obviously named 'Mary Morgan'. But a flashier title was deemed necessary for the film, along with a flashier leading lady. Younger, blonder, sexier.

Marilyn and Arthur had landed earlier that day at London Airport, and this was the official photocall. Out of the corner of her eye, Vivien watched as Marilyn primped for the press: pouting, wiggling, batting her eyelashes. Instinctively, Vivien felt that they had little in common. She found the younger woman's breathy sighs and wide eyes rather hackneyed and déclassé; there was very little breeding or elegance about her. But she couldn't be sure that Larry felt the same way. Vivien would have been lying if she'd said she didn't feel threatened.

However, despite the tangible buzz around the breathy, beautiful newcomer, Vivien had an ace up her immaculately tailored sleeve.

'How are you feeling, Vivien?' shouted a reporter.

'I'm feeling very well, thank you.'

'When's the baby due?'

'Just before Christmas,' she beamed, as flashbulbs popped and security milled around. 'A festive angel.'

Forty-two-year-old Vivien had announced her pregnancy two days ago. She was a little over four months along, and she was ecstatic, quite visibly glowing. The miracle she'd prayed for was now a reality.

'Sir Laurence, are you hoping for a boy or a girl?'

'We want a girl,' Vivien cut in, speaking over her husband in her excitement. 'We've even decided on a name – Katherine.'

'What if it's a boy?'

'It won't be. I can tell,' Vivien rested one hand instinctively on her still flat stomach.

The reporter smiled wolfishly, his gaze running along the celebrated quartet. 'Is Marilyn going to be godmother?'

Vivien's smile slipped momentarily as Larry laughed politely. 'Well, it's an interesting idea…' he began, before Vivien took over.

'Oh no. The godparents have already been chosen, so it's a definite no, I'm afraid.'

Vivien smiled tightly at the assembled press, as Marilyn beamed her megawatt red-lipped grin, seemingly oblivious to any tension.

Chapter Forty-Three

London, England

January 1958

'Are you sure you have everything, darling?'

'Yes, quite sure. Don't fuss, Vivien.' Larry's tone was irritable.

Vivien couldn't help it. She'd been hovering around him all morning in their new apartment in Eaton Square, helping him pack one moment, berating him for leaving the next.

'Well, I suppose this is goodbye then.'

'Yes, I rather think it is.'

The two of them eyed one another but Larry turned away first, pulling on his Mackintosh and trilby. He looked dashing, rakish, still the handsome man she'd fallen in love with. But now everything was changing.

Larry was heading to New York, to perform in *The Entertainer* on Broadway, which would open in two weeks. The show had enjoyed great success in the UK, playing to sold-out crowds at the Royal Court before transferring to the West End then touring. It was a new type of play by a controversial young playwright, gritty and realist, and there'd been no role for Vivien; she was too old to play Larry's daughter, too beautiful to play his downtrodden wife.

Impulsively, Vivien threw her arms around her husband, pulling him close, trying to inspire a reaction. It was like embracing a marble statue, his body language cold and aloof as he disentangled himself from her.

'There's something I need to tell you.' Larry's voice was casual, conversational. 'I'm in love with Joan Plowright.'

Vivien recoiled as though she'd received a physical blow. In some ways, the news was hardly surprising; there'd been rumours for some time that Larry and his much younger co-star were having an affair. He and Vivien were living separate lives, and Larry had always turned a blind eye to her dalliances. But for him to be *in love* with Joan... It was impossible. He *loved* Vivien. He would never love anyone like he loved her, she insisted to herself. She was Lady Olivier, and the two of them were indelibly linked in the public mind. Viv and Larry. Larry and Viv. The Oliviers.

Oh, Larry might be infatuated with this up-and-coming actress, enthralled by her youth and captivated by the new generation she represented, but he would always come home to Vivien. Let him sow his wild oats in New York, she told herself. Get this little indiscretion out of his system.

'All right, darling. Have a safe flight. Call me when you land.'

Vivien ached at the thought of the two of them together in America. She doubted Joan had ever been before, and Larry would be seeing it through her eyes, fresh and youthful, the two of them making new discoveries together, creating memories as he once had with Vivien. They would be planning their future, exhilarated in the first bloom of love.

Vivien bit her lip, the physical pain a distraction. Her Roehampton training lingered just beneath the surface and right now she was glad of it, able to suppress her emotions, standing stoic and self-possessed.

'Goodbye, Vivien.'

Larry didn't kiss her as he left the apartment. Vivien watched from the sash window as he emerged onto the street and climbed into the waiting car. She gripped the window ledge tightly, wanting to scream. An emptiness yawned inside of her. She wondered if the situation would be different if she'd been able to have his baby. She'd miscarried at five months; the baby had been a boy. The grief had tipped Vivien into another manic episode, which she'd dealt with by attending parties and drinking heavily, barely sleeping. She almost couldn't blame Larry for finding solace in the arms of another woman – one who was younger, easier, devoid of the troubles that plagued his wife.

Even Peter Finch had deserted her; he'd respectfully kept his distance when she'd announced her pregnancy, and the subsequent breakdowns had been too much even for him to cope with. She'd heard that he was dating an actress almost twenty years younger than Vivien, and the rumours were that it was serious.

Vivien watched as the car joined the traffic and crossed the square. She thought how ironic it was that she'd felt threatened by Larry working with Marilyn Monroe, yet in reality the beautiful Marilyn had driven him to distraction with her ever-present acting coach and her tardiness on set. It was the plain, northern Joan Plowright who'd been the one to unexpectedly win his heart.

Vivien turned from the window into the elegant apartment she'd decorated especially for herself and Larry. She would do what she always did when real life became too terrible to deal with: she would throw herself into work.

———

'Jack! How wonderful to see you again.'

'Vivien! I can't tell you how much I'm looking forward to working with you.'

They kissed on both cheeks and beamed at one another.

Vivien had first met John Merivale in 1940 when he'd played Balthasar in the Oliviers' production of *Romeo and Juliet*. The play had seemed like the obvious choice for two young actors who were madly in love, but it was a critical and commercial failure, and the pair made heavy financial losses.

Now, almost twenty years later, Vivien and Jack were to be co-stars once again, in *Duel of Angels* on Broadway. He'd aged of course – they both had – but he was still handsome, tall and broad-shouldered, his dark hair showing no signs of grey.

'And how's Larry?' Jack asked cheerily.

Vivien faltered. She opened her mouth, but no reply came.

Diversion came in the form of the director, Robert Helpmann. He clapped his hands once, for attention, and the cast turned to him, ready to begin rehearsal. Vivien smiled apologetically at Jack, hiding her relief. There would be time to explain later; the whole world would know soon enough.

Vivien linked her arm through Jack's as they strolled through Central Park. It was a bright, blustery New York day, and Vivien wore a headscarf and sunglasses, with a smart lavender woollen coat. The two of them had been shopping; Vivien wanted to buy presents for all of the cast and crew and had spent a small fortune in the department stores on Fifth Avenue. The bags had been sent on ahead to the apartment where Vivien was staying, and now she wanted to stroll back through the park.

'Darling, there's something I wanted to ask you,' Vivien said, thoughtfully, as they crossed Gapstow Bridge, the pretty stone arch that traversed the Pond. Around them, the metal and glass skyscrapers reached up to the heavens, the elm trees abundant with their final blossom of the season.

'Of course. Anything.'

'I have to visit my doctor tomorrow. I wondered if you might come with me. It's for ECT,' she explained, in response to Jack's quizzical expression. 'Electro-convulsive therapy.'

'Oh, Vivien,' Jack breathed, sympathy and sadness in his tone.

'It's quite all right,' she assured him. 'It's for the best. But… I'm rather frightened, you see.'

'Of course I'll come with you. I'll always look after you,' Jack said softly, squeezing her hand.

It had been three months since they'd reunited – *Duel of Angels* had received good notices, and the plan was to tour in the US – and in that time, Jack and Vivien had grown increasingly close. If Jack didn't always understand Vivien's behaviour, he accepted it. He'd adored her twenty years ago, and he realised now that he was falling in love with her. He believed that she loved him too, though perhaps not in the same way she loved her husband; she still kept Larry's photograph on her bedside table, still talked of him incessantly. Even today on their shopping trip, she would point out a tie, or an aftershave, that she thought Larry would like, then her face would fall as she realised it was no longer her place to buy him these items.

As they walked, Jack felt the box in his inside pocket push against his ribs. The thought of it, and its contents, made him feel nervous; he planned to give it to Vivien later, after he'd had it engraved. He hoped she would love it. Whilst she'd been distracted in Cartier, he'd purchased a small medallion of St Genesius, the patron saint of actors. Between Jack and Genesius, Vivien would always be protected.

'Thank you,' Vivien said, and he could hear the sincerity in her voice. 'It always leaves me feeling so strange afterwards. Like I'm myself, but not me. I'm calm, but I can't seem to access everything… I can't always *feel*.'

'Does it hurt?'

Vivien nodded, and Jack could tell she was fighting to keep her composure.

'It leaves… marks. Burn marks. On my temples. My dresser will have to use thick make-up to cover them, or do my hair differently to hide the redness.'

'Oh, my poor darling,' Jack breathed. He longed to gather her to him and kiss away her troubles, but they were in public, and Vivien was still a married woman.

They walked on in silence, arriving back at Hampshire House, the iconic Art Deco building on the southern edge of Central Park where Vivien had rented an apartment. As they entered the lobby, decorated to resemble a London townhouse, the concierge greeted Vivien and handed her a letter. It was postmarked London, and Vivien immediately recognised Larry's hasty, rather messy handwriting. She pulled the letter from the envelope, turning ashen as she read the words.

'Vivien,' Jack cried in alarm, suspecting that she might be about to faint. He helped her to the lift, recognising the signs of an imminent breakdown, knowing he needed to get her back to her rooms as soon as possible. She thrust the letter at him as the elevator began to ascend, and Jack skimmed over it, embarrassed at being party to the intimate words, devastated on Vivien's behalf by Larry's request. Although it wasn't a surprise to either of them, Jack knew she would be inconsolable. All he could do was be there to pick up the pieces of her shattered heart and glue them back together, though the cracks would always be visible.

Chapter Forty-Four

London, England

December 1960

The London divorce courts were intimidating, panelled in dark wood, the Royal Coat of Arms high on the wall above the judge, the barristers in their gowns and wigs. Vivien sat quietly on a bench, twisting her gloved hands nervously in her lap, as she listened to Roger Gage – Joan Plowright's husband – give evidence.

Neither Larry nor Joan were present; both were in America, so it was only Vivien and Roger attending today's proceedings. Roger was an affable-looking man, aged around thirty, and rather plain in appearance. He didn't stand a chance, Vivien thought, somewhat uncharitably. Joan would have been dazzled by Larry, just as she herself had been all those years ago, by his dynamism on stage, his vision and insight, his pure, undiluted talent.

Vivien listened attentively as Roger gave evidence. She sat upright and stiff-backed, her face pale, though she looked elegant as always in a red-and-black checked suit paired with a wide-brimmed hat.

'And on what grounds do you wish to divorce Miss Plowright?' the judge asked. He was grey and jowly, with pince-nez glasses on his bulbous nose.

'Adultery,' replied Roger Gage, his voice clear and calm. Like the rest of the characters in this unhappy quartet, Roger was, by trade, an actor.

'And whom are you naming as co-respondent?'

'Sir Laurence Olivier.'

Vivien swallowed, twisting her hands more intensely than ever.

'And do you have evidence of this?'

'Yes, my Lord, I have a signed statement from a private detective who confirms that he found my wife and Sir Laurence in nightclothes in a London apartment last June.'

The detective was then called to the witness stand and affirmed that he had indeed discovered the two parties as described. Vivien watched the spectacle play out; she would have been amused, had the situation not been such a cheerless one. It was farcical, a mere charade, and the detective's performance no more real than Vivien's on a West End stage. But divorce could not be granted without fault or reason, and the standard procedure was for the adulterous parties to be found in a somewhat compromising position.

'Lady Olivier, Miss Vivien Leigh.'

Vivien rose to her feet, more nervous than for any performance. Her shoes clacked noisily on the floor as she walked over to the witness box to be sworn in, her hand on the Bible as she swore to God Almighty.

'Lady Olivier, Sir Laurence has stated that your conduct in the matter has not been entirely blameless,' Larry's lawyer began, as Vivien bowed her head and her own counsel rose to his feet.

'My Lord, I'd like to admit as evidence a written declaration of two instances of adultery committed by Miss Leigh, which she has freely admitted. One took place in London, the other in Ceylon. However, Miss Leigh reconciled with her husband following both of these adulteries, and we contend that this constitutes a condoning of the acts by her husband.'

The judge nodded and turned back to Vivien. 'Lady Olivier, do you have anything to say on the matter?'

Vivien cleared her throat. It felt dry, but she declined the glass of water that had been placed in front of her. She sat up straighter, pulling down her shoulders. 'Two years ago, I became aware of rumours that my husband and Miss Plowright were romantically involved... Stories began appearing in the newspapers... Three months later, my husband confessed to me that he was in love with Miss Plowright...'

Vivien could no longer hold back the tears and bowed her head as she cried, dabbing at her eyes with a white handkerchief.

The judge nodded once again. 'There will now be a short adjournment. We'll reconvene in ten minutes.'

Vivien left the witness stand and returned to her seat. She didn't want to leave the room, she didn't want a drink, she didn't want to speak to her lawyer. She simply wanted this nightmare to be over. And yet, at the same time, she didn't, because when all of this was finished it would officially be the end of twenty years of marriage to the man she still loved with her entire being.

Vivien glanced up in alarm, pulled from her thoughts as the judge re-entered the room. He had the authority to determine who was to be awarded the divorce and decided in favour of Vivien, decreeing that Larry was liable to pay the legal costs of both Vivien and Roger.

Just like that, the illustrious marriage of one of the most celebrated love affairs of the twentieth century was over.

Outside, a gauntlet of press was waiting. Vivien kept her head down as she slipped into her chauffeur-driven silver-grey Rolls Royce; she'd bought it on a whim some years earlier, and adored its purr and prestige. Right now, she would have preferred something a little less distinctive.

The traffic was bad, and the journey from The Strand to Eaton Place seemed to drag. Vivien wished she'd brought Jack with her; even if he couldn't come into the court room with her, he could have waited in the car outside. Though if the reporters had seen him, she reasoned, it would have caused a scandal that might have harmed her case. No, this was a journey she had to make alone.

The long drive at least gave her time to reflect on the end of her second marriage – and what a marriage it had been. It had lasted more than twenty years and captured the imagination of people worldwide. They had been 'The Oliviers', glamorous and adored, respected and at the top of their game. But now it was over. The emotions of the day had taken their toll and Vivien was exhausted. She felt old. She felt like a failure.

The Rolls pulled up outside Vivien's building in Belgravia. Inside, Jack was waiting for her and she threw herself into his arms, sobbing on him until his shirt was almost transparent. He didn't speak, didn't judge, but was quietly supportive, letting her cry.

Vivien didn't know what the future would hold now that she was no longer married to Larry, but at least she had Jack. He would look after her and protect her, she felt sure of it. She was incredibly grateful to have this kind, gentle, handsome man in her life.

The band struck up 'Dixie', and Vivien was cheered by an excited crowd as she stepped off the plane in Atlanta, Georgia, swathed in a fur coat with a bonnet-style hat. It felt like the premiere of *Gone with the Wind* all over again, but this time Vivien had returned for a gala to mark the centennial year of the American Civil War. Reuniting David O. Selznick and Olivia de Havilland, *Gone with the Wind* was to be shown as the highlight of the event and, much like the premiere, there would be balls and parties and speeches, with fans flocking to Peachtree Street, where the motorcade had driven back in 1939.

Though the mood was celebratory, Vivien couldn't help but feel it had been a mistake to come. Everything reminded her of Larry. They'd been so young and in love, but now everything had changed. The Georgian Terrace Hotel where the cast had stayed, and which had played host to the premiere celebrations, now looked tired and run down, falling into disrepair. It was somehow fitting, and Vivien found it incredibly depressing.

'And what part did you play in the film?' a young reporter, who looked as though he hadn't even been born when *Gone with the Wind* was released over twenty years ago, piped up eagerly with the question and Vivien gave him a look of disdain.

'Tell me, have you even seen the film?'

'I'm afraid not, ma'am. I've heard it's rather long, and I couldn't spare the time.'

'Then, sir, we have nothing to say to each other on this or any other subject,' Vivien replied coldly.

The question, and the boy's ignorance, struck at the heart of her fears: that she was old, forgotten, irrelevant. Clark Gable, Leslie Howard, Hattie McDaniel and the book's author, Margaret Mitchell, had all died in the intervening years, forcing Vivien to confront her mortality and her legacy in the cruellest way. Yes, the town was quite literally full of ghosts, Vivien thought.

Watching herself on screen at the gala was a form of torture. It was impossible not to contrast the beautiful, youthful girl with the woman Vivien had become, her forty-seven-year-old self quite unable to compete with the eternally twenty-six-year-old beauty committed to celluloid. She wished that she'd encouraged Jack to come with her. When Vivien had received the invitation, she'd imagined that she would be quite able to go without him, with only her friend Radie Harris for company. Jack and *Gone with the Wind* belonged to two very different parts of her life that she would rather keep separate. But now she saw that it had been a mistake. She needed his support; she'd been foolish to think that she could face her past without him.

Vivien felt a wave of relief when the celebrations were over and it was finally time to leave Atlanta, and as she boarded the plane to return home, the crush of reporters and fans was as large as ever. She stopped on the steps to smile and wave, blowing kisses to the crowd, her spirits buoyed by their good wishes.

'Miss Leigh,' one of the reporters shouted eagerly. He had dark hair and a pencil moustache, and he waved to catch her attention. 'Miss Leigh, do you have any comment on the happy news?'

Vivien frowned. 'What news?'

'That Sir Laurence Olivier and Miss Joan Plowright were married today in Connecticut.'

Vivien gripped the railing tightly, afraid that her legs might buckle beneath her. It was as though she'd taken a physical blow, the wind knocked out of her. She supposed she'd always known it would happen, but having the news confirmed – and so unexpectedly – was shocking, the ultimate confirmation that Larry would never again be hers. She was furious that he hadn't had the decency to forewarn her, but had let her find out from a journalist.

Vivien fought to keep her composure, though when she opened her mouth, nothing came out. She tried again, her voice low and uncertain. 'No, I… No comment.'

Chapter Forty-Five

London, England

July 1967

'… Happy birthday, dear Vivien, happy birthday to you!'

There was cheering and applause as Vivien blew out the solitary candle on her birthday cake, a delicious-looking Victoria sponge made by her housekeeper.

'Darling, I'm glad you didn't put fifty-three candles on there, we'd have had to call out the fire brigade,' Vivien quipped, as everyone laughed.

'Can I have a piece of cake, please, Grandmama?' asked Neville politely. He was eight now, and had been joined over the years by two brothers, Rupert and Jonathan.

'Of course, darling, but you must learn the art of patience. We need to cut it and plate it first…'

As the housekeeper sliced the cake and poured cups of tea, Vivien looked round at the group that had assembled for her birthday: her mother, Gertrude, and her daughter, Suzanne, with her husband, Robin, and their three children. There was the costume designer Beatrice Dawson, known affectionately as Bumble, with whom she'd become great friends in recent years. And, of course, Jack. Vivien caught his eye and he was instantly by her side, solicitous as ever.

'Can I get you anything?'

'No, my darling. I have everything I need right here.'

He reached for her hand, and she took it gratefully, that small gesture conveying more than words ever could.

Despite never wanting a great deal of fuss on her birthdays, for she was less than enthused about growing older, Vivien felt content, delighted that her loved ones had made the effort to travel to Sussex to be with her today. She'd been heartbroken when Larry had decided to sell Notley Abbey but, in hindsight, it had been the right decision. It held too many memories, and not all of them were happy. Five years ago, she'd viewed Tickerage Mill, a traditional Queen Anne house whose grounds included a fishing lake and a bluebell wood. She adored the property, and it had become her sanctuary in the wake of her divorce.

'Right, everyone,' Vivien called, putting down her teacup and clapping her hands. 'The rain's stopped. Let's all go outside for a walk. I don't want to be cooped up inside on my birthday.'

The children scrambled towards the door, racing through the higgledy-piggledy old house, as everyone bundled into rain jackets and Wellington boots. Vivien tied a silk scarf over her head, putting on her sunglasses before stepping out into the glorious gardens beside the lake. Everything felt fresh and cold after the rainfall. The air was damp, and Vivien could feel it in her lungs. The dogs ran around, barking in excitement, with the boys following behind. Vivien linked her arm through her daughter's.

The two of them had grown much closer in recent years; Suzanne felt that her mother had mellowed, no longer prioritising her ambitions and her career above all else. From Vivien's point of view, she found an adult daughter much easier to relate to than an infant, and she'd learnt to cherish the meaningful relationships she'd developed with her family and close friends, preferring to host guests at her home in the country than attend flashy parties in London.

'How's everything with you?' Suzanne asked. 'Any interesting work on the horizon?'

'As a matter of fact, yes.' Vivien's voice was gravelly now, a combination of age, cigarettes and the gin she was so fond of. 'I've been offered the role of Madame von Meck, Tchaikovsky's mistress, in a film of his life. It starts shooting in January, in Moscow of all places.'

'Goodness. Are you going to accept?'

'I'm not sure. There've been rumblings about an Edward Albee play too. We'd start rehearsals next year, then tour the provinces before opening in London in the summer.'

'You're not planning to slow down then?' Suzanne was only half-joking.

'Never, darling.'

'But are you sure you feel well enough?'

Vivien was still plagued by violent mood swings, agreeing to ECT when she began to feel they were out of her control. In addition, she'd been suffering from colds and coughs, and feared a flare-up of tuberculosis.

'Oh, yes,' Vivien insisted. 'Besides, I think it will be good for me to get back to work.'

They were circling the lake, reaching the furthest point from the house, when the sun crept out, its presence welcome on that damp November day. Vivien felt the change of seasons more than ever, dreading the cold of winter which made her health worse. Her breath caught in her throat and she began to cough, struggling to catch her breath as the spasms wracked her body.

Suzanne looked on in concern. 'Promise me you'll see the doctor when you get back to London.'

'It's quite all right, darling. I'm perfectly fine.'

Suzanne turned to Jack. 'You'll take her, won't you? You'll make sure she goes?'

'I'll look after her, I promise.'

Jack put his arm around Vivien and held her close. She relaxed into him, feeling his strength, his presence bringing her comfort. She appreciated him more than he would ever know.

———

The car dropped Jack outside 54 Eaton Place and he bounded up the stairs, eager to see Vivien. She was already in bed, as he'd expected, sitting up against the pillows, looking pale but beautiful. He kissed her and sat down on the bed beside her.

'How are you feeling?' he asked.

Vivien had recently been coughing up blood, and when the doctor had X-rayed her he'd been alarmed to see a large black hole on her lung. She was put on bed rest for three months, told to cut out alcohol and cigarettes, and warned to keep visitors to a minimum. Her forthcoming performance in *A Delicate Balance* by Edward Albee had been postponed until she'd recovered.

'Oh, I'm all right, darling,' she smiled tiredly. She had clearly spent the evening reading, the counterpane littered with books and newspapers. 'How was the show?'

Jack was performing in *The Last of Mrs Cheyney* in Guildford, a commitment he'd taken on before Vivien fell ill.

'Fine,' he said easily. 'Nothing of note. No gossip.'

'I'm disappointed. I rely on you to bring me news of the outside world.' She waved her hand towards the window, indicating the city beyond.

'I'm sorry,' he laughed. 'I'll pop to the kitchen and get myself some supper quickly, then I'll be back.'

'Very well, darling. I have Poo Jones to keep me company,' Viven said, stroking her beloved Siamese cat on the bed beside her. 'I'll be quite all right until you return.'

Jack blew her a kiss and padded along the hall to the kitchen. There was pea and ham soup in the fridge – Cook had obviously made it that day – and he warmed it up on the stove, buttering a slice of bread to accompany it.

Jack had grown to love Vivien deeply. He knew that part of her would always be in love with Larry – he'd been her great love, and nothing could compare with the star quality of the Oliviers – but that had been a different time, and it was impossible to go back.

Larry had married Joan six years ago, and they'd had three children in quick succession; they still appeared very happy, but so was Vivien, he reflected. She was close to Suzanne, to Leigh, and to her mother, Gertrude, and saw them regularly. She seemed content with her life, even if she couldn't work at the moment. She still had dozens of friends with whom she regularly corresponded, she was a voracious reader, and she kept her mind sharp with crosswords and puzzles. She no longer had the burning ambition of her youth, but she didn't need to prove anything to anyone. Vivien had done it all.

Jack washed up quickly in the sink – it would save the housekeeper doing it tomorrow – mulling over what the future might bring. He was thinking of proposing to Vivien. He knew that they would be together for ever. Yes, Vivien had her problems, but he knew how to manage her and he was more than willing to take care of her. It would be a comfort to Larry too, to know Vivien was being looked after; Jack knew that Larry liked and respected him, and would heartily approve if they were to formalise their relationship.

Perhaps, Jack mused, when he'd finished his show and Vivien was feeling stronger, they could go on holiday. The south of France, or Italy perhaps, where the warm climate would help Vivien's TB.

Jack switched off the light and retraced his steps along the corridor. As soon as he reached their bedroom door, he knew. He raced into the room to see Vivien lying on the carpet beside the bed; it looked as though she'd tripped and fallen. Jack didn't know it then, but her lungs had filled with fluid, making it impossible to breathe, almost like drowning.

Jack cried out, falling to his knees as he tried to revive her. But deep within him, he knew it was too late.

Vivien was gone.

Chapter Forty-Six

SONIA

Figeac, France

August 1957

'Here's your Negroni, *querida*. Made French-style with the local Armagnac.'

'Oh, that looks marvellous, darling. Thank you.'

Sonia sat back on her lounger and took a sip of her drink, feeling wonderfully relaxed. The goldfinches were singing in the beech trees, the balmy air scented with end-of-season lavender. It was early evening, but she'd started drinking at lunchtime.

Sonia was staying with her friend, Julian Pitt-Rivers and his glamorous Spanish second wife, Margarita, in the heart of the French countryside. Since George's death, Sonia had become increasingly reliant on her wide network of friends on both sides of the Channel. The life that she'd envisaged for herself – in Switzerland, administering to her husband's every need whilst he wrote novels that would change the world – had been snatched away, leaving her adrift, and she'd passed the seasons aimlessly in Paris, in St Tropez, on the Italian coast.

Sonia had met Julian through her good friend the writer

Michel Leiris, and he'd invited her to spend the summer at his chateau in the Lot. She'd idled away her days visiting the pretty little mediaeval town nearby, shopping in the markets, cooking, reading and swimming. She'd attempted to write a novel but given up numerous times, proving to herself beyond doubt that she was never meant to be a writer. Thus her stay had been enjoyable but without any real purpose, a state that seemed to reflect her life over the past few years.

'Michael should be arriving any moment. Ah – talk of the devil,' Margarita laughed, as he came striding across the lawn, Julian beside him. Sonia rose to her feet and studied Michael Pitt-Rivers from behind her sunglasses as he drew closer. He was handsome and debonair, with swept-back dark hair and slightly protruding ears. He'd turned forty that year – a year older than Sonia – and to her he looked like the quintessential Englishman, far more handsome than his younger brother Julian.

She held out her hand, but he kissed her on the cheek.

'Michael, this is Sonia,' Julian introduced them. 'Or have you two met before?'

'No, we haven't. Though I've heard of you, Mrs Orwell,' Michael said, a smile playing on his lips.

Sonia arched an eyebrow, feeling the remark was rather close to the bone. The press had dubbed her the 'Widow Orwell' since discovering that George had changed his will three days before his death, making Sonia his sole heir. She'd been accused of preying on a vulnerable, dying man, of depriving his son of his inheritance, which Sonia found terribly unfair. George hadn't confided in her about his plans – if anything, she'd have been grateful to receive a warning of the poisoned chalice she was to receive. Whilst she was flattered and humbled that her former husband had placed his trust in her, she'd been left with the monumental, imposing task of how best to protect his legacy.

Once again, just like her time at *Horizon*, Sonia found herself under attack by others – namely, men – who were certain that they were better placed to take charge of George's work, resenting

Sonia's influence and power. She'd had to fight to retain control, declining lucrative offers she sensed George would have disapproved of, doubting her instincts, making enemies with every decision. It was exhausting and dispiriting.

If the truth be told, she missed George terribly, not realising at the time how much of her future had been bound up in the plans that they'd made. She'd drifted, rootless, since his death more than seven years ago now, having short-term affairs but never finding love.

'I've heard of you too,' she returned archly, and Michael had the good grace to laugh.

'You know, you shouldn't believe everything you read in the newspapers. Although in my case it was mostly true – albeit exaggerated by the carrion crows at the *Daily Mail*.'

'I don't doubt it. Eggs with a side of scandal for Middle England,' Sonia smiled.

Margarita clapped her hands together. 'Well, now everyone's acquainted, shall we have dinner?'

Sonia and Michael got to know one another well during long boozy lunches and late intoxicating evenings. She found him more relaxed, more fun, than his younger brother, though Michael was clearly a country boy at heart, never happier than when he was talking about his plans for the family's vast estate which took in great swathes of land across Wiltshire and Dorset. He talked of the beauty of the landscape, of his duty to his tenants and the concept of *noblesse oblige*, of the environment and his obligation to future generations. Sonia was charmed by his earnestness and the description of his lifestyle, which sounded idyllic. She'd always thought that her fulfilment would come through helping a literary man, but with Michael she could see a twin purpose: to help him manage the estate *and* restore his reputation.

'So how was prison?' Sonia enquired breezily one night when Julian and Margarita had already retired. She and Michael were sat on the terrace enjoying the warm evening, drinking and smoking, accompanied by the hum of cicadas and the occasional hoot of an owl.

'A breeze, compared with the army,' he quipped. He'd had a long and distinguished military career with the Welsh Guards, having served in the Second World War and risen to the rank of Major. 'In all seriousness, it's rather similar. Your life is restricted, regimented. You have to follow the rules. The men were very good to me, though, as were the guards.'

'Well, you were famous.'

'It's fair to say that my notoriety preceded me,' he smiled, and Sonia laughed. 'But really, the whole trial was ridiculous. I was being made an example of. And because of who my family are, it was open season for the press.'

Michael Pitt-Rivers was the great-grandson of the celebrated army officer and archaeologist Augustus Pitt-Rivers, who had donated much of his collection to a museum in Oxford that bore his name. Michael and his brother Julian had had a difficult start in life; their mother had left them when they were little more than boys, running away to become an actress and leaving them in the care of their father, a prominent fascist and eugenicist.

Five years ago, Michael had scandalised the country when he and his friend, Peter Wildeblood, had spent the weekend with two young RAF servicemen at the country estate of Michael's cousin. The two airmen later claimed there had been 'abandoned behaviour', with Michael and Peter standing trial for buggery. Michael was sentenced to eighteen months in Maidstone jail.

'It's terrible what they did to you,' Sonia said earnestly.

'Well, hopefully times are changing. I understand Lord Wolfenden's report is almost ready – it'll be published next month – and the rumours are that he'll recommend some major changes to the law.'

'I don't know you well, but I feel so proud of you,' Sonia

insisted. 'Homosexuality shouldn't be a crime. What you did was so brave. I can't imagine what you've been through.'

'My reputation's been rather dragged through the mud. But what good did a reputation ever do anyone anyway?'

Sonia laughed, then they both fell quiet. Overhead the sky was an inky black, a thousand stars splayed across it with abandon.

'Do you know what would really set the cat amongst the pigeons?' Sonia said thoughtfully, as she lit a cigarette and inhaled. 'If you were to marry.'

'What?' Michael chuckled at the thought of it.

'Imagine it – one of the key defendants at the centre of the country's most notorious homosexuality case gets married, living his life quite happily with a woman. Wouldn't they all look like fools?'

'But whom could I possibly marry?'

'Who better than someone whose reputation is already as damaged as your own? Someone who the press thinks has no scruples about marrying whomever she wants. You'd be rehabilitated, and those vultures couldn't say a damn thing.'

There was a long pause. Finally, Michael smiled. 'I suppose that would be quite a lark. You know, Sonia, I like your way of thinking.'

'Cheers to that,' said Sonia, raising her glass.

'Are you absolutely sure you want to do this?'

Bay was staring at her sister with undeniable concern; she looked so serious that Sonia wanted to laugh.

'Yes, I am,' Sonia insisted, taking a large slug of the gin and tonic sitting on the dressing table. 'I mean, I'm absolutely terrified right now, but surely that's normal before getting married, isn't it?'

Bay frowned. 'You don't have to do it, Sonia. I know you like to be contrary and controversial, but—'

'He's brilliant, Bay. So clever, and passionate. I adore him.'

'But your life will be so different from everything you know.'

'I'm moving to Wiltshire, darling, not to the moon. I think the idea of living in the country sounds rather fun, and we'll entertain every weekend. All of our friends will come and stay with us, and I'll still travel regularly to London and Paris. I won't become a hermit.'

Bay didn't look convinced. The sisters were in a hotel room close to Kensington Register Office, where, in half an hour's time, Sonia was due to marry Michael Pitt-Rivers.

'I'd love to see you truly happy. Marrying for love. You have so many admirers, surely you could find someone more suitable?'

Sonia thought of Maurice, the man she'd loved desperately, who she'd believed was her soul mate, who wouldn't leave his wife for her. They'd crossed paths a few times over the years, but their affair hadn't been rekindled. Their moment had passed, and Sonia had reconciled herself to the fact that a conventional life wasn't for her. As with her marriage to George, she could accept a relationship based on intellectual admiration and a degree of obeisance, willing to suppress her wants and needs for a nobler cause.

'I *do* love Michael. I know that probably sounds crazy to you, and it's difficult to explain, but I *do* want to marry him. I honestly think we can be happy together.'

'Sonia, he's a homosexual,' Bay whispered, glancing round nervously as though someone might imprison her purely for saying the words.

Sonia threw back her head and howled with laughter, so hard that tears came to her eyes. When she finally calmed down, she picked up her gin and tonic once again, finished the glass and poured herself another with shaking hands. 'Of course I know that, darling. I'm not an idiot. But it doesn't matter. Our relationship isn't based on sex, or conventional love. What Michael and I share is more profound. It transcends the prosaic, defies the everyday. It's based on respect and understanding and a mutual appreciation and affection.'

'And isn't it fortunate that he's not a pauper?'

Sonia gave her sister a hard stare. 'I'm not interested in his money, or his estate. I thought that you of all people would understand that about me.'

'I do. But most people won't, and they'll judge your motives. Didn't you have your fill of that with George?'

'Oh, bother what people think. Do you think I'd be marrying Michael in the first place if I gave a damn about the narrow-minded public's opinion of my life? Besides, it's a jolly good wheeze and yah boo sucks to everyone who's looked down their noses at the two of us. The newspapers will choke on their own hypocrisy.'

'It's marriage, not a game. You don't have to go through with it merely to make a point.'

'But it *is* a game, don't you see that? An utterly meaningless piece of paper that magically bestows respectability.'

Bay paused, and Sonia knew her sister was wrestling with herself, wondering how far to push the issue. The mantel clock ticked loudly in the silence, the time for decision growing nearer.

'You're doing it again,' Bay said quietly.

Sonia gulped down her drink, hoping to calm her nerves, aware that her behaviour was bordering on the manic. 'Doing what?'

'Trying to save someone.' The words were out and Bay had played her trump card. 'It's since the accident, isn't it? In Switzerland. Ever since then it's like you've been trying to make up for it. Trying to save someone – to save *a man* – like some figure from Greek mythology doomed to keep repeating the same action. You don't *have to*, Sonia. You're allowed to be happy.'

Sonia closed her eyes, trying to hide from the accusation. She knew Bay was right, but she didn't want to hear it. Everything would be fine, she thought blithely, she would make sure of it. Besides, like she'd said, she did love Michael, and he loved her in his own way, she supposed. He certainly wouldn't be the first gay man to enter a heterosexual marriage; half the establishment were living the same lie.

'Please, Bay. I need your support, not your judgement. I know what I'm doing.' Tears prickled at the corners of her eyes.

'Darling, I don't want to upset you.' Bay enfolded her sister in a hug, then stepped back and looked at her. 'You look beautiful, by the way.'

'Thank you,' Sonia smiled. She'd had her long blonde hair cut into a shoulder length bob, leaving behind the girlish ways of her youth for a more mature style. She'd chosen a white silk dress with cap sleeves and a cinched waist, covered in a black floral print. A string of pearls encircled her neck, and the day was warm, so she needed no wrap or jacket.

'I'm just saying that—'

'No. No more.' Sonia shook her head and finished her drink, a light coming into her eyes as she made a concerted attempt to shake off her melancholy. 'Are we ready? Do we have everything? Then let's go. It's time for me to get married.'

Chapter Forty-Seven

Wiltshire, England

January 1960

Sonia peered into the age-spotted mirror. It was so cold that her breath against it caused a fog.

It was still only early evening, but it was pitch-black outside, with ice already forming on the mullioned windows. The fire in the grate was close to dying, merely a faint orange glow emitting from the embers. The housekeeper should come round shortly to make it up before she left for the evening, and she would tidy the bedroom too. The room wasn't to Sonia's taste – it was far too old-fashioned, with a heavy wooden four-poster, tapestries on the walls and paintings of hunting scenes and ancient ancestors. But her taste wasn't to be taken into consideration; the house had likely looked this way for centuries, and an interloper like her could do little about it. As for her husband, he slept in a separate room, across the hall.

Sonia brushed her hair and applied a slick of lipstick. She and Michael were throwing a dinner party, and Sonia wanted to look nice, but even in her thick velvet dress with Michael's old long johns underneath, she was still freezing, and threw a tattered, moth-eaten cardigan over the top.

She was putting a lot of pressure on herself to make tonight's soirée a success. She and Michael hadn't been getting along well of late, and she wanted to rectify that. She'd promised herself that she wouldn't drink too much, that she'd make a real effort with his family and friends. She would be the perfect wife so that he, in return, could be the model husband.

Their marriage had started so well. After the wedding they'd honeymooned in Southeast Asia – Sonia had celebrated her fortieth birthday by visiting Angkor Wat in Cambodia – and they'd been giddy with happiness, delighted by their own cleverness. Michael was an ideal travelling companion, and they traded stories and ideas, discussing the big issues of the day, perfectly pleased with one another.

As they had planned, they decamped to live in the countryside on Michael's estate, and Sonia made regular trips to London and Paris to see her old friends. Yet, as the months passed, the wheels had started to come off their marital vehicle. Sonia didn't quite fit into Michael's world, and he was increasingly less tolerant of hers. She'd been photographed by *Vogue* magazine as the lady of the manor, but it felt uncomfortably like playing a role and the distance between her and Michael continued to increase.

Once again, Sonia was struggling to find her role and her purpose. Michael didn't seem to need her as she'd once thought he'd might, and their lives were largely lived separately. She found herself thinking of her first marriage, pondering how different her life might have been had George lived. She would have been by his side as he rose to even greater heights. And she would have been a stepmother, taking on responsibility for his dear son, Richard.

Sonia's thoughts had increasingly turned to Richard in recent weeks. Clearly he was too young at the time of his father's death for George's literary works to be left to him, but Sonia couldn't help but wonder if he'd blame her for how everything had panned out. She thought about visiting him – he'd be sixteen now, on the cusp of adulthood, and she wondered what *his* dreams and ambitions were – but she was too afraid of his reaction, scared to open that can of worms.

Perhaps she would write to him, she thought, as she put on a pair of pearl earrings that had belonged to Michael's grandmother. She'd occasionally visited him, in the depths of western Scotland, where he lived on a farm with his aunt Avril – George's sister – and uncle Bill. Sonia had taken seriously George's stipulation that Richard must always be provided for; he'd had an excellent education at Loretto, Scotland's oldest boarding school, and she'd ensured that his aunt and uncle never went short of money. But Sonia had always been involved in his life from a distance, and now she found herself dwelling on how she'd missed out on a maternal role, how dearly she would have loved to—

There was a knock at the door and she turned around as Michael entered. He was wearing a dinner jacket and bow tie, his dark hair slicked back.

'You look… handsome,' Sonia smiled winningly, hoping to win him over with a compliment.

His gaze drifted over her with indifference. 'You look… cold.'

'I *am* cold. It's fucking freezing in here. You can afford a country pile, but you can't afford enough coal to let the fire burn all day?' Sonia hadn't meant to criticise, but her reaction was instinctive. So much for her vow to be the perfect wife.

Michael gave her a long, hard stare but refrained from snapping back. 'Come on. Our guests will be here any moment. We wouldn't want to deprive them of your scintillating conversation.'

'Fuck! The apple pie!'

Sonia leapt up from the dinner table, raced through to the kitchen and yanked open the door of the Aga to see black smoke

400

pouring out. Grabbing the oven gloves, she pulled out the sorry-looking pie and swore once again.

Minutes later, she emerged back in the wood-panelled dining room carrying a tray with dessert plates of apple pie and a large jug of pouring cream. Nine pairs of eyes turned to her expectantly.

'If it were fillet steak, I'd say it was overdone, but cover it in cream and I'm sure it will be fine,' she trilled, as she handed out the portions to her guests. There were polite murmurs of thanks, but an awkwardness hung in the air. Cutlery clinked against china as Sonia resumed her seat at one end of the table, with Michael at the other. Toying with her food, she watched as he took a mouthful then pushed the plate away, grimacing.

'I'm sorry, Sonia, but that's inedible. This whole fucking meal has been inedible, in fact. I don't know why you gave Mrs Carter the night off.'

Sonia's face burned with humiliation. She glanced round at her guests: Michael's brother Julian, with Margarita; her own brother, Michael Dixon, who lived nearby with his wife Nora; Sonia's good friend the novelist Ivy Compton-Burnett, with her companion Madge Garland; and Roger Prewitt with his wife Annie, who were farmers on the Pitt-Rivers estate. Michael liked to invite the tenants – he'd known some of them all his life – but Sonia struggled to make conversation with the country folk, finding they had little in common. All had their heads down, all were pushing their food around their plates.

'I wanted to do something nice,' Sonia said defensively.

'Well it wasn't nice, was it?' Michael held up a spoonful of charred dessert, dripping with cream, and Sonia noticed how prettily the black and white contrasted. 'It was fucking awful. Don't any of you eat it.'

'It's not so bad. Better than anything I could make,' Ivy put in loyally. But neither Sonia nor her husband were really listening; this argument was about more than burned apple pie.

Sonia dropped her fork. It fell onto her plate with a clatter.

Without breaking eye contact with Michael, she picked up her wine glass and drained the contents.

'Could you refill my glass, please, darling? It seems to be empty.'

Wordlessly, Michael stood, pushing his chair back across the rug and walking the length of the table to Sonia. No one spoke, and the ticking of the grandfather clock in the hallway outside could be heard. He refilled Sonia's glass but by the time he'd returned to his seat it was empty again.

'Darling,' she called, far too brightly. 'Could you refill my glass?'

Michael sat down heavily. The room was beginning to swim in front of Sonia's eyes, its timbered ceilings and gilt-edged paintings softening and warping. She'd always felt like an interloper here, she realised, however much she'd tried to make the thirteenth-century hunting lodge feel like home. This was Michael's world, not hers.

'No,' he said succinctly.

'Do be a good host, my love. I'd rather like a gin and tonic, if anyone would care to join me.' Sonia glanced around the table invitingly.

'But why should I be a good host when you're such a terrible hostess? Roger, would you feed this slop to your pigs?' Michael brandished the plate towards him.

'I… um…' Roger looked deeply uncomfortable, as Michael turned his fire back on Sonia.

'You know which ones the pigs are, right? Pink, with snouts and a curly tail. Oink oink.'

Sonia coloured; some of her questions when she'd first moved to the countryside had been rather basic. 'Except sometimes pigs wear tweed jackets and come with country houses,' she spat back.

'Oh, Sonia, this is getting tiresome. Do shut the fuck up. *Please*.'

'Don't speak to me like that,' Sonia hissed.

'You know, I was discussing with a friend the other day how

marriage is of no benefit to the man. I do wonder why we still bother.'

'No benefit? Your clothes are washed and pressed, your house is kept clean and tidy, there's always food and drink in the pantry and you never have to think about any of that, so tell me again how that's of no benefit.'

'You think *this*...' Here Michael tilted his plate and let the apple pie slowly slide onto the tablecloth. '... is acceptable? My mother did a better job of looking after me and she walked out when I was three.'

'That's enough, Michael,' Julian said warningly, seeing that Sonia was on the verge of tears. And if she didn't start crying, she would likely lash out in anger.

'Thank you so much, Sonia,' her brother said, getting to his feet. 'But Nora's getting tired and we'd better be heading back. We have an early start tomorrow.'

Sonia nodded, not looking up, as her brother and his wife moved towards the door. The others did the same; there was a general, embarrassed, scraping of chairs, a grateful abandoning of the food.

'Thank you, Sonia. I had a lovely evening,' said Annie politely.

'I'll give you a call tomorrow.' Ivy kissed her on the cheek and squeezed her arm reassuringly.

The silence was deafening once everyone had left, the tension unbearable. Michael shot her a look of disgust and went to walk out of the room, but Sonia grabbed his arm.

'Please... don't... I'm sorry. I don't want it to be like this. I don't want us to argue.'

'Well, we seem to be rather good at it. That was certainly an epic display.'

Sonia searched his face for a trace of humour, but he looked furious. 'I'm sorry,' she apologised again, knowing she had to be the one to capitulate if he was going to grant her request. 'I'm on edge... I know why. I've been thinking about it and... I think we should have a baby.'

Michael couldn't have been more surprised if she'd announced she intended to become a nun. His astonishment turned to anger. 'Don't be ridiculous. Is that supposed to be a joke?'

'I want a baby. I want *your* baby,' Sonia pleaded, utterly serious.

'That was never the arrangement. You know that I—'

'But I love you,' Sonia interrupted. 'You've made me fall in love with you. This whole situation is so fucked up that the least you could do is this one thing for me.'

'Is this because your mother's just died? Is it some hormonal or genetic need to reproduce? I thought that only happened to men.'

'How dare you.' Sonia was incensed that he could treat Beatrice's death so casually. She'd passed away shortly after Christmas, and it had affected Sonia far more than she'd expected. 'You *owe* me. I restored your reputation.'

'I never asked you to. I was doing just fine without a reputation. Besides, no one fell for it – we're a joke. The faggot and his social-climbing wife, that's what they say about us. What is it with you marrying men you don't love, hmm? Are you offering some kind of service? Or did you want my money and surname the way you wanted George's?'

Sonia slapped him. 'I hate you.'

'I don't care.'

'I want a baby,' Sonia whispered, feeling that she might be on the verge of a nervous breakdown. Recently she'd become fixated on her desire for a child. She was forty-one years old and knew it was likely nature playing a cruel trick, her body's last opportunity to try and procreate.

As she'd confided to Vivien, over a decade ago she'd had an abortion, an act that was still illegal in the UK. She was lucky that she'd had money and hadn't had to endure some terrifying backstreet invasion with a knitting needle. At the time she'd felt liberated, believing it to be the only option for a modern woman.

Now she wondered if she should have kept the baby, if it would have been a boy or a girl, if she could have successfully taken care of both of them. She had so many godchildren and she adored being around them, but what she wanted most was a baby of her own.

'Perhaps if you were so interested in having a child you could have taken on George's son. Given him some of the inheritance that was rightfully his.'

'Fuck you.'

'And wouldn't you just love to.'

The remark was cruel, but Michael showed no remorse. He walked out of the door as Sonia's legs buckled beneath her. That was the moment she knew her second marriage was over.

What felt like hours later, Sonia picked herself up off the floor. The house was in complete darkness; she'd heard the front door slam and the roar of a car engine, and surmised that Michael had left. Her limbs felt sluggish and she moved slowly as she worked through the mental checklist of what she would need, gathering what she could find in the cupboards: a bottle of gin, sleeping tablets, opiates, sedatives, tranquilisers.

She sloped back through to the grand dining room. It had the air of the *Mary Celeste*, with abandoned plates of food lying where they'd been left, congealed apple pie in pooling cream, a yellowing stain on the tablecloth where Michael had unceremoniously dumped his dessert.

Sonia sat down at the head of the table, settling herself in her husband's chair, wondering what it must be like to be Michael. To be a man. To hold all the power. How did *he* get to decide whether *she* had a baby? Fucking patriarchy. Well, this was one decision she was going to make by herself and Michael couldn't do a damn thing about it.

Sonia opened the gin and took a comforting slug, enjoying the familiar burn in her throat. Then she turned her attention to the tablets, choosing a selection, methodically swallowing them one by one.

Chapter Forty-Eight

London, England

August 1965

'Oh, Sonia. It's beautiful!'

'It'll do.'

Her heels echoed on the wooden floor as she turned in a slow circle, taking in number 153 Gloucester Road, in South Kensington. It was a two-storey, terraced, white stucco property, with a downstairs bay window and a tiled pathway leading up to an imposing front door, moments from Tregunter Road where her mother had run the boarding house over twenty-five years ago. Inside it was cosy and traditional, the walls painted white, the fireplaces stone. Sonia would turn it into a home, as she had always done.

She had been living in Paris until very recently and it was the first time she had seen the property, bought as part of the settlement in her divorce from Michael, which had been finalised earlier in the year. She split her time between France and England and, whilst Bay knew that her sister was always happier in

France, Sonia was determined to make a go of life in this new house.

'A new start,' Bay smiled.

'To do what?' Sonia wondered.

Bay's eyes widened, but she tried not to betray her anxiety. She knew that Sonia was fragile right now, and had attempted suicide twice in the past few years. The first took place when she was still living with Michael at the manor house in Tollard Royal. For two days, it had been uncertain whether Sonia would make it through, but she'd survived and the incident had been hushed up. The second took place when Maurice Merleau-Ponty had died unexpectedly in 1961. Sonia had always referred to him as the love of her life, and Bay knew that his death had left her wondering what the point of life was. The man she'd adored, whom she considered to be her soul mate, hadn't wanted *her*. He hadn't left his wife, hadn't felt the overwhelming urge to be with Sonia, the way she had with him. And now he never would.

Over the past few years, Sonia's friends had been dying – often through suicide – at an alarming rate: Alfred Métraux, Michel Leiris, Georges Bataille. It might have been the aftermath of the war, or that the artistic temperament was unnecessarily prone to early death. Whatever the cause, Sonia wasn't immune, and now that her divorce was finalised Bay recognised the signs of depression in her sister.

'I don't know what to do with my life. I don't know what my purpose is. If I was a painter, or a writer, I would have a purpose, but I'm not. I've tried, but writing isn't for me.'

They were walking round the pretty little house, throwing open curtains and windows, letting in the light and air. Outside, at the back, was a small patch of garden. The sisters went out and stood in the sunlight; it was impossible not to feel positive and optimistic on such a beautiful day.

Bay smiled. 'You know what your purpose is, Sonia. It's George.'

Sonia looked at her quizzically.

'He left everything to you. There's a hunger out there for him – people want more writing, more articles, more information. Do something with it.'

'I set up the archive,' Sonia retorted, and Bay was pleased to see a little of her old spark return. 'And he expressly forbade me to engage a biographer.'

'You have all his documents, his journalism, his correspondence. Your legacy is *his* legacy. It's your duty. You're the only one who can do this.'

'I'm not sure—'

'Sonia!' Bay interrupted and her tone was sharp. Sonia stared at her in surprise and alarm. 'I've tried the gentle approach, and that didn't work, so I think it's time you heard a few home truths.' Bay's breath was coming fast; it was rare for her to get so impassioned, but on this occasion, Sonia needed to hear what she had to say.

'You might not believe me, but I know you better than anyone. I've certainly known you longer than anyone,' Bay went on. 'Do you have any idea how frustrating you are? You're *so* clever and *so* talented, and I feel like I've spent my life watching you *waste* everything you've been given. Instead of going out there and creating your own work, all you've done is helped other people – and most of them really didn't need or deserve your help. They were quite happy to take the credit, and leave you feeling that your contribution was minimal.'

'That's not exactly what happened…' Sonia began.

'No? Because that's what it looked like from the outside. And it also looks like you've spent the last few years feeling sorry for yourself, and aimlessly drifting, when you could have been doing so much more with your time. I know you, Sonia, and you need two things to function at your best – your friends, and your work. And I think you need a new project.'

Sonia squinted in the sunlight and looked up at her sister. 'Have you finished?'

'No, actually.' Bay knew that she was likely to infuriate her sister, but she'd held back for too long. If she didn't speak now, she might not get another opportunity. 'I know I've said it before, but I think it all goes back to Switzerland, when you were... what, seventeen?'

Sonia nodded, her eyes full of anguish.

'Ever since the accident, you've been looking for someone to save. A man. You think that if you can do that, then you'll be miraculously cured of all the guilt and all the remorse that you've carried ever since. But it wasn't your fault, Sonia! It was just a terrible, terrible accident and you did the best you could. I saw how much that hurt you, how you changed when you came back, and I don't think you ever really recovered.'

Sonia swallowed, fighting back the tears.

'And then you married George, and did everything you could to try and save *him*. And then Michael... Christ, Sonia, you married a homosexual man to save him from society's judgement, and you expected him to fall in love with you...'

Sonia didn't respond, taking in everything that Bay had said, knowing it was true, and that her sister had said it all out of love. She stood up and the two of them embraced, Sonia burying her head in Bay's shoulder, longing for comfort.

'I just wish you could be happy,' Bay murmured. 'I wish you'd found love, with someone who could love you back, unconditionally.'

'I think it's too late,' Sonia sniffed.

'It's never too late,' Bay replied, smoothing her sister's hair away from her face.

'So what do I do?' Sonia pleaded, wishing she could abdicate responsibility for her own life and let her sister take charge. 'Tell me what to do, Bay.'

'You need a purpose, a focus, and for you, that's your work. Look, you've spent years as a successful editor, and if you took on George's archive, that's how you'd have to view it – the biggest editorial project you've ever undertaken. George is respected, but you can put him amongst the greats. *You* can make George Orwell one of the most celebrated writers of all time.'

Sonia wiped her eyes and stared at her sister.

Three years later, Sonia was the guest of honour at a small dinner at Simpson's in the Strand. It was being thrown to celebrate the publication of *The Collected Essays, Journalism and Letters of George Orwell*, which ran to four volumes, spanning the decades from 1920 to 1950.

Sonia was jumpy and skittish, drinking her wine at an alarming rate. Ian Angus leaned across and patted her hand reassuringly.

'Relax, Sonia.'

'I just keep thinking, what have we done?' she confessed. 'Did we do the right thing? Would George have approved?'

'He would have been so pleased and proud with how you've handled everything. He knew what he was doing, leaving everything to you.'

'Thank you,' Sonia smiled, his kindness cutting through some of her reservations.

Ian had been her co-editor when putting together George's work. He was an astute, unassuming man who'd helped her set up the Orwell Archive some years earlier, and she trusted his judgement implicitly.

'The early reviews are excellent,' Ian told her.

'Are they? I haven't dared read them. I thought the *Observer* might be rather harsh as I turned down their offer of serialisation.'

'David clearly didn't hold a grudge,' Ian commented.

David Astor, one of the few to attend George and Sonia's wedding in the hospital room at UCH, was the owner of the *Observer* newspaper, and had offered Sonia a considerable sum to reprint one of George's essays. Sonia, afraid that they might somehow distort it, had said no.

'But some of the others might,' Sonia replied, as the waiter took away her plate. She'd barely eaten anything, unable to calm her churning stomach. 'Honestly, Ian, you wouldn't believe some of the approaches that I've had – and had to turn down. I feel like I'm going mad, trying to preserve George's legacy. I'm fighting every day to stay true to his spirit; not to edit anything he'd want to keep, or include something he wouldn't. I've had offers from Hollywood, from West End theatres, from Broadway producers, from television directors, all wanting a piece of George. He couldn't have even imagined this when he was writing.'

Ian remained quiet, letting Sonia speak, knowing it was cathartic.

'And I'm the bad guy once again,' she continued, taking another gulp of her wine. 'Just like when I was at *Horizon*. If I turn down their advances – literary or otherwise – then I'm a bitch, I'm hard-nosed and calculating, I'm the grasping Widow Orwell. They'll throw all those insults – and worse – at me. But I won't waver from what's right. I'm doing all of this for George.'

'I know you are, Sonia. And you're doing a sterling job.'

'Thank you,' she repeated sincerely. She looked around the table at the other guests – all male, all influential, all confident of their place in the world in a way that she would never be – and thought of where she'd come to in her life. Sonia had celebrated her fiftieth birthday just days earlier and, despite her best efforts, had found herself prone to introspection as she contemplated the milestone.

In some ways, her life was far from what she'd anticipated. A girl like her wasn't supposed to achieve anything of note; the Sacred Heart of Roehampton had raised its pupils to be wives and mothers – and Sonia had done neither successfully. But she *had* been married to one of the most important writers of her generation, and he'd entrusted her with his body of work. Not only that, but she'd reached a position of considerable power and influence at *Horizon*, and been part of the celebrated literary set in both London and Paris.

Her thoughts turned unexpectedly to her fellow pupils at Roehampton, to those others who had gone on to defy expectations and lead unconventional lives.

She recalled Vivien, whose untimely death last year at the age of fifty-three had shocked the world, the lights extinguished in all West End theatres to mark her passing. The last time Sonia had seen her, all those years ago at The Ivy, it had been clear that Vivien was unwell, but she'd appeared so luminous and vital that it was impossible to believe she could be gone. Vivien had lived and loved on a grand scale, but privilege and wealth hadn't been enough to shield her from unhappiness, from mental illness, from tragedy. Sonia found herself wondering whether Vivien's great success, so lauded and applauded, might have contributed to her troubles. Would her demons have been so consuming if she hadn't been on the world stage, at the top of a precarious profession with its demands and instability?

And Vivien's friend Maureen, whom Sonia had admired from a distance at school and whose story she'd followed in the newspapers over the years, had blazed a trail, daring to making her own choices heedless of scandal or convention. Yet she'd known deep unhappiness and misfortune, dealing with the deaths of those closest to her, her career at the mercy of the Hollywood machine that valued youth and beauty above all else.

Despite Sonia's reservations and uncertainties about her own life, she believed in the old adage that it was better to regret what you'd done than what you hadn't. Buoyed by the thought, she tapped her glass and got to her feet. The men around the table looked at her politely, quietening down to listen to her.

'I'm going to keep this short. Don't worry, I won't run to four volumes,' Sonia joked, causing a ripple of laughter. 'But I'd like to propose a toast. To one of the greatest writers of this century. To the reason we're all here today. To George Orwell.'

'To George,' everyone echoed good-naturedly.

To Sonia's surprise, Ian rose to his feet beside her. 'And *I'd* like to propose a toast,' he added. 'To the woman whose hard work, commitment and talent have led to the publication of these four wonderful books. Whose unfailing dedication and unflagging devotion to her late husband's memory mean that he will finally be recognised as he should be. To Sonia.'

Sonia looked around the table, grateful to her friend and unexpectedly touched by his gesture. She couldn't say that she had ever found true love, or true happiness, in her life so far, but right now, her feelings of pride and pleasure would suffice, as her colleagues raised their glasses in a toast:

'To Sonia.'

Thinking of her Roehampton friends, and of all the women who'd forged their own path, whose failures and achievements were entirely on their own terms, she smiled, murmuring under her breath, 'To all of us.'

Author's Note

The Socialites has been something of a labour of love for me. I first had the idea more than twenty years ago, and have tinkered with it endlessly ever since, so a huge thank you to One More Chapter for finally giving it a home.

Despite its long gestation, the first full draft was pretty dire, so massive thanks to my superb editor, Jennie Rothwell, for not giving up on it and pinpointing exactly what needed to be done. Huge appreciation too for Nicola Doherty, whose editorial touch was light yet unfailingly accurate. Both women shaped it into a book that is immeasurably better than the one that started out. Thanks too to the whole team at One More Chapter for all that they do.

I am, as always, hugely grateful to my wonderful agent, Emily Glenister, for her unfailing hard work and support.

And, of course, a huge thank you to my family and friends, and to everyone who bought *Well Behaved Women* – it is very much appreciated. Special mention to Ross, for giving me time and space to write, and keeping everything under control whilst I'm locked away in my writing zone. I couldn't do it without you. And to Leo & Jessica – by far the best things I've ever created.

I'm also beyond grateful to the women who inspired me,

without whom there wouldn't have been a book. I've been a fan of Vivien Leigh since I was a child and first stumbled across *Gone with the Wind* on the television, which saw me glued to the screen for the next four hours!

A George Orwell obsession came later, in my teens, and I was intrigued to learn that Sonia had attended the same school as Vivien. Thus, the seeds of an idea were planted...

I knew less about Maureen, but quickly came to appreciate her drive and tenacity and talent.

Most of all, I was fascinated by the fact that all three women had experienced this strict – almost traumatising – institutional education, and were expected to do little more with their futures than marry well and bear children. Instead, they went on to lead incredible, immensely successful lives, mixing with the cream of Hollywood, the West End and literary London, yet each had their tragedies and heartbreaks to overcome.

The joy of fiction is that I've been able to employ some artistic licence to interweave their stories in their later years. I'm not aware that Vivien and Sonia ever saw one another again after they'd left Roehampton, though it's possible their paths may have crossed in London society circles.

And whilst Vivien and Maureen *did* work together on *A Yank at Oxford*, it doesn't appear to have been a happy experience; Vivien was, by all accounts, rather jealous that Maureen (the bigger star at the time) had a larger dressing room and higher billing. The two certainly didn't continue the friendly relationship of their childhood.

Over the last twenty years, I've had time to read a lot of books on all three women. The below is a selected bibliography with some of my favourites if you want to find out more about Maureen O'Sullivan, Vivien Leigh or Sonia Orwell:

1. *Maureen O'Sullivan: "No Average Jane"* – David Fury
2. *What Falls Away: A Memoir* – Mia Farrow

3. *A Strange Kind of Loving* – Sheila Mooney (Maureen's sister – a fascinating account of life in Ireland in the early 1900s)
4. *Vivien Leigh: A Biography* – Anne Edwards
5. *Vivien: The Life of Vivien Leigh* – Alexander Walker
6. *Truly Madly: Vivien Leigh, Laurence Olivier and the Romance of the Century* – Stephen Galloway
7. *Confessions of an Actor* – Laurence Olivier
8. *My Father Laurence Olivier* – Tarquin Olivier
9. *The Girl from the Fiction Department: A Portrait of Sonia Orwell* – Hilary Spurling
10. *Lost Girls: Love, War and Literature: 1939-1951* – D J Taylor

ONE MORE CHAPTER

YOUR NUMBER ONE STOP
FOR PAGETURNING BOOKS

The author and One More Chapter would like to thank everyone
who contributed to the publication of this story...

Analytics
James Brackin
Abigail Fryer
Maria Osa

Audio
Fionnuala Barrett
Ciara Briggs

Contracts
Sasha Duszynska
Lewis

Design
Lucy Bennett
Fiona Greenway
Liane Payne
Dean Russell

Digital Sales
Lydia Grainge
Hannah Lismore
Emily Scorer

Editorial
Simon Fox
Arsalan Isa
Charlotte Ledger
Bonnie Macleod
Jennie Rothwell
Tony Russell

Harper360
Emily Gerbner
Jean Marie Kelly
emma sullivan
Sophia Wilhelm

International Sales
Peter Borcsok
Bethan Moore

Marketing & Publicity
Chloe Cummings
Emma Petfield

Operations
Melissa Okusanya
Hannah Stamp

Production
Denis Manson
Simon Moore
Francesca Tuzzeo

Rights
Vasiliki Machaira
Rachel McCarron
Hany Sheikh
Mohamed
Zoe Shine

**The HarperCollins
Distribution Team**

**The HarperCollins
Finance & Royalties
Team**

**The HarperCollins
Legal Team**

**The HarperCollins
Technology Team**

Trade Marketing
Ben Hurd

UK Sales
Laura Carpenter
Isabel Coburn
Jay Cochrane
Sabina Lewis
Holly Martin
Erin White
Harriet Williams
Leah Woods

**And every other
essential link in the
chain from delivery
drivers to booksellers
to librarians and
beyond!**